Praise for Anna Lee Huber's Verity Kent mysteries

"Readers looking for atmospheric mystery set in the period following the Great War will savor the intricate plotting and captivating details of the era."
—*Library Journal* (Starred Review)

"Action-filled. . . . Huber offers a well-researched historical and a fascinating look at the lingering aftermath of war."
—*Publishers Weekly*

"A historical mystery to delight fans of Agatha Christie or Daphne du Maurier." —*BookPage*

"Huber's historical mysteries are always multilayered, complex stories, and *Penny* is an especially satisfying one as she interweaves social commentary and righteous feminist rage into the post-War period. With a perfect blend of murder, mystery, history, romance, and powerful heroines, Huber has yet to disappoint." —*Criminal Element*

"A thrilling mystery that supplies its gutsy heroine with plenty of angst-ridden romance." —*Kirkus Reviews*

"Masterful. . . . Just when you think the plot will zig, it zags. Regardless of how well-versed you may be in the genre, you'll be hard-pressed to predict this climax. . . . Deeply enjoyable . . . just the thing if you're looking for relatable heroines, meatier drama, and smart characters with rich inner lives."
—*Criminal Element*

re praise.

"Huber is an excellent historical mystery writer, and Verity is her best heroine. Sidney and Verity are a formidable couple when they work together, but they are also very real. They don't leap straight back into life before the war but instead face many obstacles and struggles as they readjust to married life and postwar life. Nonetheless, the love between Sidney and Verity is real and true, and the way that Huber creates their re-blossoming love is genuine. Topped off with a gripping mystery, this will not disappoint."

—Historical Novel Society

"I loved *This Side of Murder*, a richly textured mystery filled with period detail and social mores, whose plot twists and character revelations kept me up way past my bedtime. Can't wait for the next Verity Kent adventure!"

—Shelley Noble, *New York Times* bestselling author of *The Beach at Painters' Cove* and *Ask Me No Questions*

"A smashing and engrossing tale of deceit, murder and betrayal set just after World War I. . . . Anna Lee Huber has crafted a truly captivating mystery here."

—All About Romance

"The new Verity Kent Mystery series is rich in detail without being overwhelming and is abundant with murder, mystery, and a bit of romance. The plot is fast-moving with twists and turns aplenty. Huber knows what it takes to write a great mystery." ***—RT Book Reviews***

"A captivating murder mystery told with flair and panache!"

—Fresh Fiction

THE COLD LIGHT OF DAY

Novels by Anna Lee Huber

Sisters of Fortune

The Verity Kent mystery series

This Side of Murder

Treacherous Is the Night

Penny for Your Secrets

A Pretty Deceit

Murder Most Fair

A Certain Darkness

The Cold Light of Day

THE COLD LIGHT OF DAY

ANNA LEE HUBER

KENSINGTON PUBLISHING CORP.

www.kensingtonbooks.com

KENSINGTON BOOKS are published by
Kensington Publishing Corp.
900 Third Avenue
New York, NY 10022

ISBN: 978-1-4967-4008-3 (ebook)

ISBN: 978-1-4967-4007-6

First Kensington Trade Paperback Printing: October 2024

10 9 8 7 6 5 4 3 2 1

Printed in the United States of America

For my sisters-in-law:
Amanda, Bekah, Cathy, and Kayla.
Sisters in more than marriage.
You are each unique and beautiful to me,
and I'm so blessed to call you family.

CHAPTER 1

Truth will ultimately prevail where
pains is taken to bring it to light.
—George Washington

June 1920
Dublin, Ireland

The street was quiet. Too quiet.

After the tumult that had come before—the rumble of military lorries, the scramble of people to clear the vicinity where they were headed, the pushing and shoving of those crowding the tram—any normal citizen might have breathed a sigh of relief upon turning into this calm, deserted street. Instead, I felt a keen sense of exposure.

There were no more throngs to conceal myself within, no more ordinary Dubliners bustling about with which to blend. I feared my drab garb, lowered head, and slumped shoulders wouldn't be enough to project the image that I was but another weary soul trudging home after a long day. Particularly when anyone peering out of the tall shutterless windows of the Georgian brick townhouses on this street southeast of the city center would find only me to scrutinize.

There was safety and anonymity in numbers. A fact I'd learned well during the war. In my work as a British intelligence agent, slipping back and forth from the neutral Netherlands across the border strung with electrified barbed wire into Belgium, I'd come to intimately understand how one was at more personal risk from the German occupiers in wide-open spaces and quiet narrow alleys than the lively town square.

Here, too, the Irish rebels seemed to have learned this lesson. Their murder gangs most often struck in crowds, assassinating their targets in well-populated areas where they could then blend back into the populace as they made their escapes. Even the members of their Volunteer Army used the masses to cover some of their activities. As seemed to be the case that afternoon when they'd raided a British garrison in the city for weapons. Hence the lorries filled with troops rushing northward, albeit much too late.

I'd listened to a pair of men discussing the incident on the tram. Whether they were actual members of the brigade who had plundered King's Inn for guns and ammunition or simply part of the crowd that had cheered them on afterward, I didn't know, but they were definitely on the side of the republicans. As were many of the people riding the tram car if their nods and remarks of approval were anything to judge by. Others, like me, kept their faces turned away and their thoughts to themselves. Though I was careful not to view their neutral expressions as indications of disapproval rather than greater circumspection. After all, at least some of them must have been aware that enemy informants could be standing in their midst, listening to everything they said. There was always someone willing to snitch on their neighbors for a few measly quid.

But on this quiet street there was no lilting refrain of Irish brogue to accompany me, no clatter of carts, or rattle of bicycle chains, or ringing bells from passing trams as in the busier thoroughfares. And this being a residential street, there was no foot traffic from those drawn to the theaters, pubs, and restaurants in the evening. Only the clack of my footfalls ringing overloud in my ears, and a snatch of birdsong to punctuate it. I looked up as a pair of buntings flew overhead, making their way toward the trees ringing Fitzwilliam Square.

My intelligence training asserted itself, and I strained to hear any telltale signs that I was being followed while continuing to trudge forward, determined not to give myself away. But my heart was pounding too loudly in my ears. I was out of practice, and Dublin was new territory for me.

Territory where, as a prominent, well-to-do British citizen, I should have been safe. But at the moment, the city was a snake pit. One teaming with revolutionaries and the forces the British government had sent to squash them. I wasn't yet certain from which I was most in danger, but there was a risk from both.

Approaching the corner with a narrow alley, I resorted to an old trick. Lowering my worn bag to the pavement, I bent down on one knee, ostensibly to tie a shoelace which had come undone. Under the cover of this gesture, I searched the length of the street in front and behind me for anything suspicious. However, it was empty, save for a gentleman some two hundred yards in front of me already turning the corner into the square.

Grasping my bag, I darted into the alley, fairly confident I'd not missed any tricks someone trailing me might have employed. The edifices of the Georgian houses were flat, leaving little architectural elements for someone to conceal themselves behind, except for perhaps the odd pillar flanking one of the arched doorways. It seemed probable that a republican would have carried on toward me with their characteristic audacity, while a British intelligence officer would have resorted to his training—feigning interest in the building architecture or pretending to call at the nearest address. Given the street's desertion, I instead elected to proceed as planned.

Tucked away behind the stately townhouses gracing Fitzwilliam Square, the mews revealed the far less auspicious side of these homes. Barely wide enough for a coach or now a motorcar to pass through, the lane was lined with walls and fences, as well as former carriage houses, which for the most part had been converted into garages. Though, at least one stable must have remained, for I heard the distinctive whicker of a horse somewhere nearby. I knew that behind several of these walls grew impressive floral gardens because I'd spied them from a window above. From the vantage of the mews, the only indications of such were the odd vine allowed to trail over a fence or the periodic whiff of a gardenia carried on the breeze. Otherwise, the surroundings were naught but stolid brick, wood, and dusty cobblestones. Even the slice of blue sky visible above seemed small and meager.

Approaching the T-junction with another lane, I turned to look behind me. For after I carried on from here, I would be boxed in. The mews ended at exactly the place I didn't wish to lead anyone. Here, once again, the places for concealment were minimal, but I stood watching the entrance to the mews until a motorcar passed along the street beyond. Then I turned and lengthened my stride—even though my shoes pinched—intent on reaching my destination. I cast one last glance over my shoulder at the place where the lane made an abrupt right turn, before moving directly toward the next to last gate in the wall on the left.

There, I paused, taking a deep breath and issuing myself a stern scolding. I hadn't seen or heard anything to indicate that I was being followed, yet like the greenest agent, I was allowing my nerves to get the better of me. Here in the mews, no one could see me or my jittery movements, but once I stepped through this gate, I would be exposed to the eyes of anyone who happened to look out from the upper windows of the neighboring homes. I had to appear exactly as I pretended to be—a care woman sent to look after the Coxes' house while they were away.

Setting my shoulders, I opened the gate and slid through,

careful to latch it firmly behind me. Then I walked calmly up the path that bisected the overgrown garden and circumvented the piles of masonry situated to one side of the rear servants' entrance.

This area of Dublin was often more sparsely populated during the summer months—the owners and tenants having departed for their country estates or traveling abroad—but with the ongoing unrest and disturbances, it was even more deserted than normal. Many of those who did not need to be in Dublin because of civil obligations had fled to safer climes. The Coxes were just such people, abandoning their Upper Fitzwilliam Street home in the midst of a renovation, which had also ground to a halt. I supposed they didn't see the point in going to the expense of completing the task when the building might be damaged by either republicans or British forces. Whatever the case, it suited my purposes perfectly.

Entering the house, I made my way silently past the scullery and kitchen to the staircase. Several of the floorboards groaned loudly when stepped upon, but I'd learned to avoid them. I climbed three stories to the uppermost floor. A thick rug muffled my steps as I entered the bedchamber on the left.

The heavy drapes inside were pulled tight over the windows, blocking the light from the sun still high in the sky on this June evening. However, I had moved about in the chamber often enough in recent days to navigate the dim interior. I was crossing toward the tapestry hung low across the far wall when something shifted in the shadows to my right.

My heart kicked in my chest as I pivoted into a stance to meet my attacker. Only to be blinded by the sudden flare of a torch switched on, though I caught enough of a glimpse of the person holding it to identify him, before shying away.

I muttered a rather unladylike curse. "Bloody hell, Sidney."

"Apologies," my husband replied, lowering the beam to the floor.

I blinked, trying to clear the spots before my vision. "What are you doing here?"

"You were late, Verity," he stated almost accusingly. "And given all the excitement in the northern part of the city, I started to worry you'd been detained. I thought it best to at least come through to be sure there wasn't any trouble on this end."

I noted then that Sidney was already dressed in his evening attire, his dark hair that was prone to curl, ruthlessly tamed by pomade. "You heard about the raid at King's Inn, then?" I asked, reaching for the edges of the dusty tapestry, its floral motif unremarkable at best.

"The moment we returned to the city. Lawrence and Glengarry were furious."

It made sense that two British military officers would be angered by the news that one of their garrisons in the heart of Dublin had been successfully raided by the Irish Republican Army, the IRA. Or, as the British preferred to still call them, the Volunteers, not wishing to convey status upon them or make these rebel skirmishes sound any more warlike than they already were. But there was something in Sidney's tone, despite its seeming impassivity, that made me think there was far more he wasn't saying.

I lifted aside the tapestry to reveal a hole in the wall behind it. A hole that, quite fortuitously, the former contractors had accidentally knocked into it, leaving an opening between this upper story bedchamber and the one in the house next to it. That house happened to belong to the Courtneys, old acquaintances of our friend Max Westfield, the Earl of Ryde, who had been happy to rent the property to us for the duration of our stay in Dublin, as they had fled for warmer and calmer climes. The only contingency was that we had to either repair or tolerate the temporary hole, as well as any ongoing construction that might resume in the home next door.

Far from inconveniencing us, we'd privately been elated

by the hole, as it would suit our purposes perfectly. Indeed, promptly upon our taking possession, Sidney and his valet and former batman, Nimble, had set about enlarging the hole and knocking out the back wooden panel of the wardrobe in the Courtneys' guest bedchamber before positioning it in front of the opening.

I gathered my skirts in my hand and began to scramble carefully through the hole and into the wardrobe before pushing open the doors to climb out the other side. Sidney soon joined me before reaching back inside to slide the coats hanging there back into place, concealing the hole. The tapestry on the other side served the same purpose.

We recognized our contrivances might not escape notice during an exhaustive raid by the British forces, which were perpetuated nearly nightly as they searched for revolutionaries, arms, and incriminating documents, but presumably our reputations and those of the loyalist Courtneys would offer us some protection against such an indignity being carried out. More pressingly, it was meant to mask our clandestine activities from the other members of our household staff we'd hired since our arrival in Dublin. They'd been told I was writing a book and that I wished not to be disturbed while I was working. Only Nimble was permitted on the upper story to tidy up or bring me tea. It was one instance in which my reputation for eccentricity came in handy.

"What time is it?" I asked Sidney, glancing about the room for a clock as I removed the coat I'd donned for my disguise.

"Gone half past six." He opened one of the drawers in the bottom of the wardrobe and took the garment from me to carefully fold it to be stored there. "And it will take at least a half an hour to reach the Viceregal Lodge. Probably longer."

I muttered another curse, struggling to hurry with my clothes. "Why couldn't this dinner have been scheduled for another night?"

"I hesitate to point out that you could have opted *not* to

venture out today, knowing you would be pressed for time later," he declared lightly as he took my hat.

"How could I not?" I paused to demand. "We've already lost so much time," I bemoaned, turning back to the buttons of my blouse, with which I was growing increasingly frustrated. "Who knows what sort of trouble Alec has gotten himself into by now? Whether we'll ever be able to extract him. Blast it!" I raged, tugging at the hem of my top.

Sidney's hands reached out to still mine, before drawing me toward him.

"I'll smudge your coat," I sniffed, remembering at the last that I'd used a tinted cream to make my complexion sallow as part of my disguise, muting my normal glow of health.

He relented but his deep midnight-blue eyes continued to hold mine, steadying me. Only briefly did they dip to finish slipping the last button free on my blouse. "I take it you had little luck today."

"None," I grumbled, and then sighed, forcing myself to be honest. "But then, I didn't truly expect any. Not when such an effort takes time. Rushing would only place all of us at greater risk."

Few truer words had ever been spoken about intelligence work. But agents grew antsy, and superior officers demanded results too quickly. Such impatience had spoiled more operations and exposed more agents to suspicion—and at times death—than I could count.

"I only wish we could have begun sooner," I finished, sinking down on the edge of the bed to remove my shoes.

It had been nearly six weeks since we'd learned that my friend and former fellow spy, Captain Alec Xavier, had dropped out of contact with his handler. He'd been sent into Ireland by C, the chief of the Secret Intelligence Service, or SIS, to infiltrate the republicans, and in particular, Michael Collins and his inner circle, if he could.

If anyone could do it, I was certain it was Alec. After all, the man had insinuated himself into the German Army years before the war had even begun and masqueraded as a staff officer among their ranks in Brussels. I'd worked with him multiple times and was fully aware of his capabilities. He was a master at shifting personas and concealing his thoughts, his legendary charm smoothing over any rough patches.

But Alec wasn't without his faults, and Michael Collins, a member of the executive council of Sinn Féin—the Irish nationalist political party controlling Ireland's shadow government—and the director of intelligence for the Irish Republican Army, was no ordinary target. For one, Alec could be rash and reckless, sometimes failing to look before he leaped. For another, he was provocative, enjoying stirring the pot. This characteristic might go over well with these Irishmen, who seemed to give as good as they got. But then again, it might just as surely get him killed.

I couldn't stop thinking of the look in his eyes the last time I'd seen him in London when he'd hinted that he would be sent to Dublin. That I might be also. There had been something unmoored, something that made me fear he wouldn't be as careful as he'd been in the past.

It hadn't eased my concerns when Byrnes, the agent Sir Basil Thomson, the director of intelligence for the Home Office, had sent to catch Collins, had instead been killed by his quarry—or more likely, by members of Collins's intelligence staff—and then exposed as the spy he was. I'd never had the same confidence in Brynes that Thomson did, but it was still a shock to hear, and had increased my apprehension for Alec.

So when C had reached out through his secretary to inform me that Alec had disappeared, neither I nor Sidney had required much convincing to travel to Dublin to try to discover what had happened, albeit in an unofficial capacity. Of course, all of this was further complicated by the fact that Alec had not been sent to Ireland at Thomson's behest, but rather C's. As such, he hadn't been working in conjunction with the intelligence service at Dublin Castle or the intelligence officers who worked under the political branch in the G Division of the Dublin Metropolitan Police. Consequently, neither were Sidney and I.

Sidney sat down beside me. "You couldn't help the fact that Groβtante Ilse passed away just as we were preparing to leave London. No one could," he reminded me gently.

My beloved great-aunt's death hadn't been a shock, for we'd known because of her illness that she was living on borrowed time, but it had still struck me like a blow, and the timing couldn't have been worse.

"You would never have forgiven yourself if you'd missed her funeral," he murmured. "And neither would your mother."

I grimaced, knowing this to be true. Relations with my family, particularly my mother, had been strained when I hadn't returned home to Yorkshire to mourn when my brother, Rob, was killed. But then we had been in the middle of a war, and my intelligence work had taken precedence. Work I was forbidden by the Defense of the Realm Act from ever telling my family about. Sidney had only found out because of the indiscretion of a colleague. But while my duties at the Secret Service had been important, my inability to accept the finality of Rob's death had been as much a factor.

However, I had since accepted the truth and reconciled with my family, and I was reluctant to shatter that amnesty. Though that hadn't stopped me from feeling conflicted while we remained in Yorkshire, and acutely aware of the passing of time and the fact that Alec could be in trouble. Eventually we couldn't delay the matter any longer. Not when the updates from C were increasingly discouraging.

When we'd made our excuses for our departure, most of my family had assumed the reason we were bound for Dublin was because of Sidney. After all, he was a decorated war hero, having received the Victoria Cross, as well as the heir presumptive to his uncle's marquessate. In their minds, I supposed it seemed natural that he'd been asked to consult with the military on the Irish situation. A notion we didn't disabuse them of. Only my older brother Freddy had eyed me askance, letting me know he suspected at least part of the truth, but I knew he would never breathe a word to the others.

Sidney's arm wrapped around my waist. "But perhaps more importantly you need to hear that *Xavier* would not begrudge you our delay."

My chest tightened, wanting to believe him. "That's easy to say now, but what if we discover the worst?"

Sidney shook his head. "Don't take on that burden. Not when we don't yet know what's happened to him. He could very well be hale and hearty, just unable to pass his intelligence reports the usual way. We could hear any day now that he found another way to get in contact with C."

I had to concede this was possible, but it did little to ease my mind.

CHAPTER 2

Twenty minutes later, give or take a minute or two, we were speeding south down Pembroke Street in Sidney's Pierce-Arrow, drawing looks from those we passed. It was difficult, after all, to remain inconspicuous tooling about in a carmine-red roadster, especially one that was the envy of many a motorist.

Before our arrival in Dublin, Sidney and I had discussed at length the best approach to our investigation here. Since it seemed unlikely we could pass unnoticed for long—our faces having graced the pages of newspapers the world over, both the society columns and in relation to some of our investigations exposing treason and murderers—it had seemed foolish to even attempt it. Besides, why cut off your nose to spite your face? We could gather what information we could as social darlings, gaining access to people and places most could not, while simultaneously masquerading as lower middle-class Irish to learn what we could from the streets.

It also gave us the added benefit of hiding in plain sight. After all, who would ever suspect two virtual celebrities of being intelligence operatives? The very suggestion seemed laughable. Or at least, I hoped it seemed so, to the rebels and Dublin Castle alike. The true nature of my intelligence work during the war had only ever been known by a few, so even if someone at the Castle knew of my past involvement, it was doubtful they believed me capable of more than typing and translating.

So, subscribing to the notion of in for a penny, in for a pound, we'd decided to ship Sidney's Pierce-Arrow to Ireland, as well as pack some of my more glamorous clothing. Such as my current gown of emerald satin which was covered in a black beaded lace overlay with a cape that gathered and fell from my shoulders, and highlighted rather than concealed the scooped back of the satin underlayer. The evening being a fine one, Sidney had opted to lower the roadster's roof, which helped to blow-dry the dampness at my hairline from my harried ablutions. It would also provide me with a ready excuse for the unruliness of my auburn bobbed waves.

Sidney navigated around Royal University and Harcourt Railway Station, bound for the South Circular Road that would skirt the edge of Dublin just inside the ring of the Grand Canal. In the distance, we could see the blue smudge of the Dublin Mountains. We passed numerous bicycles, a couple of horse-drawn carts, and a tram, but there were few motorcars occupying the road alongside ours, at least in comparison with London. It was undoubtedly due to the lingering effect of the protests over the implementation of motor permits late the previous year by Dublin Castle—the British government's seat of power in Ireland. Not only were drivers required to have a license, they also must display a permit with their personal details and photograph. It was all part of the effort to thwart the rebels from using motorcars for their illegal purposes. Though, that hadn't stopped the raiders at King's Inn from loading their confiscated arms and ammunition into two motorcars as they made their getaway.

The farther west we swept, circling the outskirts of the city, the more rural our surroundings became. The landscape was dotted with trees, fields, and an old mill, as well as a few quarries. We also passed several of the military barracks that dotted the outer edges of Dublin, as many of them were built close to the canals, which more or less formed a ring around the city, allowing them to be easily resupplied.

Sidney honked the horn jauntily to a pair of army lorries we passed outside the gates to Wellington Barracks. Several of the soldiers hung over the sides to wave and gesture, probably more interested in my husband's Pierce-Arrow than the two of us. I smiled reflexively as we hurtled past, but an uneasiness stole over me as I watched the lorries recede in the wing mirror. For all that those boys were ours and would have drawn good cheer and well wishes back home in Britain or along the pockmarked roads of northeastern France near the Western Front, this was Ireland.

There—in Britain and France and Belgium—they'd been wanted. Here, a large proportion of the population resented their presence. They didn't stand and smile and wave when those soldiers and their like—the so-called Black and Tans, drafted to supplement the dwindling ranks of the Royal Irish Constabulary—rolled through the streets of the city in their lorries and tenders on patrol or bound for some building to be raided. Rather, the Dubliners cowered, or scattered, or jeered and hurled cabbages at them. They viewed the troops less as their protectors and liberators and more as occupiers.

"You've gone quiet," Sidney remarked.

I didn't want to share my troubled thoughts. So instead, I occupied myself with tying a scarf around my head. My hair had seen enough wind, and I hoped the covering would tame it at least to some degree.

When I didn't respond, he took to probing more directly. "So what route did you elect to take today?"

We'd already discussed the matter at length, but given the struggle I'd had just convincing him to allow me to venture out alone in disguise, I wasn't surprised he wanted to know if I'd deviated from the plan. Never mind that I'd already acceded that, from a strategic standpoint, it made sense for him to know where I was, lest any problems arise. After all, Sidney and I were the only reinforcements each other had.

"I stuck to the scheme," I said. "But I also realized rather quickly that it's faulty. Wandering about the city for hours on end isn't likely to gain me anything but aching feet. So, instead, I chose a few locations Alec mentioned in his earlier reports. Places where he suspected the proprietors of being sympathetic to the republican cause or where he'd witnessed some of the rebels gather."

"Which locations?" he inquired, not sounding as satisfied with this course of action as I was.

I adjusted the Indian shawl draped around my shoulders. "Vaughan's Hotel, Rutland Square, the Wicklow, and St. Stephen's Green."

"Won't your turning up there repeatedly draw suspicion?"

"A respectable young woman new to the city, minding her own business? I think not."

As a rule, men discounted women, especially when they weren't behaving disreputably. It was why we made such excellent agents, regardless of the prejudiced prevailing opinion about women throughout the service. I liked to believe C was different, but truth be told, I wasn't certain *he* even fully appreciated my abilities, despite the fact he continued to trust me with these clandestine assignments. But of course, I'd been the one to first seek his assistance on an urgent matter pertaining to my war work, and every inquiry since then had been an extenuation of that.

I'd been demobilized more than a year ago, along with most of the other women who'd served in the intelligence services during the war. Demobbed and told to go home and keep our mouths shut. Which we did, despite the aspersions some of the officers had cast to the contrary. So every assignment I'd taken from C since then was not officially sanctioned.

Sidney turned to look at me briefly. "You didn't ask any questions, then?"

"Of course, not." I waited to explain until he'd maneuvered the motorcar around a cart piled high with hay. "Nothing would be certain to draw suspicion faster and seal their lips tighter. Better to be reserved and quiet, but polite. Unthreatening. Then they'll either begin to forget I'm there, and hopefully let something slip within my hearing, or grow curious and start asking questions themselves."

"And you can play the damsel in distress?" he surmised.

"Fretting about my missing 'cousin,' and uncertain how to go about looking for him? Yes," I confirmed, referring to the story we'd concocted about Alec's relation to me. We couldn't exactly go about telling people we were looking for a missing British Intelligence officer. "It may take more time to achieve results, but it will be safer and more effective in the long run."

Not to mention the fact that it would give me a chance to better attune my ear to the Irish vernacular and perfect my accent. Relying on my current ability, I was afraid I would give myself away if I uttered more than a few words at a time. In Belgium, I'd never feared detection because I'd grown up speaking French and German with a Walloon accent, as we'd frequently visited my Großtante Ilse, who'd lived just over the border in Westphalia, Germany. But the Irish dialect was unfamiliar to me, and even with as good an ear as I had for languages, I knew I had much to learn.

"You *have* thought this out."

The surprise in his voice sparked my irritation. "Yes, shocking, I suppose, considering I've done this a time or two."

My derisive quip seemed to have landed squarely, for a few seconds later his hand reached out to grip mine. "Sorry, Ver. I know I should have more faith in you, and I *do*. But . . ." He broke off, grimacing as he struggled to explain himself. "The stakes have changed, haven't they?" He darted a glance at me. "I mean, I wasn't with you behind enemy lines during the war. I didn't have to watch you evade the Germans and their grasping fingers. I didn't even know it was happening much of the time. And our investigations since then have been more about avoiding a few nefarious figures, not potentially an entire *populace* full of them."

"I'm not going to do anything foolish, Sidney," I assured him. "We're here to find Alec. Once that's done . . ." I couldn't finish the sentence, knowing the matter wasn't as straightforward as I wished.

We drove on in brooding silence for a few minutes before Sidney dared to break it. "To tell you the truth, I thought Alec would contact us himself by now. Or at least, that he'd contact you. After all, we haven't exactly been keeping a low profile." He gestured to indicate the Pierce-Arrow and I supposed all the conspicuous trappings of our life.

I didn't want to admit it, but I'd expected the same. And it troubled me. Surely if Alec were alive, if he were able to reach out, he would have done so once he'd realized we were in Dublin. Which meant that either he was in another part of the country, or more worrying, he was unable to approach us either because of injury, some sort of incarceration, or . . . death.

I'd considered the possibility that he no longer trusted me—that *that* was the reason he hadn't made contact—but I'd swiftly rejected it. When his position within the German Army had been compromised and he was in danger of being detained and summarily executed, I'd ventured back into Belgium at great personal risk to extract him and guide him to safety back in Holland. That wasn't something someone forgot.

"He hasn't, has he?" Sidney asked, interrupting my agitated thoughts. "Contacted you?" he clarified.

I scowled. "No."

Sidney's gaze locked with mine for a short moment before turning back to the road.

I wanted to begrudge him the question, but I couldn't entirely fault him. It would be like Alec to reach out to me privately and not Sidney. Because of our past and our mutual rapport, operating undercover together in the German-occupied territories. And because I'd once shared his bed during the dark days after I'd learned of my husband's alleged death.

For fifteen months, Sidney had allowed me to believe he was dead as he recovered from a nearly fatal bullet wound delivered by a fellow British officer, and then pursued a nest of traitors. We had since worked to heal the hurt of that betrayal, as well as some of my own, including my very short-lived intimate relationship with Alec. It had not been easy, and Sidney and I still had a distance to go, but we now knew that our bond would not break, and our marriage was the stronger for it.

However, relations between Sidney and Alec were complicated, to say the least. So sometimes Alec strove to avoid the inevitable tension by communicating with just me. Nonetheless my husband should have known I would never keep such a thing from him.

I scrutinized his profile—his square, resolute jaw and high cheekbones—trying to decipher what he was thinking. Sidney had always been good at masking his thoughts, keeping himself in a constant state of vigilance—a holdover from the war. He presented himself as an easygoing man-about-town to others, but I knew better. Only in sleep did he relax. And sometimes not even then.

"There's also the matter of those phosgene cylinders," Sidney said as he decelerated into a sharp turn.

As if I could forget. We'd learned about the missing poisonous gas nearly seven months ago, and while we'd recently confirmed they'd been taken to Ireland, all trace of them had since vanished, despite numerous sources—including Alec—searching for them. The idea of them being used against either the military or the populace here featured prominently in my most recent nightmares.

But I didn't want to discuss them now. Not when I had to play the role of the sparkling socialite in short order. So I ignored the loaded comment and instead posed a question of my own. "What of you? Did you have any luck today?"

"With the horses? Yes." He adjusted his hands on the driving wheel. "But not with the rest."

"Your chums didn't have anything interesting to say?"

"Not anything worth repeating," he muttered.

Though I was curious, his voice forbade prying, and for once I obeyed.

Since arriving in Dublin, Sidney had discovered a number of his acquaintances had been stationed here, either in military or civil service positions, and we'd decided it would be good for him to make contact with them. He'd attended a race meeting with a pair of them today while I'd ventured out in disguise.

"Well, if you managed to win more than you lost, then I suppose you at least didn't embarrass yourself as you feared," I murmured lightly.

Horse racing was not of great interest to my husband. Yet, here in Ireland, horse racing was a celebrated pastime, especially for gentlemen with money to throw around. Now, if they'd been racing motorcars, then Sidney would have been as keen as mustard. But there was a reason he had enlisted as an infantry officer and not in the cavalry.

Thank God for it! The cavalry corps had suffered horrendous losses during the war, and essentially been rendered obsolete by the middle of the conflict, for a cavalry charge could not hope to withstand a machine gun barrage.

Even so, like most gentlemen, Sidney had been taught to ride at a young age and could acquit himself quite admirably in the saddle. In fact, he was an expert polo player. With that came a knowledge about horses which allowed him to at least enjoy the feat of the thoroughbreds, and saved him from making any foolish remarks.

The tension he was holding in his shoulders seemed to ease a fraction as he tossed an affectionate look my way. "I did well enough."

Wry amusement curled my lips, for I knew that look. "By which you mean you came out ahead of them both."

He shrugged with a self-satisfied smirk.

Crossing over the River Liffey, we finally came in sight of Phoenix Park. The massive park at the northwestern edge of Dublin housed numerous important buildings, including the Viceregal Lodge, the Chief Secretary's Lodge, and the Magazine Fort, as well as operating as a garden and green space for Dublin's residents. As Sidney navigated a series of turns, I scrutinized the wide variety of trees, shrubs, and flowers in the flush of June. A towering obelisk—a memorial to Wellington—dominated one plain near the central avenue.

At the outer edge of the park, numerous military and constabulary installations overlooked the otherwise peaceful setting, including barracks, a military hospital, and the headquarters of the Royal Irish Constabulary—the RIC. As Sidney stopped to allow an electric tram before us to disgorge its passengers, we noticed a perimeter of soldiers blocking the entrance to the park. Having yet to visit this part of Dublin, I didn't know whether their presence was typical, or if the lord lieutenant's dinner party had prompted extra security measures. Of course, there was one other explanation.

"I suppose the raid at King's Inn has them on high alert," Sidney remarked softly.

"As I understand it, the Volunteers got away with a number of weapons," I replied, joining Sidney in his scrutiny of the troops.

"Rifles, hand grenades, and over a thousand rounds of ammunition. Not to mention two machine guns."

My eyebrows arched skyward, and I was about to ask him how he'd come by this information so quickly, when we began moving forward again. I supposed the answer was obvious. Lawrence and Glengarry must have been informed by their colleagues on their return to Dublin, and Sidney had overheard.

He pasted a pleasant expression on his face as we rolled to a stop before the cordon. "Good evening, Captain. What seems to be the trouble?"

"Shinners, sir," the officer who stepped forward replied, using one of the derogatory names applied to the rebels. It was a corruption of the dominant Irish nationalist political party's name, whose members had formed their own government in early 1919 and declared themselves representatives of the Irish Republic rather than taking their seats in the British Parliament. Sinn Féin was pronounced "shin fayn," from which was derived the slurs "shinner" and "shins." Though it was the IRA who formed the fighting branch of the rebellion, and who had caused the trouble at King's Inn that day, most British didn't bother to distinguish between the political rhetoric and the army, instead lumping them all together. Indeed, there was much crossover. But while most of the fighting men in the Irish Republican Army also supported Sinn Féin, not all members of Sinn Féin espoused the tactics of the IRA.

"Now, surely, you don't suspect me of concealing weapons in the boot," Sidney quipped.

Several of the soldiers eyeing the Pierce-Arrow appreciatively chuckled, but the officer didn't appear amused. "It's merely a matter of form, sir. These shinners are sly little devils."

"Of course," Sidney replied good-naturedly.

"I suppose you're on your way to the dinner at the Viceregal Lodge, Mr. Kent," the officer remarked casually, letting us know he was aware of who we were. There was a glint of something akin to disapproval in his eyes as he turned to gesture for his soldiers to let us through. "Best hurry, or they'll begin without you."

Sidney reached for the shifter, and turned away, all but

dismissing the man as he eased his foot off the break. "That's doubtful."

I was unused to my husband displaying such arrogance, even though he wasn't wrong. But then the officer had plainly gotten under his skin. In truth, I was equally surprised by the officer's reaction to Sidney. Most soldiers—most men, in general—seemed to revere my husband. He'd always been the type of man that others wanted the good opinion of, and his status as a war hero had only increased that. But the captain had clearly been unimpressed.

As we motored down the lane which cut through the center of Phoenix Park, I debated whether to say anything, but Sidney already knew what I was thinking.

"He was suspicious."

I turned to him in mild alarm. "What do you mean?"

"Of why I'm here. In Dublin," he clarified.

"I don't know why he should care."

Sidney sighed as we passed the turn to the Zoological Gardens. "Because I'm Sidney Kent, the War Office's golden child," he scoffed. "And why on earth would they send me to God-forsaken Ireland unless there was a good reason. One that officer isn't sure he'll like."

"Except the War Office didn't send you."

"No, but he didn't know that. And if he did, then he'd only assume that means the director of intelligence sent me. In either case, that officer and others like him are suspicious."

I pondered this for a moment. It had seemed inevitable that there would be some who questioned our presence here, but I'd expected it more from the officials we were about to encounter at the lord lieutenant's dinner than the general rank and file.

"Did we make the wrong decision?" I asked, pressing my hands to the smooth leather seat. "Should we have tried to conceal our being here?"

"Only to come under even greater suspicion once our

presence was inevitably discovered?" Sidney shook his head. "No, Ver."

"But if our own men think you've been sent by either the War Office or Intelligence, then some of the rebels are bound to think so, too. What if they come after you?"

"They won't," he pronounced with quiet certainty.

"You can't know that."

"I can," he countered stubbornly before adding, "but if they do, they won't live to regret it."

I took this to mean he was carrying his Luger pistol with him about town despite the restrictions against civilians doing so. I supposed he was counting on his connections and social standing to smooth over any difficulties.

"Is that wise?" I asked him, referring to his gun.

He turned to look at me. "I wish *you* would carry one. Just a small pocket pistol. It would make me feel better."

I sat back, frustration simmering inside me at his bull-headed obstinance. "In my experience, guns only create complications. I operated quite effectively inside German-occupied Belgium and France without a pistol." Where civilian-owned weapons had also been banned, and grounds for immediate arrest if not summary execution. "And I shall operate just as effectively without one here."

I felt Sidney's gaze on me but remained resolutely turned away. His refusal to understand that I was better equipped to confront the challenges of our current task continued to rankle. Ireland might still be part of the British Empire, but a significant portion of her population was at war with her British overseers. Our leaders could publicly deny it all they wanted, but this was no simple disaffection. And the fact that the government continued to mobilize more of the Crown Forces, even supplementing the ranks of the Royal Irish Constabulary to help combat the rebels, only confirmed they knew this.

This wasn't a conflict of clearly delineated lines and battle fronts, but one of shadows and stealth. Sidney, like the British government, might wish to contort the dispute and force it back into the nice, tidy rows of direct confrontation that the Crown Forces and her civil authorities excelled at countering, but thus far the Irish rebels had proved too savvy to let themselves be pressured into doing so. Which meant that Dublin Castle and the Crown Forces needed to adapt—*Sidney* needed to adapt—to this new form of rebellion, or they hadn't a hope of effectively counteracting it.

Maybe it was a mistake to divide and conquer. To send Sidney off to gather what information he could from his military and civil government contacts rather than accompany me on my forays to republican gathering places. But I knew my husband would immediately draw suspicion. He hadn't the acting skills I did, nor my facility for dialects, and they would see through any disguise he adopted in minutes. I'd laughed myself silly upon hearing his attempt to speak with an Irish accent. Any chance of gathering valuable intelligence with him by my side seemed slim to none.

So for the time being it seemed we had no choice but to operate separately. Nonetheless, I was wary of his military acquaintances' influence on him. I could only hope that whatever mulishness he picked up from them could be counteracted, and that it wouldn't get him killed.

CHAPTER 3

I had been a dinner guest at some of the most beautiful and palatial homes in Britain and across Europe. Places of such opulence and splendor that it was difficult to pay attention to either the meal or your dinner companion, for your gaze kept wandering to the frescos and wood carvings and artwork.

The Viceregal Lodge was not one of those residences.

Despite being the home of the Crown's representative in Ireland, it proved to be altogether rather modest and terribly bland in appearance. Save for the brilliant white of its exterior, which practically glowed in the light of the evening sun, the sprawling, blocky affair boasted only one architectural element of distinction—four Ionic pillars which held up the portico on the north façade. Though I supposed the magnificent grounds surrounding it in some way compensated for the building's lack of grandeur. An avid horseman like Lord French would find the vast park and superb stables a boon.

I had met the lord lieutenant just once, and that had been shortly after his return to England following his resignation as commander-in-chief of the British Expeditionary Force. A resignation Lord French had been all but forced to make in late 1915, before being replaced by his subordinate, Field Marshal Haig. As such, I didn't expect him to recall our brief acquaintance, but I was wrong.

"Mrs. Kent," he declared as he grasped my hand at the entry to the drawing room. "How delightful to see you again." A broad grin stretched his face beneath his magnificent white waxed mustache. His bright gaze shifted to Sidney. "And with your husband in tow, I see." He shook Sidney's hand. "I've heard a great deal about your exploits, Captain Kent. Though I don't believe I had the pleasure of meeting you at the front."

"No, sir," Sidney replied. "Though I saw you once when we were waiting to go up the line near Neuve Chapelle."

"Yes." Some gravity returned to Lord French's appearance at Sidney's mention of the battle. French had always been popular with the troops, partly because of his efforts in raising their morale by his frequent visitations to the front. He'd also seemed to take the heavy casualty figures of his men to heart. But while such empathy might be endearing, to be an effective military commander required a certain amount of detachment and ruthlessness that French had lacked.

He clapped Sidney on the shoulder. "Good man." Then he turned to offer me his arm. "Allow me to introduce you to my other guests."

French's figure was short and ran to portly, but he was known to be rather notorious with women. He'd been linked to several scandalous affairs, including one with a fellow officer's wife in India, which had nearly ruined his career. Witnessing the charm he exhibited as we circulated the room, coupled with the fact he'd been more attractive as a younger man, I could better understand his reputation. He lived almost permanently separated from his wife, instead entertaining with his mistress, the beautiful widow Mrs. Bennett.

We were introduced to a number of society figures, including Lord Powerscourt and his wife, with whom I was already acquainted, and high-ranking members of the lord lieutenant's staff, such as Captain Wyndham-Quin—who served as Master of the Horse and Military Secretary—and his wife, Helen. Also attending were a few privy councilors from the viceroy's advisory council—judges, railway directors, senior public servants, and the like—and their wives. Though their role now was more ceremonial than practical, just as Lord French's was.

There had recently been a serious overhaul of the administration at Dublin Castle, and many of the senior civil servants had been replaced. Only a few had escaped dismissal. One of them being the lord lieutenant himself. Though, rumor was, his position was shaky, and as part of the restructuring effort, many of the executive powers he'd previously exercised had been taken away, leaving him as little but a figurehead.

The former field-marshal being a man accustomed to wielding authority, I imagined Lord French was struggling to adjust to this new set of circumstances. I was quite certain he was aware of the top-level cabinet meetings currently ongoing in London, which the newspapers had reported on that morning. Meetings being attended by Dublin Castle officials and the heads of the military and police in Ireland, as well as the prime minister and his cabinet as they discussed the Irish situation. Lord French, no doubt, wished he was there rather than straining to exert even the smallest influence among the attendees at this dinner party.

Sidney and I had discussed this as we'd motored through the gates to the Viceregal Lodge, and my eyes met Sidney's and held, reminding him of it and our intentions to play this to our advantage. Reports were that Lord French was prone to a bit of swaggering, and without the senior officials here to keep him in check, our hope was that he might unwittingly reveal something that would help us to locate Alec.

Given our late arrival, we weren't given much time to work on our host or circulate among the guests before the butler announced dinner. As we made our way down the corridor toward the dining room, Helen Wyndham-Quin drew up beside me. "I love your gown," she declared. "It's positively stunning."

"Thank you," I replied. "I'd be happy to give you the name of my modiste in London if you'd like her to create something similar."

"Oh, I don't know," she demurred, though I could tell she was torn.

"It is a trifle daring," I admitted with a laugh, guessing this was the reason for her hesitation. Her own gown of steel blue, while certainly quality, was a bit staid. "But yours wouldn't have to be."

"True." Her gaze flickered over the satin and lace once more before she nodded decisively. "Yes, I would appreciate that very much." She reached up to fiddle with her pearl necklace as we turned to stroll side by side. "You must think me cowardly." She glanced over her shoulder toward her handsome husband. "Dicky always tells me he doesn't know how it is I can ride so hell-for-leather after the hounds and yet be such a mouse about everything else."

"We can't all be brave about everything," I told her. "Why, just ask Sidney what a veritable goose I become whenever I see a spider."

"It's true," Sidney sidled closer to say. "Even honks like one, from the chair onto which she's jumped."

Everyone laughed as I playfully swatted his shoulder.

He draped his arm around my waist, pulling me affectionately toward him. "Don't worry, darling. It's no worse than the way I shrieked when I found a snake curled up in one of my boots while waiting to go up the line." This drew even more laughter, including a loud guffaw from Lord French. "I received about a dozen rubber snakes as gifts that Christmas," he ruminated, keeping the amusement going.

I'd not yet heard this story, leading me to wonder if it was true or not, or if he was merely playing to the crowd. Like many returning soldiers, Sidney was reluctant to share information about his time at the front, so I gave the matter even odds. In any case, it had certainly broken the ice, and now people began to converse freely with us where before they'd been slightly stilted.

"Oh my," I exclaimed, stopping short at the sight of the dining table. A profusion of colorful blooms filled the vases at its center, spilling down across the tabletop to wind with the crystal and silverware that glittered in the light of the chandeliers overhead and the sunlight softly streaming through the windows. The sun wouldn't set for at least another two hours on this June evening. "I hope they haven't pruned every bush in the garden."

I turned at the sound of tinkling laughter.

"Don't worry, Mrs. Kent," Lady Powerscourt said. "The Viceregal Lodge's gardens are extensive."

I smiled. Her Ladyship was nearly two decades older than my three and twenty years, yet she might have passed for thirty, such was her beauty. The wide neckline of her golden gown accentuated her long, graceful neck and smooth shoulders. I suppressed a pulse of envy, knowing that, courtesy of the scar on my shoulder left by a gunshot wound, I would never be able to wear such a fashion again.

"Yet, I've heard that the gardens at Powerscourt House are beyond compare," I remarked.

In fact, her husband's estate and family seat were famed far beyond the shores of Ireland.

"They are magnificent," she conceded. "You and your husband must come stay with us sometime."

"I'd like that," I said, pleased to be so easily making inroads. Not that I'd doubted the ability of our social position and wealth, not to mention our status as social darlings and Sidney's prestige as a war hero, to attain us any invitation we might desire. But it was good to see that curiosity and suspicion about our presence in Dublin had not damaged this clout.

Truthfully, I hoped to be back in London before such an invitation was ever issued, but part of intelligence work was learning to take advantage of every opportunity afforded to you. For all that Lord and Lady Powerscourt were unlikely to have any knowledge of—or association with—Alec, they might have guests who did. And they very well might have a connection to the cunning Lord Ardmore, a fellow Irish peer, who for all intents and purposes had become my greatest nemesis. The Powercourts could know something worthwhile about Ardmore's past which could help us in the present.

To that end, I set about charming Lord Powerscourt when I discovered he was seated on my right. He was amiable, if a bit horse-mad, as a large number of the people seated at the table seemed to be. I was beginning to greater empathize with Sidney's position that afternoon, for while I enjoyed a good gallop as much as the next person, I felt little desire to dissect their every feature and antecedent or to bet on their races. Fortunately, this topic of conversation didn't reign long.

During a brief lull after we'd been served the second course, Tommy O'Shaughnessy, the Recorder of Dublin, fastened a probing stare on my husband across the table. I could well imagine him in his role as chief magistrate, addressing barristers and defendants in much the same manner. With his long white hair, he would hardly need the wig he must wear in court. "Well, now, Mr. Kent, you're a military man," he proclaimed. "What do *you* make of the trouble these republicans have brought to our fair city and country?"

"Former military man," Sidney corrected him, dabbing his mouth as the clanking of silverware all but fell silent so everyone could listen.

"Aye," O'Shaughnessy conceded, though there was a glint in his eye that suggested he wasn't certain of that. "But as a holder of the Victoria Cross, ye must be dismayed?"

"I would say . . . 'concerned' is the more appropriate word." He nodded toward the judge and several of the others. "As I'm sure you are."

A man seated across from me—one of the railway directors—

scoffed loudly. "'Concerned' is much too weak a word in my opinion. Not when they're murderin' policemen and government officials. Not when they're incitin' my railwaymen to treason."

I didn't think the recent refusal by railway workers to load munitions or drive trains with British arms or troops on board quite constituted the label of treason, but I could understand him having strong feelings about it, considering how it affected his company.

"It won't last for long," one of the other men predicted. "Not when it concerns their wages."

"Aye. Especially when I sack 'em all and bring over Englishmen to do their jobs," the railway official stated spitefully.

"Now, let's not be hasty, Frank," O'Shaughnessy cautioned.

"Maybe that's exactly what Mr. Brooke and the others should do," Lord French interjected, his white mustache bristling. "Teach these shinners a lesson. You can't defy the British Empire and expect not to suffer the consequences."

"The Germans and Austrians certainly learned that lesson," another fellow jested to the general amusement of some.

Sidney's gaze met mine briefly, and I could sense the turmoil within him, for it echoed my own. For millions of good men had died allegedly teaching them that lesson, and in Belgium some months earlier we'd learned that a good portion of them would still be with us if our leaders had swallowed their hubris and not bungled the opportunity to make peace midway through the war. Given what we knew, it was impossible not to feel cynical about the government's efforts here. Particularly knowing they'd had a much different response to the Curragh mutiny six years prior that in many ways had brought about the current situation.

"We've strayed from the point," O'Shaughnessy cautioned the others, and I wondered if he'd sensed my and Sidney's discomfort. "Ye were sayin' you're concerned." He leaned forward to prompt my husband.

Sidney took a drink, seemingly unruffled by all the attention directed at him, but I could tell he was playing for time to consider his response. "Well, naturally one can't help but be concerned by all of these policemen being shot. Not quite sporting, is it? And the burning of their barracks." He shook his head in disgust, but then tempered his words. "But these rumors about the so-called Black and Tans and their treatment of civilians are equally concerning."

"Those rumors are highly exaggerated," one man declared.

"Naught but Sinn Féin propaganda," another concurred.

But was that true? Even in the short time we'd been in Ireland, the number of reports of mistreatment—of homes being sacked or burned and civilians being assaulted—seemed to grow with each day. Of course, many of these were not reported in the British-controlled press, but some were. And others were shared by the papers which seemed to delight in defying the government's censorship restrictions.

The notion of recruiting former British soldiers who were out of work, to bulk up the dwindling and ineffective ranks of the Royal Irish Constabulary as temporary cadets, might have seemed a good one, but they'd yet to prove their worth. Particularly given these reports of reprisals. They'd been christened the Black and Tans because of their hodge-podge attire. There not being enough RIC uniforms, many of them wore khaki army trousers or tunics with whatever dark green RIC apparel and caps were available, the dark green appearing almost black. Jests had also been made comparing them to a breed of Kerry beagles, a hunting dog whose color markings were black and tan, and so the name had stuck.

"Even if they are true, it only serves them right," Mr. Brooke, the railway director, chimed in to say. "You've never seen a crowd turn deaf and dumb so quickly as in Ireland.

Even when half of 'em had a clear view of the shootin'. Tell me I'm wrong, Tommy," he challenged the Dublin recorder.

"Aye, you're right," Mr. O'Shaughnessy conceded. "The courts 've had a devil of a time findin' witnesses willin' to step forward. More often than not, they all deny havin' seen anythin', *especially* the culprits, though they sees them on the streets every day." He sniffed loudly, this time in disgust, though it wasn't the first time that evening he'd inhaled sharply. Judging from this habit and the discoloring of his cravat, I deduced he was a rather devoted snuff-taker.

"They're all complicit," a man with a salt-and-pepper beard declared, pounding the table. "Accessories to the crime. So why shouldn't they expect to share in the punishment?"

"Now, I wouldn't go that far," O'Shaughnessy demurred.

"I would," Brooke grumbled.

The Dublin recorder scowled. "Remember, they're all thoroughly intimidated, and they don't have the protections you or I have."

"Then they should speak up and get the lot of 'em thrown in jail," Brooke retorted.

Except such matters were never so simple.

"I trust Tudor will soon have the RIC and the Tans sorted out," Captain Wyndham-Quin said as he forked a bite of sole.

"Yes. A good man, Tudor," Lord French asserted, though I couldn't tell from his tone whether he actually believed this. "What of you, Kent?" he turned to ask Sidney without missing a beat. "Are you acquainted?"

"We've met," Sidney replied with what I imagined was maddening obliqueness to the men gathered at the table.

"Recently?" Mr. Brooke pressed.

Sidney swirled the wine in his glass. "Not in many months."

I looked down at my plate, suppressing a smile. It was clear they suspected Sidney might have been drafted in to assist

Tudor in his capacity as police advisor. Though why such a matter would be kept secret, I couldn't fathom.

"Aye, well, Colonel Johnstone had best get his DMP in line as well," the man with the salt-and-pepper beard groused. "One hears they're all either sympathetic to these shinners or too afraid to confront 'em."

"Ye can hardly blame 'em for not wantin' to stick their necks out," O'Shaughnessy rebutted. "The moment they do, they get shot."

"Aye, except 'tis their job!"

Glancing about me, I wondered if these men fully appreciated what a bleak picture they were painting of their security forces. The Dublin Metropolitan Police were so intimidated by Collins and his murder gang that they were all but rendered useless. The RIC were being burned out of their barracks and driven from rural outposts, all but abandoning them to the republicans' control. And the reinforcements we'd brought to Ireland to combat the problem seemed to be doing more to terrorize the population they were sent to protect than they were to enforce the law.

From the furrowed brows of a number of the ladies present and their lowered forks, it was clear they weren't unaffected by the pronouncements, and if nothing else several of their husbands were at least attuned to that.

"Perhaps another topic of conversation," one of the men in military uniform suggested after clearing his throat.

"Yes," Lord Powerscourt agreed before turning to me. "I should have issued you an invitation to our meeting at the Royal Dublin Society Theatre last night," he proclaimed. "We're proposing a fundraising drive to clear the debts affecting nearly a dozen hospitals in Dublin."

"What a worthy cause," I replied, allowing him to redirect us.

"I'm glad you think so. It's a disgrace the hospitals have been allowed to come to such a state." He then hastened to tell me about the fete they were planning to hold at the RDS grounds in October as their main fundraising event.

There was little opportunity to interject probing comments during the remainder of the meal, but when Lord French drew me aside as we all adjourned to the drawing room, insisting the lodge boasted a painting by a Flemish master I simply must see, I allowed myself to be persuaded. I trusted Sidney would note my departure and abet me in capitalizing on the opportunity this presented by keeping the others away. I also trusted him to know that I could fend for myself should Lord French's intent be to exert anything more than his charm on me.

We turned one corner and then another, making small talk about mutual acquaintances, before finding ourselves in a parlor which overlooked a broad sweep of the grounds. The sun sat low in the sky, casting long shafts of yellow light through the windows, which fell upon the painting where it hung over a bureau. It wasn't the most optimal lighting, and I was far from an expert, but I struggled to believe it had been painted by a master, Flemish or otherwise. In fact, I doubted the setting was even Flanders. But I soon discovered his showing me the painting was as much a pretense as my interest in it.

"Mrs. Kent, may I pour you a drink?" he asked, crossing to the sideboard.

"Sherry," I requested. Sherry was not usually my drink of choice, but since my arrival in Dublin I'd quickly learned that the gin available was not of the same quality as in London, and sherry seemed one of the likeliest alternatives to be found among the set of decanters before me.

I meandered aimlessly from picture to picture—some paintings and some photographs—while Lord French poured our drinks.

"Lest you think otherwise, I want to assure you that I haven't brought you here in order to subject you to the same interrogation your husband is no doubt undergoing in the drawing room."

My gaze having been arrested by a photo of the late Queen Victoria in a donkey cart outside the Viceregal Lodge perhaps two decades earlier, I was somewhat caught off guard by the directness of his words.

He offered me an artful smile as I turned to look at him, then returned the lid to the decanter of deep red port he'd selected for his own glass. "Clearly your husband has been asked here for some purpose, but I shall extend you the courtesy of not asking you to betray his confidence."

"Thank you," I replied as he handed me my sherry, curious whether he expected this *courtesy* to spur me to confess all. If so, he wouldn't be the first man I'd met who'd believed feigning understanding and indifference would convince me he could be trusted.

But rather than press this point, he merely nodded in acceptance, albeit in a magnanimous manner, and turned to squint through the window into the rays of the setting sun. Though he wouldn't have thanked me for it, I couldn't help but notice how tired and haggard his features now appeared. Despite his best efforts to the contrary, age hung heavy upon him. Or perhaps it was memory.

Given the importance of sunrise and sunset in the trenches, and the daily rituals of morning and evening stand-to, ready for attack, I knew that none of the men who had returned would ever look at those transitions from day to night and night to day in the same way as they had before the war. It was the same reason it featured so prominently in their poetry. Even now, nearly nineteen months since the armistice, no matter where we were, Sidney still found himself alert at the rising of the sun and its going down.

As field-marshal, Lord French might never have passed a night in the trenches, but he must still recognize its significance. After all, it had been his lot to issue the orders that sent so many men over the top, never to see another sunrise or sunset again.

I found empathy stirring in my breast and guarded myself against it. After all, this might be as much a ploy for information as the rest. There was little space for compassion in intelligence work.

I swiftly considered and then discarded several conversational gambits that might have led to information about Alec, leery of either revealing more than I wished to about our presence in Ireland or insulting Lord French with my awareness of his diminished role within the administration. The fact of the matter was, the longer I stood there sipping my sherry, the less convinced I became that Lord French knew anything of importance about intelligence matters within Ireland, let alone the existence of Alec. I began to wonder if there was actually anything of value he could be tricked into revealing.

Then Lord French surprised me.

"You are a diligent woman, aren't you, Verity? *May* I call you Verity?"

"Only if I can call you John," I countered archly.

A smile flickered across his lips. "Johnny, please."

I scoured his features as he continued to stare out the window, intensely curious about his remark about my diligence.

"I've been led to believe that sometimes you and your husband make inquiries into . . . delicate matters for others."

When I neither confirmed nor denied this, he continued.

"As I understand it, you were the ones who uncovered the truth about Lord Rockham's death. And you also investigated a troubling crime in Wiltshire, as well."

I could hardly deny it. Both incidents had been documented in the papers, though for good reason the full details had not been made public. As such, when Lord French spoke of the *truth*, it was unclear what exactly he meant: the truth that had been told to the press or the facts privately held by a few select individuals.

When I still failed to respond, he turned to look at me, his pale eyes studying me with great interest. Whatever he saw there must have convinced him of something, for his jaw firmed. “I, too, have something delicate I need looked into.” His eyebrows arched resolutely. “And I’d like *you* to do it.”

CHAPTER 4

It didn't require great powers of deduction to realize that Lord French was unaccustomed to having his requests denied by anyone less than royalty or a prime minister. So while my first inclination was to shrink from such a commitment even before hearing the details, I realized I had no choice but to at least consider the matter.

I set aside my glass of sherry and sank down on one of the wing chairs nearby, offering him my undivided attention. "I'm listening."

"It involves the eighteen-year-old daughter of an acquaintance of mine," he began, perching on the chair adjacent. "Miss Kavanagh was assaulted, and her hair forcibly cut by what was undoubtedly a company of rebels. I can see I've shocked you, but it's not the first time it's happened."

"That's terrible!" I was aghast at this new development. "But why?" I couldn't fathom why the IRA would commit such an act. What would be the purpose? Unless it was merely another example of the senseless violence so often perpetrated against women during wartime.

"Apparently, they took exception to the fact she'd recently begun stepping out with a soldier. A fine, upstanding fellow, I'm told."

That went some way to explaining it, though it certainly didn't justify it. I found myself outraged on the girl's behalf and concerned about precisely what actions were encompassed in that single word "assaulted." A world of meaning could be contained within it, and each connotation that flickered through my mind was more dreadful than the last.

"*And . . .*"

The heaviness of this pronouncement forced my attention back to Lord French. It was clear he didn't wish to share whatever else had contributed to Miss Kavanagh's selection.

"Her father is involved in some rather touchy matters for the government. Matters these shinners don't take kindly to."

As worded, this could mean any number of things, compelling me to pry further. "What does Mr. Kavanagh do?"

"He's a barrister, a King's Counsel," he clarified. "And he serves on the commission that oversees malicious injury and damage claims."

I frowned, uncertain why this in particular should draw the ire of the IRA. Unless they felt Mr. Kavanagh was unfair in the way he awarded damages. I could see how such a commission might be seen as corrupt, especially if it was packed with loyalists and officers of the Crown. Perhaps wounded soldiers or unionists seeking compensation for damaged property were viewed as being more often awarded compensation than their republican-sympathizing counterparts who had suffered injury or harm during an altercation or raid by the Crown Forces.

"Then you think they might have been trying to intimidate Mr. Kavanagh by assaulting his daughter?" I asked.

"It's possible. They may have taken out their frustration on his daughter, thinking to send a message."

The notion was cowardly, but not unheard of.

I shook my head in anger and disapproval. "Was Miss Kavanagh able to name her attackers or at least describe them?"

"They wore masks. But as I said, this isn't the first incidence of a young woman being assaulted and her hair cut.

They seem to prefer such tactics for warning girls to stay away from soldiers and the Tans. I suppose they fear they'll turn informant."

A fear that was not unjustified. I understood how strong the appeal of a handsome young man in uniform could be to susceptible young women. And wittingly or not, those women might allow something to slip which could compromise the republican effort. However, that did not excuse the use of such brutal methods of intimidation.

Lord French's mustache bristled. "I'm sure the miscreants involved in such acts are known by someone, if only they could be convinced to talk."

"If they can be found, does Miss Kavanagh think she might recognize them?" I queried, trying to apprehend what it was he hoped I could do.

His expression turned grave, and I realized he hadn't yet come to the crux of the problem. "She's dead."

My stomach dipped and I must have gasped, for Lord French nodded sadly.

"After the assault, she never fully recovered. Her mother said she was despondent, cowering in her room, afraid to leave the house. Kavanagh blames himself, of course. Believes he should have sent his family to the country. Not that they would have been any safer there. The Volunteers have managed to gain footholds in practically every corner of Ireland, burning the RIC out of their barracks, and taking matters of policing into their own hands. And now with the establishment of these benighted shinner courts, the matter is only getting worse." Lord French pushed to his feet, his posture rigid as he clasped his hands behind his back to stare out the window once more.

His agitation was understandable. I'd read the recent *Irish Times* article approving of the courts and their efficient administration. With each passing week, more and more local governments were pledging their allegiance to Dáil Éireann,

Sinn Féin's republican parliament, and refusing to cooperate with the British government. They were turning to the Sinn Féin's courts to adjudicate legal matters rather than the established British ones. Slowly, but surely, the Sinn Féin's shadow government was usurping control. The exception, of course, being in the unionist north, centered around Belfast.

"No, Kavanagh is not to blame, but these bloody shinners are," French pronounced. "The traitorous lot."

While I empathized with the Kavanaghs and even Lord French's frustration, I still didn't comprehend what he intended me to do, and I told him so. "Are the police not investigating the matter? Surely, they have a better grasp of the players involved."

"They claim they're doing what they can."

"But you don't believe them."

"I want to," he replied when I joined him at the window. His broad forehead was scored with creases. "I do believe they've done what they can," he added after a pause, further revealing how conflicted his feelings were. "But they're stretched thin as it is, and they're only as good as the information they're given from witnesses."

This echoed what the men had mentioned at dinner. That the populace in general, as well as many of the members of the DMP, were either too frightened of the murder gangs or quietly sympathetic to their cause, and so kept their mouths shut. Though I hoped the assault of an innocent young woman—an assault so horrific it had driven her to commit suicide—would draw enough ire that they might forget their fear and sympathies long enough to bring those responsible to justice. But if the police weren't to be trusted, then who were they to give their information to?

I supposed that's where I came in.

"You think they might tell me what they won't tell the police."

Lord French turned to look at me, the shrewd glint in his

eyes making him appear more like the field-marshal he'd once been. "As I understand it, you have sharp instincts and a knack for convincing people to confide in you."

"Who told you that?" I countered, wondering who he'd been talking to about me, though I wasn't surprised when he ignored the question, resuming his examination of the dusky lawn.

"I'd like to see the perpetrators punished for Kavanagh. For him and his wife. They deserve that."

A sense of wariness filled me. For all that I was sympathetic to the Kavanaghs and their grief, Sidney and I were merely there to find Alec, and to locate the deadly phosgene cylinders Ardmore had contrived to have smuggled into Ireland, if we could. We weren't there to investigate assault or murder or any of the other jobs which were the responsibility of the police, and usurping such a role seemed like a sure-fire way of drawing unwanted attention to ourselves, both from the republicans and the British authorities. Although, our doing so at the behest of the lord lieutenant should be a sufficient reason to the latter. Still, it was scrutiny we didn't want, particularly from the republicans.

But the lord lieutenant being who he was, I couldn't turn him down flat. Not without a very good reason. One I didn't have.

And then he played the card certain to obliterate any of my objections, followed by one calculated to compel my agreement.

"Miss Kavanagh may have killed herself in despair, but doesn't she still deserve justice? In fact, how can we deny it to her?" he implored, reaching for my hand, which he clasped between his own. "I would consider it a personal favor, in fact, if you would at least speak to the family, the neighbors. Uncover what you can."

Internally I groaned, knowing I had no choice but to agree, yet little chance of succeeding. "I will try," I said before warning him. "But I don't know that there's much I can do. This isn't London. The things that might endear me to people there won't necessarily do so here."

"My dear, Verity, I think you underestimate your charms," he cajoled. "But I understand there are limits. And I certainly don't want you to place yourself or Mr. Kent in any danger."

Except that was exactly what he was doing. As such, I felt it only right I press to the fullest the advantages afforded to me by his request.

"It would be helpful if we could speak to the detective inspector who was in charge of the investigation. Where would he be located?"

"At Great Brunswick Street Police Station, no doubt. That's where all of G Division is housed. But I'll make arrangements for you to meet with him," Lord French supplied, seeming almost cheerful now that he'd gotten his way. "Anything else?"

"It might prove useful to speak with someone at the Castle to discover what they know of the matter."

His disposition dimmed slightly, perhaps at the reminder that he was no longer in the thick of things where the administration was concerned.

"You can't tell me the wheels of bureaucracy always run smoothly here," I placated, lowering my voice as if in confidence. "Word is that there is a great deal of redundancy, and numerous instances of the left hand not knowing what the right is doing and vice versa. That everything would all work more efficiently if they simply allowed themselves to be led by a single head."

Lord French straightened to his full height. "Quite right. When I took this post, I was led to believe I would be providing that leadership, but I've been undermined at practically every turn."

That wasn't precisely what I'd heard, but if playing to his vanity got me the access I needed, I wasn't opposed to it.

"I'll see that it's done," he assured me. "Though I recommend taking your husband with you. The men you'll be speaking with are experienced officers and seasoned civil servants. Kent's clout is certain to open more doors and loosen more tongues than my word and your pretty face."

My smile tightened a fraction. That might be so. But I didn't wish to speak with just the experienced officers and seasoned civil servants, but rather their underlings. The men and women who saw and heard as much as their superiors but went largely unnoticed.

"Give me a day or two to settle matters," Lord French said. "I'll send you word."

When we returned to the drawing room with the others, Sidney didn't attempt to question me about what our host and I had discussed, though I knew he must be as curious as everyone else what the lord lieutenant had wished to say to me in private. I could tell by the glint in their eyes that some of them were wondering if Mrs. Bennett was about to be given her congé, but I'd learned the best way to squash such sordid speculation was to ignore it. Of course, it also helped when Sidney drew attentively to my side. For it made it perfectly plain how ridiculous the notion was that I would even consider becoming the mistress of a man like Lord French when I had a husband like Sidney Kent.

We departed shortly before eleven despite the lord lieutenant's offer to send an escort with us to smooth our way past any military pickets should we be stopped after the city's midnight curfew. However, we *did* accept his overture to procure permits allowing us to be out after curfew—items which might prove handy in the future. Especially if my daylight forays proved fruitless. We also departed with a handful of invitations to dinner and the theater from various other guests.

Overall, the evening had been a successful initial foray into Dublin society. At least, those who mingled with the British. Though we'd not uncovered anything concrete about Alec or the phosgene cylinders, and I'd been roped into conducting an investigation that could very well draw the wrong sort of attention from the IRA.

A fact Sidney was none too happy about when I informed him of Lord French's request as he motored us through the deepening twilight through Phoenix Park. As we neared the barracks outside its central gate, we could already see the lights of military lorries preparing to deploy either to enforce curfew or conduct a raid on some targeted block or building. One by one, they tested their Aldis searchlights, before switching them off again.

"Verity, we're not here to do favors for the viceroy," Sidney grumbled. The tires of the Pierce-Arrow squealed as he took the next turn with too much speed.

"I know that," I retorted crossly. "But I could hardly say no, now could I? Not when he said he'd consider it a personal favor." I crossed my arms over my chest and turned to glare through the windscreen. "After all, we *do* need to remain in his good graces while we're here."

Sidney heaved a sigh, but when he next spoke his voice was more measured. "I suspect your compassion for this girl, for her family, has something to do with it as well."

"Is that wrong?" I charged.

"Not at all." He turned to look at me as he shifted gears. "Just as long as your compassionate heart doesn't lead you into taking foolish risks."

I wanted to take offense at this remark, but I couldn't. Not when it was justified. After all, I'd taken foolish risks in the past out of compassion. Hadn't I entertained the same reticent thoughts earlier?

"We'll have to tread carefully. In *all* of this," I reminded him as well as myself. "But doing a favor for the lord lieutenant does have its perks."

This piqued Sidney's interest. "Such as?"

"He's arranging for me to speak with the detective inspector in charge of the investigation into Miss Kavanagh's assault. Which may give us a contact at Great Brunswick Street Police Station."

"Where the G-Men are stationed?"

Within the structure of the DMP, while divisions A through F were manned by uniformed officers assigned to a particular area of the city or county, the officers in G Division acted as a plainclothes investigative body. These detectives were assigned to one of three sections: routine crime, political crime, and carriage supervision. Those tasked with investigating political crime were the G-Men we were most concerned with, for they gathered intelligence for the British. As such, one of them may have crossed paths with Alec or at least obtained information on him from one of their touts, without realizing he was working undercover for the same side.

"I know it's unlikely the detective inspector for Miss Kavanagh's case has any knowledge of Alec or his whereabouts, but he must have contact with his colleagues on political duty. Perhaps through him we might be able to glean what the police know."

"Regardless, he could certainly prove to be a useful contact," Sidney said.

I pulled my shawl tighter around me against the chill of the night air. Even with the windows shut and the roof closed, the cool air found its way inside the motorcar. "Lord French has also agreed to arrange access to the Castle."

Sidney turned to look at me.

"So we can speak with anyone who might hold pertinent information to Miss Kavanagh's case."

"We?" he questioned pointedly.

"He recommended that you accompany me. Something I was already planning on. He suggested your reputation would unseal more lips."

He scowled. "I thought our aim was to stay *away* from that place. *Away* from the intelligence officers based there."

"Yes, but after giving it greater thought, I wonder if our avoidance would actually seem *more* suspicious."

I knew better than to take Sidney's silence as agreement.

"In any case, we're not going to be seen by the top brass as actually investigating, but rather . . . humoring His Excellency. Lord French is on the outs, and word is that much of the Castle administration is annoyed with him. So, if we're seen as keeping him happy . . ."

"And out of their hair," he deduced.

"Then perhaps, in gratitude, they'll be more forthcoming."

We drove on in silence as I allowed Sidney to process this reasoning. Of course, there was always the chance that any overt maneuvering could make its way back to Lord French, which was why it had to be handled with the utmost delicacy. However, I should have known that Sidney would grasp the implication immediately and instead narrow in on the part I least wanted him to notice.

"Who *are* we going to be seen by as investigating?"

"No one directly, of course," I replied, rearranging my skirts. "But I often find it's the underlings who have the most interesting morsels to share." Before he could object, I diverted the subject. "What of you? What happened in the drawing room while I was being propositioned in the parlor?"

From the manner in which Sidney's eyebrows drew together in the glare of the headlamps of an approaching vehicle, I could tell he didn't appreciate my joke. But it did serve to distract him.

"Do they still think you're here to assist General Tudor in some capacity?" I asked.

"Some of them might. I certainly didn't disabuse them of the notion."

I grinned. "A man of mystery. Some of them seem keen on uncovering the reason why you're here."

"Brooke was fairly chomping at the bit to know." He

frowned. "He's painting a rather large target on his back with his insistence on crushing these railwaymen and their munitions strike."

I turned to him in surprise. "You think we should concede?"

"No. This is still part of the United Kingdom, and to not be able to transport troops and supplies on the railways here is untenable. However, I can empathize with these railwaymen and their situation. The British government has been dragging its heels long enough on implementing the Home Rule the Irish were promised as soon as the war had ended." He braked, shifting gears as we came upon a slower moving vehicle, then accelerated around it. "And on the whole, I can approve of their munitions strike a lot more than I can murder gangs killing policemen in the streets."

"Except from what I've overheard, many of the British seem to think it's exclusively these murder gangs who are keeping the country in rebellion," I pointed out. "That if they could be dealt with, then the rest of the country would accept whatever terms the British are willing to offer."

In the light of the headlamps from another passing vehicle I could see that the scores in Sidney's forehead had grown deeper. "I served with Irishmen during the war. And while not all of them are republicans, not by a long shot, I know enough about them to deduce we've sorely underestimated those that are. Their intelligence and resourcefulness, the extent of their reach, and their bloody-minded stubbornness." He turned to look at me. "We have to tread with care, Ver."

Considering Alec had warned me of much the same thing in his last direct communication, I could only consider myself dually warned.

CHAPTER 5

The next morning, we took the tram to College Green and the Bank of Ireland, which was housed in Parliament House, where the parliament of Ireland had met until the Act of Union in 1800. It was an impressive structure with rounded walls of Ionic columns and a central colonnaded entrance within a quadrangle enclosed on three sides. The portico above the entrance was topped with three statues representing Hibernia, Fidelity, and Commerce.

We had visited the bank upon first arriving in Dublin, having established an account there for our purposes while we were in Ireland. However, the main reason for our patronage was the presence of Tobias Finnegan. Part Irish, part English, and wholly loyal to C, he had served as Alec's handler. A few chosen branches of the Bank of Ireland had also acted as his letterboxes, where Alec could drop off letters and reports that Finnegan would ensure reached C safely.

Finnegan was to have the same arrangement with me and, despite my qualms, I couldn't deny that from the outside it seemed sound. There was nothing suspicious about Sidney or I visiting the bank, particularly the Bank of Ireland, which had significant ties with Britain. They also had representatives regularly traveling back and forth to London who could act as couriers.

But all of these assets would prove moot if the person at the helm could not be trusted. The question had to be entertained. Had Alec severed communications with his handler and letterbox on purpose? Were they compromised? Or at the very least, had Alec believed they were?

I wasn't sure. And until I was, I'd decided our interactions with Finnegan should be handled gingerly.

He hadn't been in Dublin the first time we'd visited the bank, but we'd scheduled this appointment with him for his return. Upon our arrival, we were ushered swiftly through the space which had once housed what was supposed to have been a particularly magnificent House of Commons but had since been divided up into a series of offices, and into a larger office with tall ceilings. Light filtered down from windows positioned high on the wall, illuminating the room and the tall, angular man with round glasses.

In some ways Finnegan reminded me of Éamon de Valera, the Dáil's president, who was currently in the United States, campaigning for support from its government and the large population of Irish-Americans living there, as well as raising funds for the rebels' regime. In others, he did not. For one, Finnegan's face was smooth where de Valera's was craggy. For another, his nose wasn't as beaklike. But they both possessed a smile that I instinctively mistrusted. Fortunately, it was fleeting, for he seemed far more likable when sober.

"Mr. and Mrs. Kent, my apologies for not being here to greet you on your last visit. I was in London on business. I'm sure you can appreciate that," he told us genially, gesturing to the two Windsor armchairs before his desk and nodding to the young woman who had escorted us to his office to close the door behind her.

Indeed, we could, as well as grasping the implication that at least part of that business had included some sort of contact with C. Had we known he would be in London, we might have delayed our departure and met with him in even greater secrecy there, but we'd not discovered this detail until too late.

"Now," he declared as he settled in his large leather chair, interlacing his fingers before him. "I understand you're interested in an account opened by a Mr. MacAlister."

Apparently, we were to speak in veiled code, though I couldn't tell if this was because we were in danger of being overheard or an odd whim of the man before us. I did know that MacAlister had been the code name Alec had settled upon before coming to Dublin. Given the fact Alisdair was a form of Alexander, I supposed it was fitting.

"Yes. As I understand it, he was a regular client of yours," I replied, playing along.

"Indeed. Quite a regular depositor."

"Until recently."

Mr. Finnegan arched his eyebrows. "Just so." His gaze shifted to Sidney and back. "His last deposit was nearly ten weeks ago."

My stomach went cold at the pronouncement, though I already knew how long it had been since he'd dropped out of contact. "How regular were his deposits before that?"

"Sometimes almost daily, but never longer than a week to ten days." He sank back in his chair, adjusting his glasses. "Though we discussed the possibility that his transactions might become less punctual as his position within the company changed." He tilted his head to the side, dropping some of his pretense. "There was also some concern he was being followed."

"By whom?" I asked, speaking in a similar hushed and somber tone.

"He didn't know."

For Alec, an experienced and highly trained operative, not to be able to catch whoever was tracking him must mean they were equally experienced and well trained.

"I know what you're thinking," Finnegan said. "But I must caution you that the men Collins selected for his elite squad of assassins were well chosen. The Twelve Apostles know this city and all its twists and turns and alleys and byways like the back of their hand. They could find their way anywhere by the shortest route in the dark. They also know who's friendly in each house and business. Against that, MacAlister's training didn't mean much."

I swallowed, suddenly conscious of what we—the British—were up against.

"The Twelve Apostles?" Sidney queried.

One corner of Finnegan's mouth quirked upward. "That's the irreverent Irish sense of humor for you."

Alec must have fit in quite easily then, for I'd often chastised him for his impertinent remarks.

"Did he say how his position was changing?" I asked, returning to the other matter Mr. Finnegan had mentioned.

His amusement faded. "Not specifically. But our last meeting was brief. There wasn't time for him to elaborate."

"But he'd made contact with Collins?" I murmured softly.

"Oh, yes."

I inhaled past the tightness in my chest. This was something I'd also already known from reading Alec's decrypted reports, but to hear it directly from his handler was somehow more unsettling. Perhaps because every British agent who thus far had connived their way into the Big Fellow's sphere had ended up dead. Which was the reason C had asked Alec to attempt it without the knowledge of Thomson and the Secret Service at large. They'd suspected that in many cases those agents had been compromised by information provided from Collins's spies, who seemed to have thoroughly penetrated the ranks of the DMP and all but paralyzed them, as his murder gangs had killed any officers who dared to move against the republicans. And Collins's agents appeared to be making inroads at the Castle as well. But if no one at the

DMP or the Castle knew about Alec, then he wasn't vulnerable to exposure from those sources.

I couldn't help but agree with C's strategy. The best, and perhaps only, way to penetrate the rebels' ranks and Collins's inner circle was to send an agent whose very presence and identity was kept secret from even the British intelligence services within Ireland.

Yet, Alec had still gone missing. Had he been compromised after all? Had he fallen victim to these Twelve Apostles? Keeping his assignment clandestine from the rest of British Intelligence might have shielded him from possible exposure from within, but it had also left him vulnerable and without ready assistance should he need it.

A situation Sidney and I now found ourselves in. And like Alec, our only contact within Ireland was the man before us. A man I wasn't sure could be trusted.

It was enough to give any seasoned agent pause.

I scrutinized Finnegan carefully. "What do you think happened to him?" It was a broad, open-ended question, and I was curious how he would answer it.

"Well, as I'm sure you're already aware from my reports, I've done everything I feasibly can to uncover his whereabouts without hopelessly compromising him. It seems unlikely he was detained by Crown Forces, even if he used an alias. There have been no unclaimed bodies from victims of violence that match his description. And in any case, Collins and his squad prefer to make an example of spies and informants, leaving letters decrying their role as touts for the British. Their assassinations are quite public, too. Makes it easier for them to blend into the crowd and escape."

"And no one questions them or stops them," Sidney retorted, not so much in disbelief as disapproval.

"Rarely. But ye understand it's not so much that the public sanctions these killings as accepts them as a necessity. If they're not outright republicans, then they're in sympathy with them or at least determinedly neutral. There's very little to be gained by interfering, and too much to lose."

"Then they'd rather be controlled by a bunch of armed gunmen and a man with a Christ complex than the police?"

Finnegan's taut smile was patronizing if not outright condescending. Something that I knew would infuriate Sidney. Though to be fair, my husband was oversimplifying an extremely complicated issue. "With the gunmen, the public is left alone to go about their business as long as it doesn't interfere with the republican cause; while the police are part of the Crown Forces who raid and ransack their homes, impose curfews, execute blockades and searches, make false arrests, and generally disrupt their lives. Not to mention these reprisal killings." His voice became tinged with sarcasm. "Yes, it's difficult to see why they would prefer the gunmen."

Sidney's brow lowered as he eyed Finnegan with suspicion. "You sound sympathetic."

"No, but I can appreciate the average Dubliner's mindset," Finnegan replied, unruffled. "As could MacAlister. He wouldn't have lasted as long as he did if he hadn't."

"Then you think he's what? Dead?" I asked, sensitive to his choice of words.

He turned to look at me, seeming to consider his words with care. "I honestly don't know. Perhaps he's been sent to a different county. Somewhere in the West Country. We do know that men from Dublin have been sent to other parts of the country to train their IRA leadership and recruits. Perhaps he had no choice but to go, or he believed there was something important to be learned there."

Such as the location of the phosgene cylinders Ardmore had contrived to have smuggled into Ireland. Ardmore's former lackey, Lieutenant Smith, had told us as he was dying that they were taken to Dublin, but that didn't mean they hadn't since been moved.

Finnegan's voice softened. "But I can't deny that death is a distinct possibility."

I nodded, having already acknowledged this, but I wasn't prepared to accept it as truth without proof. Swallowing the lump that had formed in my throat, as delicately as possible I broached the question that I'd wanted to ask since we'd arrived. "Could he have believed your role as his handler or that of the bank were compromised? Could he have severed contact for a different reason?"

A frown creased his forehead. "Maybe." It was difficult to tell if he'd taken offense or if the manner in which his fingers drummed against his large oak desk was simply an indication that he was seriously considering the question. "But there were other contingencies in place. Other ways he might have contacted C to inform him of his suspicions. Ways that are unknown to even me. From what I've been told, he didn't utilize those either." His pale gaze turned direct. "I'm sure you were given similar contingencies."

Sidney turned to me in surprise, and I had to dig my fingernails into my palm to fight a telltale blush—a curse of my auburn-hued hair I'd had to find creative ways to circumvent. For Mr. Finnegan was correct. There was a librarian in Capel Street I could call upon—but only under the direst of circumstances—and a seemingly innocuous address near Hampstead Heath outside London I could post a letter to. Truthfully, I'd considered the idea of attempting to convince this librarian to act as a letterbox for certain messages so that they need not all go through Finnegan and the Bank of Ireland, but I'd not yet decided whether that course of action was either feasible or for the best.

Regardless, I'd not informed Sidney of either. Not because I didn't trust him, but because it had been impressed upon me that these were instructions for me alone. Which had led me to believe Sidney had been issued similar separate instructions. But perhaps I'd been wrong.

In any case, I couldn't refute Finnegan's assertion. Alec's failure to contact C in any other way was not an encouraging sign. Even if he'd been sent to another county he might have managed to post a letter.

Or maybe not. After all, he might have been sent to a rural area with nothing but small towns, where everyone knew each other's business, including that of strangers. If he posted a letter to England from such a backwater, everyone would know about it, and that would instantly place him under suspicion.

I felt frustration bubbling up inside me. "Then you have no better idea where he is than we do."

He began to shake his head, as a thought occurred to me.

"Do you have the address where he was lodging?"

"I have *an* address," Finnegan qualified, and then squashed any hopes I held. "But it's doubtful he's stayed there since the early days of his arrival in Dublin. Not regularly anyway. Many of the members of the IRA and Sinn Féin, particularly their leaders, move about frequently, catching sleep where they can. Those who don't either risk arrest or are among the more moderate members of their movement. As such, they're perfectly aware that the government allows them to remain free in hopes their influence will curb the radicals' more extreme impulses."

Finnegan looked from me to Sidney and back again, his mouth pursing in displeasure. "Frankly, I don't know why you were sent here."

I frowned, startled by his bluntness.

"I don't see how there's anything you can do. You're certainly not going to take up MacAlister's efforts, and you're too well-known to be of much use gathering intelligence."

Though I was tempted to make some acerbic comment, I bit my tongue. He wasn't the first person to underestimate me, and it was doubtful he would be the last. And in the end, their foolish disregard always worked to my advantage. Let him believe what he wished. He would soon learn better.

But Sidney wasn't so accustomed to being underrated. "Well, now, that's not your purview, is it?" Sidney remarked drolly, though his dark blue eyes glinted with irritation. "So why don't you let us worry about that, and you focus on"—he glanced to the side dismissively—"whatever it is you do here."

If Finnegan had taken offense, he didn't show it, but as we began to gather ourselves to go, he halted us. "There is one more thing." From the twist of his lips and the manner in which he scrutinized me, I could tell that whatever it was didn't exactly please him. "I believe Alec left you a message."

I sat upright.

"Why didn't you say anything sooner?" Sidney demanded.

"I was working my way around to it," he said.

We both scowled as he rose from his chair and crossed the room toward a set of file cabinets. Reaching into his pocket, he extracted a set of keys which he used to unlock one of the drawers. He extracted something before closing and re-locking the drawer. When he returned to his desk, he set a small metal box before me. Affixed to its front were four dials with numbers. If spun to the right number combination, the box would open. A combination that, presumably, I was supposed to know.

I looked up at Mr. Finnegan in question, for surely, he had more instructions for me.

He sank into his chair, his jaw set in stern lines. "MacAlister said to tell you that the combination is the date you first saw Collins."

I heaved an aggravated sigh. The cheeky blackguard! I could have cheerfully strangled Alec right about then. Leave it to him to word his clue so that it would stir up trouble for me. He could have simply said it was the date we'd last met, but apparently that wasn't controversial enough. No wonder Finnegan was eyeing me with mild censure, and the manner in which Sidney's right knee jogged up and down communicated how displeased he was to discover yet one more fact I'd failed to share with him.

But I didn't defend myself to either man. Not then. Not when doing so would just make me look guiltier. Instead, I lifted the box into my lap to input the date in late October when Alec and I had seen Collins striding away from Downing Street with two of his intelligence officers, up to some sort of mischief, no doubt. I had been attired in my fashionable garb, and Alec had rightly pointed out that I was too conspicuous, so he'd set off to tail Collins and his men through the streets of London alone. But not before ensuring I noted all three men, particularly Collins. At the time, I'd thought it peculiar that Alec was so insistent. As if he'd believed someday I would need to identify him. Now, it seemed alarmingly prescient, and not a little unsettling. Especially since that was the last time Alec and I had spoken.

The lock snicked open, and I lifted the lid, staring down in bafflement at what was inside. Sidney leaned closer to see, but Mr. Finnegan waited for me to lift the key from the box to show him. A sensation of déjà vu settled over me, and I realized this was the second time Sidney and I had unearthed a key from a metal box, though this time the unearthing was merely metaphorical. Last time, we had literally dug a battered golf ball tin from the ground in Norfolk to find a key Max's father, the late Lord Ryde, had buried there for him to find. We had yet to discover what that key was for, but the fact it had been found during a hunt to find the proof Lord Ryde had hidden of Lord Ardmore's perfidy, a hunt that had led us to one of the barrels of phosgene cylinders Ardmore had endeavored to have smuggled to Ireland, led us to believe it was important.

Alec had also been there in Norfolk when we'd uncovered the key, I recalled. Which was where he'd gotten the notion for this little ploy, no doubt. Except I hadn't the foggiest idea what this key opened either.

Fortunately, Finnegan did. "If I'm not mistaken, that is the key to Mr. MacAlister's safe deposit box," he informed us with a puzzled frown.

I could tell he was entertaining the same question I was. Why the complexity? Why two locked boxes when surely one would have served? Unless he hadn't trusted his messenger.

Finnegan's frown deepened and he rose again from his chair. "Come with me."

He led us back through the labyrinth of offices and down into the depths of the building where the space around us echoed with our footsteps. With a nod and a word, he guided us past a guard and into a room lined with walls of little doors, each one affixed with a gold-plated number and two slots for keys. Most of the boxes appeared rather shiny and new, but there was one section on the right that looked tarnished and rather old. The metal was more ornate but scratched in places, and the key holes were larger.

"We've recently upgraded our boxes," Mr. Finnegan explained, noting my interest. "Though we've retained a few of our older boxes for loyal customers who have not yet come into the bank to move their belongings to a new one." He swiveled to look at me. "MacAlister's would be among the new boxes. There should be a number inscribed on the key which corresponds to the correct box."

Locating this, I read the numbers aloud.

Finnegan approached the bank of boxes in the far-left corner and slid what appeared to be a master key of sorts into one of the slots. "You'll need to insert yours in the other slot."

I did so, finding the key slid easily into place, and then I turned it.

Finnegan stepped forward to open the door, sliding the lock box from inside. Then he swiveled to set it on the table behind us.

This was not the first time I'd used a safe deposit box, so I knew it was protocol for the bank employee to withdraw in order for the patron to view or retrieve their items in privacy. I suspected Finnegan prided himself on his professionalism, and yet I could read the indecision on his face. He wanted to remain, to discover what Alec had concealed inside. In the end, his professionalism won out.

His nostrils flared as he stepped back from the table. "I shall leave you to it." Then he turned away and strode quickly from the room, almost as if fleeing the devil himself.

"Had he been in the Garden of Eden in place of Adam, I don't think he would have taken the fruit," Sidney quipped, apparently having also noticed how tempted Mr. Finnegan had been.

I elbowed him lightly in the ribs. "With a remark like that, you'd fit right in with the irreverence of those Twelve Apostles."

He rubbed his side as if I'd actually injured him and I shook my head, turning my focus to the box before me. All I needed to do was lift the lid to see what was inside, but for some reason I hesitated. It being Alec who'd deposited the contents, it really could be anything. Though I had to think there was a good reason for his secrecy.

In my mind, I could see Alec on that last day in London when we'd parted ways, he to shadow Collins and his men—as he'd been doing in one way or another since—and me to return to Sidney. His dark eyes had burned with an uncomfortable intensity, as if searing my features into his memory as I'd told him to be safe. I'd wondered then, as I wondered now, if he'd believed our goodbye might be permanent. And if so, how permanent?

I inhaled a shallow breath, trying to remove the notion from my thoughts, but it clung like a burr.

"Just open it, Ver," Sidney coaxed gently.

I nodded, deeply grateful for his solid presence at my back.

The lid opened with a click that seemed overloud in the silent chamber. Just as the safe deposit box seemed overlarge when I looked inside to discover naught but a small, folded piece of foolscap. I lifted it out, my heart rising into my throat as I gingerly unfolded the paper to read Alec's near illegible scrawl.

I knew if I disappeared they would send you after me. Just as I knew that you would come.

Go home, Verity. This isn't Belgium. If I'm missing, then I'm dead or as good as. So go home. Forget me. Live your life and be happy. That's all I want. If you feel guilty, name your firstborn son after me, and we'll call it even.

But don't get involved. This isn't your fight. And catching Ardmore isn't worth your life.

Kent, make her go.

Reading over my shoulder, Sidney snorted, presumably at the firstborn son part, but I could find little humor in the missive. Not when even Alec seemed to believe that whatever his fate had been, it was dire. It was all I could do not to weep.

CHAPTER 6

Sensing how fragile I was, Sidney didn't speak as he led me out of the bank and down Grafton Street. He'd correctly deduced that what I needed was fresh air, not to be squashed inside an overcrowded tram. So we set off arm in arm down the busy thoroughfare. The morning was a fine one, and the shops and restaurants bustled with business. Bicycles and carts rattled past, but few motorcars, and no trams after the line veered east down Nassau Street around Trinity College.

Even without trying to, we attracted attention. Sidney in his Saville Row tailored three-piece suit and tall, dark good looks was arresting enough, but I also knew my Parisian fashions and bobbed hair turned heads. My red-violet and white ensemble boasted intricate embroidery along the collar and down the back of each sleeve and the rich shade of red-violet that colored the underside of my broad-brimmed hat accented the auburn hue of my hair rather than clashing with it. But the notice we garnered only made it all the more imperative that I retain control of my emotions.

So I forced my awareness to the people passing by, cataloging mundane features and searching for the familiar, including Alec. For no matter what he'd written, I wasn't yet ready to give him up for dead. I glanced distractedly down the street in the direction of the Wicklow Hotel, doubting I would make it on my round that day of the haunts where

Alec had mentioned seeing Collins in his reports. I wondered how useful this information would even prove now. After all, if Alec had been found out, wouldn't Collins have changed his routine?

Far from straight, Grafton Street gently arched its way southward, lined with stolid four- to five-story buildings in shades of brown and cream, and occasionally the same red brick that adorned the Woolworths department store. Ultimately it led to the northwest corner of St. Stephen's Green near the Gaiety Theatre where we were to join the Wyndham-Quins for a play in a few days' time. The Green was the largest park in the city, at least on the southern side, and so filled with people out for a stroll on such a lovely day.

We passed beneath the massive Fusiliers' Arch into the Green, and looking overhead, I could see the names of deceased Royal Dublin Fusiliers inscribed along the underside of the arch. I also spied a few bullet holes in the limestone. Remnants of the rebellion that had broken out across Dublin on Easter Monday four years ago, I suspected. I remembered hearing that one of the positions the rebels had initially seized was St. Stephen's Green. The same rebels who continued to call the Fusiliers' Arch "Traitor's Gate" today.

Sidney turned our steps to stride along the lake that spanned the northern sector of the park, and I felt my shoulders relax as the tranquility of nature enclosed around me. Ducks and moorhens dotted the surface of the water and trees lush with greenery overarched the pathways bordered with beds of geraniums, petunias, and a few late-blooming tulips. Breathing in the sweet air, I allowed it to work its magic, soothing the grief and fear balled up inside me. But I also felt it stoke something unexpected: a deep well of anger,

Perhaps recognizing the shift in me, Sidney tilted his head toward mine. "Do you want to talk about it?"

"What I *want* is to ring *MacAlister's* neck."

Sidney turned to look at me, amusement rather than concern sparkling in his eyes. "Careful. Xavier might enjoy that too much."

This pronouncement was so unexpected, so ridiculous, that it startled a laugh out of me. "You're probably right." I exhaled in weary aggravation, turning to gaze across the small lake toward the far shore. "But seriously, what on earth was Alec thinking? To take on an assignment that he expected to fail? And if he took such elaborate precautions to write and arrange for me to receive such a note, then he expected to fail." I shook my head. "It's just not like him."

"Even men as devil-may-care as Xavier can catch a whiff of lethal intuition," Sidney reasoned.

"And not fight against it?"

"His note doesn't mean he didn't try to prevent it, Ver."

I fastened a sardonic glare on him. "Alec Xavier. The man who waltzed among the highest ranks of the Germany Army for nearly six years—four of them during the war. The man who set about to charm and cultivate your friendship the moment he met you, despite knowing he'd slept with your wife."

He frowned. "While you believed I was dead. A fact I *led* you to believe."

"Yes, a very important distinction," I agreed, for we'd both come a long way in forgiving one another for our wartime failures and rebuilding our marriage after four and a half years of separation and deception. "But not to the point I'm making. Alec doesn't take unnecessary precautions. He doesn't plan ahead."

"Seems to me like it didn't prove unnecessary."

I glowered at him.

"And what about this incident when you saw Collins." His gaze turned pointed. "I'm guessing that somehow involved Xavier."

"That was purely by coincidence," I retorted, having expected him to broach this subject at some point. "We were strolling down Horse Guards, comparing notes after the incident at Littlemote, when Collins suddenly appeared."

"In London?" Sidney seemed genuinely unsettled by this.

"Yes. And before you ask, I didn't purposely keep the contingencies for emergency communication from you." I faltered. "Or rather, I did. But . . ." I glanced about us to ensure no one was within hearing distance. "That's only because I believed you'd been issued your own instructions. That's always how it's worked in the past. Each operative is given distinct directives separate from their partner's, both for their own protection and that of the intelligence service, in case the other operative is captured or defects. I simply presumed this was the same." When Sidney didn't speak, but continued to stare straight ahead of us, his jaw tight, I clasped his upper arm between my own, trying to make him understand. "It's not that I didn't trust you. I do. But when you've blindly followed directives for years, when you've taken an oath to do so, it's difficult to stop."

Sidney reached across his body to press his hand to mine. "I get it, Verity," he assured me. "Truly, I do."

I exhaled in relief. Though relief quickly turned to consternation. "But they didn't issue you a similar set of instructions?"

He cleared his throat. "Actually, they did."

I drew back. "Then why . . . ?"

He adjusted the brim of his trilby hat. "The same reason you didn't tell me, I suppose."

I narrowed my eyes. "Yet, you seemed surprised and, dare I say, aggrieved when Mr. Finnegan suspected it of me."

He fidgeted with his hat again, obviously uncomfortable with the question. "Because I didn't know you'd been given your own instructions, and I suppose I expected you would have mentioned it if you had. Not the specifics," he hastened to clarify. "Just generalities."

I released him, crossing my arms over my chest. "And yet I didn't expect *you* to mention it. I trusted you to know what information was necessary I be told and what wasn't."

We strode side by side in brittle silence for several moments before he spoke in a low voice.

"You're right. I should have trusted you. But in my defense, this is the first time we've been deployed as if we were real operatives."

I turned to look into his earnest eyes.

"This investigation may be no more official than the others we've undertaken for C, but you can't deny that this one feels different."

He was right. I couldn't. A fact which caused me no small amount of uneasiness.

Sidney guardedly eyed the men seated on a bench along the path. "Maybe it's the fact that for all that this is still British soil, it feels like hostile territory. Or maybe it's the fraught nature of our quest and the very real possibility that the quarry we seek may be dead."

I swallowed against the urge to refute this, despite knowing what he said was true.

"Whatever the case, I apologize," he finished with a sad smile.

I threaded my arm through his again, telling him no more needed to be said. We were nearing the edge of the lake, and through a gap in the trees I spotted the imposing red brick edifice of the Shelbourne Hotel. We had stayed there for several nights before moving to the townhouse off Fitzwilliam Square.

"What do you want to do, Verity?"

I tipped my head back to peer up at him past the brim of my hat, noting the furrow of his brow as he continued.

"Because I'd like to do nothing more than to use the excuse Xavier has provided and bundle you back to safety in London. But I won't. Not unless that's what you want."

I spotted an open bench several steps in front of us. "Let's sit," I urged, wanting a few moments to gather my thoughts. The directness of his question had caught me off guard, but I was relieved to hear that he was open to my opinion.

He led us to the shaded spot beneath a plane tree, waiting for me to sit before settling beside me. His gaze swept up and down the path, cataloguing the other occupants of the park much as I was doing.

"Well, Ver," he prompted.

"I can't deny that I'm frustrated by the way matters are progressing, but you already know that." I sighed. "Nor can I deny that Alec's letter distressed and angered me." My hands tightened into fists, feeling these emotions rear up inside me again. "*However*, I can't just leave it at that. I can't just walk away without answers. I can't just . . . *abandon* Alec to his fate. I *know* this isn't Belgium." I held no blame for Alec's position being compromised here. Not like I'd believed in Belgium. "But that doesn't absolve me of my responsibility to him, as a friend and fellow agent." I pleaded with Sidney, hoping he would understand.

"And what if there are no answers?" he asked gravely. "What if there is no trail to uncover, no body to find?"

His words pinched in my chest, but I knew it was a possibility I had to face. "I can be reasonable. If the trail remains cold, if matters become too dangerous . . ." I forced the next words past my lips. "Then we'll return to London." I reached out to clasp his hand with mine, squeezing it. "But we have to *try*. We've barely begun."

He nodded, squinting into the sun as he lifted his head. "There's that promise you made to Lord French to see to, as well."

"And the phosgene," I added quietly.

He turned to look at me, examining my features. "I noticed you didn't say anything to Finnegan about it."

"Because I don't know if he's been debriefed."

"And because you're not sure you trust him."

My eyes widened. "Was it that obvious?"

"No, but I know the way you think." He sat back, propping his ankle over the other knee. "And given the facts before us, it would be illogical not to question his reliability."

"There's been no sign of the phosgene from our SIS sources, but we know it was transported to Dublin. Smith told us so two months ago in Belgium. And given the fact he was dying, betrayed by Ardmore, I don't think he was lying."

"Any word from George?"

I shook my head.

George Bentnick was one of my dearest friends, and one of Britain's foremost cryptologists. He'd worked in OB40, Naval Intelligence's codebreaking department during the war, though he now served as a mathematics professor at Oxford. I'd sent George the bloodstained journal Smith had handed me just before he breathed his last, trusting he could crack the code contained within far quicker than I could with my rudimentary skills. However, thus far it had eluded even him.

"The last time we spoke, he told me he's fairly certain the code is a book cipher. But without knowing the book the cipher derives from, it's nearly impossible to decrypt." I scowled, even as a fellow zoomed past on his bike, jauntily lifting his cap to me as he offered me a cheeky grin. "You would think that's something Smith might have mentioned."

"Ah, but then he was taunting you, wasn't he?" Sidney reminded me. "Implying you might not be sharp enough to decipher his journal."

I ignored this remark, and the fact that Smith thus far had been proven right. "We need to learn more about him. After all, we know very little about Lieutenant James Smith, in truth. Perhaps if we did, we'd have a better idea what book he might have chosen."

"Unless it was chosen for him."

I glared at him in irritation, for he was not helping to solve the problem. "Perhaps we should send a cable to Max in London. He did promise to assist us however he could from that end, and he does have connections at the War Office. He might be able to gain access to Smith's file."

Max also had a vested interest in seeing Ardmore thwarted and brought to justice. After all, Ardmore had killed his father after making him an unwitting conspirator to treason. If only we could locate the hidden stash of evidence the late Lord Ryde had left for his son. If only the clues he'd crafted for him to do so hadn't been so obscure.

Nonetheless, our chief concern for the moment in that regard was finding those phosgene cylinders and ensuring they weren't used to some terrifying purpose. And Smith's book was our most promising lead. If uncovering more information from his military records would allow us to finally decrypt it, I knew Max would jump at the chance to help.

"The cable will have to be worded carefully," Sidney cautioned.

On the chance it was intercepted—by Ardmore's informants or someone else.

"I left an entire shorthand sheet with him, and as it happens, *Smith* and *War Office* are both on it."

He smiled at the pleasure I was obviously taking in my own forethought and cleverness. "Then write out what you want me to send, and I'll either drop by the telegram office myself or send Nimble."

"What are your plans for the rest of the day?" I asked as we rose to our feet and set off toward the northeast corner of the square.

"I'm supposed to meet Glengarry for lunch at Jammet's. But what of you?"

"I may venture north of the Liffey for a time." I trusted he knew that this meant I would be donning my disguise and dropping by Vaughan's Hotel on Rutland Square to see if anyone interesting turned up. Given Alec's letter, and the fact

Sidney was already anxious to whisk me back to London, I felt even more pressure to uncover something. And soon!

I considered also dropping by the library on Capel Street where my emergency contact was supposed to be located. Dressed in my disguise, there was less danger of exposing the place to any risk, and I wanted a chance to see it, should we decide that Finnegan and the Bank of Ireland were untrustworthy and elect to switch letterboxes.

As we crossed the street at the corner, headed toward Lower Baggot Street, I felt a prickle along the back of my neck. Having become strongly attuned to my instincts during the war, I wasn't about to begin ignoring them now. As unobtrusively as possible, I began to survey the pedestrians striding along the other side of the road, as well as those I could see behind us in the reflection of the windows we passed.

"You think we're being followed," Sidney murmured less in question and more in confirmation that he sensed something was off as well.

"Possibly," I replied, recalling the debriefing reports I'd read detailing how Collins's murder gang often worked. They would split into pairs or teams, often trailing a target down opposite sides of the street, waiting for just the right opportunity to close in for the kill.

"They wouldn't do anything in such a crowded street."

My nerves tightened. "Of course, they would," I hissed, unable to believe my husband's naivete. That was precisely their modus operandi. Hadn't he just heard Finnegan remark upon it?

"Not to two of society's darlings," Sidney retorted. "Collins understands what bad press that would make."

I breathed a little deeper, for he spoke the truth. If nothing, the rebels were keenly aware of the power of propaganda. As such, they carefully calculated how each killing might influence both the Irish public that supported them and the world's opinion at large. Killing the policemen and intelligence officers who were out to stop them might be one thing, but it would be hard to sell the idea that the deaths of a war hero and socialite recently arrived in Dublin were necessary to the cause.

So, if they were following us, then it must simply be to gain information.

Or perhaps it was someone from British Intelligence detailed to follow us. After all, they were equally ignorant of what Sidney and I were doing in Dublin. As such, doing anything to reveal that we were aware of their presence could prove detrimental to our efforts. It would be better to carry on blithely, no matter how much it strained the nerves.

Fortunately, Upper Fitzwilliam Street was not far, and we arrived without incident. Though that didn't stop me from climbing the steps a trifle more quickly than necessary and hurrying through the slate-blue door Sidney held open for me. We were greeted by the sight of Nimble and the Irish maid we'd hired, arguing over a basket laden down with linens.

Nimble had served as Sidney's batman during the war and now acted as his valet. He was a rather large, hulking fellow. One whose appearance was not helped by the scars blistering the left side of his face near his hairline and the loss of part of his left ear from a shell explosion. However, he was gentle and reserved, spare with his words, and as loyal as the sunrise. It seemed the maid, Ginny, hadn't yet realized this, considering the wariness that shone in her wide eyes, though it said much about her that she was brave enough to argue with a man more than twice her size. However, it was unlike Nimble to quarrel with others, especially the members of the female staff.

As I removed my gloves and dropped them on the petticoat table, I was able to deduce that what they were wrangling over was Nimble's offer to carry the basket of heavy linens down the stairs to the servants' quarters where the laundry would be collected. Ginny seemed to either take offense at the offer or believe it too unmanly a chore, but Nimble had never cared for such niceties. Not when all he saw was a woman struggling with a heavy load.

Both looked up with a start as Sidney closed the door, evidently not having heard us enter. They straightened to attention, Nimble's expression turning to chagrin while Ginny merely looked guarded and uncertain. But then she and Mrs. Boyle, the cook, had never eyed us differently. I kept hoping their regard would thaw, but it had yet to do so. Thus far, we'd declined to hire more staff, hoping our stay in Dublin would be brief, and conscious of the fact that the greater the number of people working under our roof, the more difficult it would be to conceal our covert movements. We might have considered bringing our housekeeper Sadie Yarrow, but she was an anxious sort, not at all suited to clandestine work. So we had left her in London to take care of our flat there.

Being well acquainted with his valet's disposition, Sidney took in the situation at a glance. "Best let him," he advised Ginny. "He's only trying to help."

Her cheeks reddened, but she didn't object further when Nimble hefted the heavy basket as if it weighed no more than a feather. It was evident he could have carried the small bucket, too, but he left that for her to grasp as she led him down the granite steps with rigid shoulders. I turned to Sidney as they disappeared from sight, the sound of Nimble's clumping footsteps still audible. A smile quirked the corner of my lips. For Nimble was not his real name, but it was what everyone called him, even though nimble was what he was not.

"You don't think he's becoming sweet on the maid, do you?" I teased softly to be certain they didn't overhear me.

Sidney's expression when he looked up from his examination of the letters laid out across the petticoat table clearly conveyed what he thought of this. It was true, Nimble treated Mrs. Yarrow much the same way, and yet their relationship was more like that of a mother and son, despite the fact Mrs.

Yarrow was no more than a decade older. However, Ginny was a pretty girl with fair hair and features, and she was close to Nimble's age. It was entirely possible she might turn his head.

"Anything of interest?" I queried, stepping closer to allow my eyes to skim over the handwriting on the missives. Our correspondence of the greatest importance would be coming from Finnegan and the Bank of Ireland, not through the regular post where it might be intercepted.

"There's a letter from your sister," he replied, absently passing it to me.

I felt a twinge of guilt knowing Grace had been disappointed when we'd had to postpone her visit to stay with us in London. I still hoped we might return before her next school term started, but there were no guarantees.

"I'll read it later," I said, tucking it into my pocket.

He nodded, engrossed in his own correspondence. Though he looked up at the sound of Nimble's lumbering footsteps ascending the stairs to rejoin us. "I've a cable I need you to take to the telegraph office," he told him as he reached the entrance hall.

"O' course, Cap'n," Nimble replied affably.

Sidney had ceased to ask his valet to stop calling him by his former rank in the army. Whether because of pure stubbornness or genuine obliviousness, Nimble seemed incapable of remembering not to.

"Give us ten minutes," he told his former batman as he followed me toward the staircase.

As I began to climb toward the private sitting room where I kept my letter writing implements, my gaze dropped to the space between the banisters, colliding with Ginny's. She was staring up at me from the ground floor below, but flinched as I caught sight of her and then hurried away. I couldn't help but wonder whether she'd been intentionally eavesdropping, and whether she intended to put that information to any use.

CHAPTER 7

It was several days before I heard from Lord French. Long enough for me to almost forget my promise to the man, such was my absorption with finding Alec, or barring that, at least the phosgene cylinders. I'd spent as much time as I dared in Vaughan's Hotel and the Wicklow, not wishing to draw the *wrong* sort of attention, as well as several hours each day wandering the streets and squares Alec had mentioned in his reports. While I saw much to concern me, none of it pertained to either of my objectives.

Sadly, I appeared to be growing as accustomed as the other Dubliners to dashing out of the way of military lorries filled with the motley-dressed Black and Tans as they careened through the streets, seemingly heedless of any pedestrians they might hit. They sat back-to-back, their guns pointed outward, prepared for any sort of trouble, and occasionally fired off a volley of shots just because they could, it seemed. I'd yet to witness the ambushes they were so wary of, but I'd heard them in neighboring streets and seen the resulting scatter of innocent bystanders rushing away from the scene. Apparently, the Dublin brigades of the IRA were fond of waylaying passing lorries, tossing some sort of improvised explosive inside and then letting off a barrage of gunfire on the soldiers as they leapt from the vehicle. Then the Volunteers would scatter to the winds, disappearing into the fleeing crowds before they could be caught or wounded themselves.

All of this, of course, resulted in some injuries and casualties, simply from being in the wrong place at the wrong time. At any hour of the day or night, one heard gunfire, and nowhere was truly safe from the searches conducted by the Crown Forces—be it a raid on your home or a random street or bridge sectioned off with barbed wire so passing citizens could be searched. Thus far, being female and respectable looking, I'd been allowed through these barriers without harassment, but others were not so fortunate. I'd seen the rough treatment the Tans subjected some of the men to, seemingly for no reason other than they were Irish and fit their view of what a rebel might look like.

Not all of the supplementary police were so callous. Some of the former British soldiers were polite and carried about their duties with civility and almost a sense of embarrassment that they were subjecting the populace to such treatment. But for every upstanding soldier there seemed to be another who took pleasure in the task of bullying and belittling those they were supposed to be protecting, not just policing.

This treatment contrasted sharply with what Sidney and I experienced when we ventured out on the town in our glad rags each evening. We dashed from restaurant to theater to nightclub to private party, all with the greatest of ease. If we were exposed to the sight of even the smallest of contretemps, it was smoothed over by the jaunty laugh of an officer and the assurance that whatever was happening to the poor bloke he'd brought on himself. I couldn't help but be reminded of the evenings I'd spent on Alec's arm, pretending to be his latest Belgian paramour, as we mingled and danced and dined with his fellow German officers at the Brussels establishments the German Army had taken over for their own use. All while the real Belgians outside lived in terror of their occupiers, near starvation from their meager rations.

Then, I'd barely stomached it. Now, it was even harder.

But Sidney and I continued to smile and laugh and toast, subtly plying what information we could from others and gritting our teeth behind our lips when their aspersions turned foul. More and more, the drinks we tipped back became necessary to take the edge off the shame and anger which seemed to have settled permanently in my gut; however, I was careful never to get corked. That way lay only trouble, for drunks couldn't be trusted to hold their tongues.

Still not having received our permits, we obeyed the curfew, not wanting to test the limits of our status. Yet even when one evening the hour drew a shade too close to midnight for comfort, we were waved through a barrier being erected, with nothing but hearty laughs and the confession of one cheeky corporal that he kept a photograph of me torn from a magazine hanging inside his locker. For all the special treatment we received, had we been deluded enough, we might have chosen to believe that other parts of the city were not nightly subjected to almost a state of siege, as members of the Crown Forces carried out their door-to-door searches armed with rifles and pistols, and Crossley tenders rigged with machine guns.

The more time I spent among the regular people of Dublin, the more I listened to their amiable chatter and shared in their laughter and overheard the harrowing stories of their encounters with the overzealous Black and Tan, the more I admired their pluck and spirit. It was difficult not to be drawn into their lives, particularly as they began allowing me to share them. The hoteliers at both the Vaughan Hotel and the Wicklow had taken it upon themselves to draw smiles from me seated quietly at the end of the bar where I usually perched. When I was alone, they would chatter amiably, sharing anecdotes about their lives and families, or they would include me in the banter they held with other regulars, urging me to join in their razzing. I engaged with them cautiously, testing my growing familiarity with the dialect, but wary of giving myself away. However, they'd yet to afford me the opening I needed to ask about my "cousin" until the day Lord French's letter arrived.

I hadn't read it, though it was burning a hole in my inner pocket. I'd been leery of carrying it with me, but leerier of leaving it behind where Ginny might find it. I didn't even know if she could read, but I'd been suspicious of the maid ever since I'd caught her eavesdropping. As such, I'd been even more cautious of what was left lying around.

I was thinking of this and Lord French's request, and the kindness of the older woman seated next to me on the bench in Rutland Square the day before, insisting I take a slice of bread from her lunch because she'd decided I was too thin. I was feeling balled up inside, and not attending to what Peter, the hotelier at the Wicklow, was saying, when I suddenly realized he'd stopped talking. At first, I feared he'd recognized me, but then I realized his gaze was too empathetic for that.

"What is it, lass? You've been comin' here for more'n a week now, sayin' nary a peep, but I can see the worry hangin' round ye." He leaned his elbow on the bar, gesturing for me to draw nearer. "So tell ole Peter what's ailin' ye. Maybe I's can help."

I hesitated, knowing that if I appeared too eager, I would ruin the work of the past eleven days. Alec's early reports had relayed his suspicions that hotel employees were passing information to Collins and his intelligence staff or acting as couriers. A hotelier at the Wicklow had been mentioned in particular, and while he hadn't shared his name, I had a strong hunch it was Peter.

"'Tis my cousin," I began softly, repeating the words I'd rehearsed over and over, mindful of the accent and the musical lilt of the Irish tongue. "He got himself into a bit of trouble back home," I confessed, dipping my eyes. "And I heard he come to Dublin." I trusted he would infer that trouble involved the IRA, and when the RIC's search for him had grown too heated, he'd been forced to flee the area. There were many such men in the same predicament. "But I don't know where. And I don't know where to look."

Peter didn't say anything at first but continued to scrutinize me as I fidgeted with my empty teacup. When he reached for my cup, silently nodding to ask if I wanted another, I began to fear I might have overdone it or flubbed the accent. I shook my head, and he whisked the cup and saucer away and into a bin beneath the bar before swiping a towel over the smooth wooden surface where they'd set. I almost wished then that another customer would appear, distracting him and affording me an escape, but the pair of men at the opposite end of the bar still had half their pints to drink.

Peter leaned his elbows against the bar once more, though he seemed reluctant to meet my gaze. "Must be important to find him for ye to come all this way. Alone."

There was definitely suspicion in his voice, but there was nothing for it but for me to continue to brazen it out. "Aye," I replied in a small voice.

His dark eyes slowly lifted to search my face before dipping meaningfully to my abdomen. "Are ye sure he's yer cousin?"

I blushed at the implication, and Peter flushed in turn. Though not gray-haired yet, he might have been old enough to be my father, and for all his good-natured jesting and swinging the lead, he adopted the persona of more of an uncle to the young people who stepped up to his bar. As such, I could tell how uncomfortable it made him to ask such a question, and despite the embarrassment, I decided not to disavow him of his assumption. Not when it just might get me the information I needed.

However, that didn't mean I confirmed it either. At least, not in words. Instead, I turned to the side, seeming to struggle with myself. I knew this would be seen as proof enough.

"Can ye tell me what he looks like? And I'll see what I can

do." His lips compressed into a compassionate smile as he took in my features. "He must be a handsome devil."

I blushed again, taking this as the compliment he meant. For why else would a woman as attractive as me have wasted my time with him.

I described Alec for him and called him by his code name MacAlister. If Alec had gone off-book and chosen a different name than planned, I had no way of knowing it. Just as I had no way of knowing if the county I'd alleged we were from was correct either. A short time later, I made my departure, deciding it would be best not to linger lest Peter change his mind. He'd asked me to give him a few days to ask around.

I'd returned to our townhouse, too distracted and flushed from my success to be of much use elsewhere. There was also Lord French's letter to peruse. Upon returning through the hole concealed in the wall of my "writing room," I sat down on the edge of the bed to read it. Though I'd returned earlier than usual, Sidney found me there a short time later.

I glanced up in surprise as he entered. "Was I too loud?" I murmured, conscious of the fact that, while there was little to worry about from Mrs. Boyle, who rarely ventured past the kitchen, Ginny moved through most of the rooms in the house—cleaning and dusting and changing linens—even if we'd instructed her not to disturb the uppermost floor.

He shook his head, eyeing the paper in my hands. "What's that?"

"From Lord French." I lifted the two cards that had been contained inside. "Our permits to be out after curfew."

"As promised." Sidney sat beside me, taking the permits to examine them. "What else does he say?"

"That he's arranged for me to pay a call on the Kavanaghs tomorrow morning, and afterward to speak with DI Burrows at Great Brunswick Street Police Station." I turned to him. "Will you join me?"

He straightened as if aghast. "And miss tomorrow's race meeting?" He heaved a mock sigh. "I suppose if I must."

I began to refold Lord French's missive. "If it's too much trouble . . ."

"No, no, no," he interrupted, continuing to sound self-sacrificing. "No, I understand where my noblest duty lies."

I arched a single eyebrow at him, letting him know he was laying it on a bit thick. "How was your ride this morning?" I asked, beginning to remove my coat.

Sidney had risen even before me to drive out to Phoenix Park to go riding with the lord lieutenant's Master of the Horse, Dicky Wyndham-Quin, and a few others. "Quite nice, actually," he surprised me by replying. "Though not fruitful." He pushed back the lock of dark hair that stubbornly fell across his brow despite his best efforts to tame it, and I noted his cheekbones had gotten a bit of color from the sun. "But what about you? No luck either?"

"On the contrary . . ." I relayed my conversation with the Wicklow hotelier. Or rather, most of it. I decided there was no need to inform my husband that Peter had assumed I was MacAlister's lover rather than his cousin, and that I was in a delicate state. Particularly without a husband to claim the babe.

"Progress, indeed," Sidney declared as I finished changing back into my fashionable green and white checked drop-waist tea dress.

I stowed my disguise in the bottom of the wardrobe and when I returned to my feet, he draped my long string of pearls neatly around my neck.

"But you know that doesn't mean he'll uncover anything," he cautioned gently.

I could see the concern reflected in his midnight-blue eyes. Though we hadn't discussed it, I knew he could tell that our time here weighed on me, and not simply because Alec and the phosgene cylinders were still missing.

"I know," I assured him, and then decided to change the subject. "Any word from Max?"

Sidney had planned to stop by the Bank of Ireland that morning, where we'd instructed Max to send his correspondence to us, care of Tobias Finnegan. He shook his head and I frowned. "I'm beginning to think he misunderstood the assignment."

Sidney chuckled. "It's only been a few days, Ver. Give the man some time. Besides, I do believe he had to contend with all the pomp and circumstance surrounding Trooping the Colour."

I'd forgotten the ceremony celebrating the king's birthday was the previous Saturday. Had we been in London, Sidney, no doubt, would have been invited to attend in service dress. Perhaps he *had* been invited, but if so, he'd said nothing to me about it.

Regardless, it was a startling reminder that on that same day a year ago, I'd set off from London, still believing my husband to be dead, and unable to face the spectacle that was to take place—the first Trooping the Colour since the war began. So I'd fled from London, driving west to stay with a friend before carrying on to that fateful house party on Umbersea Island when I'd discovered Sidney's deception and the reason for it, and nearly died trying to set it all to right.

For a moment I couldn't speak, the significance of the anniversary being a little too much for me. For that had been when I'd first seen Sidney's beloved face after believing I would never do so again, at least not this side of the grave.

Sidney's brow creased. "Ver?"

I struggled to clear my throat, and my voice was slightly wobbly when I replied. "It's just, I left London the day of Trooping the Colour last year."

I didn't need to say more, for I could see that Sidney understood, pulling me to him and tucking my head beneath his chin. I allowed him to hold me that way for some time while I battled the foolish tears filling my eyes.

"June eighth," he said.

I sniffed, pulling away to look up at him in confusion.

"That's the day we saw each other again. Well, technically I saw you on June seventh." Because unbeknownst to me, he'd been posing as a gardener at the estate where I was staying. "But June eighth is the first time I held you again." An impish glint lit his eyes. "Until you flung me away."

"For good reason," I contested, tempted to fling him away now.

But Sidney only pulled me closer, silencing any further protests with his lips. And tongue and teeth. When his mouth left mine to nibble along the line of my jaw, I managed to murmur, "I can't believe you remember the date."

He pulled back to look down at me. "It's seared in my memory. As is the date I last saw you before I left for the front that last time." I felt the intensity of his gaze clear down to my toes, which curled in their oxford pumps. "I remember every moment with you." Then his smile turned slightly wolfish as he lowered his mouth to my ear. "Even the first time you . . ."

"Sidney," I chided, suspecting I knew what he was going to say, though the breathless tone of my voice likely ruined any hope of correcting his behavior. Not that I was certain I wanted to.

"Where are we promised tonight?" I asked the next time my lips were free.

"Dinner with the Greenwoods," he replied, pressing open-mouthed kisses to my neck behind my ear, a move that was almost guaranteed to leave me witless. "And then dancing . . . with Lawrence and his girl."

Unfortunately, I retained enough of my faculties to realize what a tedious meal it could prove to be if the chief secretary persisted to pontificate in his overly affected and hyperbolic manner. I nearly groaned aloud, and not in enjoyment of Sidney's efforts, though I rather liked Lady Greenwood. At least the dancing would be fun, and a chance to cut loose with the other gay young things eager for a few hours of forgetfulness, particularly as the dance halls were one of the few places where a sort of general truce reined and the Crown Forces—albeit in mufti—could dance a rag next to a Volunteer without an altercation. Or so it seemed to me. But perhaps I was too optimistic.

In any case, we still had several hours before our reservation for dinner, and I decided there was only one way I was going to make it through a meal with Sir Hamar Greenwood, and that was if Sidney had already coaxed me into a near comatose state.

"Come help me draw a bath," I urged him with a smile.

I didn't have to ask twice.

CHAPTER 8

The following morning, though we didn't have far to venture, we were almost late to our appointment with the Kavanaghs. They lived on Herbert Street, not far from St. Stephen's Church, or the Pepper Cannister, as it was fondly called, on account of the steeple's shape. Their home was typical redbrick Georgian, though I had little time to observe more than that before being hustled inside out of the rain.

I had only myself to blame for the lingering queasiness in my stomach as we were shown up the stairs to the drawing room. And I supposed the flask of gin Lieutenant Lawrence's latest deb, Sally, had brought with her to the dance hall to spike our lemonades. I'd allowed my relief at finally making progress with the hotelier in gathering information about Alec to eclipse my better judgment. While I hadn't drank past the point of insensibility, I'd nonetheless been glad Sidney had been with me to ensure I hadn't let anything sensitive slip.

Sally, on the other hand, had taken her quest for forgetfulness a bit too far. She was a lovely girl, but if she wasn't careful, her carousing with British soldiers might land her in serious trouble. Trouble like Miss Kavanagh had faced. I wished now that I'd been more responsible and tried to temper Sally. She might very well have ignored me, or called me a flat tire, but I still should have tried.

Photographs covered the wall to the right at the top of

the staircase. Recent family portraits, I surmised, from the clothing and hair styles. At the center of the collection hung a respectable family with a father, mother, daughter, and son. To the left, the daughter—a young woman of perhaps eighteen—gazed back at me. Her eyes seemed to convey she held a secret. Or perhaps that was merely my whimsy. Perhaps she was merely amused by the photographer. From the shading, I suspected her eyes were blue and her hair dark. The young man to the right of the family portrait—the brother—exhibited the same coloring, looking handsome in his khaki uniform for the Irish Guard. I wondered if he'd made it back from the front. It would be far easier if he had.

The maid waited patiently while I studied the photographs and then gestured for us to enter the room at the front of the house. A man and woman—the father and mother from the central photograph—rose to their feet as we entered. Much like Mr. O'Shaughnessy, the city recorder, Mr. Kavanagh boasted white hair and a mustache, though his were neatly trimmed. He was tall and slim just like his wife, and while her dark hair was now threaded with gray, I could see that I'd been correct about her children's coloring, for they'd inherited it from her.

They both moved as if they were swimming through syrup, as if the weight of their collective grief had somehow changed the viscosity of the air. I felt my own blithe and limber movements slow in response, the muscles along my back and shoulders even straining to keep a proper posture.

"Thank you for coming," Mrs. Kavanagh told us as we sat in a pair of French provincial chairs set at right angles on opposite sides of the sofa from which they'd risen. However, I could tell from her tightly clasped hands and the speaking look she gave her husband that she was purely being polite.

Obviously, someone had overstepped, and I could only assume it was Lord French. He'd insinuated that the Kavanaghs had requested his help, but if that was true, I suspected that was in the form of his pressuring the police, *not* enlisting the aid of a war hero and his intrepid wife, no matter that we'd been splashed across the newspapers a time or two for solving crimes. I had no desire to intrude on these people's grief or to make it any worse, but now that we were here, we could hardly retreat without saying something.

"We are not what you expected." The words were out of my mouth before I could think better of it, deciding there was enough duplicity to go around these days without our adding to it.

Sidney seemed as surprised by my words as the Kavanaghs, though my tone had been kind.

"I don't know what you mean," Mr. Kavanagh began at the same time his wife said, "We mean no offense."

I held up my hand to stay their words, even as they exchanged abashed looks. "None taken. I suspect what you were hoping for was something—or rather, someone—more official. Whereas we are just trying to do a good turn since Lord French asked us to speak with you."

"Yes, I see that now," Mrs. Kavanagh confessed. Her hands carefully smoothed the black fabric of her skirt over her lap. "But I don't see that there's anything you *can* do."

I smiled softly. "Then why don't you simply tell us about your daughter?" I glanced over my shoulder in the direction we'd come. "Was that her photograph by the stairs? She's a beautiful girl."

"Yes. She was," her mother replied, her gaze fastened on the wall dividing the drawing room from the corridor as if she could see through it to the pictures hanging there. "Sweet tempered, too. Always kind and looking out for others. Never caused us a moment of trouble." She turned briefly to her husband. "Except, well . . ." She shook her head, carrying on as if she'd not spoken those words, though I was curious what she'd stopped herself from saying. "Katherine *loved* flowers."

"Primroses, especially," Mr. Kavanagh contributed.

His wife nodded, her voice shaking as she continued. "And poetry. And music." She gestured toward the doors open to the adjoining room. "She was an accomplished pianist."

I could see the Dublin box piano situated along one wall near the windows.

"She would play for hours every day." Mrs. Kavanagh's voice was barely more than a whisper, and as her words fell away leaving only silence, I could sense the physical ache the absence of her music caused them. It was like a tangible presence, a void that the piano's runs and chords had once filled. It made the air almost unbearable in its stillness, so I sought to fill it.

"Did she have many friends?"

Mrs. Kavanagh seemed almost startled by the question. "Oh, yes. More so when she was younger. But she was always well-liked."

Mr. Kavanagh reached over to clasp his wife's hand. "She took her brother's death hard," he said, confirming my fears. He turned to Sidney. "Passchendaele."

It was all that needed to be said. For there had been some battles so horrific, so ravaged by casualties, that one word was all that had to be uttered.

My eyes immediately riveted to my husband, alert to any signs of distress. Because I knew Sidney had been at Passchendaele as well. That he'd lost nearly his entire company and barely survived himself. That it still haunted him. I suspected it always would.

I could see the strain that Mr. Kavanagh's pronouncement caused Sidney. I could tell how rigidly he held himself, how he struggled to master and mask his reaction. My initial instinct was to go to him, but I knew that he would not thank me for it, so I stayed put.

Finally, he swallowed, the cords of his neck working hard. "Was he part of the First or Second Battalion?"

"The First."

Sidney nodded, and clearly this meant something to him, but he did not explain.

Mr. Kavanagh exhaled a weary sigh. "And her cousin returned changed."

All of our men had returned changed. How could they not, after everything they'd witnessed?

"For the worst," Mrs. Kavanagh muttered in the direction of her feet.

This remark surprised me, though perhaps it shouldn't have. For every person sensitive to the struggles our returning soldiers had faced there was another who either failed or refused to understand why those men couldn't simply leave the war behind. That, or they had been too blinded by the propaganda our government had spread to grasp how unspeakably appalling it all had been. Mrs. Kavanagh had lost her son, so it was natural that she might feel some resentment and a corresponding lack of sensitivity to the struggles of those who *had* returned. Nonetheless, it still shocked me to hear her voice it out loud.

Unless my assumption was false, and her nephew returning changed had less to do with shell shock and the general disillusionment of war than another factor.

Mr. Kavanagh rested his hand over his wife's, squeezing it, perhaps to recall her to whom she was speaking. By this gesture alone, I knew I would get no further information about it. That is, if there was any more to be gained other than confirmation that she was a grieving mother.

"We understand she was stepping out with a British soldier," Sidney remarked. "Was he part of the Irish Guards as well?"

"No," Mr. Kavanagh replied. "Delagrange is stationed at the Castle. Special assignment."

Which could mean any number of things. After all, there was a company barracked at Dublin Castle that served several purposes, and there were any number of specialized units also based there. The headquarters of the DMP and

RIC were even located within the castle walls. But I couldn't help but note that someone detailed to intelligence work might describe their position in just this way, especially since the service had been reorganized under new leadership based at the Castle.

Whatever the truth, it would behoove us to find out more about this Delagrange. And now that we had his name and base, it would be much easier.

Mrs. Kavanagh closed her eyes, her head still bowed. "The lieutenant was devastated when he heard what was done to her. Katherine . . . she didn't want to tell him. But it wasn't as if she could *hide* it." She looked up, glaring at the ends of my bobbed tresses where they curled beneath the brim of my cornflower-blue hat. It was obvious she disapproved. "I'm sure things are different in London, but here in Ireland, we women do not cut our crowning glories."

I could feel both men watching me, as if anxious how I would respond to such an implied insult. But I was not about to take a grieving mother, who had recently lost *both* her children, to task. Especially not when what she'd said was true. The trend for bobbed tresses, which was still almost exclusive to the young and fashionable even in London, had yet to spread to Dublin. Otherwise, the IRA would not have adopted the policy of cutting women's hair to shame them into compliance. Not only was it a deeply personal invasion of their body autonomy, but it also marked them, almost like a scarlet letter.

Of course, it grated that the underlying notion of Mrs. Kavanagh's condemnation was the implication that by simply choosing to trim my own hair I was tarring my respectability. However, she was far from the first person to inform me both directly and indirectly that they found my hairstyle too forward or mannish. Even my own mother had made her opinion clear on the matter.

Nevertheless, I liked it short. I liked the ease and freedom of its upkeep, of no longer being bound to a dressing table bench for untold hours every week while a maid swept it up into one coiffure or another. I liked how smashing it looked with the new styles of hats coming out of Paris. Styles which were not suited to mounds of hair affixed at the crown or along the nape of the neck.

But I told Mrs. Kavanagh none of this. She didn't want to hear it. Only to make her point that any modest, self-respecting woman, as her daughter had been, would have been shamed by the act of having their hair cut. And ashamed to let her beau see it thus. While the entire notion infuriated me, my feelings would not change the facts of the matter at hand.

"And how did Lieutenant Delagrange react?" I asked steadily, refusing to be bated.

"He was naturally outraged on her behalf," Mr. Kavanagh answered. "I . . . I had to make him see reason when it seemed he was bent on retaliating at random in kind." He glanced at his wife. "Katherine was particularly agitated by the notion."

Which spoke well of her. She didn't want any woman to face the same ordeal she had, even if they were friends and family to whoever her attackers had been.

"Did Delagrange listen?" Sidney asked.

Mr. Kavanagh glanced at his wife's profile. "We never heard of any such reprisals."

But would they have been reported? Such crimes often went unreported out of fear of the public disgrace they unfairly brought on the women. I imagined this was doubly so in cases where it was women sympathetic to the republican cause attacked by members of the Crown Forces. What incentive did they have to inform the British authorities if they believed no justice would come of it?

"You mentioned Katherine was agitated," I broached with care. "And I know how difficult it can be to think clearly during such a . . . situation."

Mrs. Kavanagh stirred in alarm, fluttering her hands.

"But did she recognize anything about the men who attacked her?" I pressed, even as she suddenly pushed to her feet. "Did they mention anything distinguishable?"

"I . . . I'm not discussing this again. I'm not!" She began to pace in tight circles. "What's the use. We already know those rebel extremists did it. We already know *why.*" Her eyes as they slid toward her husband were tinged with a hint of malice. Malice she soon directed toward me. "And you *don't* know. You couldn't." With this she strode from the room, leaving her husband staring dejectedly after her.

"Please," he murmured in a broken voice after a few tense seconds. "Just go."

He pivoted to face the window, and Sidney and I did as we were asked, allowing the maid to lead us back down the stairs to the front door. I considered asking her a question or two as she handed Sidney his hat, but then decided we'd done enough damage for the day. We turned our steps toward Merrion Square, in hopes of catching a tram to Great Brunswick Street.

"Well, that could have gone better," Sidney murmured in what might have been the understatement of the year.

I gave a derisive laugh. "Yes, Lord French really stepped in it this time. Or rather, forced *us* to step in it." I was none too happy with the lord lieutenant at the moment.

"Clearly, the Kavanaghs did not expect *or* desire our assistance. Not like Lord French implied."

I shook my head. "He should have communicated matters better. Both to us *and* the Kavanaghs." I crowded closer to Sidney as we navigated around a large puddle in the pavement, the rain still drumming down against the umbrella he held over our heads. I was grateful for my buckle galoshes.

"Now I have to wonder how receptive DI Burrows will be to our questions."

"No worse than the Kavanaghs, I imagine. He has to at least present the image of being cooperative."

Because of who we were. Because the lord lieutenant had made the request he speak with us.

I sighed. "That doesn't make it any less a potential waste of time."

I wondered if Peter was at the Wicklow. I wondered if he had uncovered any information for me. At that very moment, I might be learning a clue to Alec's fate. Instead, I was traipsing across the city to speak to a detective inspector who very likely resented our interference.

Sidney peered down at me. "Don't fret, Ver. At least we tried."

I answered his gentle smile with a tight one of my own. "I suppose that's all we can do."

His gaze shifted to the vicinity of my ear. "And I like your hair bobbed. It suits you."

I squeezed his arm, appreciating this considerate attempt to reassure me. "Don't worry. I didn't take Mrs. Kavanagh's aversion to heart." I frowned. "Though I can't imagine her horrified disapproval of her daughter's shorn tresses did much to console Miss Kavanagh's distress."

Curse these men who had decided cutting women's hair was a justified action. And curse the society who colluded in the weaponizing of shearing women's hair by dint of the fact that somehow its length was an indication of virtue.

Sidney nodded to a pair of passing women. "Maybe Mrs. Kavanagh was so preoccupied by what happened to her daughter's hair because she couldn't bear to focus on the other details."

I was surprised by the insightfulness of this response. I'd wondered what the other details of Miss Kavanagh's assault were, but I'd not dared to ask Lord French or the Kavanaghs.

But perhaps Sidney had discovered them another way. "Do you . . . ?"

He cut me off before I could finish my question. "No, but it bears consideration." His face was grim. "Perhaps Burrows can tell us."

If even he knew.

I didn't say this aloud, but by the deep furrow in Sidney's brow, I wondered if he shared the same concern. However, his thoughts appeared to have gone in a different direction.

"What Mrs. Kavanagh said. You don't know, do you?" He turned to look down at me, fear and uncertainty reflected in his eyes, and I realized what he was asking.

There were many things about my years as a British intelligence agent that I'd not shared with Sidney. Just as there were many things about the years he'd spent in the trenches along the Western Front that he'd not shared with me. Sometimes those oversights weren't on purpose. Other times it was because the information was too sensitive. But there were a few details I'd withheld because I knew they would hurt Sidney, and heaven knew he had already been through enough. This, however, was not one of those things.

"No. Not like Miss Kavanagh." My words were stilted. "But I've told you how some of the German officers' hands had a tendency to wander. And we were trained . . . quietly, unofficially . . . by fellow female agents on what to expect, on how to handle ourselves if that should happen." I turned to look directly at Sidney. "Because heaven forbid, we ever admitted to a male within British Intelligence that we'd ever had sexual contact with the enemy. Even if it had been rape. We would have been tarred as an enemy collaborator and tossed out of the service like so much rubbish."

I turned away to stare at the trees surrounding Merrion Square as we approached it. "I learned how I needed to keep my head, even under the worst of circumstances, lest in a moment it all be used against me."

Sidney didn't speak, and I was too lost in recollection of colleagues who had failed to remember this to their own detriment. And not just from the cruel whim of the Secret Intelligence Service and the British government, but more dangerously, from the Germans. When I did return to the present, I looked up to find his expression drawn in stark lines.

"But the simple answer is, no. No, I don't truly know," I said, making it as plain as I could.

His eyes searched mine for evidence of well-meaning deceit, and I tried to peer back at him as openly as possible. When he turned away, I didn't know if this was in acceptance that I was telling the truth or recognition that he knew he wouldn't be able to tell if I wasn't.

CHAPTER 9

Great Brunswick Street Police Station was located in a large stone building across from Trinity College, about a block from O'Connell Bridge and the River Liffey. As we entered the building, I expected there to be some sort of extra precautions or security measures, considering the fact Collins and his murder gang had targeted and killed a number of the G-Men on political duty when they were based in this building. One detective had even been shot just outside in the street. Given that, it seemed only natural that anyone crossing the threshold would at least bear a greater amount of scrutiny than usual from the officer posted near the door, but the young policeman allowed us to pass with barely a glance.

Even the man at the desk paid us little mind. That is, until we gave him our names and asked for DI Burrows. Then, his interest perked up enough to give my features a thorough once-over before passing Sidney an envelope. I thanked him despite my confusion, having presumed we'd be directed to an office or interview room of some sort, not handed a missive. But maybe Burrows had been called away on another police matter.

I crowded close to Sidney to read the hastily scrawled message on the piece of foolscap tucked inside. It requested we meet Burrows at the corner of Grafton and Nassau Streets.

This wasn't far, lying just on the opposite side of Trinity College, but it *was* inconvenient. Particularly as it was but a stone's throw from the Wicklow Hotel, which I had been haunting as my alternate persona searching for answers about Alec. As such, I was leery of being noticed and connected to the Irish maid Dearbhla Bell, the code name I'd chosen for myself. Especially since my disguise was not as pronounced as those I'd used during the war.

However, Sidney seemed oblivious to this concern, instead huffing in annoyance, and muttering under his breath about the presumptuousness of the detective as he led me from the building back out into the rain.

"Maybe there are too many prying ears at the station," I proposed, mindful of the spies Alec had alleged Collins had placed in key positions all over the city, such as the DMP.

"*Or* he's testing our willingness to be seen in public, speaking with a policeman," he suggested, looking both directions before hustling us across the street.

I supposed he was thinking of the notice recently released by the IRA's General Headquarters, ordering all Volunteers and citizens of the so-called Irish Republic to support the boycott of the Royal Irish Constabulary issued by the Dáil, the republicans' shadow government. An order to ostracize members of the RIC had been made more than a year before, but this most recent directive called for an intensification of that policy, forbidding interaction of any kind with not only the RIC, but anyone associated with them, including their families. The edict had even gone so far as to call the RIC "a portion of the Army of Occupation."

The DMP, while the acting police force within Dublin, were separate and distinct from the RIC, and they had not been mentioned as part of the boycott. I had to believe this was for a reason. Likely because Collins's bullying tactics and the threat of his murder gangs had already thoroughly neutralized them. But that didn't mean Sidney's suspicions weren't correct. Perhaps Burrows *was* anxious to test our loyalties.

We were walking too fast to converse comfortably, but as we made our way across Nassau Street, I heard my husband vowing, "If a show of loyalty is what he wants, then we shall give it to him."

Before I could ask what he meant by this or come to any understanding of why this notion had irritated him so much, we reached the corner indicated. We'd barely stepped up onto the curb when a short man of about sixty in a neat gray three-piece suit exited Yeates and Son to approach us. He wore no spectacles, making it seem doubtful he'd entered the eyeglass shop to make a purchase or request a repair. Rather, I suspected this was DI Burrows, and he'd merely stepped inside to escape the dreary weather.

His expression was good-humored enough as he introduced himself in a gentle Irish brogue, his lips curling into a pleasant smile beneath his waxed mustache. But his eyes were watchful, waiting to see how we would acquit ourselves. Sidney soon gave him good reason for that vigilance.

"I don't know what else I can be tellin' ye," he said. "But I'll try."

"Surely not here," Sidney insisted, and I thought at first he was referring to the rain. But rather than return to the shop or turn our steps toward a café I spied on the opposite side of Grafton Street, he pivoted toward the south. "This way." Then before either the detective or I could object, he began pulling me along in his wake. I hadn't even time to look to see if Burrows had followed before I was propelled into a narrow lane.

Shops also lined this passage—ones I might describe as less reputable—and there was a fetid odor lingering beneath the scent of damp bricks and wet wool. Where Sidney was leading us, I could only guess, but I surmised he'd learned of it from his army friends. Near the end of the alley, he pulled open the door to a narrow storefront.

Inside, I was immediately struck by the smell of stout and tobacco and the fact that the pub was far larger inside than it had appeared from the outside. Given the relatively early hour—it being only midday—I wouldn't have expected such an establishment to be crowded, but there were a fair number of men seated at its tables. A sprinkling of those present were dressed in British army uniforms, but many of the others were attired in suits or workingman clothes.

It took me less than five seconds to realize what this place served as, and every last ounce of my reserve of self-possession not to stumble or otherwise give myself away as Sidney led us toward a table. My skin flushed and then went cold as the eyes of at least half a dozen men tracked me across the room. It was doubtful that women often frequented this pub, particularly at this time of day.

No, they would not be welcome in this company. Not when it was populated by British Intelligence officers and their touts—local informants paid for the information they provided. Anyone here not eager to collaborate with the British Secret Intelligence Service would soon find themselves in an awkward, if not outright dangerous situation. This must be Kidd's Back, I realized. Alec's reports had mentioned it and its location off Grafton Street, but he had never dared venture there. Not when he was likely to be recognized.

I wanted to throttle Sidney. He'd known I wanted to avoid drawing the interest of any former intelligence colleagues, and this was most definitely not the way to do it. DI Burrows also looked distinctly uncomfortable as he took his seat at our table, and I couldn't blame him. Sidney might be irrefutably proving his loyalty to the British Empire, but he was also quite possibly painting a target on the G-Man's back. Though

I had to wonder, as my gaze skittered over the occupants of the room, whether any of Collins's men were brave—or suicidal—enough to enter into this veritable lion's den.

Sidney removed his battered silver cigarette case from his inside pocket—a gift from me after our wedding before he left for the front. He removed one of his specially blended Turkish cigarettes before offering the case to Burrows. The detective declined. Meanwhile, I was trying to gather up the tattered remnants of my aplomb, hoping I appeared even a fraction as at ease with my surroundings as my husband did.

Having lit his cigarette, Sidney leaned back in his chair to take a long drag before blowing the smoke toward the ceiling. He ordered drinks for both of us—the detective having once again refused—before addressing the business at hand. "Now, the inquiry into Miss Kavanagh's attack. I'm sure you appreciate that Lord French is taking a particular interest in the matter, so your full cooperation would be much appreciated."

As threats went, it was skillfully done, but I wasn't certain such tactics were necessary. In truth, I feared they might actually be detrimental to convincing Burrows to assist us. His reaction was self-contained, but for the space of a moment I thought I spied a mutinous gleam in his eyes. His jaw was certainly set in a hard line.

"As I told ye, I'll try."

Sidney's stare clearly communicated he was not impressed. "When were you called in to investigate?"

"The followin' morn."

"Did it happen during curfew?" I interjected softly.

He nodded. "She . . ." He rubbed his hand down over his face, exhaling. "The entire household was in quite a state."

Sidney's demeanor sobered to one more befitting the solemnity of the topic of our discussion. "How severe was the attack?"

The detective inspector's brow furrowed, indicating he

understood what he was asking. "She had bruises from where she'd been restrained, and I suspect she was struck at least once across the face." His voice had lowered so as not to be overheard and I had to strain to hear him. "Her hair was cut, right to the quick in some places." His gaze dipped to the scarred wooden table. "As to anythin' else, I can't say. If there was more . . ." He shook his head. "They didn't report it."

This wasn't surprising. I'd already recognized that if an even more intimate assault had occurred, it was doubtful the Kavanaghs had reported it and made it public record. Yet, in and of itself, that was not proof that anything more had occurred. So we had no choice but to hope that Miss Kavanagh hadn't suffered more.

Sidney tapped the ash from his fag into the dish on the table. "Did Miss Kavanagh recognize any of her attackers? Were there any witnesses?"

Burrows waited until our drinks were delivered to the table and the server departed before responding. "She claimed not to, and from the state she was in when I tried to speak with her . . ." Even under the dim lighting, I could see how pale he'd turned. "I believed her. As to witnesses, none stepped forward."

"Too intimidated?" Sidney queried after taking a long drink of his stout.

"In that neighborhood, I should say 'tis less likely. But . . ." He shrugged one shoulder, glancing about him guardedly for the first time since we'd entered the room. "Maybe their reach is longer than I'd like to think."

And by "their," I knew he meant the IRA.

His eyes seemed to lock on something—or someone—across the room, though I couldn't see who it was. "The Big Fellow casts a long shadow," he murmured in a hushed voice.

Sidney cast me a glance that was rife with impatience. "Do you have any suspects, then?" he asked. "Any specific names, that is?"

Burrows turned back to us slowly. "Nay. As I said, there were no witnesses. And they left no telltale evidence behind."

"But how did they gain access to Miss Kavanagh after curfew?" I pressed after taking a sip of the gin-fizz Sidney had ordered for me and then setting it aside. The gin was once again subpar, and they seemed to have forgotten the lemon juice. "Did they force their way into the house?" This was something we'd not had a chance to ask the Kavanaghs.

His brow pleated. "They'd attended some sort of dinner party that evenin', and when they returned Miss Kavanagh couldn't sleep. So she'd gone out to their garden for some fresh air. That's where it happened."

"It's gated?" Sidney asked.

"Aye. And locked. But the walls are easily scaled."

I pictured the layout of the townhouse we'd rented on Upper Fitzwilliam Street for comparison, wishing I'd been able to at least see the proportions of the Kavanaghs' back garden. "And no one inside heard anything?"

"Not that they claimed."

I supposed it was possible. If the assault happened at the rear of the garden. If Miss Kavanagh hadn't made much sound. Or had been *forced* not to. Maybe that was when she'd been struck across the face.

"And mind ye, all that I'm tellin' ye came from Mr. and Mrs. Kavanagh," Burrows cautioned us. "Miss Kavanagh barely uttered a word durin' our interview and was ultimately escorted from the room by her maid, she was so distressed."

Sidney set down his drink, a bit of foam clinging to his upper lip. "You think there's more than what they told you?"

"Or that they altered what their daughter told them?" I added, phrasing the query in a slightly different light.

"I don't think anythin'." He crossed his arms over his chest. "I'm merely informin' ye the facts I was able to gather."

Which wasn't much. And if he was never granted a proper interview with Miss Kavanagh, then he'd not even been able to mine her for the barest scraps of information. Things that she might not have realized she'd noticed, but when put together can begin to form a picture. I doubted he was allowed to examine her injuries or her hair closely either, so he wouldn't have been able to tell anything distinctive about the implement they'd used to cut it.

Yet I also couldn't blame her parents for wanting to shield her from the pain and embarrassment of such a conversation. Except by doing so, they'd only hindered the possibility of their daughter's attackers being apprehended.

"I understand His Excellency wants this matter resolved," Burrows proclaimed crossly, drawing the attention of some of those seated closest to us. "And sure, I could name a whole raft of suspicious fellows, but that's not goin' to tell ye who really did it or give ye the evidence to make it stick." His voice lowered. "Or are ye only interested in roundin' up any likely rebel?"

From the cynicism that curled his lip, I deduced this wasn't the first time such an arrest had been made.

"We only want to prevent what happened to Miss Kavanagh from happening to anyone else," I told him sincerely.

The look he gave me in return suggested he wished me luck with that. I supposed it was a rather naïve assumption that one arrest could stop these assaults, but it was at least a start.

"Then I wish ye luck," he stated, pushing to his feet. He reached across the table to shake Sidney's hand before nodding deferentially to me. "Should ye think of anythin' else . . . ye knows where to find me."

I watched as he navigated around the tables and out the door, back out into the rain, and then heaved a sigh. "Why did I expect this to be easy?" I asked no one in particular.

"It's a sad case," Sidney remarked casually. "But I'm not sure what French expects you to do about it. Not with so little to go on."

I turned to glare at him, not having forgotten how angry I

was that he'd brought me here. Thus far, it appeared I'd been fortunate that no one present was aware of my history with the Secret Service, but a quick survey of the tables nearby told me I'd drawn plenty of attention, from agents and touts alike. I ignored them, like I did most unwanted stares, instead focusing on hustling my husband out of there.

"What is it?" he asked, stirring my ire with his seeming obliviousness.

"May we go?" I bit out around a tight smile.

His gaze flicked toward a British officer seated to our right. One who had been eyeing me a little too keenly; the glasses littering his table and fags piled in the glass dish at his elbow told me he'd already been there for some time.

Sidney took one last drag of his own cigarette before stubbing it out. But before we could rise, a familiar voice cut across the bass rumble of all the others.

"Verity Kent. As I live and breathe, is that really you?"

CHAPTER 10

There was nothing for it but to smile and feign delight while inside I was cursing. "Bennett? Why, how marvelous!" I turned to clasp the hand Lieutenant George Bennett held out to me and proffered my cheek for him to buss. His mustache bristled against my skin. "How are you?"

"Very well. Very well, indeed," Bennett replied, gazing down at me in open curiosity. He had a long face and a narrow nose, and the propensity to stand about with his mouth hanging open—sometimes by a half an inch, sometimes by two. But for all that, he was a relatively good-looking fellow who had inherited his coloring from his Dutch mother.

"My husband," I said, gesturing to Sidney. "I believe you told me once you were acquainted."

Sidney shook his hand. "At Oxford together, weren't we? At least for a time," he queried, evidently recognizing him. "Magdalen?" he asked, inquiring of his college.

Bennett nodded. "Good memory. Particularly as I wouldn't have described myself as notable." He chuckled. "Not like you." He sank down, uninvited, in the chair DI Burrows had vacated, crossing one leg over the other as if settling in for a chat. "But what on earth brings you to Dublin?" His eyes were avid with interest, though I didn't miss the tinge of mockery beneath his veneer of appeal.

What I wanted to do was tell him to go jump in the Liffey,

or something far less polite, but I understood that I had to play the game. Sidney might have gotten us into this bloody mess, but I had to be the one to get us out of it.

"Oh, just seeing the sights," I declared casually, lifting my gin-fizz to take another bitter swig.

"Like you did in Rotterdam," he retorted dryly.

I arched a single eyebrow at this reference to my clandestine war work.

"Dry up, Verity," he declared with a chuckle, though I wasn't the one who'd been talking. I could tell I'd annoyed him. His eyes narrowed at the corners. "I know your husband's been read in."

"Read in to what?" Sidney asked with such perfect artlessness that I nearly forgave him for his dimwittedness in bringing me here. As it was, I was hard-pressed to withhold my amusement, especially when Bennett's face flushed with irritation.

"Alright, I'll play along. And I suppose the two of us are just old associates from London. That I coordinated with . . . what was it? That firm of importers and exporters you worked for during the war." This had been one of the fronts the Secret Service had used to conceal its activities.

Now, I was the one growing annoyed with his need to demonstrate how well informed he was. But of course, he'd always been that way. Even when he was stationed in Holland during the war. I'd actually warned Captain Henry Landau, my superior inside Holland, of it, fearful Bennett would unwittingly give intelligence to the German agents also crawling all over the neutral Netherlands. Fortunately, my interactions with Bennett there proved to be minimal, moving in and out of Holland as quickly as I had, eschewing the main office as I prepared to either slip through the heavily guarded border into occupied Belgium to liaise with our agents there, or sail across the English Channel dodging U-boats and their deadly torpedoes to report back to London. However, Bennett was fully cognizant of the role I'd played. One of the few people who was.

And what rotten luck he was here now.

There was no telling what he might report back to the Castle and ultimately to Sir Basil Thomson in London. This was not a complication I needed. I would have to walk a very thin line. Redirect his attention toward something of greater intelligence value.

Or perhaps, "misdirect" was the appropriate word, I decided, as an idea occurred to me. One spurred by my most recent interaction with Peter. For Bennett wasn't a bad sort, just pedantic and prone to bragging. He was an engineer like his father, and while detailed and methodical, lacked imagination. Which would hopefully play into my hand.

I glanced at Sidney out of the corner of my eye, hoping he was quick to catch on. For this would all go much smoother if he helped the fiction along.

"Or maybe you first introduced yourself at the canteen," I replied offhandedly to his baiting, as I'd volunteered at one outside Victoria Station during the early months of the war. I lifted my glass to take another drink and then grimaced, setting it aside.

"Not to your taste?" Bennett inquired.

I turned away, shaking my head wearily. "Nothing seems to agree with me lately."

His chin perked upward, and I could tell he believed he'd caught the scent of something. And when his gaze dipped to where I'd seemingly unconsciously pressed a light hand against my lower abdomen, I knew that smell was exactly the one I wanted him to catch a whiff of.

I lifted my face to my husband. "Perhaps you were right about this meeting," I murmured wanly.

Any fear that Sidney would not grasp my intention was

swept aside as he leaned close, draping his arm protectively around the back of my chair. "I warned you it might be too much," he gently reproved. "Especially this early in the day."

"I know."

"It seems it was a fool's errand anyway," he groused.

Meanwhile, Bennett was absorbing all of this like an old harpy listening to her neighbors bicker. Periodically, he cast a look over his shoulder toward a man with a broad forehead and a dark mustache who watched us all avidly. He had the look of the typical intelligence agents Thomson preferred, and I suspected Bennett would be reporting everything we'd said to him as soon as we departed.

"Sent to keep ole Frenchie in line, eh?" he quipped to Sidney, but my husband merely glared at him in mild irritation.

"Sorry to cut this reunion short," he told Bennett. "But I'm afraid you'll have to excuse us."

"All this smoke." I waved my hand in front of me. "I'm afraid it's turning my stomach."

"Of course," Bennett replied, rising politely to his feet as we stood to depart.

Sidney tossed some money down on the table before taking my arm.

"Another time," I said, offering Bennett a taut smile.

He bobbed his head almost cheerily. "When you're feeling better."

A tall, gaunt man was entering when we reached the door, and he paused to hold it open for us. I peered up at him almost absently, so intent was I in playing my current part, but there was something in his bearing that made me take a second look. He returned my regard stonily, and then carried on into the pub as Sidney and I exited into the damp alley. While Sidney opened his umbrella, I pondered why the man had seemed so familiar. There had been something almost tragic in his expression, something cynical as well, which I had seen often in the faces of our Tommies returning from the front.

Perhaps it was that which had so arrested me, but I filed his face away in my memory to contemplate later regardless.

Sidney took my arm again, guiding me down the alley back toward Grafton Street. "What was that all about?" he asked once we'd put some distance between us and Kidd's Back.

"*That*," I bit out sharply, no longer concealing my fury, "was me extricating us from a delicate situation."

"By pretending to *be* in a delicate condition?"

I scowled up at him, nearly turning my ankle on an uneven stretch of pavement. "I realize *you* aren't well acquainted with Lieutenant Bennett," I explained, keeping my gaze trained on the ground. "But I assure you, *he* is well acquainted with *my* history, specifically with the SIS. And he is precisely the type of man we needed to avoid drawing the notice of. And Kidd's Back is *precisely* the type of establishment he frequents. So why on earth did you drag me and DI Burrows in there?"

Sidney didn't respond immediately, and it took all of my self-control not to continue raging at him as we turned the corner onto Grafton Street. I knew from experience that the more I berated him the deeper he would retreat into stubborn silence until we were both stomping about the house, slamming doors and drawers, and muttering uncomplimentary things under our breaths. So I bit my tongue and forced myself to turn my attention to my surroundings. Saturday was market day, when most Dubliners ventured out to do their shopping. As such, the streets were bustling with people despite the rain.

Eventually I was rewarded for my forbearance when Sidney conceded. "I wasn't thinking. Not about that anyway. Just—" He broke off and I risked looking up at him now that we were on smoother pavement. His mouth was tight and his brow troubled, but whatever words he was searching for, seemed to be slow in coming.

We passed a man loitering under the awning of a shop, smoking a cigarette, and I turned away, tilting my head ever so slightly so that he couldn't get a clear look at my face beyond the brim of my hat should he happen to pay us any notice. Sidney, on the other hand, plowed on ahead, heedless of who might be watching. Concern welled up inside me, for this wasn't the first time I'd noticed how indifferent Sidney was to his surroundings.

To be sure, there were some advantages to the concept of hiding in plain sight, but only if it was played to our advantage. We had to make concessions. Be seen when we wanted to be seen, and conceal ourselves when we didn't, albeit not overtly. Go about our business, but be mindful of who might take an interest, and circumvent their expectations.

The only thing Sidney seemed to be doing was meeting and exceeding those expectations. But then, he'd been leading a very different daytime existence than I was. One filled with race meetings and canters through Phoenix Park, long lunches and visits to the Kildare Street Club, games of tennis and football matches. Most of the time he said very little about what he'd done or what his companions had said, unless it was pertinent to our search for Alec and the phosgene cylinders, but I could see that at times something lay heavy in his thoughts. Just as now.

"Does it have something to do with Lawrence and Glengarry?" I questioned when words continued to elude him. "With the others?"

He pulled me close as we hurried across the intersection toward the station where even now a tram idled that was bound in the direction we wanted, letting off and taking on passengers. We hastened our steps to catch it. Given the rain, the lower level was even more crowded than usual, but we managed to find a spot standing near the stairs which led to the upper deck. Sidney gripped the railing to steady himself while I held on to him.

The damp of everyone's garments and the heat from so many bodies packed tightly together made the air muggy, but for all that, it wasn't entirely unpleasant. At least, not while I could press close to Sidney's solid form and smell the musk of his cologne rather than the onion the fellow a few steps away was eating like an apple.

Much of the general discussion I could hear was about the results of the county and rural council elections which had occurred earlier in the month. The outcomes had been posted that morning in the newspapers, and though I'd not had time to read the articles in full, it was obvious they had been a rousing victory for Sinn Féin and the republicans. The loyalist and unionist papers could try all they might to put a more palatable tint on the story, but the fact of the matter was that all but four county councils in the north were now under Sinn Féin and nationalist control, and eighty-five percent of rural districts. When asked to speak at the ballot box, the Irish had responded with resounding support for the rebels.

I couldn't say this was entirely a surprise as it merely confirmed and expanded the control Sinn Féin had gained in the parliamentary elections of late 1918. What interested me was the government's response. After all, they'd postponed and then promised the Irish at least a measure of Home Rule once the war was over, but we were closing in on two years since the armistice and the matter was still unresolved. Of course, the demands of the Irish populace had now gone beyond a desire for just Home Rule, but surely the more moderate factions would be amenable if the government came to the table with a reasonable offer.

Given this atmosphere and our crowded confines, I didn't continue to push Sidney for answers, but that didn't mean I'd stopped thinking about it. As we trundled past the green campus of Trinity College and the railway offices lining Westland Row with its terminus, and on around Merrion Square, I ruminated on his remark about giving the detective inspector a display of loyalty. I'd not had the chance to ask him what he'd meant, but now I wondered.

By the time we exited the tram near the corner of Baggot Street and Upper Fitzwilliam Street, the rain had lightened to little more than a drizzle. Still, I used it as an excuse to stroll close to my husband's side as he held the umbrella aloft. The better to hear him when I returned to the matter of his reckless behavior and whether it had anything to do with the umbrage he'd taken at Burrows asking us to meet him on a public street corner. "As a show of loyalty," I said, repeating his words.

"Partly." He frowned. "Or maybe mostly."

I waited for him to elaborate, but either he believed this was answer enough or, more likely, he was being evasive. But why?

"Did someone say something? Or perhaps they just *implied* something?" After all, he was spending much of his time with a great deal of privileged, linear thinkers. I'd heard enough talk from Lawrence, Glengarry, Wyndham-Quin and their like to grasp that they were of the mindset that Ireland was part of Great Britain and would forever remain so, and as such these rabble-rousing rebels needed to be put in their place by whatever means necessary. There wasn't much subtlety in their or their commanding officers' approach.

"Not directly," he hedged. "There has been some amount of poking and prodding as to what I'm doing here." He turned to peer across the street at the man whose steps seemed to almost shadow ours. However, he was carrying a briefcase and an umbrella, so I'd already ruled him out as a concern. It would be difficult for him to quickly draw a gun with both hands occupied. "And it's been suggested a number of times that perhaps I should take up a commission here in a more official capacity."

I realized with a jolt that he was speaking of enlisting. "Do you *want* to rejoin the army?"

"No." He scoffed. "Heavens no!"

After the war, after everything he'd been through, I could hardly fault him his vehement reaction.

"Truth be told, I pity the poor devils who answered the call to come here. I don't see an easy way out of this. For anyone." He lowered his gaze to the pavement before us. "But I do admit to some feelings of uncertainty. I am"—his lips clamped together as he appeared to search for the right word—"unsettled."

"I know what you mean," I admitted. I was unsettled as well. By the things I was observing. By the things I was learning from sources who were not rigidly controlled by the British. By the attitudes and behaviors of those who should know better. And it was all compounded by the seeds of mistrust that had been planted by everything we'd learned during our previous investigation. Yet, I didn't know what to do except press on and focus on our immediate tasks—finding Alec and the phosgene.

"What have you told them? When they poke and prod and suggest you take up a commission, that is," I clarified.

"Nothing." His expression seemed to convey some surprise that I'd even asked. "I figured that was the best tack. To allow them to believe whatever they want to believe." He diverted us closer to the terrace of Georgian houses on my right as a motorcar sped past, spraying water from the puddles in the gutters. "They all think I'm here on special assignment anyway, and it's doubtful anything I say will change that. So why not let them go on believing it?" His eyes met mine. "At least it diverts the suspicion away from you."

"And when you go waltzing into a place like Kidd's Back with me on your arm, it all but confirms it. For the murder gangs as well as the Brits," I added wryly.

He shrugged a shoulder in indifference.

"You're supposed to be more careful, Sidney," I protested. "I know you've an image to maintain, but *not* at the risk of your life."

"I take as much care as I need to. Though, I am sorry I exposed you to Bennett's notice." His gaze dipped to my abdomen. "But was it really wise to give him the implication that you're expecting? Won't that make him take more of an interest?"

"On the contrary, Lieutenant Bennett is nothing if not a stodgy traditionalist, like most of the men in the Secret Service. At least, when it comes to the roles and capabilities of women. He'll believe that my being in the family way precludes me from being involved in any clandestine work. Both because you would never allow it and because it would render me incapable." My mouth twisted in scorn. "Either he'll choose to keep this juicy piece of gossip to himself or, more likely, he'll report it to his superiors. It's only a matter of time before we'll know."

"You aren't, are you?"

I peered up at Sidney's earnest face.

"Expecting?"

I scowled.

"It's a legitimate question."

"No, it's not. I would think you would know me better than to believe I would inform you in such a ragtag manner."

"Of course, I do. But . . ." He left this remark hanging, and I supposed I could concede him his point. Though that didn't stop me from being annoyed. "I remind you, this pretense wouldn't have been necessary if you hadn't dragged me into Kidd's Back. We were fortunate Bennett appeared to have overheard something of our conversation about Lord French. Let's hope he continues to believe that's why we're here."

"Speaking of French," Sidney remarked as we reached our rented townhouse and he released me to extract the key from his pocket. "What are you going to tell him?"

"Are you asking me what I'd *like* to tell him or what I'm actually going to say?"

Alerted to the menace in my voice, Sidney turned to smile at me in commiseration as he fitted the key in the lock.

"The truth," I answered simply. "The Kavanaghs don't

want us investigating, and without more information, there's little we can do."

He held the door open for me. "Do you think he'll listen?"

"I don't see that he has a choice."

"We'll lose our ruse."

"True." I hadn't thought of that. "But maybe we won't need one much longer."

I could tell from Sidney's expression that he was less optimistic of that than I was.

CHAPTER 11

Monday morning, I awoke with the sun, too anxious to sleep. Not when I was hopeful of learning something important that day, and uneasy it might not be the news I wanted to hear. So I climbed from the immense four-poster bed which dominated the master bedchamber. *Climbed* being the optimal word, as it required a set of custom-made wooden steps to scale the mattress. It certainly wasn't to my taste, but then, most of the furniture in this Dublin townhouse was not, and being a temporary rental, it needn't be.

I turned to see that Sidney was still asleep. He was lying on his stomach, his arms thrown up around his pillow, the muscles in his back and shoulders displayed in impressive relief in the golden morning light as the silk sheets pooled down around his hips. The sight almost made me clamber back into the bed to trail my fingers over the lines and contours of his bared physique, shrapnel wound scars and all, but a glimpse at his face arrested me. He was relaxed, as he only truly ever was in deep slumber. His vigilance released, his full lips were slack, his heavy brow and high cheekbones smooth. Knowing that, I couldn't wake him. Even if he ultimately might have been edified by my early rousing.

Instead, I tiptoed into the dressing room to perform my morning ablutions, donning a butterscotch-yellow skirt and matching print blouse and a black straw hat. With a quick swipe of lip salve, I was out the door and bound for the tram to retrace our route from two days' prior. It being too early to visit Peter at the Wicklow, I instead decided to pay a call on Mr. Finnegan at the Bank of Ireland to deliver my latest report for C and discover if he had any news or confidential correspondence for us. The bright sunlight heralded the start to a warm summer day, and it lifted my mood. Surely something good would turn up today. It simply had to.

The talk on the tram was of the continued ambushes of RIC barracks in more rural areas of the country by the IRA, and the shooting of several police constables in the West Country. There had also been some local agitation among the unions about the ongoing munition and railway strikes, but I was becoming accustomed to such occurrences, and was determined not to let them deter my optimism.

Upon reaching the bank, I was immediately shown back to Mr. Finnegan's office where he greeted me with a strained smile. "Ah, Mrs. Kent. I was just thinking of you."

"Is that because you have information for me?" I asked, unsure what his demeanor meant.

He straightened from where he'd been leaning over his desk. "Of a sort." His gaze flickered toward the door left ajar by the clerk. Out of a sense of propriety, no doubt, but there was always the chance someone might be listening.

I moved a few silent steps closer, and Finnegan lowered his voice, speaking in his own sort of code.

"A mutual friend bade me inquire whether"—he cleared his throat uncomfortably—"there is a bird in the nest?"

For a moment, this oblique manner of speaking confused me. I deduced easily enough that our "mutual friend" was C, but my mind being on locating Alec or, barring that, the phosgene, I couldn't work out how either implication figured into birds or nests. It was the pale wash of color that crested Finnegan's cheeks as I stood staring at him in bafflement that finally directed my thoughts in the right direction.

My first reaction was surprise. "Well, that traveled with admirable speed."

I'd insinuated to Lieutenant Bennett that I was pregnant less than forty-eight hours ago. Yet, that information had been conveyed not only to his superior at Dublin Castle, but also on to Director Thomson in London, and then to C, and back to Finnegan in Dublin. Of course, British Intelligence wasn't hampered by the inability to use cables, albeit transmitted in code.

Finnegan's eyebrows lifted over his wire-rimmed eyeglasses, perhaps seeing this as confirmation. Something I swiftly disabused him of.

"The answer is no. There is not," I stated clearly. "It was a necessary ruse."

This last remark only made his eyebrows arch higher, and I couldn't tell if he was reluctantly impressed, or he disapproved. "Because if there is," he intoned warningly, definitely disapproving, "my instructions are to pack you up and . . . transfer your account back to London."

This, I had not expected. And from C of all men. Not after I'd worked faithfully for him for nearly four years of war, taking on increasingly more fraught and difficult duties and assignments. And what of the almost two years since and all the unofficial work I'd undertaken on his behalf? I was here, was I not, when formally I had no cause to be. Yet, one whiff that I was possibly expecting a child and that rendered me obsolete?

I inhaled sharply through my nose, struggling to restrain my temper. "There is not," I reiterated in crisp tones.

"Are you certain?"

Clearly, Finnegan harbored a death wish, for if looks could kill, my glare before he'd uttered those words would have singed him, and the one that followed would have incinerated him on the spot.

"Tell . . . our *mutual friend*," I managed to ground out

without raising my voice like I wanted to, "that the source of that rumor was Lieutenant George Bennett, and he will understand."

At least, he should.

If nothing else, C's reaction proved my ploy was successful in theory. As long as Bennett and the others continued to believe I was merely there in a support role to Sidney, who was there at the behest of Lord French or someone else equally as inconsequential in their eyes. And that all depended on C not undermining my deception.

Finnegan turned thoughtful, clearly having questions about this comment, but he kept them to himself. "Mr. MacAlister told me you were a stubborn one," he said, pulling a set of keys from his pocket as he pivoted toward a cabinet on his right and unlocked the top drawer. "That you'd never take the easy way out, even if it was handed to you."

I frowned, some of my anger cooling. "He spoke of me?"

"Aye." He pulled two missives from the top of the drawer before closing it and locking it again. "You seemed to be on his mind a great deal in the weeks just before he disappeared."

I passed him my report and glanced down at the letters almost absently as he passed them to me, my thoughts still concentrated on Alec.

Why had *I* been on his mind? Was it because he'd had a premonition of what was coming and that I'd be sent to look for him? But if so, then why hadn't he done whatever he could do to prevent it? Or perhaps he had and it simply hadn't been enough.

Dash it, Alec! What did you get yourself into?

I thanked Finnegan for the letters, tucking them inside my leather handbag as I began to back away.

"A word of advice, Mrs. Kent," he murmured, stopping me. From the set of his lips, I could tell he was reconsidering, and I braced myself to hear another insulting presumption. "It was clear to me—though he strove to hide it—that Mr.

MacAlister cared for you a great deal. I feel fairly confident in saying that, if he were here now, his chief desire would be to see you safe. Don't let your stubbornness cloud your judgment. Particularly when those you seek to help would wish it otherwise."

I didn't respond to this speech, just glared at him and turned and left. On the one hand, I felt oddly emotional, while on the other I wanted to rage. So, in the end, I decided it was the better part of valor to say nothing.

I stumbled out into the bright sunshine, clutching my handbag close as I waited for the next tram. It was bound in the wrong direction, but I didn't mind. I simply wanted to sit and think for a time. So I took a seat next to the window, turning away from the other passengers to discourage conversation.

At first glance, it seemed strange that Finnegan's warning should affect me so strongly. After all, he was only reiterating the same message conveyed by the letter Alec had left for me in his safe deposit box. Finnegan hadn't been privy to its contents, so he hadn't known Alec had already made his wishes known. But while the letter had been troubling, it had at least been true to his disposition. On the other hand, it was so utterly unlike Alec to share such personal things with another person, let alone someone like Finnegan. It was true, as his handler, Finnegan was the only person in Dublin Alec might have felt he could trust. In a moment of extreme distress or weakness, he might have been driven to confide in him.

Yet, in his six years embedded with the German Army it didn't seem he'd ever done such a thing. Not even to me when we'd operated as cohorts and faux lovers. At least, not until we'd escaped Belgium and become lovers for one night in truth. Since then, he'd entrusted one or two things to me that I suspected he hadn't shared with anyone else. But Finnegan hardly seemed the type to inspire such trust.

I could be honest enough with myself to wonder whether part of my skepticism stemmed from jealousy that Alec might have relied on someone else in such a manner, but then dismissed it. I understood perhaps better than anyone what pressures he had been facing, for I'd undertaken similar assignments. He *should* have been able to trust his handler.

The problem was, *I* still hadn't decided if Finnegan was trustworthy. And since I hadn't made up my mind about him, I struggled with the notion that Alec had. Which meant that either I was wrong, or Alec had been fooled, and as much as I didn't want it to be the latter, I couldn't dismiss the possibility.

Dash it all, Alec! I mentally cursed him again. For coming here. For getting himself into trouble, undoubtedly because he'd been too rash. For leaving me infuriating messages. For making me care.

That was the crux of the matter, wasn't it? My life and his were too intertwined. Because of our history. Because we understood each other in ways others couldn't. Not even Sidney.

I loved Sidney. I was faithful to him and our marriage. Nothing was going to change that. But blast it all, I loved Alec, too. In a different way. But no less potent.

I couldn't walk away. And that wasn't pure stubbornness talking.

I blinked my eyes, refocusing my attention outside the window, and realized we hadn't traveled as far as I'd feared. We were somewhere along Dame Street, amidst the warren of narrow lanes that made up the Temple Bar area south of the Liffey. I'd gotten a bit lost amidst the ramshackle jumble of buildings—many of which had seen better days—the first time I'd ventured here during one of my strolls. Because of that, and the fact the area lay practically in the shadow of Dublin Castle, I hadn't yet been back. I'd reasoned that it was an unlikely place for any rebels like Collins and his men to linger. But a sight outside the tram's window made me revise this notion.

A tall man stood on the corner of one of the lanes, smoking a cigarette as he waited for another chap to catch up with him. He was rather lean, his clothes hanging on him as if he was little but a skeleton. Even from a distance there was something about him that captured my notice. As he turned with the other man to proceed down one of the streets leading toward the river, I realized why.

He was the man from Kidd's Back. The one who'd held the door for us. And I recognized now why he'd seemed so familiar to me even then. For I'd seen him once before. In London of all places. He'd been strolling along Horse Guards with none other than Michael Collins—Britain's public enemy number one.

Alec hadn't told me to take note of the two fellows strolling with Collins, but I had anyway. Force of habit. One of them had been named Fitzgerald, a man I'd heard little about. But the other had been Liam Tobin, who according to Alec's reports, operated as Collins's right-hand man.

I straightened, unable to stifle my surprise, and then scrambled to my feet, moving toward the doors to exit at the next stop. If those around me had taken note, I hoped they would assume I'd been caught daydreaming and feared I'd miss my stop. As I exited the tram and looked up, I realized I was in front of City Hall, at the very gates to Dublin Castle.

The City Hall had been built into the slope of Dame Street, so that part of its pedestal was taller than the other and the columned Portland stone façade could be made level. But behind it lay the massive complex of buildings which made up Dublin Castle. I'd yet to enter, as Sidney and I were still waiting for word from Lord French that we would be allowed within. Security surrounding the seat of the British government in Dublin was understandably tight.

Striding back east, I turned to peer down Palace Street toward its main gate. DMP officers in their rounded hats as well as members of the military police flanked the arched entrance and a narrower door set into the stone to the left, examining the papers of those waiting to enter.

Yet, no more than a few hundred feet away, I'd spied one of the most wanted men in Ireland loitering calmly on a street corner. A quiver ran through me, not only at the rebel's courage and audacity—something I had to reluctantly admire—but also at the realization of what they were willing to risk.

Because I knew from experience how difficult it was to triumph over a people who were convinced of the justice of their cause, and whose spirit refused to be crushed. Had I not lived among the Belgians and French for part of the war, witnessing firsthand their resistance to German rule? Their readiness to suffer for freedom. Their resolve not to give up hope.

While doing my research before coming here, I had read a report evaluating the Irish character. While I'd not agreed with everything the analyst had written, for his Anglo-Protestant prejudice was transparent, I had been struck by what he'd described as a marked inclination toward martyrdom. How they believed that the glorious death of those who came before only furthered the cause of those who came after, carrying the torch forward, so to speak. They'd had hundreds of years to perfect this way of thinking. It was a legacy they carried espoused in their stories, poetry, and songs. A living, breathing reminder.

Seeing Tobin on that corner had driven this home for me. For how did one triumph over a people who were prepared to die for their convictions? How did one squash the spirit of their cause when for every rebel you killed, another two or three were inspired to take their place?

As I neared the corner where I'd seen Tobin disappear, I began to realize how foolish it had been for me to leap from the tram. What had I expected to do? Trail him in my fashionable attire?

In any case, he was now long gone, having disappeared into the labyrinth of medieval streets. I briefly considered crossing the street and trying to pick up his trail, but then I lost my nerve. Perhaps later I might return in my guise as Dearbhla Bell, an Irishwoman newly arrived to Dublin to search for her cousin, but attempting to follow a republican as Verity Kent was the opposite of discreet.

So I returned to College Green and boarded another tram, this time headed in the correct direction. By the time I returned home, Sidney was just finishing his breakfast.

"And where have you been so bright and early?" he asked, taking a drag from his Turkish cigarette as he finished his coffee.

"The bank," I replied, mindful that our maid, Ginny, was about. She'd met me near the door, taking my hat and gloves, and my order for breakfast.

"Planning to do some shopping?"

"Yes, I saw the most darling hat in a shop window the other day."

All of this was said purely for Ginny's benefit as she brought me some toast, an egg, and a fresh pot of tea. Mrs. Boyle had clearly anticipated my usual. I smiled at the maid in thanks as she bustled from the room.

"Would you let Nimble know I've a task for him?" Sidney told the lass before she could scurry out of sight.

She dipped her head in acknowledgment.

He waited until the count of three before leaning forward to stub out his fag in the pewter dish at his elbow. "That should keep her busy for a time. Now, what did you *really* withdraw?"

I'd not yet had a chance to examine the two missives, being distracted by Finnegan's remarks about Alec, and then too conscious of those who might be watching to extract them from my bag before arriving home. I did so now.

"One is from C, courtesy of Kathleen." Having already

spoken with Finnegan, I could guess what the chief concern of that message was. I straightened at the sight of the handwriting on the second. "The other is from Max."

Sidney rounded the table to stand behind me as I unfolded it.

Max had written in his usual conversational style, relaying anecdotes about mutual friends and acquaintances in London, as well as his sister, niece, and nephew. I smiled reflexively, able to see him seated at his desk in his study, his head bent over the paper, softly chuckling to himself. Finally he worked himself around to sharing the information we were most anxious to hear.

I'm sorry to say, Smith's file is missing.

Sidney muttered a curse behind me shortly after I'd read those words, letting me know he was keeping apace with me.

The clerk assisting me searched for it, but as of my writing to you, it has not been located. Either it was misfiled, misplaced, or removed entirely. I think we all know who the likely culprit is, but of course, there's no evidence to implicate him or anyone else.

"Ardmore must have known there was something compromising in Smith's file. Or at least, feared it." I uttered a curse myself. "I should have thought of it sooner. Maybe we could have nabbed it before Ardmore did."

Sidney grasped hold of my shoulders. "Or maybe the file has been missing for far longer than Smith has been dead. There's no point in berating yourself about it. None of the rest of us thought of it either. We assumed, like you, that his journal would tell us all we needed to know."

And it still might. If only we could decode it.

I sighed heavily, returning to the letter in hopes that Max

had still been able to uncover something useful, but thus far his other inquiries into the man had proved fruitless. Even a visit to Detective Chief Inspector Thoreau, who had assisted us on a few cases in the past and was aware of our efforts to locate the missing phosgene cylinders, had yielded no results. So whatever file the police might have had on Smith—if they had any—had also been removed. A fact which would not be utterly surprising, as the director of intelligence was also head of Scotland Yard's Criminal Investigation Division.

However, Max, being the thorough individual he was, hadn't left matters there.

Given your present tasks, I've also taken it upon myself to adopt a greater interest in the issues surrounding that country at large, and speaking with my contacts within the Cabinet and Irish Office, I've learned some troubling things.

My interest piqued, I turned to the next page only to find a valediction, urging us to be safe and that he would write more soon, along with his signature. Blinking in surprise, I flipped back to the page before. A line at the bottom had been crossed out, but I'd thought that was Max self-editing. However, flipping through the pages of the letter again to see if they were out of order, or I'd skipped one, I began to come to a more startling realization.

"They redacted the contents of his letter," I stated, shuffling the papers once more, though I knew I hadn't missed anything. "They censored his words." I could hardly believe what I was saying, such was my shock and growing outrage. "Look here. The last page is even shorter than the rest, as if they cut off the top."

Sidney was quiet, but perhaps this discovery was less jarring for him. After all, as his company's commanding officer, one of his duties had been to censor his men's letters home from the front, to remove sensitive material.

But we were no longer at war. And Max was not some green soldier writing home and unwittingly giving away his battalion's position or sharing more gruesome details of trench life than the government wanted to become public knowledge. I was an intelligence agent, for God's sake! A distinguished veteran in my own right. Yet, they'd not only opened the mail I'd requested sent by confidential channels and read it, but censored it!

I was beyond angry, I was livid!

Had they censored Alec's correspondence as well? If so, maybe it was no wonder he'd stopped trusting his handler.

"We need to know what information Max discovered from his government contacts," I said, turning to look up at Sidney. "We need to know what they didn't want us to find out."

I could read in Sidney's eyes that he was thinking of the same thing I was. Those documents we'd uncovered in Belgium. The ones that had proven our government's culpability in prolonging the war. The ones C had been so anxious for me to destroy before I read them.

And here he was again, keeping information from me. Another of the already frayed threads of trust woven between us snapped.

Sidney nodded in solidarity. "Your alternate letterbox?"

"No. And not yours either," I insisted. "Those will still be couriered through official channels." I turned back toward Max's letter where it lay next to my untouched plate of breakfast. The telephone and telegraph would be no better, controlled as they were by the government and prone to interception. "I think we must risk the mail."

I knew that at times the IRA managed to seize the mail, but as long as we were conscious of that fact, the hazard could be mitigated.

Sidney sat in the chair next to mine. "We'll need a trusted go-between we don't think either side is monitoring."

Which eliminated my known friends and colleagues within British Intelligence, as well as any family and Sidney's former fellow officers.

"It has to be Etta," I whispered.

Not only was Etta Lorraine the best jazz singer this side of the Atlantic, but she'd acted as an informant for me during the war and since. Yet, I'd never shared her name with British Intelligence, knowing they might discount her reports, despite the fact they were some of the most accurate I received. She and Max were already well acquainted, and she sang at Grafton Galleries, a nightclub in Soho. As such, no one would find Max's visiting such an establishment or her speaking with the Earl of Ryde suspicious.

"But just to be safe, we'll have her address her letters here to Nimble," Sidney suggested, hearing as I did his valet's distinctive clumping footsteps on the stairs.

I nodded. "I'll write to Max and Etta immediately after breakfast." Which had now grown cold. My own fault.

Sidney's gaze dipped to C's letter, still untouched in my lap. "Maybe his missive explains."

I cast him a sharp look, doubting an adequate explanation existed. "I'll read it after breakfast."

He reached out a hand to clasp mine where it rested on the table, the empathy in his gaze enough to make maudlin tears threaten for the second time that morning. But I refused to give in to the urge, lifting my spoon to tap at the shell of my egg while Sidney spoke to Nimble.

CHAPTER 12

Something had happened during the time since I'd returned home after seeing Mr. Finnegan at the bank. Something that had made the populace on edge and brought the Black and Tans out in force. I noticed them as I approached the Wicklow Hotel on foot, taking a somewhat circuitous route past the Gaiety Theatre and South City Market. Since our visit to Kidd's Back, I'd decided that it was best to avoid Grafton Street the next few days and to deviate my path more often in general, lest I draw undo notice.

I didn't know whether something particular had happened—whether Collins's murder gang had shot another policeman, or the IRA had made another raid for arms like the one at King's Inn or ambushed the Crown Forces—and I didn't dare ask anyone. On the tram, I might have overheard snatches of conversation, but having taken it that morning, I'd decided it wasn't worth the risk, lest someone note the similarities between Verity Kent, social darling, and Dearbhla Bell, the Irish woman from County Antrim searching for her cousin. So I hurried on, highly attuned to those I passed and conscious of those who might be highly attuned to me.

I didn't bother to hide my nerves, as the women like the one I was attempting to portray all eyed the lorries speeding through the streets bristling with Tans, their weapons pointed outward like the spines of a hedgehog, with unease. Sometimes it seemed to me that the drivers were *trying* to hit pedestrians. The wider, busier streets risked being cordoned off for enforced searches, but there was also safety in numbers. Whereas in the narrower, quieter streets one risked being caught alone with a Tan or two on foot patrol. However, by keeping my head down and shoulders hunched, and affecting a shuffling, shambling stroll entirely unlike my generally graceful, confident stride, I'd found I could typically pass by without drawing their notice beyond perhaps their satisfaction in my fear and my acknowledgment of their power over me.

Of course, there was always the risk that in allowing my anxiety sway, it would cause me to make a thoughtless error in truth. But my anger over C's actions in censoring my letter still burned in my gut, muting my apprehension, but perhaps also making me more reckless than normal. Otherwise, I might have turned back after noting the general atmosphere of the city. However, I'd waited three days to seek out Peter again at the Wicklow, and I refused to wait another day to learn if he'd discovered anything.

As I neared the hotel, striding down the narrow pavement of Wicklow Street, I could see a cluster of Tans at the junction with Grafton Street ahead and praised myself for my forethought in choosing not to approach the hotel from that direction. However, my celebration was short-lived as it became evident that they were making some sort of search of the entire street, progressing building by building. Regardless, there was no turning back now. Not without drawing suspicion. So I hastened inside the unassuming building, finding it more crowded than usual. Clearly, I wasn't the only one seeking refuge from whatever trouble was brewing without.

Weaving my way through those milling about in the lobby and restaurant, I was pleased to discover a stool still open at the bar. It wasn't at the end, as I preferred, but near enough. I smiled tightly at the handsome man with a fresh complexion and a cleft in his chin who had turned to me with interest as

I settled in my seat, then looked away pointedly, not wishing to be drawn into conversation. At least, not with him.

Peter was busy at the other end of the bar, so I pulled a small book of Psalms from my handbag. Though I'd found that the act of reading usually did little to discourage men from trying to talk to me, once they discovered my choice in reading material, it deterred a good portion of them. Unfortunately, this handsome fellow was not one of them.

"Aye. Confrontin' that lot outside 'tis enough to make anyone want to turn to the Good Book." He gestured with his head toward the door, making a lock of light brown hair fall over his brow.

I acknowledged that I'd heard his remark with a look, but said nothing in response, returning to the words on the page before me.

He leaned closer, and I did my best to ignore him. Though his softly worded, but emphatic decree of, "Excellent choice," made it difficult to do so.

My eyes focused on the words I'd only been pretending to read, discovering I'd flipped to the pages of the fifty-eighth and fifty-ninth Psalm. I found myself wondering to which he referred, for one was a prayer for vengeance and the other a prayer for deliverance from enemies. Either might apply, but they said very different things about the person invoking them. I was about to risk asking the man what he meant when Peter bustled over.

"Miss Bell," he proclaimed. "'Twasn't sure I'd see ye today, what with all the commotion."

"Dearbhla, please," I reminded him, having asked him to call me as much during our last conversation in hopes that the familiarity would help inspire his trust. I'd practiced saying the Irish name often enough that now the pronunciation "derv-la" rolled off my tongue with ease.

He seemed a bit harassed, though I supposed that could be because of all the customers. Even now, a man raised his arm at the other end, signaling him. He nodded, telling the chap he'd seen him, before turning back to me.

"Tuh usual for a day such as this?"

The usual being either a cup of tea or a wee dram of good Irish whisky. But I knew he was referring to the latter. I'd not been able to stomach either the sherry or gin they'd stocked, but Peter knew his whiskeys.

I dipped my head in confirmation, watching as he spun around to collect the bottle from the shelf. Watching his quick movements, I worried my risking the agitation in the streets would be for naught, that Peter wouldn't have time to impart anything he'd learned.

Something of this must have been communicated to him, for as he set the glass before me, he leaned close to tell me in particular, "I'll be back with ye as soon as I help these gents."

For two more men had already raised their hands.

Telling myself to be patient, I lifted the glass and took a small swallow, welcoming the burn as it slid down my throat and spread outward from my belly. I could feel the handsome fellow on my right eyeing me.

"Dearbhla, is it?" he said.

I turned to glare at him, for I certainly hadn't given him leave to use my name.

However, his sparkling eyes revealed he was undeterred. "That means 'true desire,' doesn't it?"

I'd chosen it because its meaning was a form of truth, just as the meaning of my real name Verity. But that didn't mean I wished to discuss it, no matter how likeable the fellow's expression.

"My name means 'twin,' though I don't have one." He tilted his head. "Least, none that I was ever told about."

A smile slipped past my lips at this bit of absurdity, making Thomas, or perhaps Tom, grin even broader. Or I presumed that was his name, unless there was an Irish form.

A commotion near the door made us turn our heads, but

it was merely a pair of men knocking into something and almost oversetting it. The woman with them scolded them laughingly for their clumsiness. All the same, it had set my heart to beating faster, and increased my urgency to hear whatever Peter had to tell me and depart before the raid reached the hotel.

I turned back to my whiskey, forcing myself to take another sip rather than tossing the entire contents back as I wished. Tom also turned to his drink, some sort of dark stout. Probably a Guinness.

"No help for it now. They'll have set the barricades up at St. Andrew's and Clarendon, boxin' us in, to be sure."

My mouth went dry, but Tom seemed unfazed, tipping back his glass to take a long drink. Or maybe he was just good at feigning it.

"Nothin' for it but to let 'em go about their business," he murmured, and I couldn't tell if he was ruminating for his sake or mine.

"Do ye know what they're lookin' for?" I ventured to ask.

"What else? Shinners."

"Can't find 'em any other way. They keep slippin' through their nets," the older man on my other side interjected in a thick brogue. "So they're takin' to castin' randomly in hopes they'll catch a better haul." He cackled. "'Twon't work. Ole Mick is quicker 'an tat."

Tom smiled but didn't comment.

Meanwhile, I sat twisting the fringe of my shawl. Normally, I would have forbidden such an impulse, but I decided it would be in keeping with Dearbhla's personality. I found myself facing the impending raid with dread. If I were recognized, not only would it ruin my chance to learn anything about Alec's fate, but I also risked incarceration. At least, for a short time. Presumably C would vouch for me if pressed, but there was no guarantee.

My thoughts drifted to C's letter and his admonitions for

placing him in such a prickly situation, not only because I'd allowed myself to get in the family way, but also because I'd run into Lieutenant Bennett. As I'd predicted, the missive was focused on ordering me home if I was harboring a little fugitive and warning me to steer clear of Bennett in the future if I was not. He even went so far as to question his own wisdom in allowing me to take on such an assignment, as if *I* had been the one to contact *him* when Alec went missing and not the other way around. Given this, my confidence in C was not exactly at high tide.

I also knew there were a number of men within the service who would like nothing more than to see me fail—whether they were aware of my current mission or not—and they were certain to view my detention as confirmation of their own prejudices against the abilities of female agents. C's secretary and my friend, Kathleen Silvernickel, who had taken the dictation and typed out the letter on his behalf, had even risked warning me of who those men might be—though I knew them already—by notating in small letters at the bottom, *LB v DT & MD*. Lieutenant Bennett via Director Thomson and Major Davis. The fact that Davis, as C's second-in-command and my biggest detractor, was somehow mixed up in this was less of a surprise than it might have been. The last thing I wanted to do was give him validation of his bias. Not when one of my sincerest wishes was instead to make him eat crow. To stuff it down his throat.

No, it was definitely best not to get caught.

And the best way to do that was to follow Tom's advice. Remain calm and let the Crown Forces conduct their search. To panic and attempt to run or conceal myself would only single me out.

I looked up as Peter returned, swiping down the bar in front of me even as his eyes strayed toward the door. "Another?" he asked with a glance at my near empty glass.

I shook my head.

"Right," he murmured, for I never drank more than one. He leaned closer. "Well, lass, I know ye was hopin' for better news." He could barely meet my gaze. "But I haven't been able to turn up anythin'. Not on the name ye mentioned."

"Maybe he used a different one," I suggested, battling my disappointment. That didn't need to be feigned.

"Maybe," he conceded, though he didn't sound optimistic. "I'll keep askin' around. About the name *and* your description of him."

I nodded, for there was nothing else I could do.

Peter cast a sidelong look at Tom then. One I was hard-pressed to read. Perhaps it was watchfulness, mindful of the man's eavesdropping. But there seemed to be another element to it. Speculation maybe. A hope that perhaps Tom might solve my problem. Not in finding my "cousin" MacAlister, but in giving the baby Peter believed I was carrying a name.

The irony of Peter having assumed I'd come to Dublin to search for MacAlister because I was pregnant, and the fact that Bennett believed I couldn't be there on any sort of assignment precisely because of it, had not escaped me.

Before any more could be said, there was an abrupt shift in the atmosphere. Voices fell silent and bodies stilled. Following Peter's eyes toward the door, I realized why. A group of men dressed in the motley uniform of the Black and Tans had entered the lobby, hesitating for but a moment before fanning out to stand in the various doorways to prevent flight. The two men blocking our immediate exit from the bar area of the restaurant seemed like decent enough chaps, but for their rifles.

We could hear two men speaking with authority in the lobby, and I presumed these were the men in charge informing the employees of the Wicklow of their intentions to search the premises. Much as I wanted to turn to face the bar and focus on finishing my whiskey, I knew that such an act would draw attention when everyone else was watching the door. So I sat stiffly, waiting to see what would happen.

The older man next to me began to cough, the force shaking his entire body when he couldn't stop. I turned to Peter, suggesting a glass of water might help. But when I turned to pass it to the man, it nearly slipped from my grasp. For the man standing in the doorway, issuing instructions to a handful of men, was none other than Lieutenant Bennett.

I may have uttered a curse as I dipped my head, turning to the side, lest Bennett look up and notice me, for Tom's attention riveted on me.

"I take it ye don't approve of that fellow," he said with some levity.

Having given that much away, there was nothing but to brazen it out. I lifted my eyes to meet Tom's guardedly. "He's not what I would call . . . respectful."

It didn't take long for Tom to work out what I was implying, and his humor transformed to something of deliberation and then determination. He lowered his head so that his mouth was close to my ear. "What they'll be lookin' for mostly is single men. And single women they believe they can pester without objection." He paused as if to emphasize his next statement. "But they don't care none about married folk."

I grasped what he was suggesting, though I stifled my own reaction. For as much as I wanted to jump at the proposal, I couldn't help wondering if Tom had ulterior motives. Perhaps he was just as eager for a reason to pass through their inspection unnoted. But then, wouldn't everyone?

In any case, I didn't really have a choice. I couldn't be caught. Especially by Bennett. To pass up Tom's offer would be the height of folly.

So I turned my head to meet his gaze just inches from mine and nodded minutely in agreement, praying no one around us who'd heard Peter address me as Miss Bell would give us away.

Tom slid his arm around my waist, murmuring again in my ear. "Feign distress."

I realized what he meant and angled my body as if I was

seeking protection from his. He smelled of soap and something unexpectedly sweet. Between the brim of my hat and his broad shoulders, my features were mostly shielded from view. Behind Tom, I caught a glimpse of Peter scrutinizing us in what I interpreted as silent approval before he hurried toward the opposite end of the bar. There a tall man with dark hair was addressing Bennett and his cohort in a cheerful manner. "Ye look like ye could use a drink."

While they were distracted, Tom ushered me toward the door where the Tans were fanning out to search. "Must we remain?" he asked politely when it was our turn, keeping a protective arm around me. "My wife is understandably unsettled."

The temporary constable must have given Tom but the barest of glances, for the next thing I knew, I was being led through the door and out through the lobby. I looked up as we emerged in Wicklow Street, discovering his prediction had been correct. Barbed wire had been rolled out across the intersection with Clarendon Street, as well as the opposite ends of Wicklow at Grafton and St. Andrew's Streets. Black and Tans milled about with their weapons slung over their shoulders while others worked in tandem with plainclothes men to search the surrounding buildings. I deduced that most of the men in mufti were intelligence officers of some sort, intent on finding wanted rebels, weapons, or any papers or evidence that might prove worthwhile.

I did my best to ignore what was happening around me, but it was difficult when a pair of men to our right were being questioned in strident voices, and another was being shoved as he was marched toward a lorry. A woman's voice raised in distress rang out from the building on the left. If I'd thought it was hard to walk away from the plight of another human being under duress from the Germans in Belgium so as not to compromise myself or our intelligence network, this was worse.

The Tans manning the barricade at Clarendon Street allowed us through with the barest of inspection, and then Tom and I were striding through the small crowd that had gathered to observe the proceedings, muttering angrily to themselves. Tom's arm remained firmly around me until the curve in the lane took us out of sight of Wicklow Street and anyone who might have been watching. Even then, he kept my arm linked with his and I did not shake it off, grateful for the assistance as my knees felt a bit wobbly.

"I couldn't help but overhear Peter say ye were lookin' for someone," he said as we passed a tobacconist, the rich scent of its custom blends wafting out to us. He smiled encouragingly. "I may not be as well-connected as Peter, but I'd be happy to help if I can."

My gait had begun to feel steadier, and I disengaged from him further as I considered his offer. While it was true that it might be easier to find answers with more people asking for them, I also knew very little about the man. Even his ready assistance in helping me escape certain recognition by Bennett—an act which would normally have spoken in his favor—might have been done more for his own benefit than mine. As such, I was wary of trusting him.

But time was crawling by, and we still had no definitive leads on Alec's whereabouts. The longer we stayed in Dublin, the more balled up I became inside. Sidney, as well. With the end of the war, I'd believed I'd left behind a world of military cordons and dodging foot patrols of soldiers, no matter that they were our own boys. As much satisfaction as I'd taken from doing my bit, as much as I'd enjoyed the adventure, I had not relished the terror and mental anguish. Yet here it was all coming back to me, and I didn't like it. I didn't like it one bit.

So I inhaled a shaky breath and took a chance. "Aye, my cousin." I explained briefly who MacAlister was and what he looked like, sharing even less than I had with Peter.

When I finished, Tom patted my hand where it rested against his arm. "Like I said, I've not as many friends as Peter, but I'll do what I can."

"Thank ye."

He nodded. "How can I contact ye with what I've learned?"

I'd anticipated this question, and had no intention of sharing my address. "I drop by the Wicklow most days. Or Peter could tell me."

"Aye, but I'd avoid the Wicklow for a few days, were I ye. What with the Tans raidin' it."

Except this seemed counterintuitive to me. Now that the Crown Forces had searched it, they were more likely to leave it alone, at least for a time, and move on to other targets.

"Maybe we could meet somewhere else. Somewhere quieter."

"Where?" I asked, careful to keep my skepticism from my voice.

He appeared to give the matter some thought, but I suddenly began to wonder if it was all a ruse. "A park, maybe. St. Stephens or . . . wait. I know. There's a library. On Capel Street. No one would bother us there."

Except now my instincts were on high alert, for my emergency contact happened to be located at the library on Capel Street. Perhaps he'd only been thinking of the book of Psalms tucked in my bag. Maybe that had been his reason for suggesting a library. Regardless, I was now on guard, and wary of meeting the fellow. But for the moment there was nothing for it but to agree to the meeting in three days' time. I simply wouldn't show.

He offered to walk me the rest of the way home, but I refused, and we parted ways at the intersection with South King Street. However, I lingered for a long time in St. Stephen's Green, not trusting that I wasn't being watched. Then I took a meandering route home.

CHAPTER 13

Though I had begun the week with such high hopes, things only grew worse. First, a district inspector in the RIC was shot and killed outside his home in County Wexford. It was rumored that part of the reason he was executed had been the DI's torment of prisoners who had surrendered after the 1916 Rising, but he'd also been diligent in his persecution of the Sinn Féin and rebels.

Riots broke out in Londonderry along mostly sectarian lines—Catholic nationalists versus Protestant unionists—and lasted for more than a week. Coverage in the newspapers mostly favored the unionists, but of course, with many of them being British controlled and subject to government censorship, that was to be expected. The London-based *Sunday Times* also recounted a supposed incident where two girls were outraged by members of Sinn Féin when their mother refused to hand over her farm to them. A person no less august than Arthur Griffith, who was acting as president of Dáil Éireann in de Valera's absence denied this account, calling it "obviously a vile, infamous and malicious falsehood."

Even so, it brought Miss Kavanagh again to the forefront of my thoughts. I had been at a loss as to how to proceed with the investigation into her assault, and I told Lord French so when I saw him again at the Irish Derby. The three-day race meeting at the Curragh had almost not happened as two hundred of the stable lads had gone on strike over their pay just days before the derby was scheduled to begin. However, the dispute was resolved, and the Irish Derby continued as planned.

Sidney and I had motored down from Dublin, joining the lord lieutenant and several members of his household, as well as a few members of the Irish nobility inside the Royal Stand. We might have boarded the train, but Sidney had been anxious to take his Pierce-Arrow out for a spin in the Irish countryside. The weather being mild and sunny, I wasn't about to argue.

The Curragh was located southwest of Dublin near Kildare, and in fact was known not only for its racecourse, but its horse training in general, as well as being the principal military garrison in Ireland. The garrison where the Curragh mutiny had occurred in March of 1914 when the army corps officers under the command of General Gough had informed the British government that they would not enforce Home Rule within Ulster. After decades of attempts, the bill for Irish Home Rule had been poised to finally pass through both houses of parliament—and in fact, it did in September 1914—despite heated opposition from some of the northern counties which comprised the ancient province of Ulster. But despite Gough and the other officers' blatant refusal to uphold the law they were sworn to protect, the British government took no action against what, in effect, had been a revolt, and instead moved to placate the emboldened unionists in Ulster, suspending the implementation of Home Rule for the duration of the Great War, which had by then broken out across Europe. A law they had yet to implement nearly two years since the armistice, as they were *still* placating the Ulster unionists.

Much of the current discontent stemmed from that mutiny and the events that followed, a fact that Sidney and I had both heard British officers and soldiers bemoan, cursing

Gough and the others for landing everyone in this mess. I had to empathize with those who expressed these views, for they had no choice but to do their duty and make the best of a bad lot. They had no illusions that they would be met with the same leniency and forbearance as Gough and his fellow mutineers if *they* refused to do their jobs. They knew full well that they would be strictly disciplined if not arrested outright. Having served as an officer of the British army during the war, Sidney was fully cognizant of how British military discipline worked. Or rather, how it was supposed to work.

There were many who would argue the issue was far more complicated than that, and it undoubtedly was. But that did not alter what the average Irishman or average British soldier believed. Or change the fact that the British government had bungled the matter badly. Were *still* bungling it. Or the fact that politicians still continued to manipulate matters to their own advantage at the expense of the people they were meant to govern and protect.

As the Crown's representative in Ireland, Lord French held the place of honor in the Royal Stand, reveling in the moment. Soldiers from the local garrison had been called out in force, positioned throughout the grandstands and enclosures, ready for any trouble the IRA might have planned to disrupt the event. I noticed quite a few officers, including Dicky Wyndham-Quin, among the race goers within the separate elevated covered stand, which formed the most prestigious viewing point. However, many of them were distracted by debates over the merits of the field of competitors and consumed with placing their bets.

Knowing Lord French was an equally avid horseman, I hadn't anticipated having much of a chance to speak with him on more weighty issues. So I was surprised when he beckoned me over. His gaze lingered appreciatively on me in my cornflower-blue and white georgette ensemble with matching loose-brimmed hat sporting a spray of daisies along its band.

"Have you had a chance to look into that little matter for me?" he asked.

That's when I'd informed him of my interviews with the Kavanaghs and DI Burrows, careful to keep my voice light and even, lest he detect my simmering aggravation at his drawing us into concerns it seemed the Kavanaghs had no desire for us to be involved with.

But Lord French just shook his head sadly. "These rebels and their intimidation tactics. It's diabolical."

"I don't think it's that," I replied flatly, wondering how he'd formed such an assumption about their lack of cooperation from what I'd just told him.

"Oh, I assure you, it is part of it." He patted my knee. "Perhaps you haven't been here long enough to see it, but these blasted shinners and their murder gangs are behind most of the things that are wrong in this country." He scowled, shaking his head, before turning back to me with a sigh. "But I suppose guilt may play some part. After all, Kavanagh initially didn't want to take his position on the committee. I had to convince him."

This explained why Lord French was so anxious to see the perpetrators of Miss Kavanagh's assault prosecuted. I could tell by the deep furrow in his brow that he felt some sense of guilt, too.

"However, I suspect it is more Mrs. Kavanagh's shame you're butting up against than anything. She's a good woman, but like most ladies of her ilk, bound by strict propriety." He shook his head, and I suspected he was thinking of his mistress and his current living arrangements. Mrs. Kavanagh would certainly not approve. "It traps them in such rigid bindings of respectability that they cannot see beyond their own offended sense of order and decorum to recognize that one does not always bring disgrace down upon oneself."

I knew now that he was speaking of her daughter. How Miss Kavanagh had done nothing to invite such an assault.

Yet that very fact rocked the core of propriety her mother's life had been built upon. As long as you were righteous and good, and behaved as you should, nothing bad could befall you. Had Mrs. Kavanagh spent even the briefest amount of time in war-torn occupied Belgium, she would have recognized the fault in this logic.

Lord French lowered his voice further. "I would never suggest that her sense of embarrassment and disgrace played a factor in her daughter's decision to take her own life, but . . ." He appeared to struggle with his words. "As I understand it, she did not make life easier on her." His gaze met my own. "And I think she carries a measure of guilt for that. She was so intent on brushing it under the rug while her daughter lived that she cannot allow it to be revealed to the light now that she's dead."

There was a painful yet astute logic in this observation. One I felt was far more credible than any amount of supposed intimidation by the IRA. Though I did wonder where he'd gotten his information. Mr. Kavanagh?

He patted my knee again. "Speak with Mr. Kavanagh alone. I suspect you shall find him more cooperative and communicative then."

I nodded, not being averse to the suggestion, though I was still not convinced it would yield results. But I would confront that when the time came.

"As for Burrows," he continued with a fierce frown, "I'm convinced the entire DMP are duds. If they're not working for Collins outright, then they're essentially in collusion with him. They look the other way, and no more of them get shot."

Given the number of G-Men Collins's murder gangs had already assassinated, it was difficult to fault them for taking the threat seriously. Especially when the British had yet to adopt effective countermeasures. Those who had been threatened or survived previous attempts on their lives, were now either retired or relegated to the walls inside Dublin Castle.

"If I had my way, they'd all be sacked," he declared.

And replaced by Black and Tans, no doubt.

His voice turned bitter. "But I've been overruled. They're Johnstone's problem." He turned to me. "Speaking of which, I've managed to secure you and your husband access to the Castle." His gaze flitted toward where Sidney stood speaking with Lord Powerscourt and another gentleman. "There was some resistance to your presence, but I told them to bugger off. I'm the lord lieutenant, aren't I?" He harrumphed, his impressive mustache quivering.

This proclamation brought a smile to my lips.

"Should they give you any trouble, remind them of that."

"I will," I promised.

"Good. Now, run off and place your bet before it's too late."

I complied, though I had no intention of betting on the horses. Sidney placed only a minor wager on He Goes, winning a modest sum when that thoroughbred thundered across the finish line first. As at any horse race, it was difficult not to get caught up in the excitement of the moment, and I found myself cheering along with the others and smiling broadly as Sidney accepted congratulations from those who had picked other horses to wager on.

I was leaning against the front of the box, laughing at something Helen Wyndham-Quin had said when a face in the crowd below caught my eye. He turned away at nearly the same moment I spied him, so I couldn't be certain of what I'd seen, but I could have sworn it was Tom. I kept my gaze trained on his hat, but so many of the men were wearing the same flat caps that all too quickly I lost him in the milling throng.

There was no cause for alarm, I told myself. Many people had traveled down from Dublin that day for the Derby. Tom could be one of them.

I had not seen him since the day he'd escorted me out of

the Wicklow to avoid being caught by Lieutenant Bennett, but then I'd also altered my routine, spending less time at the hotel, and at an earlier hour than previously. Peter still had no news about my "cousin" MacAlister, and he hadn't mentioned Tom to me. But I was still wary of the fellow and his connection to the library on Capel Street.

Sidney brushed my elbow with his fingers, questioning me with a look. Clearly, my sudden interest in the crowd had not gone unnoticed. However, I wasn't about to alarm him with unfounded suspicions. Not when Tom's presence here—if it even had been Tom—could be entirely natural. Instead, I threaded my arm through Sidney's, smiling in reassurance as he led me toward an officer who had hailed him across the box.

I cast my gaze over the crowd one last time and then vowed to push the matter from my mind, accepting a glass of champagne from the steward circulating among the guests.

Nimble was waiting for us when we returned to Upper Fitzwilliam Street, and from the looks of it, he'd been lumbering back and forth across the entry hall for some time. At our entry, he abruptly pivoted mid-stride, bursting with importance. However, he didn't immediately rush into speech, having been too well trained during his time in the army as Sidney's batman.

"Nimble," Sidney said by way of greeting, eyeing his valet with interest as I set my reticule and gloves on the petticoat table.

"Cap'n," he replied, drawing a swift breath to speak. "Did ye 'ave a good day, sir?"

"Yes. Even won a bit of blunt." Sidney set his hat on one of the hall chairs, then turned and latched the door. "Has Ginny left for the day?"

Nimble nodded. "And Mrs. Boyle has retired to 'er room." It was located off the kitchen. "But she said to rouse 'er should ye wish anythin'."

He looked at me in question before answering. "No, we grabbed a bite to eat near Naas. Let's retire to the parlor then, shall we?"

I led the two men up the stairs to the parlor, where curiously enough a landscape painting of Curragh Chase hung over a satinwood console table. Having now been to the famous plain, I could better appreciate the piece of art. I settled in a chair near the dormant hearth. Hand-painted pole screens from the eighteenth century, which had been used to shield ladies' complexions from the heat of the fire, flanked the fireplace on either side, still ready for use. Rather than sit, Sidney stood with his arms crossed and his hip leaned against the sideboard, as if undecided whether to pour himself a drink. I supposed it depended upon whatever Nimble was so anxious to tell us.

"What is it?" Sidney prompted his valet.

Nimble stood just inside the door, his shoulders stiff and his arms pressed tightly to his side. I'd noticed before how he adopted the habit of many polite, larger men of trying to restrict himself to the smallest space possible, lest he break something, even when standing in a room as expansive and uncluttered as our parlor. Though it could also be a byproduct of the war, having lived in the tight, squat confines of dugouts and trenches.

As always, he was spare with his words. "This came for ye, Cap'n," he declared after removing a letter from his pocket and holding it out to Sidney. His gaze flicked sideways at me. "Or maybe for Mrs. Kent."

I realized then that it was from London and pushed hurriedly to my feet to move toward my husband. True to expectation, the missive was addressed to Nimble in Etta's distinctive scrawl. Finally, word from Max! It was unopened, and I set about tearing the envelope with my fingernail as soon as Sidney passed it to me.

"You weren't curious?" Sidney teased the younger man.

"Nay. I knew what 'twas." He scratched at his hairline on the left side of his face where blisters scarred his pale skin. "Don't know if it means anythin', but I did catch Ginny studyin' it."

I looked up in surprise.

"The outside, anyway." He dipped his head toward the letter. "Don't think she opened it."

No, it appeared untampered with. But that didn't mean her interest wasn't noteworthy.

"*Can* she read?" I asked, wondering if her presence might prove a problem in the future.

Nimble shrugged, and I allowed the matter to drop. After all, it was difficult to know whether the maid's curiosity stemmed from the origin of the letter or the fact it was delivered to Nimble. I wasn't oblivious to the looks they cast each other's way—or *didn't* cast each other's way, as it may—when they were both in the same room. For the moment I was more interested in the contents of the letter.

Sidney dismissed Nimble with a soft word while I unfolded the missive. Etta had included a note in her effusive style, agreeing to the subterfuge I'd asked of her, and requesting that any future assistance I desired from her be as demanding as having handsome gentlemen pay her calls in her dressing room. Though, she felt I should urge Max to bring her more gifts. Simply to enhance the deception, of course. I couldn't help but smile at her playful banter, but my good humor swiftly fled when I opened Max's enclosed message.

He confessed his own anger and bafflement at the SIS's redaction of his remarks about the discussion concerning the Irish situation during the cabinet meeting on May 31st. His contact had merely reported that the violence in Ireland had reached such a pitch that several of the cabinet ministers were espousing the idea of some sort of martial law for the entire island. That they'd tacitly agreed that the court system was collapsing. The assizes in many areas had failed utterly, and trials by jury couldn't even be attempted because either jurors declined to take part or the government didn't trust them to bring in a just conviction. Far from praising the courts like the press had, the cabinet instead condemned them. Though I supposed that was only to be expected, as the Dáil was their rival shadow government. Correspondingly, the Royal Irish Constabulary had become increasing demoralized across the country, precipitating the resignation or retirement of many policemen, and necessitating further recruitment to the temporary cadets—or Black and Tans—to shore up the numbers.

While it was true that something like two hundred murders had occurred and yet no one had been executed for the crimes, it dismayed both Max and me the way the cabinet danced around the truth. They insisted that Ireland had a problem with violence, not a rebellion. That their primary aim should be to crush the thugs they alleged were being paid to commit murder and arson. That they struggled to believe that the civil courts could do this via due process because Irish Catholics couldn't be relied upon to rigorously impose justice on revolutionaries.

"Good Lord," Sidney muttered in disgust, having read over my shoulder. "Do they not even listen to their own sources?"

I had to agree. Everything we had read to prepare us before coming to Ireland, and everything we'd witnessed since then, did not support these findings.

"And can you explain to me how you cannot have a rebellion yet have revolutionaries the populace refuses to prosecute?"

I let my hand fall to my lap, shaking my head.

Sidney began to pace. "I'll tell you what, the average soldier, policeman, and officer knows perfectly well this is a rebellion. An armed conflict. A war. Our government is merely batting around semantics for the sake of public image."

Once again, I had no counter argument. Nor was it entirely clear why the Secret Intelligence Service had redacted all this from Max's previous letter. We already knew the civil courts were failing and that the RIC was crumbling, hence the need for the Black and Tans at all. Their opinions of the cause of the problem and proposed solution were frustrating and disheartening, but not so much so that they should have feared us finding out.

"Maybe the SIS censor was simply being too aggressive," I heard myself suggest out loud, already doubting it before the words were even uttered.

Sidney halted before me, staring down at me with a single arched eyebrow that communicated what he thought of that suggestion.

"Then why redact this information?"

He tilted his head in thought. "Maybe there's more to it than Max's informant told him. Or maybe there's more to come that, when fitted into this context, will divulge more than they want you to know."

I nodded, supposing I would have to accept that reasoning. At least, for the time being.

"Whatever the case, we need Max to continue to plumb his informant for information. There will undoubtedly be more to report. And soon." I crossed to the secretaire, intent on writing to tell Max so.

"I'll inform Nimble he has a letter to post at first light. One he should keep concealed until then," he added, obviously thinking of Ginny and the interest she'd shown.

CHAPTER 14

The following morning, I had another missive for Nimble to deliver, as well, though this one in person. Determined to fulfill my obligation to Lord French, I dashed off a note to Mr. Kavanagh requesting a private conversation with him. I still wasn't convinced he would share more with me than before, but I decided the matter couldn't be dropped until I tried at least once more. Then, if still no new information had come to light, I would inform Lord French that I'd done all I could.

I was debating what route I should take that day in my disguise and whether to risk a visit to the Wicklow when Nimble returned with Mr. Kavanagh's urgent response. His wife was visiting her sister in Glasnevin for the day, and he would be happy to receive me if I was able to come before three. Upon reading this, I wasted no time in donning gloves and a smart hat with part of the brim rolled up and the other half flat, setting out on foot for Herbert Street.

It was but a short distance, though I tucked an umbrella under my arm in case the overcast skies signaled rain. As usual, Baggot Street bustled with trams, bicycles, pedestrians, and the occasional motorcar or horse cart. Though today, one half of the pavement was also taken up by a group of soldiers in uniform strolling down the opposite side of the street deeper into the city. As they were laughing and jesting with one another, their hands thrust into their pockets informally, I suspected they were at ease rather than intent on some duty. Probably bound for the theaters and pubs and other entertainments offered on Sackville Street and the area around College Green. They'd no doubt come from Beggars Bush Barracks a short distance away, beyond the canal which circled the city. But that didn't make the disturbance their presence caused any less.

Dubliners purposely avoided sharing the pavement with them, dodging traffic to cross to the other side. One young woman who had been walking and reading at the same time became particularly anxious to cross once she noticed them, nearly stepping into the path of an oncoming bicycle. I supposed she feared being labeled a totty or a tart, as I'd heard that girls who even dared to walk on the same side of the street as British soldiers, let alone fraternize with them, were called.

I wondered if Katherine Kavanagh had faced the same stigma. Though she had been part of a different social class. One tied to the Anglo-Protestant Ascendancy who had controlled Ireland for hundreds of years, and still did, despite their being in the decided minority across much of the island. This was something the republicans were certainly trying to change. Hence the reason for some of Ulster's unrest, as the counties clustered near Belfast were the only ones where Protestants were in the majority.

Given the manner in which the soldiers' very existence seemed to agitate the populace, I expected the reasons for my own tension were derived from those around me. However, as I turned the corner into Herbert Street, leaving all of that behind, the sensation lingered. Was I being followed?

I glanced about me as unobtrusively as possible, but even on this quieter street there were too many pedestrians to tell. Especially if the person tailing me was well trained. This street was mainly residential, so my favorite tactic of observing the reflections of those behind me in the large glass windows at the front of many shops would not work, and neither would my shoe trick. Being close to my destination there was nothing for it but to carry on.

The door to the Kavanaghs' home was opened just seconds after I knocked, so there was no chance to turn and naturally survey the street. The same maid as before led me up the stairs and past the family portraits hanging along the wall to the drawing room. This time it was empty, but the maid promised Mr. Kavanagh would be along shortly.

Before she could hurry away, I halted her. "Wait, please."

She turned back toward me in surprise.

"I should have said before, during my last visit, how sorry I am for *your* loss, as well." I'd noted how young the maid was and decided that if Miss Kavanagh possessed the reputation her mother had claimed, then she'd likely been kind to the staff as well. "I imagine you were quite fond of her."

"Oh, aye. All of us was," she exclaimed earnestly. "For somethin' like that to happen to someone like her." Her eyes glinted with unshed tears.

"Did no one see anything?"

She shook her head. "We're not allowed out of our rooms after curfew. Madam is very strict about that. 'Specially with us maids. Ernie only went to investigate cause he thought he heard a scream."

"Ernie?"

"Aye. Well, Earnán. But Madam makes us all go by the English version of our names. So Earnán is Ernie and Cathal is Charles. I'm Mary, so that didn't have to change."

I blinked, surprised by the amount of information she was willing to share, after DI Burrows had been stonewalled. But then Mrs. Kavanagh—or Madam, as Mary called her—wasn't here to silence her. "Is Ernie the . . . footman?" I guessed.

"Aye. *First* footman."

I nodded in understanding of the importance of that distinction, particularly to the staff.

She tipped her head to the side. "Or rather, he was. He quit a month ago."

"Not long after Miss Kavanagh was assaulted?"

"Aye, but it's not what ye think," she insisted. Her eyes were suddenly wide with regret.

"What do I think?"

"That he were somehow involved. 'Twasn't like that. Ye should've seen how upset he was. He was right fond of Miss Kavanagh. Blamed himself for not investigatin' sooner when he first heard the noises. Rattles and scuffles and the like. Thought they were scavengers pickin' through the refuse."

"He told your employer all this?"

"Aye." A furrow formed between her thin brows. "And they told him to forget it."

Now, why on earth would they do that? Why wouldn't they want him to report it to the authorities? Were they afraid they would assume what Mary had worried I had? That Ernie was the culprit. Or had Ernie seen more than Mary realized? Something they'd not wanted him to share.

Her head snapped toward the stairs where a soft thud had come from, as if someone had dropped something. She flushed. "I . . . I should go now, ma'am. I'll be wanted."

"Just one more question," I said as she began to back away. "Do you know where Ernie went?"

She shook her head. "Sorry, ma'am."

I nodded once and she hurried away to scuttle down the stairs, the white mob cap covering her hair bobbing with each step.

Once she'd disappeared from sight, I turned to enter the drawing room, contemplating how I might track down this Ernie. Or rather Earnán. I should have asked her for his surname.

I crossed toward the window overlooking the street, frowning to myself. I'd occasionally heard of people making their staff members adopt a different name than the one they'd been given, but usually that was because there was more than one maid with the same name or because their name was long or difficult to say, so they opted for a shortened form of it. But this was the first I'd heard of someone forcing their staff to use the anglicized version of their names. Though, somehow, I suspected it was more common than I realized.

The drapes over the windows had already been drawn to allow the muted daylight to lighten the room, and I allowed my gaze to sweep down the length of the street from one end to the other, as far as I could see. A few people strolled along the pavement in either direction, but none of them seemed to be paying much attention to the Kavanaghs' home, except . . . there! At the corner near St. Stephen's Church, there was a man loitering near the lamppost. He was dressed respectably in a brown three-piece suit and derby hat, and might have just been waiting for a friend, but for the glances he cast periodically toward the Kavanaghs' house.

I narrowed my eyes. He might have been one of Collins's men, but there was something about him that screamed British army. His posture, perhaps, or his mannerisms. And while it was true, there were plenty of former British soldiers, particularly from the Irish Guard, who sympathized with and might have joined the republicans in their efforts to overthrow the British, I didn't think that was the case here. This chap had received some sort of training. British Intelligence training. So why was he following me? Had my ruse with Bennett not worked as well as I'd hoped?

"Mrs. Kent," Mr. Kavanagh hailed me before I could come to any satisfactory conclusion. "I'm sorry to have kept you waiting."

"Not at all," I said as he clasped my hand briefly before gesturing for me to take a seat on the sofa while he claimed the French provincial chair next to it. "Thank you for seeing me, and on such short notice."

He dipped his head sharply, an unspoken acknowledgment of our collusion to converse without his wife's interference. "I'm not sure what else I can tell you."

Having noted the effect candor had on him before, I opted to employ it again. "I'm not sure either. But when Lord French asked me what I'd learned, he indicated there might be things you were withholding for the sake of your wife's feelings. It was he who suggested that I speak with you privately."

Mr. Kavanagh didn't appear pleased by this insight, but what man would? He rubbed his finger back and forth over his white mustache in deep thought before finally relenting. "He's not entirely wrong. Mrs. Kavanagh . . ." He seemed unable to put into words his wife's objection to discussing their daughter's assault and death.

"Understandably," I assured him.

His eyes glinted with gratitude. "What do you wish to know?"

"The night of the attack . . . I understand that it occurred in the garden. That she'd gone out to clear her head. Were there no witnesses? None of the staff?" I paused, wording my last question carefully so as not to get Mary into trouble. "Who found her?"

His pallor grew wan and his lips bloodless. "Ernie, our footman, found her. After her attackers had already fled. No one else saw or heard anything." He looked up distractedly toward the hearth, the wall of which adjoined the next townhouse. "Not even our neighbors."

"Then Ernie didn't hear or see anything?"

"No." His brow furrowed. "And before you ask if you can speak with him, you should know he gave notice some weeks ago. And I don't know where he's gone."

Except I already knew that the footman had heard something. It was a scream that drew him out to the garden in the first place. Why would Mr. Kavanagh lie about this?

"What about your daughter? What did she tell you?"

He shifted in his seat, crossing the opposite leg over his

knee. "Not much. She was in shock, you understand. And the men wore masks." He scraped a hand down his face. "The look on her face when we found her." He screwed his eyes shut. "And when . . . when . . ." He shook his head.

"When what?" I pressed, but he shook his head harder.

"She was never the same," he finally replied in a dull voice.

But there was something else. Something he wasn't telling me. Just as there had been something Mrs. Kavanagh had stopped herself from saying the last time I visited. Something about how she'd never caused them a moment of trouble except for whatever she'd stopped herself from uttering. After speaking with Lord French and hearing more about Mrs. Kavanagh's rigid propriety, I'd started to wonder if the words she'd not uttered related to the trouble her assault had caused them. That she'd realized how poorly the thought would reflect on her. But now I wondered if it was something else entirely.

Mr. Kavanagh's head hung low. "And it's all my fault."

"Because of the commission investigating malicious injury and damage claims?" I asked, curious where exactly the source of his guilt lay. "Or because you allowed a British soldier to court her? This Lieutenant Delagrange."

For some reason this question seemed to distress him. "No, no. Delagrange is an upstanding fellow. Quite the decorated officer."

But the more he protested this, the more I doubted it. It left a cold feeling in my gut.

He pushed to his feet, pacing agitatedly toward the window and back. "No, it's that dashed commission. Why did I ever agree to be on it?"

"You've received threats?"

He nodded.

"From the IRA?"

His gaze darted to me and then away. "From the rebels," he clarified, perhaps thinking I was testing him since the British government refused to acknowledge they were an army. "From Sinn Féin."

"Because they believe the commission's rulings are unfair?"

He scowled. "And they resent the Irish ratepayers being made responsible for paying the claims."

"Ridiculous considering the fact they're supporting the very men causing those damages," a voice proclaimed from the doorway. It belonged to a British gentleman with dark eyes and even darker hair, which contrasted with his pale skin. The same gentleman I'd seen from the window monitoring this house. The same gentleman I suspected had been following me.

He swaggered forward. "One would think that would motivate the potato-eaters to turn in the murderous thugs, but they've never been very bright."

I frowned, taking an instant dislike to the fellow—whoever he was—and his offensive language. Though Mr. Kavanagh's startled reaction to his presence was more than interesting. It told me who the visitor likely was before the maid ever spoke.

"My apologies, sir," Mary said, dipping a curtsy. "Lieutenant Delagrange insisted on comin' straight up."

"It's alright," he assured the maid. "Of course, he's always welcome."

But the look on Mr. Kavanagh's face was far from welcoming. In fact, I would have described it as dismaying. A dismay that Delagrange plainly took pleasure in.

Just as he took pleasure in allowing his gaze to rudely rove over my figure. "I hope I'm not interrupting," he declared.

"Of course, not," Mr. Kavanagh stammered. "Have you been introduced? Mrs. Kent, allow me to present Lieutenant Delagrange," he hastened to say before the question could even be answered.

"Charmed, I'm sure," I responded sardonically.

Delagrange's smile broadened to reveal even more of his

teeth, putting me in mind of a lion waiting to devour its prey. But I was no gazelle to be taken down. It was clear that I would get no more from Mr. Kavanagh with Delagrange present—precisely his intent, I was sure—and I hadn't the least desire to spar with the fellow. So instead, I opted to disengage.

Pushing to my feet, I moved toward Mr. Kavanagh, offering him my hand. "I've taken up more than enough of your time," I told him with a soft smile, which appeared to catch him off guard as much as Delagrange's abrupt arrival.

"Thank you for coming," he murmured.

"Please convey my condolences once again to your wife."

He blinked. "I will."

With that, I swept past Delagrange with the barest nod. The brute no doubt viewed my departure as a retreat, and therefore a victory. I'd discovered long ago that men often saw things in such childish terms. Let him think so, even though the truth was he'd disclosed far more by revealing himself and barging into my meeting with Mr. Kavanagh than anything I had done or said.

For one, his mufti attire all but confirmed my suspicions that he was part of the intelligence branch. For another, he was a posturing buffoon, puffed up on his own self-consequence, which suggested he was a rather green agent. He'd not yet experienced enough to confront his own fallibility or to appreciate the importance of stealth. Those agents out for glory and recognition never lasted long.

I shook my head, thinking of the intelligence officers in Kidd's Back and Cairo's Café and all the other places they were known to frequent. If we were able to uncover such a thing so easily, then you could bet that Collins and his men had also. I'd seen his right-hand man Tobin with my own eyes entering Kidd's Back. Those agents were arrogant fools. Fools who I feared would come to a bad end.

But the most important thing Delagrange had divulged

was how anxious he was for me not to converse with Mr. Kavanagh. For why else would he have charged into the drawing room rather than wait patiently for me to emerge? This was a mistake. For while Delagrange had interested me before, especially after noting Kavanagh's reaction to my mention of him, it was not to the degree he did now. Now, I was determined to learn just who Delagrange was and what he was so intent on hiding.

Emerging from the Kavanaghs' home, I paused a moment to adjust my gloves. Which was just long enough apparently for their neighbor, who must have been watching for me from her window, to step out her door and call to me.

"Mrs. Kent. Oh, Mrs. Kent."

She waved me closer, and I approached hesitantly, wary of the fact she might simply be nosy. But then again, sometimes nosy neighbors had their uses.

She was a pleasantly rounded woman a few years older than Mrs. Kavanagh, with a somewhat florid complexion. She'd hastily pulled a shawl over her shoulders, clasping it before her. "Forgive me," she declared with a genial smile. "But when I saw ye there, I just had to introduce myself. I'm Mrs. Gardiner." Her eyes strayed to the house I'd just departed. "I'd no idea the Kavanaghs had such glamorous friends."

I smiled tightly, debating how to answer her. Fortunately, she was the type who didn't require one.

"Callin' to pay your respects?" She clicked her tongue in empathy. "Such a sad business. When I heard what had happened to poor Miss Kavanagh, why ye could've knocked me over with a feather."

"It's all very shocking," I agreed before artfully prompting, "and so frustrating that the police haven't been able to find more witnesses to help them locate the culprits."

"Oh, aye! And believe you me, I compelled my staff to come forward with any information they felt might be helpful. That they should feel free to inform me if they felt too intimidated to speak to the police, and I would convey it on their behalf." She shook her head, a mannerism I was to quickly learn she favored. "But alas, none of 'em saw anythin'."

"Has the neighborhood experienced many disturbances from the republicans?" It seemed quiet at this end of Herbert Street, tucked away from the wider, busier thoroughfares with road bridges over the canal, but appearances could be deceiving.

"Nay. 'Tis one of the things that makes it so shocking." A shrewd glint entered her eyes. "But they say Miss Kavanagh was targeted. Because of her father."

She clearly hoped I'd remark on this, but I redirected the conversation. "I just met the fellow she was stepping out with. Lieutenant Delagrange."

"Oh, aye. Quite handsome, isn't he?"

I supposed. Though his demeanor left much to be desired.

"So sad. He was quite fond of her, as I understand." She peered over my shoulder toward the Kavanaghs' home, her expression seeming sincere, but there was something in her voice that alerted me to conflicted feelings. Or perhaps her thoughts had already moved on to other matters, for she sighed. "That family has seen more than its fair share of tragedy these last few years."

"You're speaking of their son who died in the war," I deduced.

"Aye. And their nephew."

"The one who also served?" I asked, remembering Mrs. Kavanagh's remarks about how he'd returned a changed man.

Mrs. Gardiner's gaze shifted to meet mine, like a bloodhound, able to smell my interest. "The same." She leaned closer. "He was killed by one of those murder gangs."

I stiffened in surprise, and she nodded.

"Left a note with his body and everythin'. Apparently, he was some sort of informant."

I supposed for a woman bound by such strict conventions,

her nephew getting himself murdered, regardless of the circumstances, was enough to earn Mrs. Kavanagh's disapproval.

"When did this happen?" I asked.

"Oh, a few months ago." She considered the question. "March maybe. Or April." She shook her head. "I do know Miss Kavanagh took his death hard. Poor girl."

I understood what she was saying. That this also helped explain the young woman's despair and perhaps contributed to her taking her own life. I realized then that I didn't know how Miss Kavanagh had done it. It was an incredibly delicate question. One that there had never been an appropriate opening to ask in either of the charged conversations I'd held with her parents. But perhaps the neighbor might know.

"How did she do it?" I murmured softly. "How did she take her own life? As I'm sure you can appreciate, they don't wish to discuss it."

"Of course, of course," Mrs. Gardiner replied. "'Twas a bottle of pills. Some sort of sleeping medicine, I believe." She arched her eyebrows in criticism. "Something the nurse they'd hired to care for her should never have left where she could reach it."

Yes, that did seem like a terribly elementary mistake.

Having uncovered everything I felt I could and perhaps satisfied some of the neighbor's curiosity, I excused myself, continuing south down Herbert Street. I'd noted a young woman watching us from a window across the street, and debated whether I should detour toward her home. It seemed maybe she had something to tell me as well. But when I turned to look directly at her again, she shrank away from me.

Or maybe it was from the man who called out my name, hurrying to catch up. It took all of my self-control not to groan in irritation at the sound of Lieutenant Delagrange's voice. Apparently, the eejit didn't know when to leave well enough alone.

I didn't pause or break stride, but Delagrange didn't take the hint, reaching my side soon enough. "I suggest you keep your distance from the Kavanaghs in the future."

"Oh, yes? Why's that?" I asked in a bored voice. Truly, his behavior was becoming terribly predictable. I practically had to stifle a yawn.

"Because it's distressing to them. So, if you know what's good for you . . ."

I couldn't withhold a sigh at this last remark—such a cliché threat—and Delagrange broke off, perhaps in surprise. "You *do* know who asked me to speak with them in the first place?" I inquired, straining to maintain my patience.

This query was met with silence, leaving me with reluctant curiosity as to whether he didn't know or if he had simply failed to think his actions through.

Sadly, the predictability continued as he doubled down. "I suggest you ignore Lord French's flights of fancy. Everyone knows he's nothing but a figurehead. Couldn't get the job done in France, and he couldn't get the job done here either."

"Shall I convey your thoughts to him?"

This succeeded in wiping the smirk from his face.

"More pertinently, are you actually suggesting I disregard the wishes of the lord lieutenant—the Crown's representative here in Ireland—be he a mere figurehead, or not?" I scoffed. "You won't last long if you're that politically and socially unsavvy."

He suddenly reached out to grasp my arm, pulling me to a stop, and forcing the people walking several paces behind us to swerve to avoid us. "I am not a man to be trifled with," he snarled, staring down at me menacingly, ignoring the looks we were drawing from passersby.

My heart kicked hard against my ribs, but I refused to be intimidated. "Let go of my arm," I demanded in a low voice.

In response, he squeezed tighter, and I knew I would find bruises there later.

"Or would you rather I scream?"

These were not the streets of German-occupied Brussels. People here would not be afraid to come to my aid. Not when I was a respectable upper-class woman signaling my distress. Even now, from the corner of my eye I could see several people considering interfering.

It took a second longer than it should have for him to realize it, but the lieutenant finally released my arm. I immediately turned away, giving him the cut.

Such was my fury, that I had to force myself to take measured steps down the pavement, nodding in gratitude and reassurance to those still watching us. Truth be told, I would have liked to do nothing more than land the brute on his backside, or knee him where it counts. I could have done it, too. But that would have drawn too much attention and revealed too much about my own abilities.

No, there were better ways to deal with men like Delagrange. A letter from Sidney to Lord French, Chief Secretary Greenwood, and Under-Secretary Anderson, for good measure, would see the lieutenant put in his place and warned away from me. I would have sent a letter to Colonel Winter, Delagrange's more direct superior in Intelligence, but Kathleen had warned me what an oily snake he was. He'd probably approve of Delagrange's methods. Better to go over his head. Or rather, adjacent. Director of Intelligence Thomson would likely have approved as well.

Which reminded me why I had to tread so carefully, and how closely I had to watch my back. Even from the men who should have been my allies.

CHAPTER 15

As the month of June drew to a close, matters in Ireland only seemed to worsen. There had been more raids on RIC barracks, more policemen killed, but this time they were followed with major reprisals by the Crown Forces. In Bantry, County Cork, an invalid was shot dead, and a number of houses and businesses burned. In Fermoy, also in County Cork, where a large military barracks was located, the town was looted and burned, in retaliation for the capture of General Lucas, a brigade commander. Outrage over the worsening reprisals continued to increase, even reaching as far as India, where two companies of the Connaught Rangers mutinied in protest.

Assemblies were held in places like Naas to reinforce support for the dockers and railwaymen who continued to refuse to handle or transport munitions or military and police personnel. New duly elected county councils continued to come out in support of the Dáil Éireann, which persisted in meeting covertly despite having been proscribed by the government. While meanwhile in the north, the Ulster Volunteer Force was being revived by officials, a move to reorganize and control the already existing loyalist vigilante groups operating throughout the ancient province. This was a somewhat alarming development, one that the British government would surely put a stop to, leaving the policing to the Crown Forces rather than a transparently sectarian group.

There were also worrying developments in our little corner of Dublin. Peter, the hotelier at the Wicklow, still had no news to share of my "cousin's" whereabouts. Nor did I collect any useful information from the other places I frequented. I was beginning to second-guess my strategy. It seemed I might have more luck in my guise as Dearbhla in the evenings, but it would also expose me to more risk. Plus, Sidney and I were often issued invitations to dinner or the theater or other venues in the evening. Invitations we felt compelled to accept, though I was even beginning to doubt the wisdom of that.

I was also almost certain that Ginny had snuck into my "writing room" one day while I was out. The room she'd been strictly forbidden to enter. I could only hope she hadn't found the hole at the back of the wardrobe and instead had assumed I'd simply left the house without her noticing. Regardless, I'd had to ask Nimble to keep a closer eye on her.

The day Sidney and I finally visited Dublin Castle was not particularly auspicious. Heavy, overcast skies signaled there would soon be rain, and there was some agitation among the population as newsboys on the street corners cried the latest headlines—a failed ambush in Skibbereen and a bombing in Cork City. As we approached the Palace Street gate, the main entrance to the Castle, I could see canvas screens had been erected above the ornate cast-iron gates, presumably as an extra security measure to prevent snipers from neighboring buildings being able to see inside the Castle complex. The bomb-catching meshwork stretched across the archway—of particular importance that day—was being inspected, as were the barbed wire and sandbag protections.

About twenty yards from the gate, a mantrap stood open in the pavement. A swift look down inside showed a pair of Royal Engineers moving about. I was to learn later that the River Poddle ran beneath the Castle walls and that wire entanglements had been erected over the subterranean stream to keep the rebels from gaining access that way. I could only imagine the concern this must have caused the authorities that the IRA might utilize this weakness in the Castle's defenses, either to sneak in or blow it up from below. The underground river also explained the dank smell I soon discovered permeated the place. Water even seeped from the stone walls in places—a fault in its construction.

The gate house to the left of the main arched opening was accessed through a smaller door also constructed of iron, and manned by an assortment of DMP officers and military police. They checked our passes and our names against a list of visitors and then we were allowed to enter, being directed toward the offices housing the headquarters of the DMP. Almost immediately to the right, I noted a long, narrow alley within which a number of men appeared to be milling about. However, my attention was swiftly diverted to the Lower Castle Yard several dozen yards before me.

I was at once struck by the hum of activity. The massive courtyard was filled with armored cars, tenders, and lorries—rows upon rows of them—and even a tank. Some of them rumbled in idle as men tinkered with them, issuing forth plumes of exhaust, but most sat quietly, waiting to spring to life. Meanwhile, soldiers in the all too familiar shades of dark green and khaki gathered in groups, jesting with one another, cigarettes dangling from their fingers, their metal badges and revolvers flashing in the stray beams of sunshine that occasionally managed to penetrate through the clouds. Here and there, civilians and uniformed officers darted between the massive complex of buildings and through a gate to the right, which I presumed led into the Upper Castle Yard.

Most of the buildings were constructed of brick, at least on the exterior: a Georgian remodel, as I understood it, meant to blend with the rest of the city. Directly across the lower yard stood the Chapel Royal and the medieval-looking round Record Tower from which the Union Jack flew. From our vantage, I could just make out the muzzle of a machine gun aimed between the parapets and trained on the Palace Street gate in preparation for any attempted invasion. The other buildings surrounding the yard housed the RIC headquarters, the Treasury Office, the British Army's Dublin Command, a central telephone exchange, a coach house and stables, and the DMP headquarters.

Rather than be caught gawking, Sidney laced my arm with his, guiding us toward the chief commissioner of the DMP's office. However, I found my gaze continuing to stray toward the gate leading into the Upper Castle Yard, or the "Devil's Half-Acre," as it had been dubbed by the Irish after centuries of contentious and sometimes violent British rule. It contained the sumptuous Viceregal State Apartments, the Privy Council Chamber, and the offices of the chief secretary of Ireland and undersecretaries, as well as residences for some of the staff. The intelligence office was also, no doubt, contained within. Not that I wished to see it.

Several of the soldiers turned to watch us as we passed and I flashed them a smile. As I'd been dressing that morning, I'd acknowledged that we couldn't hope to pass unnoticed. Not together. So I'd decided the best thing to do was give them all something to talk about. By doing so, my presence would seem less suspicious. I knew my sage-green gown with frilled skirt and crisscross neckline with lavender accents was both flattering and eye-catching, precisely the combination I needed.

I noticed then a sprinkling of men dressed in plain clothes standing amidst those in uniform, deducing they were either intelligence officers or G-Men. I didn't recognize any of them, so presumably we didn't have a personal history. At least, none of them gave me more than the admiring stares I normally received from men.

A man in the starch-collared DMP uniform, with polished buttons marching up the front of the tunic and a shiny buckle cinched at the waist, greeted us as we entered the chief commissioner's office. He showed us through an interior door to the larger office of his superior. Edgeworth-Johnstone was a sportsman of great prowess, particularly in fencing and pugilism. He'd won numerous titles in his younger days, and still cut a trim and dashing figure now at nearly sixty. His uniform was much like his clerks', albeit with far more gilding and ornamentation about the collar and across the shoulders. He had a flared pyramid mustache and a head of sparse, closely cropped hair, but I came to realize that his most distinctive feature was his heavy, triangular-shaped eyebrows, which emphasized the natural downturn of his lips and made him look like he was perpetually frowning.

He rounded his desk to shake Sidney's hand before clasping mine very properly. "A pleasure to meet you." He gestured for us to have a seat while he resumed his. "I understand you have some concerns for me. Speaking of which . . ." He tapped a folder on his desk with his flat hand, his manner turning more serious. "Your letters were received," he told Sidney. "And your concerns addressed. Lieutenant Delagrange has been warned to stay away from Mrs. Kent." His gaze shifted between us. "Though I trust that's not what this meeting is about."

"No, it isn't," Sidney answered on our behalf. We'd already agreed it would be better for him to probe elsewhere for more information on Delagrange, and also best for him to do most of the talking during this meeting. "As you may already know, the lord lieutenant asked us, as a personal favor, to look into the assault of Miss Katherine Kavanagh."

The commissioner indicated with his head that he was aware.

"We've spoken with Mr. and Mrs. Kavanagh, who are still justifiably distressed, as well as your man in charge of the investigation into the incident—a Detective Inspector Burrows out of Great Brunswick Street—but none of them were able to tell us much." He eyed the other man shrewdly. "Given the importance of Mr. Kavanagh's position, we thought you might be able to tell us more."

Johnstone sank back in his chair, considering us carefully before speaking. "As I understand it, His Excellency is most concerned with apprehending the culprits who perpetuated such a fiendish crime. To that end, I can tell you that a witness was found."

I sat forward in surprise, turning to Sidney as he repeated, "A witness?"

The commissioner nodded, opening the file immediately in front of him on his desk. I arched my neck, trying to catch a glimpse of the papers inside.

"Yes. Let's see . . . A footman, it appears. One who worked for the Kavanaghs."

Earnán.

"He stumbled upon the end of the attack, and while he couldn't identify the men's faces because of their masks, he heard enough of their accents and discussion to recognize they were from the local brigade of a republican group that calls themselves the IRA."

I found it interesting that the commissioner was speaking to us as if we didn't already know who the IRA were, as if we weren't highly aware of the intricate ins and outs of the struggle. He closed the file, sinking back in his chair again. I wished I could get my hands on its contents.

"Burrows didn't inform us of any of this," Sidney informed him with furrowed brow.

Johnstone clasped his hands before him. "Because DI Burrows didn't know. This information was obtained by a different source."

The furrows deepened. "Do you mind telling us who, so we might speak with him?"

"I'm afraid that's classified."

Which meant that he was an intelligence officer. Or the tout of one.

"But I assure you their report was quite thorough. I doubt that there's more to be learned from that avenue." The commissioner tapped his thumbs together. "And as I understand it, the footman soon left the Kavanaghs' employ. Too frightened the IRA would retaliate if they learned he cooperated with the authorities."

Definitely Earnán, then, though we still didn't have his last name.

"Could you at least share the footman's name?" I asked. "Or is that also classified?"

His smile was patronizing. "I'm afraid so. Secrecy is of the utmost importance in these sorts of matters, Mrs. Kent." He turned to Sidney. "If you want my advice, leave this matter to us. I've already told His Excellency as much. We'll be on to the culprits soon enough."

With that, we were essentially dismissed.

"I suppose that corroborates at least some of what you learned the other day," Sidney murmured as we descended the stairs.

"But neither Mary nor Mr. Kavanagh mentioned that Earnán had seen the men or heard their discussion," I countered.

"Maybe he was afraid to tell them."

I turned to look into Sidney's expectant gaze, having to cede he could be correct. If the assailants knew that Earnán had heard them, if he'd been frightened enough to leave the Kavanaghs' employ, then he might have been just as eager to protect those he left behind. I frowned, though more often than not, I found that leaving people in ignorance placed them at more risk, no matter how noble your intentions.

We emerged to much the same scene in the Lower Castle Yard, and while I wanted nothing more than to explore the complex further, specifically venturing into the upper yard, I knew we no longer had an excuse to be there. I allowed my eyes to linger on its edifices, racking my brain for some justification.

Which was when I spotted the woman striding purposefully across the yard, a stack of folders clasped before her. A female clerk or typist. One of, no doubt, many who worked in the Castle, performing many of the same tasks I had during my initial months with the Secret Service in London during the war. Applying for such a position would be foolhardy. No one of my social and marital status, not to mention my reputation, would ever be accepted. There was no longer a worldwide war going on and a necessity for such exceptions. And attempting to do so in disguise would be even more imprudent. However, if I befriended one of these women, I might be able to learn more from *them* or perhaps even be invited on a tour. Such things were done no matter the rules. Though I would have to choose carefully.

When the woman turned to anxiously survey the yard, showing she wasn't quite as self-assured as she first seemed, and then affixed her gaze on me for a few moments, I memorized what I could of her features. She had thick, dark hair and eyebrows, and an aquiline nose. I wanted to be able to recognize her if I ever saw her again.

I was about to turn my back on the yard, when I suddenly felt someone watching me. And *not* in the complimentary manner of the soldiers milling amongst the military vehicles. Swiveling my head to the right, I caught sight of the individual standing outside the doorway adjacent to the constabulary offices. There was some distance between us, but based on his appearance alone, I knew he must be Ormonde de l'Épée Winter, the newly appointed director of intelligence in Ireland and deputy advisor to the police. The fellow looked precisely as if he'd been plucked out of a lineup and cast in his role. Short and dapper, with a monocle set in his eye, an affectation I could only imagine was meant to emulate C, much as his uninspired code name "O."

I recalled again how Kathleen had cautioned me about him during our last briefing before my departure for Dublin. "I'm telling you, Ver, he's probably entirely amoral, and as dishonest as the day is long," she'd declared with a vehemence I'd rarely witnessed from her. "Men seem to like him well enough. Even C doesn't seem to have strong objections to him, despite his being appointed by Thomson. But I'm telling you"—she'd eyed me sharply—"watch your back with that one."

"Is he a lech?" I'd asked.

"Possibly. But I'm less concerned about him grabbing your arse than him blackmailing, betraying, or selling you to the highest bidder. He's already been acquitted of murder once. And I don't think he'd hesitate to do it again if he thought he could get away with it."

Meeting his cold gaze in person for the first time, even across a courtyard, I better understood Kathleen's warning. It did put one in mind of a snake. A wicked little white one.

He didn't approach, and I had no desire for a conversation with the fellow, so I turned away, carrying on past the last streetlamp and out the pedestrian gate.

Sidney waited until we were striding past St. Andrew's Church before speaking. "Who was that unctuous chap with the monocle?"

I smiled at his description, explaining O's role. There was no need to elucidate my reasons for wanting to avoid him.

"I've been told he wants to flood the city with intelligence operatives," Sidney stated evenly. "That more and more are arriving each day."

"They've set up a special training school for them in England," I confirmed.

We crossed George's Street, navigating around a collision between a bicycle and a cart. No one appeared to be injured, though both vehicles would require new wheels. However, the drivers were creating quite a scene screaming at each other in accents so thick I could only make out the occasional curse word.

"But they won't have taught them properly how to blend in," I warned, finishing my thought.

"The other day in Rabbiatti's Saloon, I heard one of them speaking in just about the thickest Cockney accent you've ever heard," Sidney said. "He was commenting on the accent of two other fellows, wanting to know how on earth they'd picked up the Irish brogue, and how he'd been there for over a year and still hadn't been able to master a bit of it."

"Because they were probably Irish," I exclaimed, unable to contain my exasperation any longer. "They were probably Collins's men."

Having startled the woman approaching us, I allowed Sidney to pull me toward the inner edge of the pavement. "It wouldn't surprise me," he said in a low voice.

"During the war, had we sent agents into Belgium and France speaking with Cockney accents, the Germans would have picked them up in a trice," I hissed. "I can't decide whether Thomson and his cronies are so prejudiced against the Irish that they think they're too stupid to even notice the difference, or if they're simply oblivious to the fact that an Irishman is not the same as an Englishman, no matter how hard the government has tried to make that so."

"Either reasoning would fit, it seems to me," Sidney agreed, maintaining a far more even tone than I could manage.

"They're just sending over more targets for the rebels' guns," I whispered in a broken voice. Reckless, dimwitted targets like Lieutenant Delagrange, a man I'd never thought to feel sympathy for.

Sidney pulled me closer to his side, but he didn't try to convince me I was wrong. Sometimes it was better to let the truth stand, even when it smarted.

CHAPTER 16

The next day, I spent the better part of the morning contemplating our next steps. Once again, the newspapers were filled with reports of RIC patrols being attacked, barracks burned, and a more credible report of a seventeen-year-old girl from County Kerry having her hair forcibly cut and her head tarred simply because two of her brothers were members of the constabulary. There were also accounts of troubling evidence that had emerged in a court case in Derry City of collusion between the British Army and the Ulster Protestant vigilantes during the recent riots that had occurred there, which left me feeling less confident the government would halt the formation of an official Ulster Volunteer Force.

It left me wondering for perhaps the dozenth time why on earth we were in Ireland. Why I hadn't latched on to the excuse Alec had afforded me and returned to London. After a month, we were no closer to finding him, and no closer to uncovering Miss Kavanagh's assailants other than confirmation that they seemed to be members of the local IRA. But Lord French had already suspected that!

I had one last option open to me that I could think of. I'd been resistant to use it given the quid pro quo nature of the man in question, but now I felt I had no choice. So I dashed off a letter to my reporter friend asking him to meet me for lunch sometime in the next few days. Then knowing it was too late for him to respond requesting we meet that day, I climbed the stairs to my self-proclaimed writing room, locking the door firmly behind me, and donned my disguise to set off for the Wicklow. It had been some days since I'd called at the hotel, and I knew I had to stop avoiding Tom, or abandon the strategy all together.

Peter seemed happy to see me, confessing he'd begun to think perhaps I'd gone back to County Antrim, from which I'd claimed to hail. But he still had no news of Alec. "And I have to caution ye," he said in a concerned tone as he leaned against the bar. "That's usually not a good t'ing."

I nodded, understanding what he was saying.

Still I sat, sipping my drink and listening to two men at the opposite end of the bar quibbling over a recent match at Croke Park. Such was my absorption, that I didn't notice Tom's approach.

"Is this seat taken?"

I turned to look at him, recognizing he was giving me the chance to tell him to beat it. Instead, I gestured for him to sit. My senses were on high alert, waiting to see what he would do. I lifted my gaze to the glass behind the bar, anxious to see if he'd come alone or if a cohort was watching us from the other side of the room.

"You've been avoidin' me."

I'd not expected frankness, but then decided I was glad of it, responding in kind. "I have." It helped that Peter was also monitoring us closely, at least suggesting he would step in to assist should I need it.

My candor seemed to surprise Tom as well, for it took him a moment to answer. "I suppose I can't blame ye. You're a stranger to Dublin, and I did come on rather strong. 'Tis your beauty. It fair steals my good sense."

I could tell from the smile he flashed me that he expected this display of charm to melt my defenses. On a less experienced woman it might have worked, for he *was* handsome and engaging. But I'd faced down more than my fair share of rogues in at least five countries, and I was married to Sidney Kent. It took more than flattery and an appealing smirk to disarm me.

"One can never be too careful," I responded blandly, taking another sip of my tea.

He didn't say anything else at first, as if he expected me to say more. But as Peter set his dark stout before him, he tried again. "Well, I meant it when I said I'd like to help ye." He took a deep drink before continuing, the foam clinging to his upper lip. I expected him to play for time, perhaps attempt to arrange another meeting, but instead he shocked both me and Peter with his next pronouncement. "And I think I may've found somethin'."

My cup clattered into its saucer as I turned, now giving him my full attention. However, the regret plainly writ across his features drained the blood from mine.

"Rumor is there's a man of your description who went by the name of MacAlister buried in a bog in County Kildare."

My stomach pitched, but Tom wasn't finished.

"They . . . they say he was a spy for the Brits. But they may've gotten it wrong," he hastened to add as I turned to clasp the bar, lest I crumble under the weight of this news.

I'd told neither of them he was a spy, which seemed to only add credibility to the report. Was this it then? Had I finally uncovered what had happened to Alec? Were my worst fears confirmed?

Peter sprang into action, the dear fellow, pouring a glass of water and forcing it into my hand. "Here ye are, Miss Bell. Take a drink now. Aye, just like that," he coaxed as I lifted it shakily to my lips and swallowed. "Another one, now," he said, and I complied.

Lowering the glass to the bar and taking a deep breath, I had to admit I did feel better. My vision no longer seemed to fade to a point somewhere in the distance.

"There, now, you just sit here with ole Peter for another minute and then I'll ask one of our porters to walk ye home." I noticed him dart an angry glare at Tom and then toward the far doorway, but I didn't have a clear vantage in the reflection of the glass of who might be standing there. Whoever it was obviously had some connection to Tom and obviously didn't want me to see them.

This, more than anything, helped me recover my equilibrium as my mind turned over the conundrum. Why did the person near the door wish to remain hidden? Was this mysterious someone the source of Tom's information? Was Peter unhappy with them because they'd upset me, or for another reason entirely?

For that matter, how did I know that what Tom had told me was true? Yes, the detail about the man in the bog being a spy had lent it verisimilitude, but if Tom had realized who I was, if he was working with the rebels, then he might have added that for my benefit.

But if that were true, if Alec had still been alive and undetected, having simply broken off contact with his handler, then had I unwittingly placed him in even more danger? I might have very well gotten him killed. The realization was like a splash of cold water in the face.

"Nay," I finally told Peter. "Nay. I'm fine now. 'Twas . . . 'twas just the shock. I'll be alright."

"Are ye sure, lassie?" he asked, scrutinizing me closely as I gathered up my things. "'Tisn't a bother."

"I'm sure." I offered him a weak smile. "But thank ye." I turned to Tom. "And thank ye, too."

"I could walk ye—" he began to offer, but I shook my head.

I still felt a bit light-headed as I exited the hotel, but each step brought more clarity. Enough that I was able to apply my training, making quick turns and doubling back on my route, hopping aboard the tram at the last minute to ensure I wasn't being followed. By the time I'd reached the alley behind our townhouse and passed through the neighbor's gate to begin picking my way across their garden, which was becoming more overgrown with each passing day, I had determined to question everything until it was verified by an independent source. And fortunately, I knew just the person to ask.

"So ye *are* in Dublin's fair city," Michael Wickham declared when I arrived at the table where he was already seated in the little restaurant he'd selected, in Dawson Street. He rose to his feet, bussing both my cheeks. "When I received your letter, I thought for certain ye were pullin' my leg. A gin rickey for Mrs. Kent," he told the waiter. "The good stuff."

"Do they have the good stuff?" I asked as I settled in my chair, removing my gloves.

He winked. "Wait and see."

I smiled. If anyone knew where to find a decent bottle of gin in this town, it was Wick.

"But what on earth are ye doin' here?" he demanded. "This is hardly Paris in spring." His voice lowered a notch. "And I thought ye were done with all the skulkery."

"I have no idea what you're talking about," I replied blithely.

He sat back in his chair, crossing his arms over his chest. "Uh-huh." The twinkle in his eye told me he knew better, but I'd learned it was best never to confirm anything to a reporter. Not even a friend. "Just like ye were naught but a comely English maid concerned for the welfare of her French cousins when I met yet in that field hospital outside Amiens."

By chance, the table we were seated at was but one of about half a dozen, and it was tucked away in the corner near the kitchen, affording us a measure of privacy.

Wick had been injured by shrapnel while reporting on the Germans' 1918 spring offensive while I'd nearly been blown up by a shell delivering a message from HQ about a suspected traitor among a brigade's intelligence staff. I'd been posing as a French refugee, fleeing the Germans' swift advance, but been forced to improvise once it was discovered I was English at the dressing station I'd been taken to before being transferred on to the field hospital. I'd been a bit out of my head, not only from the scrambling my brain had received, but also with grief over Sidney's recently reported death. Wick had proved to be an invaluable friend and also a bolstering hospital mate, as the irreverent Irishman had made me laugh when I'd most needed it.

"I read your article in the *Irish Independent* last week," I told him. "Incisive as always."

He spread his hands as if to say, *It's what I do*.

My brow furrowed in concern. "You're not in any danger, are you? I heard the IRA destroyed some print machinery at the *Independent* some months back when they didn't like an editorial that was published." One decrying an ambush on the lord lieutenant which had happily failed in its objective to kill him.

He shrugged one shoulder. "It comes with the territory." His nonchalance didn't surprise me. It was part and parcel of the dashing, absent-minded figure he cut, with his square-cut jawline, ink-stained fingers, and windblown hair that appeared perpetually in need of a haircut.

The waiter set what appeared to be a credible-looking gin rickey before me and then withdrew. Wick watched me eagerly, waiting for me to take a drink. I almost hated to disappoint him, but in the end, there was no need to. This, indeed, was made with the good stuff.

"Told ye," he declared smugly as he observed my pleased reaction. "And just wait until ye taste their croque monsieur." He closed his eyes, anticipating a delicious taste. And this was a man who was serious about his sandwiches. "Shall I order?"

"Please do," I said with a smile. He'd succeeded in finding me the only palatable gin rickey I'd had since arriving in Dublin. I more than trusted him to order us an appetizing meal.

That done, Wick eyed me expectantly. "Now, darlin'. Not that I wasn't pleased and flattered when I received your note. But tell me what sparked this lunch invitation."

"Perhaps I simply wanted your company," I demurred.

His eyebrows arched in good-natured skepticism, and I relented. "What do you know of the assault on Miss Kavanagh?"

A slight furrow formed in his brow and his eyes took on a bit of a vacant stare, telling me he was sorting through the reams of information stored in his brain to locate the right details. "The King's Counsel's daughter? Serves on some commission. She had her hair cut. Quite brutally."

"That's the one."

He nodded. "I wanted to look into it." His eyes narrowed. "There was somethin' fishy about it. But ole Harrington warned me away." He shrugged. "And then there were other more pressin' stories to pursue."

There always was during wartime. And no matter the British government's petty dickering over the language, this *was* a war.

"Fishy how?"

"Well, the IRA got blamed almost immediately, if I recall. But the attack occurred in the garden after everyone had retired. Yet some lads from the local brigade just happened to be hangin' about when Miss Kavanagh decided to step out for some fresh air?"

He had a point. The timing was rather suspect.

"And the likes of the Miss Kavanaghs of the world are not the IRA's usual targets," Wick added.

"She was stepping out with a British officer," I observed. And there had been yet another report of forced hair cutting in the papers the day before, this time of a woman in Clonakilty who'd had a gun held to her head as it was done, just because her father and two brothers were in the British Army.

"Many of the young ladies of her ilk are," he countered. "But they're no danger to the local lads, because they don't know anythin' worth passin' on, either accidentally or on purpose."

"Yes, but that commission you recalled her father serving on is responsible for awarding malicious-injury and damage claims," I informed him before taking another sip of my drink.

This gave him some pause as he considered the ramifications. "Aye, 'tis a sensitive subject. Particularly given the fact there's evidence of collusion between the Crown Forces and Castle authorities of false and inflated claims being made."

"What evidence?" I'd heard the rumors, but this was the first time anyone had spoken to me of actual proof.

However, Wick only shook his head. Which told me that he was probably working on a story about the matter and couldn't divulge his sources. It was a story that the government and their censors would take exception to, putting Wick at risk. But then, this wouldn't be the first time he'd been sent to prison for writing a story the authorities disliked.

"Returnin' to the Kavanaghs, 'tis doubtful his role with the commission would be reason enough to provoke such a risky attack on his daughter. Not the least because Kavanagh is one of the most moderate voices on that committee."

I ruminated over this new information, recognizing the logic of his arguments. I had already been harboring misgivings about the matter, and Johnstone's claim that the Kavanaghs' footman had told an intelligence officer that he'd recognized the assailants as being members of the IRA had only increased them. This only brought them bursting to a head. Though I still had one more point to clarify.

Wick spoke before I could mention it. "What's *your* interest in the matter?"

"The lord lieutenant asked me to look into it," I responded after a brief pause.

One corner of his mouth curled cynically. "My, my. Don't we have some toplofty friends."

I frowned. "It's not like that." I reached out to fiddle with the alignment of the silverware, but once I realized what I was doing, lowered my hands to my lap. "Yes, he asked as a favor, but I mainly agreed because it seemed the girl deserved some sort of justice. If she was distraught enough to kill herself—" I broke off, inhaling a steadying breath. "It must have been bad."

Wick's scorn was replaced by something more sympathetic, something more speculative. "Aye. I'm acquainted well enough with ye to know what a soft heart ye have."

I scowled at him, and he grinned.

"Ye don't hide it very well, love. Though you've got more pluck than an entire company of soldiers combined. 'Tis why everyone adores ye so."

I flushed at this unexpected compliment. "Not everyone. Believe me."

He chuckled. "Aye. Not the ones ye cross."

"Speaking of cross," I said, lifting my glass. "The Kavanaghs' neighbor suggested one of Miss Kavanagh's cousins had crossed the IRA. That he'd been found with a note condemning him as an informant to the British."

Wick's face scrunched in contemplation again, and I could practically see him flipping through the pages filling the drawers of the file cabinet of his mind. "If so, he's not a Kavanagh. Do you know his name?"

"I'm afraid not." It hadn't seemed important at the time, but now I was kicking myself for not asking.

"Hmm. Let me do some diggin'."

I hadn't asked him to do so, but I wasn't about to turn down the offer, even if it cost me another favor in the future. This also led me neatly into my next request.

"While you're doing so, there's another body I'd like you to look into." I set my glass down carefully. "I've been told there are rumors of a body recently being found in a bog in County Kildare. That he was killed because he was a spy."

When my gaze lifted to meet Wick's, I could tell he recognized the significance of this. From the way he scrutinized my features, he might even have guessed that was why I was really here in Dublin. But for once, he didn't prod or tease. He merely accepted me at my word.

"I haven't heard of any bodies bein' found in bogs. Not in County Kildare. The Móin Alúine, I presume. And not recently." His expression turned watchful. "As for the spy bit, neither Collins nor the IRA would miss the opportunity to make a demonstration of such a John." His voice dipped in warning. "Or Jane."

I didn't even pretend not to understand. "That's not why I'm here," I assured him. "I was released from my war work almost sixteen months ago."

His stare only intensified. "That doesn't mean anythin'."

My lips twisted. "Well, in this case, it does."

He must have sensed my growing disaffection with the establishment, but once again he didn't push. "I'll ask around, but I'm fairly certain these rumors—wherever you heard them—are false."

I swallowed, struggling to restrain the immense surge of relief his words had caused me. I'd already shed more than a handful of tears the previous evening when I'd informed Sidney of what Tom had said. I wasn't going to cry again just because Wick had told me he'd probably been wrong. What that said about Tom, I didn't know. Had he purposely misled me, or had it been an honest mistake? Because of Peter's reaction and Tom's connection to the Capel Street library, I was inclined to believe the former, but the truth was, I didn't know.

Our food arrived, and we left off weightier topics while we enjoyed our meals and caught up on each other's lives. But once our plates were cleared, Wick offered me a cigarette, which I declined, before lighting one for himself. He sat back to consider me and my questions once again. "Have you come to any conclusions about Miss Kavanagh's attack?" he asked after blowing a stream of smoke toward the ceiling.

"Truthfully?" I sighed. "No. And I'm at a bit of a loss as to what else I can do," I admitted. "The family hasn't been exactly cooperative. And neither has the detective inspector in charge of the case."

He tapped a bit of ash into the dish at his elbow. "Yes, but her family aren't the only people who may have known the girl well."

I was an idiot. "Of course! At her age she was bound to have friends she confided in, perhaps even more than her parents." I wondered if I'd even seen one of them watching me from the window across the street as I spoke to Mrs. Gardiner. "You are a genius!"

He chuckled, taking one last drag from his cigarette before stubbing it out. "No, just used to bein' creative about where I find my sources."

Rounding the table, he helped me from my chair, and then escorted me from the restaurant. The day was warm and the sun bright, glinting off the rose window of St. Ann's Church. I expected Wick to confess he needed to return to the offices of the *Independent* across the river, but he continued to delay, and soon enough I discovered why.

"Far be it from me to turn into one of those frettin' hens, but a word of caution, Ver."

I looked up to find him scanning the street before us rather than peering down at me, something I found far more disconcerting.

"Collins knows you're here."

His tone sent a skitter of alarm down my spine. "You say that as if you know it in fact."

Wick's gaze shifted to meet mine, and I could see that was exactly what he meant. Of course, as a reporter, particularly for a paper that had become more and more disenchanted with the British government, even going so far as to call the Crown Forces an "army of occupation" upon occasion, he had doubtless spoken to Collins and many other prominent Sinn Féiners and IRA leaders at one point or another. Even knowing there was a natural explanation didn't make me feel any better.

"Finish whatever ye came here for and then get out," he urged. "You've friends here, but we can't protect ye forever. Not if ye prove to be a threat."

"I'm no threat," I assured him in a small voice. "And neither is Sidney."

The steely look in his eyes softened. "Even so, mistakes get made. And I don't want you to be one of them."

CHAPTER 17

Wick had given me much to think on. So much that I almost missed the look of distress on Ginny's features as she hovered in the entry hall. Only when I heard hobbling footsteps mounting the stairs from below, ones which didn't belong to Nimble, did I look up. Ginny shuffled from foot to foot, her eyes ringed red as if she'd been crying, as Mrs. Boyle—our cook who never climbed the stairs if she could help it—came to a stop beside her.

"Did ye tell her?" she asked the maid in her rolling Irish brogue.

A trickle of alarm spread through me. "Tell me what?"

The cook scowled at Ginny. "'Tis Mr. Nimble. They took him away."

The breath in my lungs tightened. "*Who* took him away?"

"The Tans," Ginny sobbed. "A pair of 'em, they was pesterin' me on my way back from the baker." She swiped at her cheeks. "Mrs. Boyle sent me to fetch a loaf of bread . . ."

"The one they sold me this morn' wasn't fit for a sow," the cook grumbled with a shake of her head.

"And Nimble must've been watchin' for me, because the next thing I knew, he came chargin' down the street, tellin' 'em to leave me be."

"I see," I said. And I did. Nimble would never abide a man mistreating a woman of any class. It was one of the instances which might provoke him enough not to mind his tongue, even when it would be wiser if he had.

Mrs. Boyle planted her hands on her hips, declaring in approval, "He's a good lad."

A fact I didn't think any of us would dispute, but it didn't tell me where they'd taken Nimble.

"What did they do?" I asked Ginny.

It took her a moment to stammer. "They . . . they started beatin' 'im." She hiccupped on a sob. "Called over some friends."

I pressed a hand to my mouth.

"Then threw him into one o' those lorries and took off with him. I'm so sorry," she blubbered, weeping in earnest.

I grasped her hand, shaking my head in agitation. Of course, it wasn't her fault, but there were more important things to be dealt with at the moment. "How long ago did they take him? And where?"

"No more than half an hour," Mrs. Boyle said. "As to where? Perhaps the Castle." She nearly spat the word.

She was probably right. If the men had been Black and Tans, then they wouldn't have taken him to the local DMP station. Dublin Castle or one of the local barracks were most likely their destination, but the Castle could tell me for certain. A swift glance at the clock told me Sidney would be home within the hour from Phoenix Park where he'd gone riding, but I couldn't wait that long.

"When Mr. Kent returns, tell him where I've gone," I ordered, snatching up my handbag and gloves again. "Tell him to come."

"But what are you goin' to do?" Mrs. Boyle asked as I turned toward the door.

The look in my eyes when I glanced back must have been frightening, for they both shrunk back half a step. "Bring Nimble home."

* * *

"I don't give a damn about your protocols," I snapped at the senior guard at the gate to Dublin Castle. "I was here not four days ago." I swiveled to point at a man standing behind him to the left. "*You* saw me enter." And then another to the right. "And *you* saw me enter. I am Verity Kent. Wife of Sidney Kent, recipient of the Victoria Cross for his service to his country, and heir presumptive to his uncle, the Marquess of Treborough." I narrowed my eyes, biting off my words. "My bonafides are quite above reproach. And I want to speak to a senior officer now. Not when one is available. Not when an appointment can be arranged. *Now.*"

"For God's sake, let her through," a thin-lipped gentleman of about forty grumbled. "She's not going to bomb the Records Tower or assassinate the chief secretary."

Still the senior guard resisted, and in another situation I might have admired his devotion to duty, but not now. Not when I was imagining increasingly awful things happening to Nimble with each passing minute.

"Will you vouch for her, sir?" the guard finally asked.

"Yes, yes," he retorted, ushering me before him. "Come with me, my dear. Now, who were you so anxious to see?" he asked as we passed through the inner door and into the Lower Castle Yard.

"A senior officer. I don't know precisely which one. My husband's valet was assaulted and arrested by a group of temporary cadets. He was coming to the aid of our maid, who they were pestering," I explained. "Mr. Kent is at Phoenix Park this afternoon, and Nimble is our only male servant. He takes his job rather seriously in his absence, protecting all the women of the household. I want him released."

The gentleman frowned. "Did he strike the cadets?"

"Absolutely not," I stated with conviction. I knew Nimble well enough to recognize he would never have turned violent, despite what his size might suggest. "He was angry, of course, but he did not express himself physically."

The gentleman continued to grimace, and I felt compelled to offer Nimble further defense. "He served as my husband's batman during the war and was injured at Riqueval."

He nodded. "Yes, I see." He gripped his attaché case tighter. "Come with me." We turned right, striding past the Treasury Office to that of the constabulary.

While not exactly leaping to attention, the men loitering inside clearly recognized the gentleman with me as one of some authority, for they rose to their feet as we passed through several outer rooms. Coming upon a partially closed door, he rapped before entering unprompted. "Smith, Mrs. Verity Kent wishes to speak with you. Apparently, her manservant was arrested under what may be faulty circumstances. The chap served with her husband, Mr. *Sidney Kent*." He leaned on my husband's name for emphasis, but I hardly noticed it or the man he was addressing, for my gaze had been captured by the other fellow in the room—O.

He scrutinized me through his monocle. "Clever of you to go to Wylie," he declared before Smith could even speak.

So the helpful gentleman was William Wylie, a barrister who acted as a legal advisor to the Dublin Castle administration. That was a bit of luck.

Wylie scowled at O. "I met her in the guardhouse, and I must say her claims are concerning." This last he addressed to Smith, who must be the man with the authority to amend this error. The name plate on his desk read Inspector General T. J. Smith, and I realized this must be the fellow they expected to retire shortly, and who they'd brought General Tudor in to replace, though for now Tudor was nominally a police advisor.

"I suppose this is regarding your husband's valet, who calls himself Nimble," O interrupted once again, to Smith's obvious irritation. "The man I was just telling you about," O informed him, either oblivious to or uncaring of his annoyance. "But truly, you must calm yourself, Mrs. Kent. You're clearly agitated and that can't be good for you in your *delicate condition*." His voice was laced with a mockery the other men seemed to miss, though they got the inference. They both eyed me with alarm, as if I might go into labor at any moment, though it must have been perfectly obvious I couldn't be far along. Evidently Bennett had spoken with O. "Would you like a chair?"

"What I would like," I replied icily, "is to not have to come down here to retrieve the manservant on whom I rely." I turned to the white-haired Smith. "Then he's been brought here?" I asked, relieved to discover that at least this guess was correct. "I want him released. Two of your temporary cadets were *harassing* my maid. He was merely coming to her assistance when they first *assaulted* and then arrested him." It took everything within me to restrain my rage and remember to use the polite official terms the government insisted upon.

"Yes, we were just discussing that," Smith replied. "My men are accusing him of attacking them first."

"Balderdash!" I stated, allowing my temper to get the better of me for a moment. "Nimble is a law-abiding British citizen. He may have gotten angry. Your men were *pestering* an innocent young woman under our employ and protection. As such, he may have raised his voice, but he would never have raised his fist to them."

"He's an awfully large fellow, Mrs. Kent."

I glared at Smith, speaking in a carefully modulated tone lest my words sound like the threat I wanted to make. "Size is not always indicative of capability."

"And your maid is an informant for the shinners," O murmured silkily.

This was no more than I suspected, though I didn't take it as confirmation. From everything I'd heard about O, he was precisely the type to lie as he saw fit in order to sew discord. He expected outrage and anger, no doubt. So instead, I scoffed.

"An informant? On what? Our clothing? The latest on-dit for the gossip rags?" I shook my head and even managed to summon a chuckle.

"You and your husband have some rather highly placed friends," O countered.

"Perhaps, but our staff and the townhouse we're renting here in Dublin are both rather modest. We're not doing any entertaining. So where exactly this maid of ours is supposed to collect information for the IRA, I don't know."

"And you're conducting an investigation on behalf of the lord lieutenant."

This appeared to be news to both Wylie and Smith, but I wasn't about to let it disconcert me. Instead, I stood blinking at O in feigned confusion. "And? Oh, wait. I see. You think we're foolish enough to leave papers lying around or discuss pertinent details in front of our staff." I smiled at him as if he were a simpleton, which was perhaps a mistake. But I rather enjoyed watching the vein throb at his temple.

"You worked for the Secret Service during the war," O bit out, finally succeeding in shocking me as well as the others. Though not because he knew of my role with military intelligence, but rather because he'd spoken of it in front of two men who almost certainly were not authorized to know such things. The Official Secrets Act forbade any such disclosure.

"Colonel Winter, I believe you must have me confused with someone else," I responded calmly, fairly confident I was reading the disapproval now blossoming across the other men's features correctly. "I worked for an import-export company who transported supplies for our troops."

I could see the blistering retort quivering on O's lips, but he must have realized he'd stepped in it, remaining broodingly silent as Wylie turned his back on him to address Smith again.

"Are there any other charges against this Mr. Nimble?"

Nimble was not his real name, but I didn't disabuse him of this and muddy the issue.

"No. Only assault," Smith replied.

"Then, under the circumstances, I recommend you drop the charges and release Mr. Nimble to Mrs. Kent." Wylie turned to me with arched eyes. "I trust we will have no trouble from Mr. Nimble in the future."

"So long as your men do not harass any of the female members of my staff," I answered tartly.

I wanted to demand the Tans who had assaulted Nimble be punished, but I recognized when retreat was necessary. If I pressed the matter, they might refuse to release Nimble, and if the matter went to arbitration, the word of those Tans would be believed to be more valid than that of our maid or most other witnesses. However, I was not about to sacrifice Ginny or Mrs. Boyle's safety. Nimble wouldn't want that.

The inspector general appeared as if he might argue, but then nodded his head in assent.

"This is highly irregular," O complained. "The fellow should be questioned first. By protocol." He turned to look at me, narrowing his eyes. "He may know things."

About us was the clear unspoken threat.

"What things?" Smith demanded.

"About this maid, for instance. Perhaps he's noticed things about her that her employers are too . . . obtuse to see."

I arched a single eyebrow at him in disdain. Obtuse, indeed.

However, I was dismayed to see that Smith was considering it. If necessary, I would threaten to go over his head, straight to Lord French. O had already mentioned our relationship to him. But first I waited to see what he would do.

Wylie shook his head at Smith, demonstrating that at least one of them had sense.

A moment later, Smith relented. "It will take a few minutes

to get the paperwork in order. Perhaps you would be so good as to escort Mrs. Kent where she might have a cup of tea," he told Wylie.

The tightness in my lungs eased a fraction, but I knew I wouldn't breathe easier until Nimble was actually walking out of the gate with me.

Though only ten minutes had passed since Wylie had left me in some sort of lounge, I found myself watching the clock anxiously. I'd managed to stomach a sip or two of tea, but the rest grew cold as I waited for Nimble. Smith had promised he would be brought to me within a quarter of an hour, and there were still five minutes to go, but still my gaze darted between the door and the clock.

The trouble was, I didn't trust O. Didn't trust him even when I could see him.

"The snake," I muttered to myself, not realizing I'd actually said it out loud until I heard the muffled giggle behind me.

I turned to find a woman preparing herself a cup of tea. The same woman, in fact, who I'd noticed across the Lower Castle Yard just a few days earlier. I hadn't heard her enter, but she must have come quietly through the door on the far end.

"You must be speakin' of Colonel Winter," she told me with a conspiratorial grin. "We all think he's rather reptilian."

And by *all* I suspected she meant all the female staff, but perhaps some of the males as well.

I smiled in return. "One expects a forked tongue to dart out at any moment to clean that ridiculous monocle."

She laughed merrily as she finished pouring hot water over the tea leaves in her cup. "I'd like to see the like. Oh, but that's a good one. I'll have to tell the other girls." Her voice had a lovely lilt. She turned to face me, brushing aside a strand of wavy dark hair that had begun to fall loose from its pins. "I'm Nancy, by the way. Nancy O'Brien."

"Verity Kent."

"Aye." Her eyes twinkled in good humor. "I've seen your picture in the papers."

"Well, don't hold that against me," I jested and she laughed again.

"That's somethin' they don't write about ye. How witty ye are."

I shrugged a shoulder. "Most of the reporters are men. And those that aren't, are usually told to focus on my appearance."

"It's what sells papers."

My voice turned wry. "Apparently."

"How do ye know the colonel, then?" she asked in a softer voice, moving closer while her tea was steeping. "They don't have ye workin' in his department, do they?"

"No, the Tans arrested my husband's valet for defending our maid from their pestering." Renewed anger sparked inside me. "The colonel didn't wish to release him."

This appeared to have bemused Nancy, for it took her a moment to reply. And then it wasn't what I expected.

"Did ye best him?"

I allowed some of the enjoyment I had felt at vexing him to infuse my expression. "Of course."

Nancy grinned.

"What of you? Are you a clerk? A typist?"

"Oh, a bit of this, a bit of that," she answered evasively.

I nodded, turning away, ostensibly to study the door. "I did much the same during the war." Out of the corner of my eye, I could see her studying me curiously. A curiosity that I hoped would keep her from examining my next request too closely.

"I know this might seem an odd remark," I said. "But I don't have a lot of friends here in Dublin. Not ones that aren't fusty and all consumed with their own consequence." I turned to look at her. "But you seem intelligent and fun. Would you want to meet me for a drink sometime?"

I could hear voices outside the door and turned toward them eagerly.

"Sure," Nancy said, drawing my attention back to her. She smirked. "Why not?"

I smiled in return, but I was too anxious for Nimble to feel much elation at securing Nancy's agreement. "I'll send you a message," I told her, rising to my feet as the door opened.

A lanky constable entered first and then stepped to the side to allow Nimble's larger frame past him.

The first thing I noted was the swelling contusion around his eye. I gasped, hurrying over to him, and grasped the sides of his face, turning it this way and that. There was dried blood at his hairline where they'd reopened part of his scar. Blood they'd evidently tried to clean up, considering the dampness of his hair and his collar.

"Ye don't need to make a fuss over me, ma'am," Nimble protested. "I'll be alright."

"I most certainly do! Where else did they strike you?"

But Nimble wouldn't answer, and the lanky constable, who was so young he still suffered from acne, only avoided my eyes. It was doubtful he'd had anything to do with what happened anyway. He'd simply been sent as the scapegoat, so to speak.

"Has a doctor examined you?"

"Aye," Nimble mumbled.

An army one, no doubt. One who would pronounce him fit even if he was bleeding all over the floor.

"Well, we'll have you checked by our own."

"That's not ne—"

"It is," I told Nimble, not brooking any arguments.

"Yes, ma'am," he relented, clearly in some sort of pain.

"Now, let's get you home."

One last glance over my shoulder told me Nancy had observed this exchange, but I ignored her, intent on seeing Nimble safely back to Upper Fitzwilliam Street. I half expected to find O standing outside the constabulary, gloating, but cooler heads must have prevailed, convincing him to remain out of sight. It was a good thing, too. Because I just might have risked being brought up on charges myself for slapping the look off his face.

We shuffled past the guards, who eyed us solemnly, and out the door to Palace Street. By all appearances, Nimble was escorting me, but I could sense the strain it caused him just to walk. I felt tears bite at the back of my eyes but blinked them away. I would not weep. Not when Nimble needed me to keep a clear head and navigate us through this late afternoon traffic. We would have to take the tram, though it would be crowded.

I was just debating where it would be best to catch it when Sidney appeared in front of us in the middle of Dame Street. He took one look at both our faces and assumed command of the situation. I didn't object or try to explain. Not then. I simply accepted his assistance.

CHAPTER 18

While Sidney and the doctor—another Royal Army Medical Corps man, but one whom Sidney was friendly with and trusted—tended to Nimble upstairs, I ventured belowstairs to speak with the rest of the staff. We gathered in the small servants' hall off of the kitchen, where I had Mrs. Boyle and Ginny sit at the table. It was clear Ginny had wept even more tears since my departure. Her face was blotchy and her eyes dim. Mrs. Boyle, on the other hand, was quiet and solemn.

I stood before them, undecided about what I should say. In the end, I opted for the unvarnished truth. "I don't care if you're an informant for the IRA." I looked Ginny squarely in the eye, and then Mrs. Boyle. "Though if you are, you should be aware the Castle suspects it. But they've been warned to stay away from you. You and Nimble," I stated in a hard voice.

Ginny blinked wide eyes, as if she couldn't quite believe what I was saying.

"However, if you get caught red-handed doing something compromising for the republicans, there may be nothing Mr. Kent and I can do. So think carefully before you agree to anything."

Mrs. Boyle's somber gaze had shifted to Ginny, telling me she either suspected or knew for certain that Ginny wasn't quite innocent of the accusations O had flung at her. But that didn't preclude her from also being culpable.

I turned my head to the side, frowning and tapping my foot as I considered how much to trust them. The truth was, I knew little about them or their backgrounds. Yet, they worked in our household, and I'd just told them I didn't care if they went on informing about us to the rebels. Which was true, but only because I didn't believe there was anything they could tell them that was particularly sensitive. Unless they'd discovered that I was sneaking out through the secret passage connecting our townhouse to the one adjacent, or they'd read one of Max's letters. Otherwise, we were smart enough to take precautions. What I'd told O was true. I'd learned long ago not to write anything down unless absolutely necessary, and to burn those notes I did receive.

Even so, the moment seemed to call for some display of faith. One that perhaps might be reciprocated. This wasn't the first time I'd found myself wanting to ask both women questions pertaining to local knowledge and opinion, and to offer a perspective different from my own. But as matters had stood, I'd known better than to expect assistance from either of them. Perhaps that could change.

"If you *are* informing to the IRA," I began, turning back to them. "I can tell you that we are not here because of the rebellion." I tilted my head. "Or not directly. Though I can understand why they would suspect it. But we're not here to foil it or stop it. That is not our purview, and I have no intention of making it such."

As I said the words, I knew it to be true. I didn't know exactly *how* I felt about this rebellion, this revolution, though I was deeply conflicted about it. What I did know was that it was not my fight, and I would not help either side win it. I was solely focused on finding Alec—dead or alive, locating those phosgene cylinders and foiling whatever Ardmore's intent was for them, and bringing Miss Kavanagh's attackers to justice, whoever they might be. None of those things required me to take action against either side.

Which was why I hadn't told the British authorities I'd seen Collins's right-hand man, Liam Tobin, on a corner near the Castle and entering Kidd's Back pub. Or relayed my suspicions that someone at the Great Brunswick Street Police Station was supplying information to Collins. Or any of about a dozen other things that had struck me as questionable. They weren't my task.

I couldn't tell how this speech had affected either woman, or whether they even believed me, but I knew that waxing on about it would not make it more convincing. Instead, I turned to Ginny. "Nimble told me some of what he heard those Black and Tans say to you."

Ginny's face was stricken.

"That more than pestering, they were actually threatening you." A fact I wished I'd known when I was demanding Nimble's release. "That they mentioned cutting your hair."

Her head dipped as if in humiliation, and I stepped closer to the table, shaking my head.

"No, no, no. Don't let them do that to you," I declared angrily. "They're the ones who should be ashamed of themselves, not you. Of all the scurrilous, revolting displays of masculine outrage. How dare they!" I turned away, gathering myself before I destroyed both women's opinions of me and my stability.

When I turned back, it was to discover them both eyeing me warily, but also with open curiosity. I chose to view that as an encouraging sign.

"I've read and heard the reports of the IRA cutting women's hair in retaliation or as a threat, but I'm beginning to suspect the Crown Forces also do it. Is that true?"

Mrs. Boyle was the first to react, scoffing. "Aye, they do. They just hush up the reports of it."

By censoring the newspapers.

I glanced at Ginny, who still seemed to be struggling to overcome her sense of shame over the incident with the Tans. "I suspect women who have been attacked by someone from the Crown Forces are also less likely to report the crime when it's doubtful anything will be done about it."

Mrs. Boyle agreed. "Aye. More likely to blame the poor girl than do anythin' to punish them that harmed her."

"When does it most often happen?" I had my suspicions, but I wanted to hear it from them.

"Durin' raids." Ginny finally spoke, her eyes trained on the table before her. "They separate ye from the others, in another corner or room, and hold the others back with guns or cudgels while 'tis done."

My heart constricted inside my chest, for Ginny spoke as if she had experience with this. Even Mrs. Boyle sensed it, for she reached across the table to clasp her hand.

I had experienced the raid at the Wicklow Hotel, or at least part of one, but the Crown Forces rarely conducted raids in the homes around Fitzwilliam Square, as most were owned by loyalists. Men like those we'd met at Lord French's dinner party—Tommy O'Shaughnessy, the city recorder; and Frank Brooke, the railway director; and their like. It was one of the reasons we'd rented this house.

But if the Crown Forces did decide to raid your home, you had no choice in the matter. If they knocked on your door—even in the middle of the night—they expected you to answer it immediately or else they'd simply ram it open. There wasn't even time to dress. And then you were supposed to follow every directive to the letter as they searched your home and your person, even rifling and overturning and sometimes destroying property. I'd heard complaints about Tans stealing things, as well. For there was no one to stop them, not even the commanding officers who should have done so. They simply looked the other way.

It reminded me uncomfortably of the raids I'd witnessed in Belgium. When the Germans came through to check that only the people denoted on the list that was required to be posted on each domicile's door were in residence. Or when they confiscated yet another round of supplies, be it food, livestock, blankets, metal, or mattresses—essentially looting the Belgians of almost all their worldly goods. By the end of the war, most of the citizens of Belgium and northeastern France were more than half starved and possessed but one or two sets of threadbare clothing, a blanket for every two to three people, and a bedstead but no mattress.

While the British Crown Forces' raids on the Irish were not to that extreme, that didn't mean the fear and intimidation were not real. Or that the Irish people weren't being deprived of valuables—both materially and intangibly.

"I take it you both know people who have been raided or assaulted?" I asked them both.

They nodded.

"And none of them have gotten justice."

They shook their heads.

I frowned. I knew this was war, and essentially civil war, at that. Yet, the government and Crown Forces seemed to all but strike out blindly much of the time. Whether intentionally or not, their policy appeared to mostly be all stick and no carrot. But I couldn't help but think that the carrot would go over much better and be far more restorative in the long run.

I looked at Ginny, thinking of how she walked home late in the evening and returned early the next morning. When she'd accepted the position, she'd seemed fine with the terms, but we hadn't really given her a choice. "Would you like for us to add board to your wages?" I asked, regretting the fact I'd never thought to ask her before.

She shook her head. "Nay. Mam needs me at home."

Needed her wages, I suspected, as much as her. But perhaps her mam was sick. Though I was curious, Ginny didn't offer more information, so I didn't pry. Still, it bothered me to think of her walking alone. It might be light in the summer, but come autumn and winter when it grew dark well before dinner and light after breakfast, I would have to come up with a solution. If we were here that long.

I pushed the worry from my head and returned upstairs to discover the RAMC surgeon was just leaving. Sidney closed the door behind him and then turned to find me watching him. He seemed tired and discouraged, but he held out his hand to me and drew me up two flights of stairs, past the parlor where Nimble had been examined and was now resting on the chaise longue—Sidney's orders—to the private sitting room adjoining our bedchamber.

We sat together on the Sheraton sofa, and he draped his arm around me, pulling me close to his side. He'd yet to change out of his riding attire, and I could smell the scent of horse clinging to him beneath that of his cologne and hair pomade as I leaned my head against his shoulder.

"I wish I'd been here," he said.

"Then *you* could have bearded the *snake* in his den," I quipped rather more sharply than I'd intended.

"The snake?"

"Ormonde de l'Épée Winter."

"Ah," he replied, not requiring any further explanation. More's the pity. "Well, whatever you said must have worked, because Nimble told me he heard someone upbraiding the men in the other room while he was being cleaned up."

"That must have been Inspector General Smith. He was rather more sensitive and sensible." Though still susceptible to puppet-strings, it seemed.

"Well, either way, I trust they've been warned away."

I lifted my head. "By Smith, but O might countermand that order." I pressed my finger to the center of his chest. "You need to speak with General Tudor and get this all sorted out." He was the man really in charge of the RIC. "And while you're at it, someone needs to take him to task for his men's deplorable behavior in assaulting women and forcibly cutting their hair. I don't care if it's in retaliation for what the IRA have done. It's brutish and cowardly."

Sidney grasped hold of my hand where I had been repeatedly stabbing him in emphasis, I was so riled. "I'll speak with him," he promised.

Though that didn't mean it would do any good. I'd met General Hugh Tudor at a dinner party. He'd been brought in to overhaul the fumbling RIC and their crumbling morale. He was a crony of the war secretary and a decided hawk. As such, he was more likely to advocate browbeating all the women in Ireland if it would bring the rebels to heel.

"Was he at Phoenix Park having a good gallop with you and Dicky, or is he back in London, chumming it up with Churchill and the others?"

Sidney's eyebrows arched at the snide tone of my voice, but he didn't comment on it. "I don't know where he is at the moment. But I'll make a point of seeking him out to speak with him. It will only further our ruse that I might be working covertly for him."

"And is the ruse working?" I struggled to keep my voice even. He hadn't been very forthcoming with any intelligence he'd learned in the past few weeks, making me wonder if there'd been any. I'd been content to overlook it, trusting he would share anything pertinent when he could, but after the day's events, I was more than a little impatient.

"Well enough that Winter tried to recruit me," he muttered dryly.

I sat up in surprise and alarm. "Outright?"

He clasped my elbows. "Is anything with him outright? But yes. Outright enough." His mouth twisted in distaste. "And in case you're wondering, I declined."

I settled back beside him, relieved but also a little confounded. I'd not known Sidney had spoken with O, and I wished he'd told me before now. "When did all this happen?"

"About a week ago." He grimaced. "About the same time I got a lead on where those phosgene cylinders might be."

"What?" I demanded, sitting upright again. Judging by his sheepish expression, I hadn't misheard. "Sidney!"

"I know, I know." He lifted his hands to my upper arms, but I shook them off. "I should have told you right away, but I wasn't certain the tip was any good. And you've been so consumed with finding Alec and getting justice for Miss Kavanagh, and well . . . I've been fairly useless in both endeavors." He rubbed the back of his neck. "I suppose I wanted to figure this one out on my own."

I scowled. "This isn't a contest. We're supposed to be a team, remember. Even if we are separated more than usual."

"I know," he repeated with a deep sigh. "It was rather illogical, I suppose."

Which wasn't like Sidney. But from the few comments he had made, I had been able to glean that the past few weeks hadn't been all fun and games. He might have been spending much of his time in pleasurable pursuits, but that didn't mean he hadn't been forced to stomach the company and opinions of people he would normally have eschewed if not outright scorned. It had turned his temperament a trifle bitter.

Relenting, I reached out to clasp his hand. "What was the lead?"

His fingers squeezed mine. "A letter uncovered during a raid from someone in the leadership of the Volunteers. It was unsigned. This person suggested that since we used poison gas during the war, we might not hesitate to use it against them. And that they should be prepared to retaliate in kind."

I couldn't fault the IRA leaders' logic. The British Army had developed and used poisoned gas on our enemies during the war, albeit not first. So if we'd been able to find a way to legitimize our using it then, what was to stop us from coming up with an excuse to use it now on the rebels? But the idea of poisonous gas being in the hands of these rebels, especially something as awful as phosgene—which essentially caused people to drown in their own beds as their lungs filled up with fluid—was still horrifying.

"The letter went on to suggest they start developing biological weapons." His eyebrows arched meaningfully. "And it also hinted at an unexpected benefactor who had a gift for them."

"Ardmore," I deduced.

He nodded. "My thought exactly."

"So if the letter is to be believed, and the benefactor is Ardmore, then he intended for those phosgene cylinders that were smuggled out of England off the Isle of Wight on the *Zebrina* and intercepted by that Irish crew off the coast of the island of Alderney to go to the republicans. But where has he been storing them the past three years? And where are they now?" I straightened to attention. "Or did you find them?"

"No. They thought they'd traced them to a bicycle shop in Great Britain Street, but it ended up being a bust."

"They?"

Sidney hesitated, telling me I wasn't going to like his answer. "Lieutenants Bennett and Ames."

I nearly cursed at his mention of my former Secret Service colleague. The one who I'd led to believe I was expecting a child, in order to escape his suspicion.

"They're good contacts, Ver. Especially if we want to locate this phosgene before the rebels use it."

"I'm not sure that I trust it in the hands of Bennett and Ames and their like either," I retorted.

"Yes, well, we Brits already have plenty of the stuff in storage," he countered drolly. "They hardly need Ardmore's stash. Let's just hope that even if compassion and human decency don't reign, that at least cooler heads will see how irreparably damaged our reputation would be across the world if we used the stuff on our own citizens."

We could never take the high moral ground with any nation ever again if we did.

But the question remained . . . "What do the rebels intend to do with it? Or are they truly only eager to have it to counteract an attack by us?" And what was to stop them from changing their minds?

Sidney shrugged.

I swiped a hand across my forehead, settling back beside Sidney so that our shoulders brushed. "I really wish you weren't becoming chummy with Bennett." I didn't trust him, and I didn't trust the IRA not to leap to the wrong conclusion because of their association.

"I never said we were becoming chummy. Simply that he and Ames have their uses."

I eyed him askance, failing to see the difference if he was drinking with them at Kidd's Back and exchanging information.

"Take your pal Delagrange."

"Pal?" I repeated incredulously.

"Bennett told me he was a bit of a wash-out in the army. That he's been chucking his weight about. But they all know why he's here and how he ended up in the intelligence unit."

"Then he's not well-liked?"

"Not by anyone with sense or seniority. At least, according to Bennett."

Who, I suspected, possessed the opinions and level of intellect of the average intelligence officer, so it was perhaps a fair assessment.

"He also said Delagrange had recently filed a malicious-injury claim." From the look in Sidney's eyes, I could tell he'd been saving this juicy morsel of information for last, on purpose.

"When?"

"Approximately two and a half months ago. He was awarded one thousand pounds. Or so he told everyone. Though he's been uncharacteristically silent as to the details of those injuries."

"This doesn't make any sense," I exclaimed, gesturing with my hands as I laid out my points, as if somehow that might make things clearer. "Mr. Kavanagh serves on the committee who reviews malicious injury and damage claims. His daughter is supposedly assaulted by members of the IRA because of it, and because she's stepping out with a British soldier. A soldier who we now know had recently been awarded compensation for one of these claims. Yet, no one mentions this despite the fact that, on the surface, it would appear to be even more evidence against the IRA. Instead, Kavanagh is wary of Delagrange, and Delagrange warns me away from the family, against investigating. Why?"

I thought about what Wick had said about their being evidence of collusion between the Crown Forces and Castle authorities in making false claims, but I didn't know how or if that fit here.

Sidney echoed my confusion. "I don't know. Though—"

I looked up at him as he broke off, waiting for him to continue.

He smiled regretfully. "When I first heard what happened today, I wondered . . ."

"If Delagrange sent those Tans to pester our staff," I finished for him. "I did, too." He'd been warned to stay away from me, but that didn't preclude him finding other ways to retaliate. "We need to know the details of that malicious-injury claim."

"That's why I arranged a meeting for tomorrow with Mr. O'Shaughnessy. You're welcome to come, too," he added when I turned to him in approval.

I considered, but then declined, trusting him. "No, in this

instance, I suspect you'll get more from O'Shaughnessy without me. *I'm* going to try to speak with the Kavanaghs again and then track down some of Miss Kavanagh's friends."

"Something Wickham said?" he guessed.

"Yes." I told him the points Wick had made about the timing and location of the assault as well.

He eyed me carefully. "What about the claims that fellow made at the Wicklow Hotel?"

I met his gaze levelly. "He hadn't heard even a whisper about it."

"Really?" I could tell Sidney was as much struck by this as I had been.

"Not about a body in a bog, *or* a spy being executed." The final word stuck in my throat, coming out a bit mangled. "But he's going to ask around."

Sidney nodded somewhat reticently. Perhaps because he knew how much I wanted the rumors to be untrue. But then that raised questions about why Tom had lied, and I had no good answers. No reassuring ones anyway.

We lapsed into silence, both occupied by our own solemn thoughts.

After a few minutes, I allowed my head to tip sideways onto Sidney's shoulder. "Should we check on Nimble?"

Sidney stirred enough to drape his arm around me. "Let him rest. He's not in any danger."

Danger. I ruminated on that word. On the concept. And wondered whether we would know if we were in danger before it was too late.

CHAPTER 19

I arrived at the Kavanaghs' door at perhaps the most inauspicious moment of the day. But then, of course, I'd planned it that way. Rain poured from the sky, racing along the edges of the streets toward the gutters and drumming insistently against the dome of my umbrella. Though that didn't stop the Kavanaghs from pretending not to be home.

I'd seen the telltale twitch of the curtains in the drawing room window after my card had been sent up. The maid's pink cheeks when she delivered their lie only confirmed it. I smiled at Mary reassuringly, letting her know I understood. It wasn't as if I hadn't expected it. Still, when I'd seen the sky darkening and smelled the approaching rain, I'd thought to take a gamble.

It had failed, and now my hem was wet despite my raincoat and buckle galoshes, but all was not lost. Mostly thanks to Ginny, who had proved more forthcoming with information this morning than she had any other. When I asked her about the homes in the area, she proved to be familiar with most of their owners and staff. Some deft questioning yielded the probable identity of the young lady I'd seen watching me and Mrs. Gardiner from her window. Miss Fiona Fairbanks.

Miss Fairbanks lived with her parents and two siblings in the house across the street and two south from the Kavanaghs. Her mother was a veritable stickler for propriety, much like Mrs. Kavanagh, and prided herself on being deeply religious, though her staff said she only knew ten Bible verses altogether, and those had been stitched onto samplers placed throughout the house. Ginny had smiled impishly, revealing a charming gap between her front teeth, when I'd correctly guessed that a number of them were from Proverbs.

Hearing all this and deducing that, as the middle child, Miss Fairbanks was likely straining against her mother's rigidity—particularly as it applied to what had happened to her friend—I took another gamble. I strode away from the Kavanaghs, ostensibly to return home, but then halfway down the street, crossed to the other side to double back. I stopped long enough at the Fairbanks residence to deliver my card and a note into the hands of one of the staff, and then continued north to the Pepper Cannister church.

Once I'd wrangled open the overly large door and stepped inside, I discovered it to be quiet and dry. The interior was deep, but not wide, with two balconies running along the sides and a number of stained-glass round-topped windows. The central window depicted the martyrdom of St. Stephen, for whom the church had been named. I wandered for a time, and spoke briefly to the vicar, who told me Mount Street, in the middle of which the church stood, had once been the place where criminals were executed, and so had been named Mount for the mounting block before the gallows. Whether this was true or not, it seemed a rather morbid name for a street. When I suggested as much, he told me Misery Hill lay just a few blocks north.

Following this history and geography lesson, I settled into a pew near the middle of the right side, allowing ample space for Miss Fairbanks to join me if she appeared. I'd begun to fear my ploy had not worked, that her grief and curiosity would not prove enough of an inducement, when I heard the swish of fabric hurrying down the aisle.

She paused beside the pew, gazing down at me, her expression one of half terror, half triumph. "Mrs. Kent?"

"Yes."

"I'm Miss Fairbanks," she stated, as if there were any doubt and I might be here waiting for someone else.

"Won't you have a seat."

She looked at first as if she might refuse, but then she removed her own raincoat, draping it over the end of the pew, and sat down beside me with a thump. I took the opportunity during this flurry of movement to study her.

She was a pretty girl, if not as beautiful as Miss Kavanagh had been. Her copper hair was neatly tied up with ribbons and pins and her face was sprinkled with freckles I suspected her mother despaired of. I sincerely hoped she didn't make her daughter take milk baths, thinking that would make them go away. Her nose was upturned and her teeth had a slight overbite, but she presented a tidy, restrained picture.

She pleated the fabric of her azure skirt as she stared straight ahead. "You said you wanted to discuss Miss Kavanagh."

"As I understand it, the two of you were friends."

She nodded, her face rippling with pain.

"Then I'm sorry for your loss," I told her sincerely.

She swallowed, but her voice still shook when she spoke. "You know, you might be the first person to tell me so." She turned to look at me then, a single tear trailing down her cheek.

My heart went out to the girl. How lonely she must be in her grief.

I extracted the handkerchief tucked in my sleeve. "Here, my dear." I patted the hand resting in her lap as she dabbed at her eyes with the opposite. "It is difficult to lose a friend. Sometimes more difficult than losing family, for we choose our friends, don't we?"

"Or rather they choose us." She tried to smile, but it emerged more as a grimace.

"Quite," I said, understanding what she was trying to convey. "I take it your family was not as sympathetic to Miss Kavanagh after what happened to her." It was not difficult to guess when the girl had not been consoled for her grief.

Her lips trembled and her brow creased as she struggled to withhold her tears. "No." She inhaled a raspy breath, before remarking angrily. "Mother . . . she said it must have been her own fault. And after . . . after she died, she said . . ." She hiccupped. "She said . . ."

I pressed my hand to hers, halting her. "I think I can guess what she said."

There were people who deemed that those who committed suicide automatically went to hell, but I had to believe that God was more compassionate than that.

She sniffed and nodded.

"But Miss Kavanagh was in extreme emotional distress, wasn't she?" I pointed out.

"Yes," she sobbed.

"Then I don't think we can say she was in her right mind."

"Maybe." Her voice trailed away along with her thoughts, and I wondered if she was thinking of something particular.

"Did she talk to you? After the assault?"

She turned to look at me, but I could tell her gaze wasn't completely focused on me.

"Were you allowed to see her?"

She blinked, coming to herself. "I snuck over to see her. When my parents were away."

"And did she tell you anything? Did she recognize her attackers?"

Her voice grew tight. "They wore masks."

"Yes, but she might have heard them speak. Or perhaps she smelled something distinctive."

"I . . . I don't know. She didn't say anything to me," she insisted, but her sudden agitation suggested otherwise.

"Miss Fairbanks," I said, and then repeated myself, waiting for her to stop wringing my handkerchief between her fingers and look at me. "You understand I'm only here to help." I peered at her earnestly. "I was asked to look into her assault, to figure out who did this to her. To ensure that whoever hurt her can never hurt anyone else. I think Miss Kavanagh would want that, don't you?"

She nodded tentatively.

"But I can't *do* that if no one will tell me what they know."

She sniffed again. "I . . . I don't *know* who attacked her. Not for sure."

"But you know something. Something that makes you suspicious of someone." I could see in her eyes that I was correct. "I'm not asking you to tell me that you witnessed who did this to her. I'm only asking you to tell me what you did see, or observe, or hear, or were told. During the day of the assault and the days before and after. Anything that might, *just might* be pertinent. Can you do that?"

She nodded, lowering her eyes to her lap as if to gather herself. But as the seconds ticked by, still she hesitated, and I wondered if she was afraid of someone. Not her parents, surely. Not sufficiently anyway, or she would never have snuck out of her house to meet me.

Then I recalled something about the day I'd seen her watching me from her window.

"Does this have something to do with Lieutenant Delagrange?"

She startled, turning to look at me with wide eyes that then turned to pleading. "Be-before we left the soiree that night," she whispered. "Kitty told me that the lieutenant had asked her to meet him in her garden after her parents went to bed. She . . . she was thinking about agreeing. But only because she had been planning to break it off with him," she hastened to add as if I might think the worst of her. "And she thought that might be a good time."

Alone. In her garden. In the dark.

I had to question Miss Kavanagh's naivete, but that didn't make any of what happened to her her fault. Though it did better explain why she had been out there in the first place.

"When you saw her after the assault, did she tell you whether he'd been there? Did she say if he was her attacker?"

She shook her head, tears streaming down her cheeks. "And I didn't ask."

Something, it was clear, she regretted. Would probably regret to her dying day, no matter what I said.

We sat silently for a time, side by side, as she grieved, and I contemplated the probability of the attacker being anyone *other* than Delagrange now that I knew he'd asked Miss Kavanagh to meet him in her garden that night. It would explain why he'd been so intent on warning me away. Though I was still baffled as to his motive and why Mr. Kavanagh seemed wary of him. I supposed he might have suspected Miss Kavanagh's intent to end their relationship, and so he'd made plans to punish her, but that seemed rather extreme. There must be more to it. Something to do with that malicious-injury claim he'd filed.

And as for that testimony Earnán the footman had supposedly given, that had no doubt been reported by Delagrange. Reported and sanctioned and *repeated* to me by Johnstone, despite the fact they knew about Delagrange's threats against me. Threats concerning the Kavanaghs. How had that not raised red flags? Delagrange had probably intimidated Earnán into quitting the Kavanaghs employ as well, just to cover his tracks.

It was all beginning to fit together in my mind, but that didn't make it proof the courts would accept. Miss Fairbanks's statement was but one piece. There was much more to uncover if we were to bring Delagrange and his accomplices to justice, starting with tracking down Earnán.

Once Miss Fairbanks had herself more in hand, I asked her to contact me if she thought of anything else, anything at all. "Even the smallest seemingly insignificant detail could prove to be important."

She nodded, and then insisted on leaving first. It was only as she was pushing through the overlarge door that I recalled I'd forgotten to ask her about Miss Kavanagh's nurse. I'd wanted her impression of her, but the girl was rattled enough without me chasing after her.

A few minutes later when I did follow her out onto Mount Street, I discovered the rainstorm had moved off, leaving behind but a muzzy drizzle. Determined to make the most of the day now that the heavy rain had passed, I set off for the Bank of Ireland. It had been some time since I'd spoken with Mr. Finnegan, having allowed Sidney to handle our affairs there. I hadn't precisely been avoiding the bank manager after our last awkward encounter, but I certainly hadn't been eager to seek him out. However, armed with the knowledge from Wick's latest message, I was curious to hear Mr. Finnegan's opinion.

The note had been delivered by a newspaper errand boy that morning. With his typical brevity, Wick had written *No bog body found,* letting me know Tom's report of such had either been fictitious or so secretive that not even Wick could discover the details. He'd also given me a name, and I could only presume it was Miss Kavanagh's cousin, the one Mrs. Gardiner had mentioned had been killed by the IRA and made an example of. But Wick had made a notation. *Daniel Keogh–irr.* I deduced the *irr* must be an abbreviation for "irregular," and this was Wick's way of telling me there was something odd about Mr. Keogh's death. Well, odder than it already was.

I'd dashed off a note, asking for more information or another meeting. But the errand boy had already run off and I had hesitated to send Nimble off on such a task while he was still recovering. He'd moved more slowly about the house that morning, and I could tell he was in pain, but he refused anything offered to him for it. Ginny and Mrs. Boyle had taken to cosseting him, and I was grateful. So for now the note still rested in my pocket, along with another for Nancy O'Brien at the Castle.

After speaking with Miss Fairbanks and realizing how imperative it was that I found Earnán, the footman, I was doubly glad I'd already composed a letter to Nancy asking her to meet me for drinks. If there was some way Nancy could get a peek into that file I'd seen on Johnstone's desk—female staff were always being overlooked—and I could convince her to do so, maybe she would find Earnán's full name and current address printed there. It was a long shot and a big favor to ask of her, especially on such a slim acquaintance, and I felt a bit slimy initiating a friendship with such ulterior motives, but such was the nature of intelligence work. It wasn't the first time I'd been forced to go to such lengths.

Upon reaching the bank, I was forced to cool my heels for a short time, enjoying a surprisingly good cup of Earl Grey tea one of the clerks brought me while I waited. When I was finally shown back to give Finnegan my latest report for C, he apologized for the delay, but I brushed it aside as inconsequential. After all, he *was* conducting actual business here in addition to his role for C. However, I didn't fail to note how anxious he seemed. It was clear something had happened to overset his customary composure.

"I've but one piece of correspondence for you," he informed me as he unlocked the cabinet where he stored them.

"Thank you," I replied as he passed it to me after closing and relocking the drawer.

I eyed him curiously as he stood stiffly by his desk, as if

waiting for me to either say something or leave. At one point, he even rocked back on his heels.

"Was there anything else?" he finally prompted. "Have you uncovered something?"

"For a time, I thought I had," I admitted, actually starting to feel unnerved by his behavior and the strangled tone of his voice. "Someone reported that the body of an alleged spy had been sunk in a bog to the west."

"Oh?"

"But I've since learned it was false. Are you quite alright, Mr. Finnegan?" I asked, unable to continue to ignore his strange conduct.

"Yes. Yes, of course," he insisted. When I continued to scrutinize him, obviously unconvinced, his shoulders crumpled. "No, Mrs. Kent. No, everything is not alright." He sank down in his chair. "Everything is definitely not alright."

I perched on one of the armchairs opposite, watching as he removed his round spectacles and rubbed his hand over his eyes. "Perhaps I can help?"

He laughed humorlessly, drawing a frown to my face. "Don't misunderstand me. It's nothing to do with your abilities. It's only . . ." He heaved a weary sigh. "Why couldn't you have just gone back to London when you were told?"

I straightened in affront, but his voice was more mournful than accusatory. Whatever he had to say next, I was not going to like it.

He replaced his glasses, looking up at me resignedly. "There's evidence that MacAlister has switched sides. That he's working for Collins himself. And that's why he disappeared and severed all communication. He feared we were on to him."

My shock upon hearing this was not as great as I expected. Which only made me angry, not only at Finnegan, but at myself. "What evidence?" I demanded.

He shook his head. "I'm not authorized to share that with

you, but surely you can see some of the pieces beginning to line up. He vanishes, no trace to be found. And yet the IRA make examples of spies and touts. He leaves behind multiple messages, telling you to go back to London, to stop looking for him." He paused. "That is what he left for you in his safe deposit box, isn't it?"

I scowled.

"A plea for you to return home. I imagine he even appealed to your husband. Right there, he risked revealing himself, all because he cares for you and doesn't want to see you come to harm searching for him." He tilted his head in thought. "Though, I suppose he might also have wished to preserve your memory of him as a hero rather than a traitor."

This struck me square in the chest.

His lips quirked self-deprecatingly. "I suppose that's why *I* was so reluctant to tell you. I wanted to preserve that memory for you, as well. Sentimental of me, I guess. But there's enough harsh reality to go around in this world. Especially these days."

"This is madness!" I finally managed to reply. "He's no traitor. Why, if you knew what he did during the war . . ." I broke off before I said too much. "I don't believe it."

"You will," he replied with a calm implacability that unsettled me. "You're a highly intelligent woman, Mrs. Kent. You'll begin to put the pieces together." His sympathetic gaze seared like fire. "You already are."

My hands flexed around the arms of the chair, wanting to hit him, to choke him. To make him stop spouting these lies.

"Go back to London, Mrs. Kent. This is no place for you. Not when Collins must certainly have you and your husband on his watch list."

I narrowed my eyes, for this felt like a threat.

"He may have restrained himself thus far for MacAlister's sake, but that won't last. Not if you keep digging. Not when they've given you every chance to back down. Those G-Men who were assassinated only received one warning, you know." His fingers tapped a rapid staccato against his desk. "This source who told you a spy had been sunk in a bog." Ending his rapping abruptly, he reached into this desk to extract a cigarette case. His eyebrows arched as he removed one, closing it with a snap. "Who do you think sent him?"

It was no more than I'd suspected, no more than I'd feared, but still it enraged me. The very idea!

Finnegan lit his fag and took a drag, before exhaling a long plume of smoke. It appeared to settle his nerves, which had been jangling since I'd entered his office. "For the sake of yourself and your husband, and any remaining affection you hold for MacAlister, go home, Mrs. Kent." He pointed with this cigarette hand vaguely toward the east. "To London."

This last statement was more than I could endure, so before I said something I would regret, I jumped to my feet and charged out of the office. Fighting tears of fury, I crossed College Green, leaping gingerly over the puddles in the pavement. I paused in the middle of the traffic island, next to the statue of Irish politician Henry Grattan, unconsciously echoing his stance with his hand lifted toward Trinity College as I pressed mine to the limestone pedestal on which he stood.

My thoughts raced, whirling through my mind faster than I could catch them. Alec, a traitor?! It seemed impossible.

And yet . . . not.

Alec had always gone his own way, sometimes imprudently. But after the lengths he'd gone to for his country during the war, I couldn't believe he would suddenly abandon all that for the likes of these rebels who were certain to fail against the might of the British Empire in their ultimate quest for a republic. Or could I?

A sickening uncertainty filled me as I lifted my face to observe my surroundings. The impressive façades of the immense buildings with their limestone pillars, the bustling traffic of trams and bicycles and carts, the hodgepodge of humanity, from ladies in silk and lace to dirty children darting about in flat caps and short pants. Two Black and Tans stood on the opposite corner, hailing to their comrades in a military lorry as it trundled past, kicking up dirt and heedless as always of those around it who scampered to get out of its way with looks of both trepidation and loathing stamped across their features.

I wasn't blind or oblivious to the problems here, to the failings of the British government, and the simmering resentment of the populace. The Irish might be considered British citizens, but always second or third class. Over my shoulder loomed the Bank of Ireland, which had once housed the Irish Parliament, but they'd lost even that with the Act of Union. They'd played the game of politics to get it back, and even though they'd succeeded, there was still no Home Rule.

When they'd forced the issue by electing those who vowed to refuse to take their seats in Westminster and instead create their own Dáil Éireann, their own parliament in Dublin, the government had reacted by proscribing it, their political party, and numerous other Irish organizations of national importance. The rebels had sent delegates to the Paris Peace Conference, asking the American president to acknowledge their rights to exist as a small nation, in accordance with the statements he'd made in his Fourteen Points, but they'd been all but ignored and told to wait to address his League of Nations—something that it was now uncertain the American Congress would even approve joining.

The ambushes and raids and burnings of RIC barracks, and the murders of policemen, I could not condone. But I also accepted their necessity when one was fighting an intelligence war. From the rebels' standpoint, they could either take out the British sources of information or wait to be picked off one by one and see the revolution crumble like every rebellion before it. There was no other option. It was a bloody, but necessary, strategy.

Having had their eyes blinded and ears deafened, the British government's solution had seemed to be to lash out indiscriminately. To recruit demobilized soldiers from the war who were desperate for work and use them to fill the shrinking ranks of the RIC and send them into the cities and countryside to police a population who was hostile to them. Time and time again, I was reminded of scenes from Belgium, of the Germans' mistreatment of the citizens of the countries they occupied. But in this case, it was *us*, the British, who were doing the mistreating. *We* were the Germans and the Irish were the Belgians.

Alec and I had both risked life and limb, time and time again, to not only ensure the Allies' victory but to see Belgium liberated. How could we not see the parallels in this situation and feel betrayed? Terribly, terribly betrayed. For what was the use of principles and high morals if one was not prepared to expect them of oneself?

So maybe, *maybe* Alec had switched sides. Maybe he *was* working for Collins. Or maybe he'd merely pretended to switch sides.

I pushed away from the statue angrily. *Maybe* wasn't good enough.

CHAPTER 20

I returned home, both surprised and relieved to find Sidney there. Until I saw that he was about to leave again. However, he took one look at my face and set his hat back on its hook.

"Won't you be missed?" I asked as he reached for my hand.

"Lawrence will understand."

I didn't argue, wanting nothing so much as to pour out everything I'd just learned to him. Which was exactly what I did once we were closeted in our private sitting room. I was too agitated to sit, instead pacing before the pair of windows that overlooked the garden. It had grown stuffy in the house after the rain, and so Sidney opened them both to the cool afternoon breeze before pivoting to sit on one of their ledges as he listened. I could hear that I was rambling as I expounded on my thoughts, but he didn't interrupt me, perhaps knowing I needed to purge it all from my head where it had begun to cycle back on itself.

When I finally did stop, making one last pivot toward him, it was to find him watching me intently. "What are you thinking?" I asked, unable to read his expression with my own worries clouding my judgment.

He pulled me toward him, draping his arms around my waist. "I'm thinking, you've given this a lot of deliberation. I'm thinking, this isn't the first time you've considered the possibility."

"It's not the first time you've considered it either," I retorted accusingly.

"It isn't," he answered steadily. "But I don't know Xavier like you do."

When I didn't respond, but simply stood there staring at the flash of my wedding ring in the sunlight and the paleness of my hands resting against the shoulders of his deep gray coat, he prompted me. "What do you want to do, Ver?"

I scrutinized his features. His sun-bronzed skin from all his outdoor pursuits and his square jaw that could lock in stubbornness. His full lips that could feather so lightly over my skin and his midnight-blue eyes that deepened almost to black when he made love to me. I knew he would do whatever I asked, and that was why I hesitated. Because my decision didn't affect just me, but also him. And it could place us both in unspeakable danger.

I grasped his face in my hands, feeling the beginnings of stubble abrading my fingertips.

Yet, I couldn't turn my back on this. I couldn't turn my eyes away from the truth. The truth about Alec. The truth about what our government, of what the rebels, of what *humanity* was capable of. I thought I'd already seen the worst of it in Belgium and France, but I was learning there were degrees to everything. And I couldn't help but feel somehow I had a part to play here, even if it was just as a witness.

Sidney smiled sadly and nodded, having read my thoughts.

"I have to know," I finally said as a tear slid down my cheek. "Beyond a shadow of a doubt."

He brushed the tear aside with his thumb. "I know, Ver."

I sniffed. "Which means I have to find Collins. That's where I'll find the truth about Alec. Dead or alive."

His brow furrowed and his hands flexed where they rested against my hips, and I knew he was fighting the urge to forbid it. For finding Collins could spell my death sentence.

There was no doubt in my or his mind that I could do it.

I knew what Collins looked like. I knew some of the places Alec had reported that he frequented, and while some of those places could now be suspect, the information contained in his earliest reports had more than likely been accurate.

If I were completely honest with myself, I had to concede that the main reason I *hadn't* found Collins yet was because I was afraid to. Which had undoubtedly hampered my search for Alec. I'd known I needed to adjust the hours of my searching and the locations I frequented. I'd known I needed to follow the trails left by Collins's associates, but I hadn't. Out of fear.

No more could I let that impede me. I had to commit now to this wholeheartedly, to embrace the uncertainty, or I might as well return to London. If our life here had been like walking a tightrope before, now it would be like doing so without a net.

"Are you certain that's the best approach?" Sidney resisted.

"It's the only one."

He continued to frown but didn't argue.

"We also still have those phosgene cylinders to locate." Though I supposed it was some relief to know we weren't the only ones searching for poisonous gas that might have fallen into the hands of the republicans. At least, Bennett and Ames and the rest of British Intelligence appeared to be aware of it, thanks to that letter they'd intercepted during a raid. But they didn't know of Lord Ardmore's involvement.

"We also have some new information pertaining to Miss Kavanagh's attacker." I relayed what Miss Fairbanks had told me about Lieutenant Delagrange asking her to meet him in the garden.

"That certainly explains some things. Then I take it you suspect Delagrange and his companions were the ones who assaulted Miss Kavanagh and cut her hair. That blaming the local IRA brigade was merely a convenient excuse."

"It looks that way. And yet Delagrange continued to show

up at their home, paying her court. Remember her mother said she hadn't wanted to see him."

Sidney scowled in disapproval. "She made it sound as if it was because her daughter was ashamed of her hair having been cut, but what if she'd not wanted to see him for a different reason entirely."

I tried to imagine what that must have been like. Had she known the man courting her had been one of her attackers? Had she told anyone? Or had she kept silent, suffering alone. I hoped that if she *had* told someone, it hadn't been her parents. Otherwise, their actions that followed were unspeakably cruel.

"It was no wonder she hadn't been in her right mind and had chosen to drink that sleeping draught when it was left where she could get to it."

"Is that how she died?" Sidney asked, and I realized I'd never told him what the neighbor had said. I could tell from his expression that he found it as unsatisfactory as I did the first time I'd heard it.

"I've been meaning to track down the nurse and speak to her about it, as well as the footman. Speaking of which . . ." I pulled the two letters I'd meant to post from my pocket. "If you're going out again, will you post these?"

"Of course." He glanced at them absently, pausing on Wick's.

"He found no mention of a bog body, and he discovered that Miss Kavanagh's cousin who was allegedly killed by the IRA was named Daniel Keogh, though he noted there was something irregular about his death. What?" I asked, having noted the paroxysm that had spread across his face. "What is it?"

"Daniel Keogh was the name of Miss Kavanagh's cousin?"

"Yes." I knew I'd spoken clearly enough before, so his reaction to his name must be for another reason.

"The malicious-injury claim Delagrange filed was against a Daniel Keogh."

"That's what Mr. O'Shaughnessy told you." In all the tumult, I'd forgotten about Sidney's meeting with him.

He nodded. "A case Mr. Kavanagh considered recusing himself from, but then changed his mind about at the last minute."

I frowned. "Definitely suspicious. But what was the timing of all of this?"

"Mid-April."

My gaze hardened. Just a couple of weeks before Miss Kavanagh's assault. "It would be good to know when Daniel Keogh's death occurred. And why Wick deemed it irregular."

Sidney tapped Wick's letter, correctly deducing its contents. "I'll also see what else I can find out. Meanwhile"—he squeezed my hip—"we're going to dinner and the theater with the Wyndham-Quins tonight."

"Oh yes," I groaned. "I forgot."

"I thought you liked Helen."

"I do, but . . ." I exhaled, unequal to the task of putting it all into words.

He seemed to understand anyway, pulling me closer. "We can never really tell who our friends are here, can we?"

I could see that this also weighed on him. "No."

A taut smile curled the corners of his mouth. "I suppose this was what it was like in Belgium."

"Yes and no. There I was never static, never in one place for long," I explained. "So it was harder to fall susceptible to the natural human desire for connection. As an intelligence agent, you can only allow the illusion of intimacy, never the actual thing."

"Except with a partner." His voice had lowered coyly, but I could see the shadow of Alec in his eyes, the knowledge of our past connection.

I draped my arm around his neck. "One you trust? To a certain degree." I stared into his eyes, letting him see my vulnerability. "But you're more than a partner, aren't you?"

"Yes. Ever. Always."

When his mouth met mine, I allowed myself to fall into the kiss, wanting to forget everything else except Sidney and my love for him.

Sometime later, while Sidney went out to run a few errands and post my letters, I removed from my handbag the missive Mr. Finnegan had given me, before I began dressing for dinner. I'd recognized it as being from one of the telegraph offices, and opened it to read the wire Kathleen had sent me in our code. It was brief, by necessity, but she was warning me that O was asking questions about me, and C was requesting my report on the encounter.

Truth be told, I'd expected as much, and I'd already encoded my version of events in the letter I'd given Finnegan earlier. O had undoubtedly painted my actions in the worst possible light, but there was nothing I could do to stop him from doing so. I just hoped those who knew better weren't swayed by whatever snake oil he'd tried to sell them.

Had I but known what was to come, I would have tried harder to enjoy that evening with Dicky and Helen, laughing over drinks at Jammet's and the players on stage at the Gaiety Theatre. I might have entered into our plans to see Pauline Frederick in *Paid in Full* at the Palace Cinema with a bit more gusto instead of wishing I was combing the hot spots Michael Collins—and hopefully Alec—frequented. I certainly would have tried to enjoy all of those flush summer days in early July just a little bit more, or at least prepared myself. For there was a storm brewing over Ireland, and if we'd thought all the things that had come before were bad, things were only going to get worse.

It began the next day over breakfast.

Since our arrival in late May, we'd begun receiving a variety of newspapers espousing all sorts of different views to keep abreast on what was occurring, including the Dáil Éireann's official daily news sheet, the *Irish Bulletin*. While it might have been written off as mere propaganda by some, most of the people Sidney and I had delicately prodded—even staunch unionists—had agreed it was largely accurate and fair-handed in its reporting. Of course, the government had outlawed its printing, but somehow it continued to evade detection, and new editions appeared on our doorstep and others across Ireland, as well as being mailed to America and other countries in Europe and perhaps even farther.

That morning, the *Irish Bulletin* and The *Freeman's Journal* published reports of the mutinies of members of the RIC at Listowel and Killarney. But it wasn't the mutinies themselves—which seemed to have been for the most part peaceful—that caused alarm, but the accounts made by the constables. It had begun in mid-June when they'd been ordered to turn over their RIC barracks to the British military, and informed they were to be transferred to other postings. An order they'd refused. But the real trouble had started when they were paid a visit by not only General Tudor but also the newly appointed district commissioner of Munster, Lieutenant Colonel Gerard Bryce Ferguson Smyth, and a detachment of British troops. Smyth had appeared in full dress uniforms, including Distinguished Service Order and Bar, and campaign medals. Whether he thought this would overawe the mutineers or make them cower, I didn't know, but I could imagine the scene at this remote RIC barracks as Constable Jeremiah Mee described it.

Smyth had then proceeded to address the constables. He'd allegedly told them that if a civilian didn't follow an order immediately or appeared suspicious in any way, for example with their hands in their pockets, that they should shoot them down. "You may make mistakes occasionally and innocent persons may be shot, but this cannot be helped and you are bound to get the right persons sometimes. The more you shoot, the better I will like you, and I assure you that not one policeman will get into trouble for shooting any man." He claimed, "Sinn Féin has had all the sport up to the present and we are going to have it now." Other purported remarks were equally disturbing,

If true, it was shocking.

"Do you know Lieutenant Colonel Smyth?" I asked Sidney.

His brow was scored with deep furrows, telling me he was equally concerned. "Not personally. But he was decorated multiple times for bravery during the war. Even lost an arm."

I lifted the paper. "I don't know anything about this Constable Mee, of course, but I can't spot any obvious deceptions in his claims. He states quite frankly at the beginning of the article that he and his fellow constables were on the side of the British, and fully anticipated us winning the war. That their objection to handing over the barracks to the military and being transferred was the fact that, after the conflict, the British would leave, while win or lose, they would have to return to live in Listowel with a potentially hostile populace. If they were going to be held accountable for the actions of the Crown Forces, they wanted to at least have some control over the way those actions were carried out, and some ability to protect their own friends and family." I paused to scan the article. "Though, I have to wonder what their political opinions are now that they're no longer members of the RIC."

Sidney continued to frown at the page in front of him, but he didn't appear to be reading it. The very notion of any commander of our Crown Forces issuing such an order was disturbing enough. It must be outrageous to Sidney, who had once served.

"Could the reports be false?" I asked, trying to maintain a healthy skepticism until I possessed all the details. When this made no dent in Sidney's expression, I probed the matter from a different angle. "Could Smyth have been speaking out of frustration?"

This succeeded in drawing Sidney's gaze. "No, I cannot believe a man of Smyth's reputation would have issued such orders without being explicitly given them himself." A muscle in his cheek jumped as his gaze dipped to the table again. "And one does not question one's orders once they're given. At least, not openly."

Seeing the bitter twist to his lips, I spoke delicately. "Does that mean you believe Mee's account?"

He scrubbed a hand down his face and then through his hair. "I don't know what I believe." He cradled his chin in his hand, partially covering his mouth as if to stop himself from continuing. "And that's what troubles me. That these orders might be real."

I understood he was thinking of more than Listowel, but the papers we'd uncovered in Belgium and the things we'd witnessed or experienced since our arrival. The letter from Max that had been redacted.

It had been some time now since Max's last correspondence. I'd known he would be busy with the Henley Royal Regatta and the social season events which surrounded it. As an earl and a highly sought-after bachelor, he couldn't shirk them all. But the lack of communication made me suspicious. Not of Max, but of the postal delivery chain we'd thought would remain undetected. Now, I wasn't so sure.

"They're recruiting former officers now," Sidney said gravely. "To supplement the dwindling police numbers."

I wondered if this was another area in which Tudor or others had tried to recruit him. Perhaps O wasn't the only one who had approached him.

"I suppose they need someone to keep the Black and Tans in line," I remarked, taking a sip of my now cold tea.

"Not for that."

I turned to him in confusion.

"They're going to form their own elite units."

"For what?"

Sidney didn't answer this, but I could tell it bothered him. And I supposed it bothered me, too. If you were going to go to the trouble of recruiting a group of experienced demobilized officers, why wouldn't you give them men to command? Why form them into their own corps? What did they intend to do with them?

"We have army battalions stationed here," Sidney ruminated. "If they're so desperate they need former army officers to maintain the peace, why not just use the existing forces they already have trained?"

"Because then it's all but an admission that it's war, not just some . . . campaign of terror perpetuated by a few extremists with guns in conflict with the police. Those paid assassins and murder gangs, as they so carefully refer to them, become a brigade, an army." I arched my eyebrows. "A rival republic." I threw down my napkin and pushed to my feet. "And while I understood their initial resistance in escalating the conflict to such, now they're doing so with a subpar force while still pretending not to."

I could only hope cooler heads would soon prevail, and an acceptable truce and plan for finally implementing Dominion Home Rule was offered. It seemed inevitable that would be what it would all come to. So why not avoid the months or years or decades of casualties and festering animosities that would occur from not doing so now?

Fortunately, cooler heads did prevail at Bellewstown that day. We drove up for the race meeting with Dicky and Helen, expecting it to be an unexceptional outing except for the winning or losing of a few pounds. However, a relatively large contingent of the British Army overran the racecourse, supposedly with the intent of deterring the Irish Republican Police force that the shadow government was encouraging to operate in the absence of the RIC, who had abandoned many of the rural barracks. Matters could have turned ugly quickly, but everyone maintained control of their tempers, and little happened but the confiscation of a few armbands and caps.

But while the crowds of Irish complied with the army's orders, I could sense the anger and resentment and mistrust fermenting behind their eyes. They weren't foolish enough to confront a superior force bristling with weapons, but that didn't mean they were cowed or pacified by the Crown Forces strutting and flexing its muscle. No, it only ground their bitterness deeper, and drove those who otherwise might have remained neutral straight into the arms of the republicans.

CHAPTER 21

Nancy spotted me before I saw her, raising her hand to wave at me from a table by the windows. I'd intended to arrive before her, but a cordon the Tans had erected over O'Connell Bridge had hopelessly snarled traffic. The impediments and searches weren't entirely unexpected given the number of IRA attacks on RIC barracks in the counties to the south and west over the past few days. In County Kerry they'd even tried to use a cannon they'd confiscated at an old castle to blow a hole in the side of one RIC post. The speeches made the day before, on Orangemen's Day, by staunch Ulster Protestant unionists like Edward Carson had only enflamed the situation.

However, I'd failed to anticipate the Crown Forces would take action that day in Dublin. I'd been forced to abandon the tram I'd been riding and walk the rest of the way to the tea shop located on a side street near Christ Church Cathedral, where Nancy and I had agreed to meet. I'd let her choose the place, given she would be taking her lunch hour from the Castle.

The shop appeared to still be doing a steady business even though it was after the rush of midday. I squeezed past a pair of matrons with wider skirts than my own, pulling my hands from my pale gray kid leather gloves as I hastened toward her.

"Apologies. A thousand apologies. I know you're on the clock."

She waved this apology away, swallowing the bite of food in her mouth. "Given that, I hope you don't mind that I already ordered. I didn't want to be stuffin' my gob whilst tryin' to chit-chat."

"Of course not," I replied, having been less surprised to find the tray of sandwiches and little cakes and a pot of tea already at the table than she might have realized. But then, my friends who had worked in the various military intelligence sections during the war and I had rarely stood on ceremony in such matters, each of us being almost too busy to eat, let alone wait about on friends to place our order. We'd come and gone from the table we frequented in the restaurant near Whitehall, designated by the government for our use, happy to snag ten minutes to catch up amidst the frenzied pace of our covert work. Those few stolen moments each day were what I'd missed most when I'd been sent out of London and into the field.

I poured myself a cup of tea while Nancy selected another sandwich from the tray. In many ways, her job was much the same as mine had been during the early years of the war, and given the current state of affairs, I imagined things at Dublin Castle were just as hectic. "Thank you again for meeting me," I told her. "I know it probably wasn't easy, especially after everything that's happened over the past few days."

She brushed a strand of dark hair that had loosened from its pin away from her temple. "You mean the article in the *Freeman*. Sure, and all, but I don't really have much to do with all of that. Though it certainly caused quite the hubbub among the brass."

I took a sip of tea, lest I blatantly ask what she *was* involved with. That was not something to be asked outright. Although, she didn't seem averse to discussing what went on at the Castle. "Colonel Winter in a hubbub. I think I'd like to see that."

She grinned. "Stop by the Castle today and ye just might. He's not happy with the press coverage of Smyth's denial."

Everyone had, of course, been anticipating a firm denial that the incident at Listowel had ever occurred. Smyth and the British government could hardly do otherwise. So whether truthful or not, many members of the press as well as the general public had been poised to doubt it.

"Rather naïve for him to expect differently," I couldn't help but remark. Particularly given the outrage it continued to cause across Great Britain and America.

"I think it offends his sensibilities to be questioned."

"Now *that* I believe," I said, selecting a sandwich for myself—cucumber and watercress.

"The girls enjoyed your quip," she told me before taking a drink. Her eyes twinkled over her cup. "I told my cousin, too, and he nearly snorted water out of his nose when I told him you'd expected the colonel's forked tongue to dart out at any moment and clean his monocle."

"He must be familiar with Winter as well, then."

"Oh, aye. He's got quite the reputation. Speakin' of which . . ." She set down her cup, eyeing me shrewdly. "Word is, ye worked for British Intelligence durin' the war."

I met her gaze evenly, careful not to show my surprise that this rumor was being bandied about. But then again, O had revealed as much to Inspector General Smith and Mr. Wylie during our confrontation. There was no telling who else he might have told. Apparently, the letter of the Official Secrets Act didn't apply to him. Only when he deemed it necessary.

Bearing this in mind, I played coy. "Is that a question or merely a statement?"

"It's whatever ye wish it to be," she countered, drawing a smile to my lips.

"Well, considering the fact that if I say no, you'll just think I'm following protocol, and if I say yes, I would be in violation of the law, there's really no point in me answering, is there?"

"Ah, but if it wasn't true, you wouldn't be concerned about saying yes, would ye? They can't prosecute ye if it's a lie."

I shook my head at her teasing logic. "Except the moment I say yes"—I glanced about me furtively—"I suspect the colonel would jump out of hiding from under that table or wherever he's burrowed into the walls, and shout, *aha!*"

Nancy's grin turned wicked. "More like, *S-s-stop right there!*"

We laughed.

"Now, that was too good of an impersonation," I jested, narrowing my eyes playfully. "I'm on to you, now. You're really spying for him, aren't you?"

Her laughter shifted in timbre as she seemed to fumble for a response. "You've got me there. Couldn't resist his monocle." Her eyes glinted mischievously as she seemed to recover herself. "Or his forked tongue."

"Ugh!" I replied, making a disgusted face, at which she laughed even harder. "Now I can never make that jest again."

Her cheeks had reddened, either from amusement or embarrassment at having made such a quip. Perhaps both. Either way, I was still ruminating on her stumble at my jest about her spying. Though it was possible her reaction had been in relation to the nature of her work. If she worked in the intelligence office in some capacity, as her familiarity with O seemed to suggest, that remark might have hit a little too close to home. Whatever the case, she was more than she seemed. That much I was sure of.

A waitress interrupted to bring us a fresh pot of tea, and when Nancy glanced at the watch affixed to her bodice, I realized my time with her was running out. She would have to return to the Castle soon, and I hadn't yet broached the subject I'd hoped to. But how best to do it? Perhaps her natural curiosity about me was the answer.

"I will say that I do miss my war work sometimes," I confessed as I poured myself another cup. "I suppose that sounds silly," I added, allowing chagrin to infuse my voice. "But it was nice to feel that I was doing something worthwhile. That I was helping." While the self-consciousness was feigned, the sentiment was certainly real. "I suppose that's why I still dabble in inquiries for other people."

"I can understand that," she replied. "It *is* rather nice to feel useful."

She turned to peer out the window, obviously internalizing what I'd said. I was about to prod at why this seemed so profound to her when she turned to ask me a question first.

"Are you involved in any inquiries now?"

"One," I confessed. "A young lady who was assaulted and had her hair forcibly cut. It drove the poor girl to commit suicide."

"How terrible," Nancy murmured, crossing herself almost unconsciously.

I nodded, leaning across the table as I lowered my voice. "The people who asked me to look into the matter believe the IRA are responsible, but I don't think so."

Her eyes were wide and clearly intrigued. "Really? Do you know who?"

I glanced surreptitiously about me, smiling absently at a man who had just risen to his feet at a table across the shop. "A British soldier she was stepping out with," I whispered. "A real nasty piece of work named Delagrange."

She blinked in recognition. "I think I know who ye mean. He works for Intelligence."

"That's him."

Her face screwed up in outrage. "He's been flirtin' with my friend Eileen, but I've been warnin' her there's somethin' *wrong* about him."

"The trouble is, an intelligence officer allegedly interviewed a footman who witnessed the end of the attack. Supposedly the footman recognized the assailants as being members of the local IRA brigade. Then rather suspiciously, he left their employ." I tapped my fingernails against my teacup. "*I* think Delagrange was that intelligence officer, and the footman noticed him. So he threatened the fellow somehow, forcing him to quit. And then Delagrange made up the entire statement to direct suspicion away from himself."

"Then you need to talk to the footman," Nancy declared enthusiastically, now invested in the outcome.

"I do, but I don't know his surname, and I've been essentially banished from the Kavanaghs' home. I think Delagrange has threatened them in some way, too," I explained, omitting the part about Mr. Kavanagh's possible culpability in the lieutenant's potentially fraudulent malicious-injury claim. I narrowed my eyes, staring into the distance. "If *only* I could get my hands on the incident file the commissioner kept referring to when we met with him. I'm sure it has the footman's full name and possibly his address." I tilted my head as if having a sudden thought. "I wonder if the detective inspector who was assigned to the case can get a look at it." I frowned. "It's doubtful, given the fact the Castle seemed to be keeping the intelligence officer's findings specifically from him. But I suppose it's worth a try."

Truthfully, it *was* worth a try, and I was a little aggravated at myself that I'd not thought of it until now. I'd written off DI Burrows as useless the moment Johnstone had told us his man was unaware of the interview that intelligence officer had undertaken with the footman. But perhaps I'd been too hasty. It was worth attempting another conversation with him.

More pressingly, I couldn't tell whether my observations had any effect on Nancy. I couldn't very well come out and ask her to take a look at the file, but I'd planted the seeds of the idea and given her all the information she needed to find it, should she wish to. I'd also hopefully given her sufficient motivation to *want* to. I disliked that I was manipulating her, but for a good cause, I reminded myself.

I grimaced in apology. "And there I've gone and lowered the tone of our entire conversation."

"'Tis alright," she assured me. "I need to be gettin' back to the Castle anyway."

"Oh," I said sadly, meaning it. "Of course."

"But let's make plans again," she said, rising to her feet. "Maybe next week. The cinema?"

"I'd like that," I assured her.

"Grand! I'll ring ye."

I departed soon after, intent on tracking down DI Burrows. This meant venturing closer to O'Connell Bridge and the Tans' barricades than I would have preferred, even in my own guise, but Great Brunswick Street Police Station was the most likely place where Burrows could be found. Or at the very least, they could direct me to where he'd gone.

Traffic at College Green and along Westmoreland was still snarled. The smell of exhaust and sun-warmed bricks and pavement clogged the air, and I found myself wishing I'd chosen less restrictive garments. The creamy gold silk and sapphire-blue-accented ensemble might have been flattering but it wasn't the most conducive to long strolls in the summer sun.

A cart carrying produce had attempted to divert the wrong way down College Street and the driver was now arguing with a pair of DMP constables trying to remedy the situation. I scanned the participants and onlookers for any sign of Burrows, and nearly collided with a man stepping out of Kennedy and McSharry.

"Pardon me," the man exclaimed as he clasped my upper arms, righting us both.

I was about to nod my head in acknowledgment before hurrying on when he addressed me by name.

"Verity Kent."

I halted, my ears ringing as I turned to peer up into the striking, but treacherous face of Captain Lucas Willoughby.

A slow grin spread across his features, obviously pleased to have astonished me. "Fancy meeting you here." Whether he'd intended it or not, I heard the mockery in his voice.

"Yes. Fancy that," I drawled, knowing full well he must have expected to find me here. In Dublin, that is. Not along Westmoreland Street.

After all, he worked for Ardmore, and I'd known there was no hope of preventing Ardmore from finding out where we'd gone. Really, it had only been a matter of time before Willoughby was sent to monitor us. Or perhaps Willoughby had been here before us, monitoring the phosgene cylinders and arranging whatever plans Ardmore had for them. The truly shocking thing was that we hadn't run into each other before now.

But perhaps that had been by design. After all, the last time I'd seen Willoughby, he'd killed one man; fatally wounded another; and threatened to shoot Sidney if I didn't hand over a report Ardmore had desperately wanted. Only when I'd called his bluff, and thrown the report into a cottage one of the men had set on fire before Willoughby could stop me, had he relented and walked away. Just following orders. Ardmore's orders. Who for some reason wanted me alive, so we could continue to play his twisted game of cat and mouse.

A former pilot and Naval Intelligence officer who had been stationed in Palestine for at least part of the war, Willoughby had now been back in northern climes for almost a year. As such, his once sun-bleached hair had darkened to a honey blond and his tan had faded to a British rose.

"You've been spending too much time indoors, Captain," I observed somewhat acidly.

He arched one of his brows sardonically. "Yes, well, I don't have friends who own as fine a stable as your husband does."

This was clearly meant to alarm me, but I was perfectly aware that some of Sidney's sporting pursuits had been published in the gossip sheets here in Dublin and even London. He could just have easily learned this from reading those.

"*Do* you ride?" I asked him.

"Of course."

But the look I returned was meant to indicate there was no "of course" about it. A barb directed at his insecurity over his upbringing, for he'd been raised within spitting distance of the aristocracy but made to understand that he would never genuinely be a part of it. Perhaps it was unworthy of me, but I rather enjoyed seeing that I'd gotten under his skin as he scowled ferociously.

I turned to peer into the window of the clothing store from which he'd emerged. It often catered to British officers—current and former—so his patronage wasn't surprising. Sidney might have even shopped there. It didn't tell me anything useful about his presence in Dublin either. Such as where he was staying or who he was associating with. But there was likely some crossover between his and Sidney's acquaintances, particularly within the military.

It was only because I'd looked toward the window that the reflection of a man across the street caught my eye. He was too far away to see clearly, but he was watching me and Willoughby, and he seemed somewhat agitated. I was tempted to turn and look at him, for he seemed somehow familiar, but I knew the moment I did he would disappear in the crowd of pedestrians. Such was my interest, that I nearly missed what Willoughby said next.

"I understand you recently lost a friend and colleague."

My gaze shifted abruptly to meet his, at first not comprehending, and then realizing he was speaking of Alec.

"My sincerest condolences."

It was difficult to tell whether he was being earnest or if he was mocking me again, so I ignored the remark and the insidious apprehension that Willoughby might know something I did not. There were enough lies and half-truths swirling about my former cohort without adding Willoughby's, no doubt, disingenuous ones.

When I turned back to the reflection in the window, the man watching us had shifted so that I could no longer see him. I darted an annoyed glare at Willoughby before turning to walk away. However, he wasn't finished taunting me.

"Mrs. Kent," he called, quickly catching up with me. "Won't you allow me to offer my escort." He glanced about us, perhaps having also sensed we were being watched. "Haven't you heard how unsafe the streets are these days?"

"Perhaps for the likes of you," I retorted, refusing to be intimidated by the suggestion.

But he merely smiled when I refused this proffered arm, tucking his hands in his pockets. "Oh, now, there you have it wrong."

I glowered at him in confusion.

"I'm perfectly safe."

What he meant by this, I didn't know. Did he think he was impervious to an assassin's bullet or incapable of being caught unawares? Or did he mean the IRA wouldn't dare to touch him? But why? Because of something he knew? Because of his association with Ardmore?

Whatever the truth, I knew better than to think he would tell me. So I kept my questions to myself and lengthened my stride. "Regardless, I do not require your assistance. Good *day*, Captain Willoughby."

This, at least, seemed to deter him, as he fell back. However, when I turned the corner, he was still standing where I'd left him, watching me.

CHAPTER 22

"Are ye *tryin'* to get me plugged?" Detective Inspector Burrows hissed as he thrust his hat onto his head and stormed out of the Great Brunswick Street Police Station.

I didn't know exactly what the clerk had told him when he'd informed him I was asking to speak with him, but Burrows had barely flicked an eyelash at me as he barreled out of the office and across the lobby. It had taken me a moment to realize I was supposed to follow, so I'd been forced to scramble to catch up with him.

"I told you and your husband everythin' I know," he grumbled under his breath.

"Perhaps, but we—"

He shushed me loudly, cutting me off. "Not here."

I frowned. Not here, but *he* was allowed to speak?

Despite my aggravation, I managed to hold my tongue, trailing half a step behind him until we reached the quay along the southern shore of the Liffey. From this vantage we could observe part of the ongoing disruption on O'Connell Bridge, which was wider than it was long, as pedestrians and vehicles tried to pass to the opposite side of the river. We moved to the concrete embankment overlooking the steely blue water, turning our backs to the traffic that bustled eastward, seeking another way around the Crown Forces' cordon. But the double-decker trams had no choice but to idle in long lines on their rails waiting for their passengers to be searched. The buildings directly across the river had been destroyed or damaged during the 1916 rebellion, and evidence could still be seen of ongoing construction and repairs.

Burrows adjusted the fit of his coat—this one a brown herringbone—and leaned forward to rest his elbows against the top of the barrier, clasping his hands together. He heaved a dispirited sigh. "Waste of time," he muttered. "Too canny are the men they're most after, to be caught like that. Which just makes it all a right headache for the rest of us." He eyed me askance. "But ye can't tell you English what for."

I didn't challenge this statement, for in many ways he was correct. In any case, I had more important things to discuss, and the inspector seemed at ease enough to let me address them. Apparently, he was more afraid of who might overhear us in and around the police station than out here on the busy public quay. Interesting.

"We spoke with the commissioner."

Burrows didn't react, but continued to watch a lorry as it rumbled past the barricades and into north Dublin. Perhaps he'd been expecting us to go over his head.

"Were you aware that they have a file on Miss Kavanagh's assault?"

Though he didn't stir, I could tell that he was listening.

"That an intelligence officer filed a report saying he spoke with a footman in the household who claimed to have recognized the assailants as men from the local IRA brigade."

His mustache bristled.

"He told us you hadn't been informed. Though I don't understand why."

He turned to look at me.

"You *are* supposed to be the detective inspector assigned to this case. Yet they let an intelligence officer interfere."

His brow lowered thunderously. "It's—" He caught himself, breaking off before uttering the name I knew must have occurred to him. The only intelligence officer who would hold such an interest in the inquiry.

"It has to be Lieutenant Delagrange," I finished for him. "I think that's fairly obvious. What's not is why they didn't tell you he intervened or allow you to follow up with the footman."

I fell silent, allowing him to ruminate on this while I watched a trio of boats tied up along the opposite quay bobbing gently on the water. On how exactly he and the DMP were supposed to apprehend the men responsible when the descriptions the footman had allegedly given of them were withheld. It was counterproductive. After all, the DMP constables were the ones who knew everyone on their beat and where to find them.

"They don't trust us," Burrows stated gruffly.

"Because of the suspects' connection to the IRA," I extrapolated.

Because there were many who believed that the Dublin Metropolitan Police had yielded to Collins and the IRA. That they were so intimidated by the murder gangs that they'd ceased to be of any use in apprehending them. Not that the DMP had ceased to operate altogether. They still did their jobs in maintaining the peace and stopping common criminals. But in regard to the republicans, they'd adopted a sort of "live and let live" policy. They didn't arrest or identify the rebels to the other British authorities, and Collins kept their names off his murder list. Given the number of DMP men who had already died, and Dublin Castle's inability to protect them, it was difficult to blame them for accepting such an arrangement. At least, I didn't.

"But in this case, I don't think that's the issue," I told Burrows. "Because I don't think the IRA was responsible."

He frowned. "You just said the footman identified the culprits as bein' from the local brigade," he argued, glancing distractedly down river toward the train gathering speed as it left Tara Street Station and crossed the bridge which skirted the Custom House on the rail line headed northeast. Great plumes of steam drifted toward the sky.

"No, I said that Lieutenant Delagrange had said he had."

The pupils in DI Burrows's eyes dilated, telling me he'd grasped what I was trying to convey.

"But no one else has spoken to this footman to verify his report, and rather conveniently, at least for Delagrange, the footman left the Kavanaghs' employ shortly after."

Burrows smoothed his fingers over his mustache as he analyzed this new information.

"You implied you weren't allowed to question the staff?" I said.

"Nay. Everythin' came to me through Mr. and Mrs. Kavanagh."

Who'd seemed to be thinking more of their daughter's reputation.

"Then you didn't meet the footmen? Or learn their names?" I asked.

He shook his head.

"Could you gain access to that file the commissioner showed us?"

His lips quirked in wry amusement. "And how exactly would I go about that? *If* I could even gain an audience with the man." He cleared his throat. "Apologies, sir, but Mrs. Kent says ye have some information on the Kavanagh case you've been keepin' from me. Might I have a look at it?" He chuckled humorlessly. "He'd toss me out of more than his office."

I grimaced, recognizing now that my question had been rather naïve. "Then, could you ask around, at least? See if anyone knows his surname or where he's gone. His given name is Earnán."

"I can try," he conceded, though he didn't sound optimistic.

I nodded, adjusting the fit of my pale gray gloves. "And I shall try to speak with the Kavanaghs' staff again." Maybe when the Kavanaghs were not at home. "We have to confirm what, if anything, the footman actually saw."

Though I didn't turn to meet it, I was struck by the world-weary expression I glimpsed on the inspector's face out of the corner of my eye. Even his shoulders appeared to droop under his dapper three-piece suit. It made me think back on what he'd said as he'd hustled me out of the police station.

"What did you mean when you asked if I was trying to get you plugged?" When I turned to look at him, I could tell I'd caught him off guard.

"Oh, well, 'tis just a sayin'—"

"I know what 'plugged' means," I said, halting his feeble attempt to minimize the matter. "And I don't think it was just a general statement on you G-Men keeping your noses out of IRA matters. I heard the tone of your voice." I scrutinized his taut features. "You seemed to have something very specific in mind."

His lips flattened, almost disappearing behind his gray mustache as his gaze strayed toward O'Connell Bridge once again. Black and Tans, in their hodge-podge uniforms with the rifles draped over their shoulders, bayonets affixed and pointed toward the sky, strode from vehicle to vehicle and sorted pedestrians and bicyclists, waving some through while others were prodded and searched.

"I don't want any trouble."

I was about to ask from who when he elaborated.

"I received a message. A warning," he explained in a low voice. "Shortly after I spoke to ye the first time. 'Twas left at my desk at the station." He avoided my eye. "Told me to lay off and stay away from you and the Kavanaghs or I'd end up with a bullet in my brain."

I blinked in surprise. "Yet you're speaking to me now."

He scowled at me. "Aye. And none too happy about it." He

glanced over his shoulder, presumably in the direction of the police station. “But better here than there.”

An interesting revelation. Clearly, he was suspicious of *someone* he worked with.

“Who was the message from?” I asked.

He scoffed. “’Twasn’t signed or anythin’. But ’twas on Dáil stationery. So who else could it’ve been but Mick Collins.”

I knew Collins and his men often delivered warnings to G-Men, ordering them to lay off their pursuit of republicans, or else suffer the consequences. So this seemed in keeping with their normal modus operandi.

Was I wrong about Delagrange then? Maybe he wasn’t to blame. Maybe Miss Kavanagh had gone to meet him in the garden, but he’d never shown up. Or maybe the attackers had heard them talking and assaulted her after Delagrange departed? Either scenario could be plausible. Otherwise, why would Collins have bothered to warn Burrows away? If the IRA wasn’t involved, why would they hinder the investigation?

The thought was troubling.

“Unless . . .” Burrows had evidently thought of something, though he didn’t like considering it. I waited for him to overcome his reticence.

He grunted. “Word is that some Dáil stationery was taken durin’ a raid on the Sinn Féin headquarters late last year. That the Castle has found some . . . strategic uses for it.”

Then the warning might not have come from Collins or the IRA, but from those who wanted it to seem like it had. Or it might be exactly as it seemed. There was no way to know for certain. Not yet, anyway.

“If you find out the footman’s name, can you send it to me by messenger?”

I could read the hesitation in his eyes. This was supposed to be his investigation, after all. He should be the one questioning the footman. But if the IRA had warned him away, or even if they hadn’t, he was in no position to take on Dublin

Castle if it was discovered the footman's testimony had been falsified.

"Aye," he agreed. "And you'll let me know what you uncover?"

I assented. After all, he deserved to know who had threatened him. The IRA or a crooked intelligence officer. I wasn't sure which was worse.

That evening and the following, I expected to catch sight of Willoughby dogging our steps. In the past, that had often been his task, turning up like a bad penny whenever we least wanted him to. But he'd not appeared at either the restaurant or the dance hall, or the dinner party hosted by Moya Llewelyn Davies.

Sidney had cursed quite eloquently when I'd told him how I'd literally collided with Ardmore's henchman on Westmoreland Street. "What is he doing here now?" he wanted to know. But the look we exchanged told me it wasn't necessary to explain.

Ardmore, and consequently Willoughby, never simply flitted about willy-nilly. There was always a purpose to their movements, always a plan. The difficulty lay in figuring out exactly what their machinations were before it was too late to do anything about them. Clearly Ardmore had significant intentions for Dublin, or else he wouldn't have sent his best man. And the most obvious answer to what those intentions were was the stolen phosgene cylinders.

Sidney hadn't heard anything more about their location, either from Bennett and Ames or any of his other contacts, and of course, I'd been distracted by other matters. Most notably, finding Michael Collins. My first two attempts proved rather fruitless, but then the rain had hampered everyone's movements. My investigation into Miss Kavanagh's assault was also stymied until either I uncovered the footman's name or Wick was able to provide me with some information that proved useful.

Meanwhile the raids and ambushes by the IRA continued. One in Dingle, County Kerry, resulted in the death of two RIC constables, and the attack on an RIC bicycle patrol in Foynes, County Limerick, caused the death of another. However, reports were that the RIC in Foynes had not been content to let this murder go unpunished, burning the creamery and other buildings in reprisal.

The Listowel Incident continued to make headlines. It was believed to have played some part in the British Trades Union Congress passing a motion supporting Dominion Home Rule in Ireland and adequate protections for minorities. It had also caused such an uproar at the Labour Party conference that they demanded an investigation into the matter, raising the question in the British House of Commons the next day.

This sparked a lively debate at Moya's dinner table at Furry Park House in Killester, north of Dublin. A number of guests supported the refusal of the House to open the matter for discussion, while others thought such a highly publicized and hotly debated incident should have at least been addressed, if nothing more than to at least make it appear as if it wasn't being swept under the rug. Whatever the truth, the incident was political dynamite, and everyone agreed that the prime minister had no choice but to promise a full investigation. In fact, word was, he'd already summoned Smyth to London to speak with him personally.

I was somewhat skeptical of this full investigation actually happening, or of the results being released. For if Smyth had really said what Mee and the other constables had reported, and if he'd merely been repeating the instructions he'd been given by his commanding officers, then the government could hardly admit it. Not publicly. But politicians often thrived on farce.

In any case, the incident was soon overshadowed. At least in Dublin.

The General Post Office on Sackville Street had been one of the buildings captured by the rebels during the short-lived 1916 uprising, being shelled and burned along with the structures surrounding it as the army fought to take it back. As a consequence, it needed to be rebuilt, and the post office facilities had been moved temporarily to the Rotunda Rink at Rutland Square.

When I boarded the tram in disguise the next morning, bound for north Dublin, I learned that the republicans had raided the postal sorting office at the Rotunda that morning and made off with a number of mail bags. Word was that they'd been the official correspondence bound for Dublin Castle, and this soon bore out to be true. Several days later, Lord French even received a few letters at the Viceregal Lodge stamped with the notice OPENED AND CENSORED BY THE IRISH REPUBLIC. Apparently, the correspondence that the rebels decided they had no use for was simply resealed and dropped in a post box.

This raid caused some a mixture of consternation and alarm. Given the uncertain loyalties of those working for the telephone and telegraph companies, mail was considered the most secure form of communication other than personal contact. And for intelligence agents working covertly or people who wished to share information with the authorities, direct contact with Dublin Castle personnel was too risky. So having their correspondence intercepted was a severe security risk. I could only imagine the amount of valuable information IRA intelligence might have been able to glean from it all depending upon the day's haul, and given the raid's success, it would undoubtedly be attempted again, be it at sorting offices, or holding up mail vans or mail carriages on trains. This could prove a sharp deterrent to potential informants.

But for much of the public not directly affected, the mail

raid merely caused general amusement. Even some of the press joined in on the satirical banter. "It would really save time if official correspondence were forwarded direct to Sinn Féin," the *Pall Gazette* wrote. While the *Irish Times* remarked, "We seem to be approaching the day when British authority in Ireland will be shaken to its base by the laughter of two hemispheres." This last troubled me, for it smacked of tugging the tail of the tiger, and I feared for some days how the Crown Forces would react to such criticism.

In any case, that morning I was more concerned with finding Collins and hopefully trailing him to a place I could corner him to find out what had happened to Alec. How exactly I planned to do that without getting myself killed, I didn't know, but I trusted inspiration would arise when the moment presented itself. I also trusted that I was too notable a personality for him to actually harm. Collins was nothing if not a man of calculation, be it in his job as finance minister, tasked with raising the national loan, or directing his men who they should assassinate. Thus far he appeared to have calculated correctly who the public would stomach being killed. As such, surely he would recognize he could never present my death in a light that was to his advantage.

I considered whether continuing on to Rutland Square as I'd planned would be best, considering it was bound to be crawling with Crown Forces. In the end, I resolved to continue, but elected to disembark the tram at Nelson's monument, near the granite shell of the GPO, and approach the square via a different route. It proved to be a fortuitous decision.

As I drew nearer to the square, I could see that a crowd had gathered. British Regulars shouldered rifles with fixed bayonets and Black and Tans had formed a perimeter around the area, keeping people back and even hampering the ability of people to reach the Rotunda Hospital. It all seemed a trifle excessive given the fact the rebels had made off with the bags of mail they'd come for a few hours earlier. It was doubtful they intended to return or hamper the investigation after the fact.

I stood along the pavement near the junction with Moore Lane, my back to Devlin's pub, a place I'd begun to frequent. Though the trade there, and the potential to overhear something important, didn't increase until late in the afternoon. At this hour, I was more likely to learn something at Vaughan's Hotel along the square. Nevertheless, I lingered in the shade cast by the four-story brick building at my back, watching the crowd and the Crown Forces' display. The day promised to be a warm one. Perhaps too warm for the rough wool coat that comprised my disguise.

I knew Liam Devlin, the publican, stood in the doorway behind me. We'd exchanged nods and I'd offered a smile to his twelve-year-old son, who'd been seemingly sweeping the front walk, but was truly more interested in observing all the excitement. His father had since shooed him back inside. The Devlins had recently moved to Dublin from Scotland, so the pub seemed an improbable fit for a rumored republican hangout, but perhaps that's exactly why it was utilized as such.

Devlin was a talkative man, so I'd heard him address a number of people in his deep, bluff voice, but something about his next remarks made me take notice. "I dinna ken," he told the fellow who'd asked after someone. "But give it to O'Reilly. He'll get it to him."

The name O'Reilly nagged at me like an annoying little brother. It meant something, though for a moment I couldn't recall. And then, like a bolt from the blue, I remembered. Alec's early reports had mentioned that a fellow named Joe O'Reilly often acted as a messenger or courier of sorts for Michael Collins. That the police were prone to overlook him because he seemed so inconsequential.

Well, I decided not to make that mistake. For if Alec had

been right, and this O'Reilly was the same one, then the "him" Devlin had mentioned must be Collins.

Careful not to tip Devlin off to my interest, I watched as the fellow he'd been speaking to approached a thin, youthful man a short distance away. He turned his head with a lively movement, revealing a thin, eager, but otherwise unremarkable face. He listened carefully to whatever the chap was telling him and then accepted something from him, tucking it into an inner pocket of his coat. A bicycle leaned against his hip, so it took him a bit of time to navigate through the crowd.

I waited, not wanting to draw suspicion by moving off in the same direction he had gone too soon after him. When he was almost out of sight, I began to tail him, darting glances over my shoulder back toward the Rotunda, as if it still drew my interest and not the man in front of me. At the edge of the crowd, he mounted his bicycle, and might have sped off, losing me, but for the fact he had to adjust the bicycle clips at the hems of his trousers. This allowed me time to draw almost even with him, so that when he rode off, I was not so far behind.

Then began a game of leap-frog, in which he would cycle ahead while I hastened to catch up. He would stop, speaking to someone or entering one building or another for a short time, and I would pull even or slightly ahead before he set off again, passing me. I made note of each face and premises as best I could, intending to return if I didn't spy Collins with my own eyes before I lost O'Reilly. For all I knew, he might have already delivered whatever that man had given him, but entering a shop or abode without knowing what I was walking into would be beyond imprudent, and I'd promised Sidney I would take care.

The moments when I leaped ahead were particularly fraught, as I had no way of knowing which direction he'd intended to go next. Yet, standing about and loitering was out of the question. At numerous points, I found myself wishing I had a bicycle of my own, but taking one of the few I spotted unattended leaning against walls or lampposts seemed too risky and liable to draw the wrong sort of attention.

Twice, I'd thought I'd lost him, only to turn the corner to find his battered old bicycle leaning against a post or to spy him coming out of a bookshop. The third time he drew out of sight, I feared he'd vanished for good. A sickening swirl of disappointment filled me, and I glanced up at the nearest street sign, trying to figure out exactly where I was. Then suddenly he appeared again, coasting out of an alley before looking both ways and crossing Capel Street, intent on something.

Tracking the direction of his movements, I could see that he was headed toward the public library. Before O'Reilly had even reached the other side, I recognized him. The man jogging lazily down the steps. It was Michael Collins.

CHAPTER 23

Though I'd only seen him once, thanks to Alec drawing my attention to him, I'd memorized what I could about Collins. He was tall and broad-shouldered with a sturdy frame, a sportsman, but not a lithe one, more of a brawler. It showed in the particular way he moved. I'd heard him described as handsome many times, but while he wasn't unattractive, I suspected as much of the appeal lay in the mystique of the man and his reputation as in his actual good looks.

On that day, he seemed particularly merry. And well he should have been, given the successful mail raid at the Rotunda and the propaganda coup of the public's outrage over the Listowel Incident. He greeted O'Reilly with a cheerful smile, one hand tucked into the pocket of a rather ill-fitting tweed suit. An old soft hat rested over his thick, dark hair, and a dust-coat was draped over his arm.

Such was my shock at actually catching sight of Collins, I stood stock-still at the corner, watching them like the greenest nitwit. Had either of them bothered to look up, I would have certainly been spotted, but luck was with me, for neither of them did. They exchanged a few words and O'Reilly passed Collins a paper, which he promptly read. Then with a satisfied nod, he moved toward the side of the steps while O'Reilly rode north.

Collins, too, had a bicycle—a rather ancient-looking thing.

Not like what you would expect the leader of a rebellion to ride. He mounted it and pulled out into the street, tipping his hat to a pair of constables on the opposite corner, cool as you please, and riding off at a fair clip down the center of Capel Street before I could even consider following. I wouldn't have been able to keep up with him at any rate.

I wondered if the constables knew who he was. I had to think they did. Which meant the Castle was right about the DMP and probably part of the RIC, as well. Collins was hiding in plain sight, the Castle just didn't have the eyes to see him, for he looked like any normal, everyday, respectable businessman. Many of whom pedaled about the city.

But while I'd failed to give chase, I had noted one particular thing about Collins's bicycle. Its chain rattled like old Marley's shackles from Dickens's *A Christmas Carol.* That was something I was certain I would recognize if I heard it again.

Alec's early reports had also supplied me with another useful piece of intelligence. He'd strongly suspected Collins had kept to some sort of schedule, pedaling about the city to various offices and rendezvous in approximately the same order and routine. If this was true, then he would be returning to the Capel Street library. And when he did, I would be ready for him. Whatever the truth about Alec, whether he was dead or he'd switched sides, he was, unwittingly or not, helping me to get closer to the truth.

"I found him," I declared softly, dropping into the chair adjacent to Sidney's in the sitting room adjoining our bedchamber. They were positioned next to a window overlooking the garden, and from this vantage I knew that he'd seen me cross the neighboring garden in disguise a short time ago.

Either Sidney had been deeply absorbed in the story he was reading in the newspaper before him or he'd forgotten my intentions, for it took him a moment to grasp what I meant. When he did, the paper crumpled as he lowered it to his lap with a start. "Did you . . . ?"

I shook my head before he could finish his question. "No, I didn't speak with him. And no, Alec wasn't with him." I brightened, refusing to be daunted. "But I found him once, and I'll find him again." I turned my head, narrowing my eyes as I peered into the summer sun streaming through the window. A gentle breeze billowed the curtains inward. "I just need a bicycle."

"Did he see *you*?" Sidney asked solemnly.

"Of course not," I retorted breezily, even though I knew perfectly well that was because of blind luck. I couldn't freeze again. And I wouldn't. The shock was over. From now on, I would maintain a clear head.

"Where did you find him?"

I opened my mouth to tell him, but then halted, uncertain if I should.

Sidney's mouth pursed in irritation. "I suppose you think I'm going to turn up there and bungle your chances."

"No. But I know you're thinking about it."

He scowled, but then grunted in concession. I knew him too well.

"Regardless, I need to tell you so you'll steer clear of there for another reason. He was coming out of the Capel Street public library." I arched my eyebrows. "Which happens to be the emergency contact I was given should Finnegan and the Bank of Ireland be compromised." This was something I wasn't supposed to share with him, but I couldn't risk it also being his emergency contact.

Sidney smoothed and folded the paper, setting it aside. "Isn't that also where that Thomas fellow from the Wicklow wanted you to meet him?"

"It is," I replied with a start, having temporarily forgotten that fact. I'd since wondered if he might be working with Collins or someone else among the rebels, but now I was doubly suspicious.

"It could all just be a coincidence," Sidney pointed out. "After all, it *is* a public library. I'm sure any number of people patronize it, be they republicans or not."

"That may be true, but it's all still a little too convenient for my liking." Or so my instincts told me, and I'd learned early on in my role as an intelligence operative never to discount them. More times than I could count, that maxim had kept me alive.

"What of you?" I asked as he removed a cigarette from his case and lit it. The sight of the battered silver case was always a little bittersweet to me. "Did you stop to see Finnegan?"

He exhaled a plume of smoke. "I did. And you were right. He asked whether you'd shared his suspicions about Xavier switching sides. Seemed *quite* anxious for us to leave Dublin."

I leaned forward. "I'm telling you, Sidney, something is *off.* That man has wanted us to leave since the moment we arrived, and while I'm accustomed to being underestimated, this goes far beyond simply doubting our abilities."

"I agree, darling. As such, I think we should steer clear of him *and* the bank for the moment. There was no correspondence for us today anyway." He rose to fetch a pewter dish from the tea table, tipping his ash into it as he set it on the table next to his chair. "I imagine you heard about the IRA's mail raid at the Rotunda."

I nodded. "Which has got me thinking. It's been some time since we received a letter from Max."

"I had the same thought," Sidney confessed. "And by all accounts, the raiders knew exactly where to go and what to nab, which leads one to suspect they had inside information. Given that there's undoubtedly republicans or at least Sinn Féin sympathizers working for the post office, it could be possible that all of our mail to this address is being intercepted, read, and then forwarded on to us."

"Yet Max's latest letter wasn't."

"Maybe it contains sensitive information."

I considered this possibility. "But I haven't noticed any telltale signs that anything delivered to us through the post had been opened. Max's letter transferred to us through Finnegan, which was censored, yes. But nothing else. And I've been trained to look for such things."

Sidney shrugged. "It's just a theory. Maybe Ryde simply hasn't had time to write. He does have things in his life to concern himself with other than us."

This felt like a mild rebuke, and I scowled, letting him know I didn't appreciate it.

"I saw Bennett and Ames again today," he informed me after taking another drag.

"Well, that explains your testy demeanor," I taunted in return.

This earned me a sharp look. "They have another suspected location where the phosgene might be stored. They asked if I wanted to tag along."

"I have to say, I'm rather relieved to hear someone else is actually looking for it." It certainly eased the pressure on us to find it. "But just so you're aware," I cautioned, "this could be O's way of luring you in."

"With excitement and adventure?" Sidney mocked. The very thing that had lured many of our men to sign up for the war. At least at its start.

"No." I met his gaze solemnly. "The chance to make a difference and prevent further bloodshed."

The cynicism slowly faded from his eyes.

"O knows you're no green recruit. That you require a far headier enticement." One that was much more difficult to turn down. "Not that that's actually what you would be doing once he had you in his employ, but the 'get a pound of flesh off the rebels' pitch wouldn't have the same effect on you."

Sidney's eyebrows arched, possibly at the scorn now creeping into *my* voice. "I forgot to mention, someone telephoned while you were out." He pulled a tiny slip of paper from his pocket, and I crossed the small space between our chairs, perching on the arm of his as he handed it to me. "Nimble spoke to them."

Fortunately, his valet was healing quite well, though his face still looked alarming, with a colorful array of bruises. Ginny and Mrs. Boyle continued to coddle him, a fact Nimble seemed embarrassed about, but I'd told him to enjoy it—that, as a man, he was bound to do something to irritate them sooner or later. This seemed to concern the dear even more than the cosseting.

I opened the paper to find a few brief words in Nimble's painstaking hand.

Wick. Croke Park. Saturday at 3.

"It appears we're going to a football match," Sidney observed after I showed it to him.

"That it does," I replied, knowing I wouldn't be able to deter him from accompanying me, and truthfully, I didn't want to. Besides, Wick wouldn't mind. "Just don't wear your Chelsea scarf," I jested. "Then you'll really end up a marked man."

"Different kind of football, darling."

"I know that," I snapped in annoyance. I may not have ever seen Gaelic football played, but I was aware it was distinct from the English version.

When I looked up, I could tell by the twinkle in his eyes that he was baiting me.

"Just for that, maybe I *will* bat my eyes at Mick Collins

when I finally approach him. 'Oh, you big, strong rebel,'" I cooed, sliding off the arm of the chair.

But I wasn't quick enough, and Sidney pulled me into his lap, locking his arms around me. "No flirting with the rebels," he ordered as I laughed. "Big and strong or otherwise."

I reached up to brush the strand of dark hair that had fallen over his forehead in our tussle back behind his ear, a coy smile curling my lips. "Perhaps if you reminded me why . . ."

I never finished the thought, for he'd already grasped the assignment, his mouth finding mine.

And he did. He most certainly did.

"Now, this is *it*!" Wick shouted to me as I stood between him and Sidney in the stands at Croke Park two days later. The stadium lay north of Dublin, just beyond the Royal Canal, between two railway lines and within walking distance of three tram routes. And a good thing, too, for it appeared to be a popular venue.

The pitch was a verdant green despite all the abuse it was taking from the players. I hadn't entirely worked out the rules of Gaelic football yet, but the best I could describe it was a cross somewhere between English football and rugby. The people in the crowded stands seemed enthusiastic about it, including Wick. Even Sidney appeared to catch on rather quickly, joining in the cheering and jeering of the match.

I was having more trouble concentrating due to the two rowdy fellows behind us who were using blistering language. Sidney had looked at me several times now, silently asking if I wanted him to say something, but I shook my head. The last thing we needed was to cause a scene. One in which our Englishness could become a source of contention. Though it wasn't like we hadn't encountered their like in England as well. As long as their flailing hands didn't smack me, I was determined to remain mum.

Though I was beginning to wonder why Wick had asked us to meet him there. Thus far, we'd been unable to discuss anything of pertinence. Not with thousands of screaming spectators surrounding us and Wick wholly absorbed in the match. My puzzled frustration must have been evident, for at one point, Wick finally leaned down to yell in my ear.

"I'm bein' watched."

I turned to him in question, for this had heightened my confusion. Did he mean now?

"Someone from the Castle. Ye heard the *Freeman's Journal* had their printin' machinery smashed by the British Army after they published that Listowel constable's account?"

I nodded.

"Well, now we're all bein' watched. A lot more closely."

He meant subversive journalists. Those who dared to report the things the British government preferred to censor. Which explained why he'd asked us to meet him at such a public venue. If the intelligence agent had followed him inside, at least they couldn't get near enough to hear what we were saying.

Some of my tension over what Wick was telling me must have been conveyed to Sidney, for he eyed us sideways, clearly wondering what had been said. However, he knew better than to ask for details until later.

I found myself curious how many of the Crown Forces were attempting to blend into the crowd in plain clothes. To be certain, most of the people there were either neutral or supporters of Sinn Féin. I suspected a healthy mix were also IRA, be they active members or allies, of which I was learning there were many. Just in the two days since I'd been trailing Collins—first to the vicinity of Upper Ormond Street, where I'd lost him again, and then to the quays opposite the river—I'd seen the variety of people with whom he interacted, all or most of whom must have known his identity.

At the half, Dublin was ahead of Kildare, much to the

crowd's glee, and the rowdy chaps behind us decided to leave the stands momentarily, much to my relief. Wick noted this, arching his eyebrows, but I didn't want to waste time discussing them when we had other matters to address. We resumed our seats on the bench, and he leaned across me so that Sidney could hear.

"The irregularity I mentioned in my note," he said, diving straight to the heart of the matter about Miss Kavanagh's cousin. "Daniel Keogh's body was found at the base of the Forty Steps."

"Where's that?" I asked.

"Just outside the Castle," Sidney answered, grasping something I hadn't yet.

Wick's gaze met his. "'Tis an alley that runs from Castle Street down to Ship Street, where the Castle barracks are located. 'Twas constructed to act as a break between the castle walls and the surroundin' properties. Namely St. Werburgh's churchyard."

Which could have posed a security threat to the Castle.

Wick shook his head. "To be sure, the boys would never have executed someone and left him on the doorstep of Dublin Castle. 'Twould be suicide."

And by "the boys," I knew he meant the IRA. Wick might have referred to them as such in case someone nearby overheard, but I thought it more likely he'd done so unconsciously. Which was something I would have to contemplate later.

I frowned. "But for someone at the Castle, someone for whom it was their turf, so to speak . . ."

Wick tipped his head to indicate he'd had a similar thought. He turned his head as if to survey the pitch. "Ye should also know, they're denyin' involvement."

"The . . . boys?" I used his term.

"Aye. Word is, he was one of their own. And the letter they found with the body, the one on Dáil stationery, 'twas a fake."

"Seized in a raid on the Sinn Féin headquarters," I supplied, thinking of the note DI Burrows had received.

"You've heard of it, then? Aye. Your lad Keogh isn't the first to receive one. The Castle has attempted the trick before to try to sow ferment among the ranks, and this latest crack won't be the last." He spoke with a certainty I couldn't question. Not if the Castle's stock hadn't run out.

Some of the players had risen from the bench to begin batting and dribbling the ball about, and Wick watched them for a moment before turning to me with a sharp glint in his eye. "So what's this I hear about a shipment of phosgene fallin' into the republicans' hands?"

I blinked at him, taken off guard. A fact I was certain Wick had been counting on.

Not so, Sidney. "That's rather concerning," he replied with his eyes still on the pitch.

"Aye." Wick studied us closely. "And I have it on good authority, you're the ones to speak to."

"What would we know about it?" Sidney asked, still playing ignorant, though I had already deduced Wick's game.

Wick's voice hardened. "Now, ye see. That's not how this goes." He turned to me. "Ver knows. I gives ye information, and then ye gives it right back. Just like those lads down there, passin' the ball."

I did know. I'd been waiting to see what favor he requested in return for the intelligence he'd shared. Though I had no idea it would be this.

"We know about the missing phosgene," I murmured. "But not who has it." I glanced at Sidney. "The Castle is alleging they're in the rebels' hands, but we don't know that for certain." I grasped Wick's arm. "And if you print that, true or not . . ."

"It'll be a propaganda coup for the Castle," he replied. His mouth pursed disdainfully, having deduced the same thing I had.

"Who told you about it?" I asked, curious who would leak such information and why.

"A contact at the Castle."

I couldn't fault him for protecting his source, but their position at the Castle called into question the motivation behind them telling Wick about the phosgene. Besides which, the only person we could link with certainty to the phosgene was Lord Ardmore, and he worked in some sort of mysterious capacity for the government. We simply didn't have enough proof of that link to be able to present it in a court of law.

More pressing was the location of those phosgene cylinders and the Livens Projector which had been stolen with them. Perhaps Wick could help with that.

"Did they tell you anything more about them? Where they might be? How they got here?" I pressed Wick, curious what else he might know.

He sat with his arms crossed over his chest, his gaze following something or someone. "Just that a shipment had fallen into rebel hands, and that you were the person to ask about it." Our eyes locked for a fleeting second, and I could tell he thought I'd lied to him when I'd told him I wasn't here for the rebels. However, there wasn't time to set him straight. Not when he stood to greet a younger man who was hurrying toward us.

It was obvious Wick recognized him, accepting the message the lad held out to him with a softly worded, "Sir." Wick's posture changed as he read it, straightening to alertness.

"Smyth was assassinated in Cork City," he muttered to us abruptly.

Lieutenant Colonel Smyth, the new divisional commissioner of the RIC in Munster, the man at the center of the Listowel Incident.

"'Twas no more than we expected." Wick scrubbed a hand over his face, heaving a sigh. "But still."

I exchanged a look with Sidney. Just the day before when we'd read that Smyth was returning to Ireland after his brief trip to London to debrief the prime minister on the situation, Sidney had expressed his disbelief, and his certainty that they were signing his death warrant. The government had made some excuse about Smyth needing to return to regulate police duty for the assizes, but it was difficult not to be skeptical. After all, if Smyth died, then Lloyd George could claim an inquiry into the Listowel affair was both impossible and irrelevant. It seemed he'd gotten his wish.

"I have to go," Wick declared, gesturing for the younger man—a messenger for the *Irish Independent*, no doubt—to follow him.

Sidney and I departed soon after. Our reason for being there was concluded, and after the news about Smyth, neither of us was interested in the match any longer. A sense of wariness filled me of what was to come. Particularly if the constables' report from Listowel was true. Had the RIC been privately encouraged to beget violence with even greater violence, to shoot on sight? Only time would tell.

CHAPTER 24

The following morning, I received a request from a surprising source. Miss Fairbanks wrote to ask me to meet her at the Pepper Cannister church just after one o'clock. I'd not held out much hope of convincing her to speak with me again, so for her to request a meeting seemed a great boon. I was due to meet Nancy at the Pillar Picture House at three, so I had just enough time to accommodate Miss Fairbanks.

I arrived to find her waiting for me in the same place where we'd sat the last time. It was quiet inside. The rain from the morning had since moved off and soft sunlight now streamed through the stained glass bathing the pews and floor in near-translucent color. The patch in which Miss Fairbanks sat tinted her copper hair magenta.

When I sat beside her, she acknowledged me with a tight smile, her hands clasped before her. "Thank you for coming."

"Of course."

When she didn't volunteer anything more, I found myself remarking on our setting. "This is a lovely building, isn't it? The sunlight through those windows . . ." I lifted my hand, tilting it left and right to watch the hues change. "It's almost tangible, isn't it?"

She eyed me quizzically, evidently not appreciating my whimsy. But then nothing I knew about her upbringing led me to believe she'd been encouraged to embrace such things.

"You said to contact you if I thought of something, even if it's small," she finally ventured to say.

"Yes." But still she hesitated, forcing me to prod her. "Have you thought of something?"

She nodded, biting her lip. Clearly, she was struggling with whether to tell me, and as our silence lengthened and stretched, I could almost feel it solidifying. Yet, I didn't know enough about whatever had occurred to her to prod her to tell me. So instead, I decided to approach it from a different angle.

"Were you acquainted with Miss Kavanagh's cousin, Daniel Keogh?"

She seemed to start, almost as if she'd forgotten I was there. "Mr. Keogh? Yes. Though . . . I'm not supposed to admit it." Another edict from her mother, no doubt. "He seemed to be a nice man. Kitty was awfully fond of him. Although Mr. Kavanagh said his politics were questionable."

"Sinn Féin?" I guessed.

She nodded. "Which was why Kitty never believed that he'd been killed by the Volunteers as a tout. She said it didn't make sense. That it was more likely he was a tout *for* them."

"What did Mr. Keogh do?"

"I don't know exactly, just that he worked for a railway."

A position which could prove useful to either side, particularly given the ongoing railway strike against transporting military material and personnel. Though, Mr. Keogh had died before that had even begun.

"Did he know Lieutenant Delagrange?"

"Oh, yes. Actually, they knew each other from somewhere before the lieutenant began seeing Kitty." She frowned. "Kitty said Mr. Keogh didn't approve of him, but I don't know why. Except . . ." Her brow furrowed. "Well, I think Mr. Keogh was a little sweet on Kitty himself."

That could explain it. Or the fact that Delagrange had

filed a malicious-injuries claim involving an incident that Mr. Keogh was part of, and he knew Delagrange was lying about the extent of his injuries.

"Mrs. Kent?" Miss Fairbanks said solemnly, her amber eyes pleading with me. "Do . . . do you think the lieutenant was responsible for the attack on Kitty?"

I answered carefully. "He seems like a strong suspect."

She searched my face, seeking something, and then lowered her head almost as if praying. "Then there's something else you should know."

Hearing the hollow tone of her voice, the hairs along the back of my neck stood on end, for I knew whatever she had to say was important.

"The day that Kitty died, Lieutenant Delagrange asked me to help him see her." She directed her words to the floor, and it was all I could do to remain still and listen. "Kitty had closeted herself in her bedchamber and she wouldn't leave it, and neither her mother nor her nurse would let the lieutenant visit her there. It would have been highly improper, of course. But . . . but he said he was desperate to see her. That he feared she thought the worst of him since he hadn't reacted as well as he should to learning of the assault on her." Her hands tightened into fists, and she pounded them on her legs. "He claimed he'd been in shock, but he didn't care about any of that now. Just her. And I . . ." She closed her eyes, shaking her head. "I thought it all rather romantic."

I rested a consoling hand on her shoulder. "So you helped him."

"I distracted the nurse long enough for Lieutenant Delagrange to slip into the room, and then distracted her again when he left."

I frowned. "And the nurse noticed none of this?" For someone who was caring for a patient who was allegedly at risk for suicide, the nurse didn't seem to be terribly attentive or observant. "What did you—" I began, intending to ask her the nature of the distraction, but Miss Fairbanks interrupted me.

"What if she didn't intend to take that sleeping medicine on her own?" She pressed her hands to her face. "What . . . what if he's responsible?" She began to weep, murmuring in a broken voice. "And I helped him."

"If that's true, you couldn't have known," I said, rubbing her back between her shoulder blades. "You couldn't have known he had such horrible intentions. And . . . and we don't know for certain that he did."

She turned to me with angry eyes, obviously not wanting me to placate her, for she was right. It certainly looked damning. Especially knowing that Delagrange was likely Miss Kavanagh's chief assailant. But there were still facts to be gathered and proof to be found, or it was merely her word against his. If only I could find the footman and the nurse.

"Do you recall the nurse's name or where she came from?"

Miss Fairbanks hiccupped, straightening. "No, Kitty and Mrs. Kavanagh only ever called her 'Nurse.' And she won't speak of her now."

Maybe not, but perhaps a member of her staff would. If I could ever gain access to the house again. But Mrs. Kavanagh was always home, and she always sent me away. I was almost to the point of resorting to asking Ginny for help.

"Thank you, Miss Fairbanks, for telling me this," I told her. "I know it wasn't easy."

She sniffed. "Kitty would have done the same for me." There was a wistful note in her voice, almost as if she wasn't sure she believed it.

I was given my second surprise of the day when I arrived at the Pillar Picture House on Upper Sackville Street. Nancy and I bought our tickets and found seats in the middle of the cinema. We chatted amicably, and as the Pathé reels that preceded every film began to play, she slipped a thin stack of papers from beneath her coat and passed them to me.

I looked at her in confusion, laughing at the almost giddy grin that had spread across her face. "What's this?"

"That file ye wanted," she leaned over to whisper.

My gaze dipped to the papers as she continued.

"The one on Miss Kavanagh. 'Tis a copy, of course, but it's all there."

I could hardly believe it. I'd hoped she might glance at it and slip me the name of the footman and perhaps the officer who had filed the report, not give me a copy of the entire file!

My astonishment must have been evident, for she giggled. "You're welcome."

"I . . . yes, thank you," I replied belatedly.

She nodded. "Now put it away."

I did as I was told, though no one around us was paying us the least attention. It was all I could do to leave it there; such was my eagerness to read it now that I had it in hand. I'm afraid I only gave the film half my attention, but what I did see was a rather sappy affair anyway, not at all to my taste. The rest of my thoughts were devoted to speculation over what the report might say. But these soon gave way to misgivings about Nancy.

Superficially, it would seem this was a triumph. To have successfully secured a friend and contact inside the walls of the Castle. One who could gain access to secure files and information. Nevertheless, I was wary.

It had simply been too easy. Nancy and I were barely acquainted. Yes, we'd seemed to have a natural affinity, but that didn't equate to trustworthiness. As an employee of the British government, she was bound by the Official Secrets Act, and yet she'd so quickly and seemingly guiltlessly stolen a confidential file for me. At least, she appeared untroubled by her actions, engrossed as she was in the film.

Maybe she felt justified in her decision to break protocol

because I had once worked for the government myself, but she had no proof that this was true, only rumors and my veiled references. Even so, I might have been dismissed from my government position because of unscrupulous actions. She couldn't have been certain what type of person she was giving the file to or what my intentions were for it, no matter what I claimed.

Yet, Nancy was an intelligent girl. That much had been clear to me right from the start. So I had to believe she knew precisely what she was doing. Which meant one of two things. Either she was doing this at the behest of someone in the government, or she didn't feel bound by the Official Secrets Act, perhaps because she was already breaking it. Maybe because she'd already sworn her loyalty to a rival government—Dáil Éireann.

The first option seemed doubtful if for no other reason than I couldn't think of anyone within Dublin Castle with the authority or desire to grant me access to the file. Not even Lord French, whose motivations for asking me to investigate Miss Kavanagh's assault would almost certainly end with my revelation that her assailants had not been members of the IRA. He was the sort of man to prefer the comfortable fiction that it had been the enemy.

That meant that Nancy was, like as not, an informant for Collins. And like as not, he'd instructed her to reciprocate our friendship and give me the file.

This troubled me, though I'd already suspected the Big Fellow was aware of my inquiry into Miss Kavanagh's assault. It troubled me because I didn't like suspecting I'd received help from the man. I was conflicted enough about him without this weighing into the matter. Of course, my feelings about Alec and fear of what had happened to him were also all mixed up in my opinion of Collins. It was difficult to separate the two.

As a former British Intelligence agent, one still working

covertly at the behest of C, I knew how I was supposed to feel. Or at least how I was supposed to operate. I should turn over everything I knew and all the evidence I'd gathered to C, regardless of what that meant for Nancy or Collins or Alec, if he was alive. But I found I couldn't do that. Not when I didn't trust how it would be handled. I knew this meant that I was stepping into dangerous territory, but most of intelligence work lay in the shadows, rarely was it black and white.

So I decided I would remain quiet about Nancy for now. I would make peace with it. Because having a connection inside the Castle would prove useful, even if I could never be absolutely certain of her loyalties. I'd worked with other such contacts before. During the war, there had been no shortage of people operating with ulterior motives, be they inside the German-occupied territories or the relative safety of London.

I turned to look at Nancy as she laughed at the heroine's reaction, smiling as she swiveled her head to meet my eye. In that moment, she seemed so artless, so unguarded, and I felt a pulse of concern on her behalf. For if she was, in fact, an informant for Collins, and he'd directed her to get me the file, then he'd rather carelessly made her vulnerable to suspicion. And if there was one thing I knew about informants, especially ones in valuable positions, you protected them at all costs. It seemed Collins hadn't yet learned that lesson, and I hoped Nancy wouldn't pay for it.

Though we had no way of knowing whether the address listed in the Dublin Castle report for Earnán Doyle was correct, Sidney and I had decided it was at least a place to start. After all, Delagrange had, indeed, proved to be the intelligence officer who had allegedly interviewed him, and he might just as easily have fabricated his address as he had the rest of the report. However, I had a suspicion the lieutenant wouldn't have risked manufacturing such a simple fact to verify. Not when he needed the rest to be believable. In any case, Doyle was a common name, and so was Ernie/Earnán. There might have been hundreds of men in Dublin who answered to such a moniker. We hadn't the time or ability to track them all down.

The address was located off Dominick Street, not far from King's Inn, and proved not to be a home at all, but a tenement. One that housed not one family, but dozens, all packed cheek by jowl into tiny rooms, some separated by little but a sheet or curtain. The sanitation facilities—what there were—were rudimentary and akin to what I would have anticipated fifty years ago in Victorian London. Yet Dubliners had to contend with them today.

I'd heard that there was a severe housing shortage, but this was deplorable. And given the fact that Ireland was under the administration of the United Kingdom, there was no one to blame but ourselves. In the cramped, filth-ridden corridors, disease must run rampant. Few of the children running about in the street had shoes, and most were wearing clothes with patches upon patches. Yet they all had cheery smiles for us as they asked for pennies and bobs.

The adults were more suspicious, eying our fine garments with understandable misgiving even though we'd worn some of our dowdiest. I began to fear we'd miscalculated, and that I should have come alone in my disguise. But then an older woman looked me in the eye and seemed to deem me worthy, or at least not a threat, and pointed me toward a doorway. She had no teeth and a deep brogue, so I struggled to comprehend.

Fortunately for us, a young man appeared in the entrance, his clothing neater and newer than most. The jaded look in his eyes spoke of weariness and deep disappointment, and I took a gamble we'd found our man.

"Earnán Doyle?" I asked, taking the lead with Sidney at my back, hopefully trying to look nonthreatening.

The man's expression turned wary, but he didn't retreat, and he didn't deny that was his name.

"Mary suggested I speak to you. She said you were the one who found Miss Kavanagh after she was assaulted."

He began to turn away.

"Please, we mean you no harm," I begged. "We only want to discover the truth about what happened."

He scoffed and spat in the dust, startling me.

"We've seen Lieutenant Delagrange's report."

His shoulders stiffened.

"We know what he *claims* you said you saw."

This comment piqued his interest, and he turned his head to look at me more squarely.

I risked taking another step closer. "I know what I suspect actually happened, but I'd like to hear the truth from you."

He scowled. "The truth? No one wants to hear the truth." Anger and frustration fairly vibrated through him.

"You told the Kavanaghs, didn't you?" I guessed, remembering what Mary had told me. "And they told you to keep it to yourself."

His head dipped, his brow furrowing in silent confirmation.

"I'm asking you not to do that. For Miss Kavanagh's sake. Won't you please tell me?"

He glanced over his shoulder toward the doorway, clearly struggling with himself. "Alright, I'll tell ye. But I won't never repeat it ever again," he warned. "Understand?" He inhaled sharply through his nostrils. "'Twas Delagrange and his mates. I could tell that straightaway, even with their ridiculous masks. He came to the house often enough, 'twasn't difficult to recognize him, though he seemed to think he'd fooled me." He crossed his arms over his chest, scuffling the dirt with the toe of his boot. "But Mr. and Mrs. Kavanagh must've told him what I'd said, for he came to see me a few days later. Told me if I ever told anyone else, I wouldn't live to regret it. That he'd taken care of Mr. Keogh, and he'd take care of me, too."

I exchanged a speaking look with Sidney, unable to believe everything Earnán had just confirmed for us. He had been the witness and connection we'd been searching for all this time.

"And you didn't tell the detective inspector any of this?" I confirmed.

"Nay, he wasn't allowed to speak with us." His face tightened in disgust. "The Kavanaghs made certain of that."

"You have to come with us. You have to tell him now," I pleaded. "And tell the Castle that Delagrange forged your statement as well."

"Nay!" He shook his head. "I told ye I wouldn't. Do ye think I don't know how this works? 'Tis their word against mine, and no one will believe me."

I pressed my hands to my chest. "We do!"

Earnán's gaze flicked over my shoulder as if to verify that when I'd included Sidney in this statement, it was true.

"And we have some corroborating evidence, that Miss Kavanagh told a friend that Lieutenant Delagrange asked her to meet him in their garden after everyone else retired." I didn't add the part about Delagrange having convinced Miss Fairbanks to help him sneak up to see Miss Kavanagh just before she allegedly committed suicide. I didn't want to muddy the waters concerning the assault.

He considered this. "Maybe, but that won't change anythin'."

"But we have to try," I insisted, growing agitated. "For Miss Kavanagh. Doesn't she deserve justice?"

"Aye. But don't we all?" He gestured to the slum, the city, the country around him. To the people living in squalor, with little hope for a better future. To those denied equal justice or declined a promotion because of their religion or social status. To the people who had played the political game correctly and yet still lost.

"I heard what happened to Miss Kavanagh, and I'm sorry. I truly am. And I pray God has mercy on her soul. Sister Mary Aloysius said it was the best thing we could do for her, and I suppose that's as true in death as life. But I cannot bring her back. And I cannot win her justice. Not as Earnán Doyle, lowly first footman, and an Irish Catholic, at that."

When I would have argued further, even drawing breath to do so, Sidney clasped my upper arms from behind, halting me. We couldn't deny that what Earnán had said was true, and we had no right to expose him to danger. Nor any right to shame him for his silence when the outcome would not change.

However, if we could secure the promise of a fair hearing—perhaps even the agreement that Earnán could act as a confidential witness—then we could return to make our plea. Until then, we had to respect his decision. Though, I had one more question.

"Who is Sister Mary Aloysius?" I asked, having the vague stirrings of an idea that I might know.

"Miss Kavanagh's nurse," he replied as if I should have known this already.

Of course! Sisters often trained as nurses, offering succor to the sick and dying.

"One of the Kavanaghs' friends recommended her. Apparently, she'd nursed someone on his deathbed for months, and yet 'kept her papish nonsense to herself,'" he added dryly.

I suspected this last was a direct quote from one of the Kavanaghs.

"Do you know where we can find her?"

"Mater Hospital, I suspect. 'Tis where she came from."

Sidney thanked him and we turned to go, but I remembered the look on his face when we arrived. It troubled me.

"When you left their employ, did the Kavanaghs give you a reference?" I asked Earnán.

The look on his face was answer enough.

I felt affronted on his behalf. “Perhaps we could—”

But he cut me off with a shake of his head. “I’m needed here.” His answer was resolute, as was the look he shared with another man a short distance across the yard.

As Sidney led me away, I couldn’t help but wonder what exactly that meant, and whether “here” included the local IRA brigade.

CHAPTER 25

"Well, that was more than we hoped for," Sidney remarked once we'd returned to Dominick Street. Soon after leaving Earnán behind, he'd removed a cigarette from his case and lit it, the smell of Turkish tobacco doing at least something to dispel the stench of this tumbledown corner of Dublin.

I tipped my face up toward the sun, feeling a jumble of elation and frustration. "If only we could convince him to testify."

"You can hardly blame the man for his reticence. Not knowing what we do." He grimaced. "Not after picking up the paper and reading what's happening elsewhere in this country."

Just in the last three days, several areas of the country had erupted in violence, and much of it was not at the hands of the IRA. In Cork City, where RIC Divisional Commander Smyth had been shot dead, and the men responsible had managed to slip away in the crowd leaving a neighboring cinema where a film had just let out, Crown Forces in the area had been ordered to patrol the streets. However, tempers boiled over, resulting in a number of attacks on civilians, including several former British Army soldiers. It didn't help when railway workers refused to transport Smyth's body north to County Down for his funeral.

In County Limerick, the IRA killed a constable during an

ambush, and the RIC retaliated by burning several buildings, including the library and creamery. Then in Tuam, County Galway, after two more RIC men were killed in an ambush, the RIC and British Army Dragoons stationed nearby embarked on a reprisal of looting, burning, and shooting, causing a great deal of destruction. In many of these cases, it was difficult to get entirely accurate information. In some instances, the newspapers obeyed the government's censorship orders while wild rumors seemed to pass about by word of mouth, such as accusations that the blood from one of the former soldiers killed in Cork was used to write the killers' regimental name on a wall close by. However, when an English reporter writing of the incidents in Tuam actually compared it to the villages devastated by the Germans in Belgium and France, I got a sick feeling in the pit of my stomach.

"It certainly doesn't encourage people to step forward and do the right thing when just walking down the street can get them killed, let alone angering either side of this conflict," I said softly.

Sidney helped me pick my way around a pile of refuse. "What's our next step, Ver?"

I knew what he was asking. As matters currently stood, it was unlikely that challenging the established narrative would change anything. But much like with Alec, I couldn't leave it at that. Not if there was anything else we could try. Miss Kavanagh deserved that much. Any future men or women who might find themselves in Delagrange's crosshairs deserved our every effort to prevent it. Anything less would be a dereliction on our part.

"I need to speak with Sister Mary Aloysius," I declared firmly. "Maybe Miss Kavanagh confided in her." My eyes narrowed. "And we need to speak to the Kavanaghs again. Though we may have to force the issue." My last three attempts to call on them had been rebuffed, but we knew enough now to threaten our way inside if necessary.

Sidney halted us just in time to avoid colliding with a bicyclist who came hurtling out of a side street.

"Apologies," the chap called over his shoulder.

Sidney dropped his cigarette butt on the pavement, grinding it out with this heel as he continued to eye the cyclist's retreating form with disapproval. "I'll pay another visit to O'Shaughnessy." The city recorder. "Perhaps he can tell me some more information about Delagrange's malicious-injury claim."

I nodded. If nothing else, perhaps we could prove the lieutenant and his mates had perjured themselves. It might be enough to throw some discredit on him.

I considered approaching DI Burrows about Daniel Keogh's murder, but it was doubtful he would be able or willing to help us. Not when the probable killer was an intelligence officer at the Castle. That would fall under the jurisdiction of O, and I had zero faith in *his* impartiality.

"I also think we should speak with Bennett and Ames."

I turned to Sidney with a scowl, but he held up his hand to halt my protest.

"I know you'd prefer to keep your distance, but they're not only acquainted with Delagrange, but they also don't favor him. They might hold some useful information about him."

I heaved an aggrieved sigh. "You have a point. Just because their intelligence on the location of the phosgene cylinders has proven faulty . . ."

He eyed me askance at this barbed comment.

". . . doesn't mean they won't have some valuable insights into Delagrange."

Sidney might think my criticism unfair, but I couldn't help but continue to harbor suspicions about Bennett and Ames continuing to involve my husband in their efforts. Yesterday's raid had proved just as fruitless as the one the week before.

"We also need to debrief Lord French," I said. "But I think that can wait until Sunday's dinner party."

He agreed as we hurried to catch the next passing tram. "I take it you intend to spend the afternoon on your other quest," he said as we began to move forward.

Sidney had taken to calling my search for Collins a quest, and it was beginning to feel like one. Though the day before I'd at least secured my own steed, or rather bicycle. And a good thing, too, for it seemed Collins rode half a dozen or more miles each day across the breadth of the city to various offices and other locations. I'd managed to tail him from Wellington Quay to the Wicklow Hotel—wondering to myself how I'd missed him all the times I'd sat at Peter's bar—and then southward, only to lose him near St. Stephen's Green.

I was, by parts, amazed and horrified at his fearlessness. He wore no disguise, standing tall and straight as he rode or marched bold as brass past the various Crown Forces, and even through police cordons. I supposed that was his dazzle-painting, his camouflage. For no one would believe that, as the most wanted man in Ireland, he would pedal carelessly through the streets, even engaging soldiers and officers in conversation. I couldn't decide if he was mad or a genius. He was certainly charming.

"Yes," I told Sidney. "Maybe today will be the day."

It wasn't.

I followed Collins as far south as Mespil Road, but then lost him again as he was headed into town. The trouble arose in maintaining enough of a distance so as not to alert him or anyone around him that he was being followed, particularly as I had to find a place to pause and loiter while he went about his business. Thus far, most of his stops had been at offices or shops or a hotel, not a pub or restaurant where I might have more naturally approached him. He might have entered the bar or restaurant of a hotel, but I couldn't be certain. I also hadn't spotted Alec, and with each passing day, my hopes began to sink lower.

It wasn't the day I spoke to Miss Kavanagh's nurse either.

When I stopped at the Mater Hospital to ask after Sister Mary Aloysius, I was told she'd gone to Rathfarnham and wouldn't return for almost a fortnight. While the distance to Rathfarnham was only about twenty miles, I received the impression that the sister would not welcome visitors. So I resolved to be patient.

But my patience was wearing thin.

"Couldn't we have met them someplace less lousy with intelligence officers?" I groused as Sidney led me into Rabbiatti's Saloon in Marlborough Street the following evening.

"Not if you want to catch them not minding their tongues," Sidney murmured into my ear as he removed my coat. The temperature had taken a dip that day, but per my husband's instructions, I'd done my own dazzle-painting, wearing something swank with one of the straight drop-waists that were so popular, so as to pretend to conceal any possible rounding of the abdomen. I had to remember that Bennett and the others believed I was expecting.

Apparently, I'd done well on my assignment, for at least half of the eyes in the room swung my way, and the other half soon followed. I knew I'd brought my jade-green gown with a beaded bodice and fringe skirt with me from London for a reason.

Sidney's hand pressed proprietarily against the bare skin of my back. "Cheer up. I'll take you dancing later."

I wouldn't say no to that. Not in this getup.

We weaved our way among the tables littered with glasses of liquor and wreathed in cigarette smoke toward where Bennett stood gesturing to us. The ceiling here, at least, was taller, so that the heat and smoke could rise. "Verity," he declared before bussing my cheek. "So glad you're feeling up to joining us."

I didn't miss the slight arch to his eyebrows or the curious glance he passed over me from head to toe as he offered me the chair he'd just vacated. However, I wasn't about to comment on my health or the status of my presumed expectant state. A fact that irritated Bennett as he turned to fetch a chair from a neighboring table, but it would have been impolite for him to ask about it outright.

Sidney introduced me to the other man seated at the table, Lieutenant Ames. Ames had a curious accent, which I soon learned was because he'd been born in the United States, though at some point he'd become a British subject and served in the Grenadier Guards during the war. He was slightly older than Bennett and possessed a broad forehead, dark receding hair, and a mustache.

Meanwhile, Bennett had signaled the publican and ordered us drinks. He seemed to be well enough acquainted with Sidney to know that he appreciated a good stout. "A gin fizz, right?" he asked me as our drinks were delivered, I presumed having taken notice of what I'd been drinking at Kidd's Back the last time I'd seen him. I smiled politely and thanked him, though I wished I could have been sipping a gin rickey from that little restaurant in Dawson Street where Wick had asked me to meet him.

"I suppose Sidney has kept you abreast of our extracurricular activities," Bennett remarked, leaning back in his chair with a second tall glass of ale in one hand and a cigarette in the other.

By this, I deduced he meant their search for the phosgene cylinders.

"It's only too bad they've thus far proved unsuccessful," I observed wistfully as I risked a sip of the gin fizz. It wasn't precisely enjoyable, but at least it was palatable in comparison to those I'd sipped elsewhere.

Bennett's eyes narrowed slightly, perhaps wondering if that was a dig at him, but I maintained an artless expression. Sidney, however, was not fooled, pressing his leg against mine underneath the table in warning. Much as I would have liked to persist in issuing veiled barbs, I recognized he was correct. You didn't poke the bear you hoped would share his catch of fish.

"Yes, but we are getting closer," Ames declared after draining his third glass of whiskey mixed with water. I noted the softening of his pronunciation and gauged he was but another glass away from being corked. I wondered how long it would take Bennett to get there.

"These shinners are craftier than they look," Bennett concurred, though he looked disgruntled to admit it. "But don't you worry."

I offered him a smile of gratitude, running my finger around the rim of my glass as I pretended to lapse into thought. "It does make one wonder though, doesn't it? How they got their hands on the stuff in the first place?"

I was curious to hear whether they'd formed any theories, and whether Ardmore featured in any of them or if he'd escaped the suspicion of everyone but us.

"Who knows?" Bennett replied. "Probably a corrupt RE." Royal Engineer. "Someone from the Irish Guards." He gestured broadly with his hands, letting me know he wasn't far off pace from Ames. He was just better at hiding his inebriation.

In any case, his assumption wasn't entirely false, considering the phosgene would have originated with the Corps of Royal Engineers. The barrels and crates smuggled off of the Isle of Wight containing the phosgene had been stamped with their mark. I supposed it was also only natural to assume an Irishman was responsible. And in a way, he was correct, for Ardmore himself was Irish. Just not the type of Irish Bennett was thinking of.

"But as I said, you needn't worry your pretty head about this one, Ver." He toasted to Ames and my husband. "We've got it covered."

Sidney's leg pressed against mine again, perhaps alerting

me to the fact my answering smile was more predatory than placating. It took a great deal of self-control not to put the fellow in his place and take him to task for the presumption of using my nickname as well. But Ames was also watching me, so I swallowed the urge and adjusted my mask to one of complacency.

I supposed it was my own fault for broaching the question, so I lapsed into silence, listening as the men bantered and bellyached. The latter largely came from Bennett and Ames, who were evidently not as pleased by their assignment here in Dublin as they'd hoped to be. It was plainly not as simple or cushy a commission as they'd been led to believe. I wanted to feel sorry for them, but some of their and the other men's remarks about the Irish were abhorrent.

Having spent enough time with intelligence officers, it was easy for me to pick out who they were among the crowd, and almost to a man they were all drinking too much. I couldn't believe that during their training no one had pointed out how risky this behavior was. Maybe they thought they were safe here, given it was largely populated with fellow intelligence officers, members of the Crown Forces, and touts offering up information. But it was both reckless and foolish. Especially when at least some of their names must have been on Collins's list for potential assassination. After all, I'd already seen his right-hand man walking into Kidd's Back. Who knew which of his men might have been sitting amongst us even then.

"You know, I was a bit concerned that bounder Delagrange would turn up here tonight," Sidney suddenly declared, evidently having decided that Bennett and Ames were corked enough. "But I haven't seen his face all evening."

This, indeed, had been a concern, for we'd figured it would be far more difficult to get information about Delagrange out of Bennett and Ames if he was there.

"Oh, he isn't all bad," Bennett said, slurring some of his

words. "I don't know what got into 'im to accost Ver." He began to snicker. "'Cept maybe he fancied 'er."

I knew for certain that wasn't it, but I played dumb. "I did hear he was recently injured, so perhaps some lingering pain made him cross and out of temper," I suggested, feigning pity.

But this comment only drew more snickers from Bennett, and even Ames cracked a smile. "'Cept whatever his injury was—"

"If he actually had one," Ames muttered under his breath.

Bennett nodded. "Wasn't all that terrible. But he stuck it to the Irish anyway." He clinked glasses with Ames.

"What do you mean?" Sidney asked with a false smile.

"He filed one of those . . . those . . ." Ames swirled his hand before him as if this might help him recall.

"Malicious-injury claims," Bennett supplied.

Ames pointed at him. "That! Applied to the Recorder's Court for compensation. Pretended to be more wounded than he was, and the committee fell for it. Paid him one thousand pounds."

Bennett laughed.

It infuriated me how they both seemed to find it all so amusing, but I merely smiled. "How on earth did he convince them?"

Ames rocked back in his chair, and I worried he might tip it over, for he was none too steady. "A bit of actin'. A bit of lyin' by his friends."

"He's lucky he didn't get caught," Sidney replied, and I could hear the beginnings of a bite in his voice. I lifted my leg, rubbing my calf along his underneath the table in silent warning.

Bennett scoffed. "Command doesn't care. Not when the money's comin' out of Irish pockets, not ours." He took a long swallow from his nearly empty third glass. "So long as we're not caught."

"Then Delagrange isn't the only one who's gotten away with it?" I asked when Sidney seemed unable to.

"Oh, no." Bennett chuckled. "Not by a long shot."

I supposed this all but confirmed that Delagrange and his mates had perjured themselves, but we still didn't know what the incident was where he'd claimed to have been injured or how Miss Kavanagh's cousin was connected to it. I looked to Sidney, needing his help to draw it out of them.

"The incident where he was allegedly injured must have occurred soon after he arrived in Dublin," Sidney began in a flat voice, gaining more self-awareness as he spoke and modulating his tone to one of more amused interest. "He's fortunate that didn't rouse suspicion. Though, I suppose it was always the raw recruits who were most likely to click it."

This statement caused me a mixed reaction. I was proud of Sidney for overcoming his evident distaste and coaxing Ames and Bennett to react in amused agreement to this statement. But I was also slightly appalled to hear him speak of the men who had died under his command in such a callous way, even though I knew it was all an act.

"Isn't that the truth," Bennett replied, and I wanted to snarl, "as if you would know," for he'd served almost exclusively as an intelligence officer in Holland.

"But Delagrange served in the army here before he transferred to intelligence," Bennett continued, not even bothering to couch matters in euphemism. "He got knocked around a bit in a skirmish with the shinner crowd outside Mountjoy demanding the release of their hunger strikers but got no more than a scrape and a few bruises."

In mid-April, the government had capitulated and, in a monumental error, released not only the political prisoners who had been on hunger strikes, but a whole host of others incarcerated at Mountjoy Prison on charges related to the rebellion. It had contributed in further demoralizing a police force that was already crumbling under the weight of the populace's boycott. So the incident referred to in Delagrange's claim must have occurred shortly before that, and Daniel Keogh had been there.

Sidney made some follow-up remarks but the look he cast my way communicated he was ready to leave. We'd gotten the information we needed, and now he was counting on me to extricate us.

"Darling," I murmured, draping myself along Sidney's side. "You promised to take me dancing."

"That I did," he agreed, though the smirk he shared with the men suggested he was indulging me. "If you'll excuse us, gentlemen."

"Of course," Bennett replied with a leer, though Ames appeared more wistful. I wondered if perhaps he might have a girl of his own somewhere. Or one he'd like to call his own.

Sidney helped me into my coat and tossed some money on the table for all of our drinks before shaking the men's hands. Then we strolled out of the saloon without a backward glance.

CHAPTER 26

Marlborough Street bustled with traffic, most of it pedestrians and bicycles, but Sidney still managed to flag us down a taxi. Otherwise, he was quiet, brooding on what Bennett and Ames had said. He was keeping himself very contained, and that as much as anything told me how bothered he was by it all.

So when he asked where I'd like to go dancing, I told him I was tired and suggested we go home instead. I could tell he didn't believe me, but he didn't argue, directing the driver to Upper Fitzwilliam Street. Nimble was surprised to see us when we returned so early, however he was too well trained to say anything.

"Everything alright, here?" Sidney asked him. They exchanged a few words as I made my way up to our bedchamber, intent on removing my shoes, which pinched.

Sidney found me there a few minutes later perched on the tall four poster bed, rubbing my foot. It was admittedly not the most alluring or ladylike of poses, with my skirt rucked up over my knees and my hair matted from removing my jeweled headband, but he had seen me looking much worse. Including covered in blood from a gunshot wound. So when he paused in the doorway to stare at me, I arched my eyebrows in query.

"I suppose it's a good thing we didn't go dancing after all," he said.

I scowled, taking offense, and hurled the shoe I still held in my hand at him.

He knocked it aside. "What?" he asked in confusion, before realizing his error. "No, I meant that your feet evidently weren't up to it. And I'm afraid I'm not the best company at the moment either." He sighed, gesturing at the shoe now lying next to the tallboy where he'd batted it. "Obviously." He closed the door with his foot and reached up to pull his bow tie loose. "But you deduced that already, didn't you?"

I descended the steps of the bed to stand on the bottom one so that I was nearly even with his height. "What troubled you the most?" I asked as I unfastened the top two buttons of his still crisp white shirt.

He turned his head to the side, struggling with something. "The way they treated it all as if it's a lark," he finally said, his dark blue eyes meeting mine, stark with shadows. "The lying and perjury and fraud. That statute is supposed to fairly compensate those who are wounded and the loved ones of those who have been killed, but they spoke about it almost as if it were some sort of slush fund." The longer he talked, the angrier he got. "And the implication that Dublin Castle is aware of it but content to look the other way since it only hurts the Irish—" He broke off, turning away again as his jaw flexed. "That's not what we're supposed to be doing here."

"Do you think the advisors and judges are content to look the other way as well?"

Men like O'Shaughnessy and Kavanagh.

"I don't know," he said. "I suppose that depends on whether they've been bribed or threatened. Maybe that's something I should ask Mr. O'Shaughnessy when I speak with him tomorrow."

His expression was bleak and jaded, and I suddenly realized how hard all of this had been on him. Having to sit there and pretend he was of the same mind. I might have donned a physical disguise to venture out into the city searching for information in order to locate Alec, but Sidney was forced to wear an invisible one day after day, masking how he truly felt about matters pertaining to this Irish situation. I was interacting with strangers who would hopefully never know who I really was, and who I would probably never see again once we left the isle. Meanwhile, Sidney mingled as himself, with men he very well might meet across dinner tables or boardrooms in the future. They were men he had perhaps respected and might even have admired. Now he was questioning those bonds of amicable feeling.

For a man who had already seen so much of the worst of humankind, who had been forced to question lifelong friendships—even having his best man shoot him and leave him for dead—it tore away a piece of my heart to watch him face such things again. And at my careless behest. He would never have been here had I not asked him to help me search for Alec. He would never have heard these disillusioning things.

I pressed my hand to his chest. "I'm sorry, darling."

"What do you need to feel sorry for?" he retorted. "You're not the one behaving like a bloody jackass."

"Maybe not. But if I hadn't—"

He grabbed hold of my hand, firmly shushing me. "No, Verity. I know what you're thinking. I can see it in your eyes. You did not force me to come to Dublin." His eyes glinted in challenge. "You couldn't have even if you'd wanted to. Nor could you have made me sit at home while you did all the inquiring. I took this on myself. And I'm better off for the knowing."

I opened my mouth to attempt another feeble argument, but he squeezed my hand, cutting me off before I could utter a syllable. "Stop, Ver. I won't hear it. We're supposed to share our lives, every bit of them. Including, in this case, the disillusionment and danger. Isn't that what you once told me?"

"Yes," I said, comforted more than I would have thought to hear him say it.

"Well, then."

I smiled shakily.

Sidney released me to shrug out of his evening coat, draping it over the end of the bed. "So, how exactly did Delagrange's malicious-injury claim lead to Miss Kavanagh's death?"

"Well, we know from Mr. O'Shaughnessy that Miss Kavanagh's cousin played some role in that malicious-injury claim, and from Bennett that it occurred during the general strike protests that occurred before the hunger strikers were released from Mountjoy in mid-April." I reached up to remove my emerald chandelier earrings, dropping them in the jewelry box on the clothes press beside the bed. "Mr. Keogh must have known Delagrange perjured himself, and he must have told his cousin, Miss Kavanagh."

"Then Miss Kavanagh tells Delagrange she knows the truth," Sidney extrapolated as he removed his cuff links. "Maybe even demands he return the money and recant his statement."

"Which Delagrange won't do."

"It would tarnish his name forever, and that of his mates who lied for him."

"And the British Army."

Sidney nodded. "Just so."

I laid my jade bracelets and emerald necklace in the box and closed it with a snap. "Perhaps she threatens to tell the truth if he doesn't." I stared down at the gilded surface, running my fingers over the pearl inlay. "So he assaults her to keep her quiet, but is careful to do so in a way that can be blamed on the IRA."

"What of Mr. Keogh's murder? Was that to silence him as well?"

"Probably." I turned to look at Sidney. "The IRA aren't claiming responsibility for his death, and according to Miss Fairbanks, Miss Kavanagh suspected her cousin was actually working *for* the IRA, not against it."

He raked his hand back through his hair, ruffling it. "That would explain Mrs. Kavanagh's disapproval of him."

"I imagine she disapproved of the manner of his death just as much," I remarked dryly. "But yes, it would." I paused to consider. "Though that also suggests Delagrange is capable of premeditated murder." The note on Dáil stationery left with the body implied definite forethought.

"If the man is despicable enough to assault and forcibly cut the hair of the woman he professes to hold affection for, and ask a few of his chums to help him do it, I can believe he's capable of just about anything," Sidney stated, his mouth curled in disgust.

"Valid point," I admitted, even as my thoughts slid to one even darker. If Delagrange was capable of all that, what would he do if she still refused to remain silent? Or perhaps the real question was, what wouldn't he do?

Seeing the look on my face, Sidney sidled closer, his voice gentling. "You're thinking of Miss Fairbanks's confession. That she helped Delagrange sneak into Miss Kavanagh's chamber shortly before she died."

"How can I not?"

His gaze shimmered with empathy, but also wariness of something else. Something he was keeping from me.

"What is it?" I asked.

"Bennett told me Colonel Winter has big plans. That he's already recruited a number of his former comrades who he knows have the stomach for the work."

That didn't sound good, considering Winter's amoral reputation.

"And he has plans to get his hands on the Dáil Loan."

While I understood the British government's desire to seize

the money the Dáil had raised in the form of a national loan to fund their shadow government, for it might very well bring the rebels to their knees, I didn't trust whatever O's intentions were for it, or that it would be returned to the proper people.

Yet, none of O's actions were our purview. We were supposed to find Alec and locate the phosgene cylinders, if possible, and get out. However, I could see in Sidney's eyes the same reticence I felt at walking away and leaving O to wreak whatever havoc he chose. And O was supposed to be one of the good guys!

He grasped hold of my waist. "But that is not our concern at the moment." His eyes searched mine. "I assume you want to confront the Kavanaghs."

His hands were warm through the silk of my gown, infusing me with courage. "After you speak with O'Shaughnessy," I confirmed. "We need to understand just how much they know." My voice tightened in anger. "Just how much they're involved."

After all, Mr. Kavanagh had nearly recused himself from the hearing over Delagrange's malicious-injury claim. And if Earnán had been telling the truth—and I believed he had, for he had nothing to gain from such a lie—then the Kavanaghs had known it was Delagrange he'd seen assaulting their daughter in the garden. They'd known and told him to stay silent about it.

Sidney squeezed my waist, bringing me out of my dark contemplations. "Tomorrow."

I nodded, but he must have still been able to tell how much all of it distressed me for he pulled me into his arms, cradling my head against his shoulder just above his heart.

Sidney set out early the next morning to speak to Mr. O'Shaughnessy before he left his home in Fitzwilliam Square with his DMP escort for the Four Courts. I'd intended to have a lie-in, but my thoughts wouldn't be silenced. Too much had happened, and there was still too much to be done. So I rose and dressed, lingering over breakfast.

I knew Sidney intended to return before mid-morning, and in any case the timing was all wrong to set off in pursuit of Collins. The day before, I'd trailed him from Mespil Road to Westland Row before losing him in the late afternoon commuter traffic. The man did get about.

I settled in the back parlor with a plate of toast, a cup of tea, and the latest stack of newspapers delivered that morning. Though I soon wished I'd allowed the latter to molder in a corner. For while the south continued to have its pockets of unrest, the north had exploded with sectarian violence. For all that the British government wanted to pretend they were being fair-handed, it was quite obvious who had the freer hand.

Lieutenant-Colonel Smyth's funeral had been held in Banbridge, County Down, with a large turnout of unionists, including General Tudor, and seemed to have gone off without a hitch. However, Protestant workers soon unleashed their discontent, demanding the removal of all Catholic workers from a number of industries and marching through the streets to provoke other businesses into doing the same. Soon loyalist mobs in Banbridge and neighboring Dromore began looting and burning Catholic-owned houses and shops, resulting in numerous deaths and injuries, while allegedly the RIC did not attempt to intervene. When assistance from the British Army was finally requested, they arrested some of the Catholics being attacked, but none of the loyalist mob.

But matters were even worse in Belfast, where riots broke out. Once again, Protestant workers demanded the expulsion of their Catholic coworkers and those who tried to defend them, attacking them and driving them from their places of work, in particular the Harland and Wolff shipyards and other industrial sites throughout the city. Nearly ten thousand were ousted from their jobs. Unrest ensued, with clashes between Protestants and Catholics resulting in dozens of deaths and hundreds of mostly Catholics being driven from their homes. What aid the Crown Forces provided seemed to have only made matters worse.

Though the violence in the south was no less concerning. A British Army lorry carrying a load of rations was attacked in County Cork, resulting in the death of one officer as well as several wounded. A joint meeting of the Leitrim and Roscommon County Councils had been raided by the army and had nearly resulted in the unauthorized hanging of two of the councilmen. At Corracunna Cross, British soldiers fired into a group of young men and women, killing two, though there were differing accounts as to who the youths were and whether the shots being fired had been provoked. And in Dublin, tensions over the railway workers' strike had flared when sixty Black and Tans had attempted to board trains at Kingsbridge station, only to have the railwaymen refuse to transport them. Five or more officials had been suspended because they wouldn't let the trains leave the station with the Tans on board. Which had delayed a number of trains, including special ones bound for the Curragh races, and caused a cascade through the system.

Word was that the British cabinet's Committee on the Irish Situation was meeting in London over the next few days, and I hoped to God they finally adopted a consistent policy, preferably offering Dominion Home Rule, as anyone with sense saw it must come to. However, Max's continued silence, despite the numerous letters I'd sent through Etta Lorraine and one coded cable, made me nervous. Perhaps they'd been intercepted by the IRA. Or maybe our work-around had been discovered by British Intelligence and they'd been withheld for the same reason Max's earlier letter had been censored. Either way, I intended to risk it and telephone Max if I didn't hear from him before the week's end.

When Sidney returned, he found me staring out the window at the bright flowers bobbing their heads in our tiny garden beneath the dreary sky. The homeowners must have had a standing agreement with a pair of gardeners who appeared at intervals to tidy up the exterior, for I'd not clipped even a blade of grass since our arrival.

I could tell almost at once that Sidney's visit to O'Shaughnessy had proved unsatisfactory.

"Uncooperative?" I queried as he joined me.

He pressed one hand to the window frame and the other to the hip of his navy-blue worsted trousers. "Rather more ignorant. Or so he claimed. But I believed him," he admitted. "If bribes were offered or threats made, O'Shaughnessy didn't receive or hear of them. And he hadn't suspected their perjury until I suggested it."

"Suggested it?"

He pushed away from the window. "Yes. Recall, we have no proof. Not when Keogh is dead, and Bennett and Ames and all the others are unlikely to repeat their stories to a commanding officer, let alone a magistrate."

"Wick . . ."

"Isn't going to reveal his sources. If they would even step forward."

My hands tightened into fists in my lap. "Then the only person who might be able to do something about it is Mr. Kavanagh, and that means his admitting he either accepted a bribe or acted out of fear."

Sidney's expression revealed the same doubt I felt—that he could be convinced to speak out against Lieutenant Delagrange, though the man should be at the forefront of the charge demanding justice for his daughter and his nephew.

"We have to try," I insisted.

He stepped toward me, holding out his hand. "Then let's go do it."

CHAPTER 27

This time we didn't give the Kavanaghs the opportunity to turn us away.

"Good morning," Sidney declared cheerily as he strode into the entry hall past a somewhat stunned Mary. He handed her his hat and umbrella before threading my arm through his and escorting me toward the staircase. "We'll show ourselves up, shall we?"

"Oh, but sir," Mary called belatedly after us, hurrying to catch up. "Sir?"

"It's alright, Mary," I told her over my shoulder, affected by her obvious distress.

As we reached the next floor, I spied Mrs. Kavanagh staring at us round eyed from the rear parlor, but Sidney carried on through the door farther along the corridor into the drawing room. "How dare you," she spluttered in outrage as she came through the adjoining door. Her gaze swung toward where Mary hovered in the doorway. "You were given strict instructions . . ."

"Not to allow us entry?" Sidney finished for her. "It's no use blaming your maid when we quite clearly forced our way inside. How could she have been expected to stop us?"

"It shouldn't be her job to answer the door anyway," I added, my voice hardening. "That should fall to your first footman." Whom they'd allowed to be threatened into leaving their employ.

Mrs. Kavanagh stiffened in affront but given the fact she was a woman who prided herself on being such a stickler to decorum, even sacrificing her daughter to it, I couldn't withhold the barbed comment.

"What is the meaning of this?" Mr. Kavanagh demanded as he pushed past Mary into the room, his white mustache quivering in indignation.

"I think you know," Sidney replied icily. "Or else you wouldn't have turned my wife away nearly half a dozen times. But by all means, eject us from your home and we shall conduct this interrogation in a far more public place at a time not of your choosing."

The Kavanaghs exchanged a speaking glance, and then by unspoken agreement, both turned to close the doors they had each entered through. They perched stiffly on the edge of the settee where they had sat when we first interviewed them, both of them gathering their wounded dignity around them like a cloak. But I had no patience for placating them.

"We know that Lieutenant Delagrange and his cohorts are the ones who assaulted your daughter and cut her hair," I stated without preamble, sitting in the chair adjacent to theirs. Sidney stood just behind me. "And we know you know it."

Mrs. Kavanagh pressed a hand to her chest. "Why of all the preposterous things to suggest? He is an esteemed member of the British military. How can you suggest—"

I cut her off before she could finish. "We spoke with Earnán Doyle, your former first footman." I would not call him Ernie, no matter what she preferred. That was not his name.

This silenced her, but only for a moment. "He's not to be trusted—"

"We also have it on good authority that your daughter agreed to meet with Lieutenant Delagrange in the garden that night after everyone retired," I continued. "That he'd asked her to do so, and she'd agreed, intending to discourage him from courting her further."

Mr. Kavanagh blinked slowly while his wife stammered. "Why of all the outrageous—"

"She knew about his malicious-injury claim," I told him. "She knew he and his mates had perjured themselves."

Mrs. Kavanagh turned to look at her husband in a way that made me think she was at least ignorant of this part.

"The question is, did you?" Sidney pressed Mr. Kavanagh.

His face had gone pale though he glared at my husband. "How dare you insinuate—"

"Did he bribe you? Threaten you? Which was it, Mr. Kavanagh?" Sidney persisted. "What made you decide not to recuse yourself from the matter, despite the fact your daughter was stepping out with the claimant and your nephew was named in the claim?"

But Mr. Kavanagh stared back at him stonily, refusing to answer. We couldn't gain access to his financial accounts without government assistance, which it was doubtful we would receive. Our only way of discovering what really happened was if he told us.

"Our nephew?" Mrs. Kavanagh retorted. "You mean that rapscallion Daniel Keogh. He's naught but a troublemaker."

"Yes, one who informed for the IRA, we understand," I supplied. "Which makes it doubtful he was killed by them. It seems far more likely that Delagrange did it to keep him silent as well. Particularly as he'd already caused trouble for him by informing your daughter of what he knew about his malicious-injury claim."

"But they found a note," Mr. Kavanagh protested, though this must have sounded feeble even to his wife's ears; she scowled at him.

"Forged," Sidney stated.

Mrs. Kavanagh scoffed. "You have no proof of that. These murderous rebels are a villainous lot who would turn on their own mother if it served them to. Maybe Daniel crossed them. Maybe *that's* why they assaulted Katherine."

"Except we know she met Delagrange that night, and we know your footman identified one of the assailants as him," I said, my voice tight with condemnation. "That he told you, and you instructed him to keep quiet about it. Delagrange certainly took the accusation seriously, for he threatened him. Scared him badly enough to make him resign his position."

"It couldn't have been Delagrange," she insisted.

"Why?"

"It just couldn't," she snapped, her hands shaking with rage and distress.

I could tell now that her obstinance was more about denying a truth she couldn't face than actually believing the opposite.

"He's a British officer from a good family. He doted on her." She shook her head over and over. "He couldn't have hurt her. He wouldn't have!"

"But he did," I stated implacably.

She opened her mouth to further protest, but I spoke first . . .

"And your daughter told you so, didn't she?"

She coughed, appearing to choke on her own denial, and her husband reached out to rub her back, offering his assistance.

But I pressed on, able to see now what had happened. "Yet you still wouldn't let her break with him. You even forced her to see him, to pretend that all was well."

The Kavanaghs looked up at me with wide eyes. Because they were being forced to relive their greatest failure, or because their secret was out? I couldn't tell which was uppermost in their minds.

"That's why she insisted on closeting herself in her room. She thought there, at least, she would be safe." For no self-respecting matron would allow a man unrelated to them in her unwed daughter's room. But then I recalled what Miss Fairbanks had said. "Except she wasn't."

This, at least, seemed to startle them.

"From herself, you mean?" Mr. Kavanagh asked.

I met his gaze evenly. "Did you know that Delagrange snuck into your daughter's room shortly before she died?"

Mrs. Kavanagh looked as if she'd been struck. "Impossible," she gasped.

"We have it on good authority, and not from a member of your staff."

"The nurse?"

"No." I decided not to tell her the source of this information. Not yet. Let her sit with the fact for a while rather than dwelling on the trustworthiness of the witness.

"Are you saying . . . ?" She didn't finish the sentence, and neither Sidney nor I completed it for her.

Maybe Delagrange forced a lethal dose of the sleeping draught into her or maybe he poisoned her water or tea. Or maybe his invasion into her most secure and sacred place when she was already in such a fragile state, proving she would never be truly safe from him or anyone else, had pushed her to take her own life. I wasn't sure we would ever know the truth. But that didn't remove fault from Delagrange or the Kavanaghs for not protecting their daughter as they should.

"You placed your reputation above your daughter's wellbeing, and it cost her her life," Sidney declared harshly. I heard him inhale a steadying breath, cooling his temper. "But you can still make it right."

"How?" Mrs. Kavanagh wailed tearfully. "It won't bring her back."

"No, but you can at least get her justice."

"And you can prevent it from happening again to some other susceptible young lady," I pleaded.

"Tell the authorities what you know," Sidney charged. "Force Dublin Castle to conduct an inquiry into the matter. You have the clout and friends to do so."

"You have a far more optimistic view of government than the rest of us do," Mr. Kavanagh derided. "But then again, you're English and an aristocrat at that." He shook his white head. "They won't open an inquiry into the matter. They won't do it because they don't want to."

He spoke with such certainty, even as a Protestant, a loyalist, and a King's Counsel, that it gave me pause. If anyone in Ireland should believe they could attain justice, it would be someone like him. Yet he still held no faith in it.

"You could at least try," Sidney replied.

"And lose everything I have left? No." He eyed us both with disfavor because we'd made him face his and his wife's failings. Because we were English. Perhaps both. "I can't stop you from pursuing this further, but I don't have to help you."

Mrs. Kavanagh nodded in agreement even as she continued to silently weep.

Recognizing there was nothing more we could say, I allowed Sidney to draw me to my feet and escort me from the room. Mary was waiting for us fretfully in the entry hall. I hated the idea that we might have gotten her into trouble, so I slipped her a calling card from my reticule. "Should they give you any trouble."

She dipped her head in understanding, palming the card and then slipping it into her apron pocket.

Then Sidney and I swept from the house and out into a deluge of rain. It suited our moods perfectly.

It was raining again two days later when we arrived at the Viceregal Lodge. Despite the sumptuous meal we were no doubt about to enjoy, I found myself feeling pessimistic about the evening. Or perhaps it was merely that I was feeling pessimistic about the entire situation in Ireland and our endeavors there.

Collins persisted in eluding me, though I'd tracked him back to north Dublin the day before. However, the rain this day was coming down too hard, and the hour I would intersect with Collins on his daily route had grown too late for me to return looking like a drowned rat and still change in time for the lord lieutenant's dinner party. I didn't want to make a repeat of our fashionable, but late, arrival in June.

Meanwhile, unrest continued all over Ireland with more raids, ambushes, burnings, reprisals, and killings perpetrated by both sides. Though not all of it was intentional. In Dublin just the day before, a fellow riding his vehicle along Victoria Quay had been accidentally struck and killed by two army officers in a motorcar. Alternatively, there could be no doubt of the intention behind the killing of RIC Detective Sergeant Mulherin, who shockingly had been shot and killed by the IRA while leaving mass in Bandon, County Cork.

Much of the discussion at dinner centered around this and the other outrages of the IRA, but I noticed few wished to dwell on the actions of the Protestants in the north or the burning of houses and businesses and creameries by the Crown Forces. In some areas, it seemed our forces had almost adopted a policy of commercial vandalism focusing on key industries—the creameries in particular. Once again, I couldn't help but be reminded of the parallels with Belgium and northern France, where crucial industries had been systematically dismantled and looted or outright burned by the Germans. It had made their recovery after the war all the harder.

By the time dinner had concluded and Lord French had asked me and Sidney to confer with him privately, I was afraid I'd fallen into a rather sullen silence. I noted we were led into a proper study this time, just as I'd noted that Sidney had been invited with me. I didn't know if this was because the lord lieutenant's mistress hadn't appreciated the speculation made about him attempting to woo me, or because he'd heard the rumors that I was allegedly expecting. Whatever the case, I was just glad not to have to make the request myself.

Lord French seated himself in a chair that was a trifle too large for his short stature, diminishing rather than enhancing his authority. The tall windows at his back offered an expansive view of the grounds, though the rainy weather had brought on an early twilight, casting much of it in shadow. He appeared to listen carefully to our report, ruffling his finger back and forth over his impressive mustache, but with each passing statement his expression grew more displeased.

Periodically, he would mutter something under his breath, and for a short time I thought we might have found an ally. However, this hope died when he glanced once at the longcase clock ticking away by the door, and then later at his pocket watch. It was increasingly evident that what we were telling him was not what he'd expected or wanted to hear, and now he wished to be finished with the matter.

"Yes, very good," he told us once we'd finished. He stood. "I shall refer the matter to Macready and Boyd. It will be up to them, and I suppose Winter, if they wish to pursue the matter."

"But, sir," I protested, rising to my feet as well even as he moved toward the door. "Aren't you concerned to hear that an intelligence officer is behaving in such a manner?"

"Our men are under a great deal of stress these days, Mrs. Kent. Particularly our officers." He nodded at Sidney. "Your husband knows what it's like. This Lieutenant Delagrange is, no doubt, in need of some guidance on how to better handle himself, but I should be greatly surprised to discover it is as serious as you fear. Regardless, the matter no longer belongs in my hands. Or *yours*." He paused in the doorway to glare at us each in turn. "Am I clear?"

Then without waiting for our responses, which I supposed were a foregone conclusion—he was the lord lieutenant, after all, and expected our obedience—he strode from the room.

It took me several moments to compose myself before I could speak, such was the haze of red that had fallen over my eyes. I had no doubt my complexion was flushed for I could feel the heat in my cheeks and across the top of my chest.

"I have been condescended to many times in my life," I finally uttered, modulating my voice. "I am a woman, after all," I quipped. "But to be treated in such a manner by the man who *asked us*"—I had to break off, inhaling a calming breath before I continued—"to investigate the matter in the first place, is beyond insulting."

I turned to find Sidney still staring at the doorway through which Lord French had exited, his brow furrowed in consideration.

"Don't tell me you agree with him?"

His gaze collided with mine. "Not in the least. But I do begin to wonder why he asked us in the first place. Kavanagh isn't a big enough fish to toady to, even if he is on the lord lieutenant's privy council. And we already know the Kavanaghs didn't request us. So why did His Excellency divert the matter our way? Why involve us at all?"

I didn't have an answer to this question, but he was right. It didn't make sense.

"You think there's someone else?" I asked.

"Maybe." He searched my features. "But either way, we're not letting this go. Not yet." His mouth firmed. "Not while I have some sway to be exerted. Or else what good is that Victoria Cross?"

I smiled faintly at this weak jest.

"Come on, darling. Let's play nice and rejoin the others."

At this remark, I glowered, wanting to do just about anything but that.

He pulled me close, murmuring into the skin at the nape of my neck before trailing his lips over it. "If you do, perhaps there's a reward in it for you."

"Is that a promise?" I countered bitingly.

His response was for my ears only.

But by the following evening I was the one promising *him* rewards in order to cajole him out of his distemper.

Upon his return home I went to greet him, arriving in time to see Sidney hurl his hat, his driving gloves, and lastly his battered cigarette case down on the petticoat table. The silver case clattered over the side, spilling its contents all over the granite stone floor.

"Feel better?" I asked upon observing this display.

He shot me a glare before bending down to pick up the fags.

"Best tell Mrs. Boyle to delay dinner ten minutes," I told Nimble, who had come clomping up the stairs at a trot. Then I retreated to our bedchamber, waiting for Sidney to join me there.

"I take it matters did not go well at the Castle," I deduced as he closed the door.

"No. The whole lot of them don't see the point in opening an investigation based purely on the word of a . . . oh, how did they put? A disgraced servant, a starry-eyed girl, and a vague presumption."

"All of them?"

"All." He removed his coat, tossing it down on the bed. "That it's a girl's and a servant's word against Delagrange's, and considering Delagrange is an intelligence officer, and men like him are giving their lives for their country every day, they would sooner trust their own, thank you very much." His sarcasm made it clear he was repeating someone else's words.

"They were referring to that officer in Bandon, weren't they?"

The evening papers had reported that an intelligence officer had been killed while trying to apprehend a suspect in DS Mulherin's murder. Though only a few of those papers had also mentioned that soldiers from the officer's regiment had begun a series of dreadful reprisals.

He plopped down on the bench at the end of the bed. "Undoubtedly."

"Then perhaps part of their refusal comes down to poor timing. Maybe if we asked—" I broke off at the sight of his face when he looked up at me. Obviously, there was more.

"One of them suggested that my suspicion of Delagrange was more motivated by his inappropriate behavior toward you."

"You can't be serious?" I demanded incredulously.

But he was.

Fury rushed hot through my veins. "After everything you've done for your country." I paced away, before pivoting to return. "Oh, I can just guess who made such an asinine suggestion."

"It wasn't Winter," Sidney said, taking the wind out of my sails. "And I won't tell you who," he added just as I was about to ask. "It doesn't matter. Because unless we can find concrete evidence of Delagrange's guilt, Dublin Castle isn't going to do anything about it."

I sank down next to Sidney. "And how are we supposed to do that when Miss Kavanagh is dead, and her parents refuse to share what they know?"

I thought of Miss Kavanagh cowering alone in her room and how desperate and terrified she must have been. The people who were supposed to love and protect her most in the world had instead been more concerned with preserving their status and concealing any perceived flaws than shielding her from a repugnant officer.

No, not alone. She'd had Miss Fairbanks and her nurse. And while I'd believed her friend when she'd said Miss Kavanagh hadn't told her anything more, I wondered if Sister Mary Aloysius might have proven a safer confidante. Though it would still be another week before she returned to Dublin, and it was doubtful Dublin Castle would find the nun a more acceptable witness than any of the others.

"So much for justice," I muttered.

"I saw Delagrange from a distance as I was departing."

I turned to see that Sidney was staring fixedly at the floor, his hands tightened into fists.

"He knows he's going to get away with it."

The statement made me feel sick to my stomach and brought a lump to my throat. "Then it's a good thing I wasn't there," I managed to choke out. "Because I very well might have taken the pistol from the nearest officer's holster and shot him."

"Don't think I wasn't tempted," Sidney jested morbidly. I knew he'd left his own Luger at home lest they confiscate it at the guardhouse.

I leaned over, bumping his shoulder with my own. "What a pair we make. Talking of justice and then joking about taking it into our own hands."

He draped his arm around me, tipping his head so it rested against mine. "Sometimes it's the only thing that makes the injustice easier to swallow," he said, and I knew he was speaking from experience. For in the trenches, there had rarely been justice dispensed. Or if there had been, one might never have known it.

I closed my eyes and prayed I could find some way to reconcile with this, at least for Sidney's sake if not mine.

CHAPTER 28

I'd lost him again, and I was thoroughly sick of it *and* myself. For this time, I only had myself to blame.

Collins had been headed northeast, crossing the Royal Canal in the direction of Clontarf when I'd allowed my attention to wander. We'd been cycling down the same street for so long, and I'd not ventured to this part of the city before. As such, everything was unfamiliar, including the bizarre configuration of the railway lines as they neared Dublin Bay. What began as a momentary glimpse of curiosity turned into a longer scrutiny and then my mind was deep in contemplation of the contents of Max's belated letter. Before I knew it, Collins had disappeared.

Even though I'd spent the better part of thirty minutes searching for him—nearly getting myself lost in the process—I was forced to admit I'd royally blundered it. My hands tightened around the handlebars of the bicycle, my knuckles turning white as I struggled to restrain my anger. Fortunately, I had a nice long ride into town to review all the curse words in my vocabulary.

Eventually even that grew boring, and my thoughts returned again to Max's letter. To say I'd been relieved by its arrival that morning was an understatement. Nimble had even dared to rap on our bedchamber door to alert us, for he'd known we were concerned. Etta's accompanying note had been glib and amusing as always, and it had confirmed that at least my letters were reaching her to be passed on to Max. Unsurprisingly, Max's missive proved the most informative.

It seemed that one brief communication from him had gone astray—either confiscated during a raid or genuinely lost to the vagaries of the postal system—but it had merely been to inform us he would be away from London for a fortnight visiting his sister and her children. That much explained, Sidney and I had propped ourselves on pillows side by side to read the meat of the letter.

I had known the British coalition government's cabinet Committee on the Irish Situation had been meeting in London, but few details had been leaked to the press. Those that had been seemed encouraging, spurring many people from all parties to begin talking openly of peace, be it in the newspapers or in person. However, Max's source had shared his inside knowledge of the committee's debates, undoubtedly expecting the young earl to keep the information to himself. The present policy in Ireland had proved to be untenable—straddling the line between war and peace—and so the committee was to discuss whether to pool all our resources toward one or the other.

But it appeared its members were split into two camps, one for peace and conciliation and the other for coercion and war. The first was comprised of a few Liberal ministers and most of the Dublin Castle administration, who urged offering a settlement which included Dominion Home Rule for Ireland, while the coercion camp—made up of mostly cabinet ministers—called for the introduction of martial law and greater resources to crush the insurgency.

Wylie, the law advisor who had helped me attain Nimble's release from the Castle, had argued that martial law would only antagonize the Irish people, and create lasting bitterness toward Britain that would strengthen with time and cause further discord. However, General Tudor, the police advisor, was firmly in the coercion camp, and contended that with additional military recruits and support he could end the outrages. As an alternative to martial law, he suggested the implementation of court-martial jurisdiction over all crimes.

Tellingly, Max's source had little hope that the peace camp would win out, even though it was comprised of the people who currently lived and worked on the ground in Dublin, contending daily with the Irish situation. Those in the war camp, except for Tudor, either spent no time in Ireland or were Protestant unionists from the north.

As someone who had lived among the Irish now for two months, I was both disheartened and wary. Some of the remarks made by those in favor of coercion had been alarming, and I could only anticipate matters here deteriorating further. The argument that the current Home Rule Bill could not be abandoned now or it would be a discredit to our government seemed disingenuous at best. Not only had the Irish been waiting for six years for its implementation, but the bill as it now stood had been so altered from the one that had originally been passed—namely partitioning off six of the northern counties in Ulster—as to barely resemble it.

Thoughts about this letter and all the things I would have liked to point out to the committee continued to tumble through my mind as I pedaled toward O'Connell Bridge. As such, the first gunshot barely penetrated my consciousness, but by the time I heard the second shot, I'd instinctively begun to cower, bending low over my handlebars. People crossing the bridge in front of me turned to retreat back toward the north, forcing me to halt in my tracks lest I hit them.

"What's happened?" I called out, over the shrieks of those fleeing, to a man who had sidestepped next to me to peer back over his shoulder toward the south shore of the Liffey. The sound of gunshots continued to echo off the buildings there. This was clearly not just another assassination where a murder gang fired a few bullets into their target and then fled the scene.

"Firefight between our boys and some Tommies outside the bank," was his succinct response before he took off.

I took this to mean the Bank of Ireland, and given its proximity to the river, I knew I couldn't risk crossing here. Not when there were bullets flying. Turning my bicycle, I pushed it alongside me as I trotted north on Sackville Street, following the panicked crowd. I glanced about me, trying to decide what to do and where to go. One woman stood against the wall cradling her arm as if she'd fallen and injured herself. Meanwhile above, curious onlookers leaned out the windows, trying to catch a glimpse of what was happening across the river.

It was only a matter of time before the streets near the scene were swarming with military lorries. They would likely cordon off the streets nearby, as well as several of the bridges, trying to catch the rebels in their net. The natural choice would be for me to turn east and try to make it across Butt Bridge before the military arrived with their barricades and barbed wire, but it was also a swivel bridge, and if it was open to allow a boat to pass, I could be trapped. I could turn west and cross the river at any of the several bridges which spanned the river upstream, but that would mean having to also divert farther south to avoid the streets surrounding the bank.

While I might have chanced brazening it out, and hope I passed unnoticed if I were stopped or hindered by a military cordon, I decided it would be better not to risk it. Not after the way Sidney had been treated at the Castle and their dismissal of our allegations against Lieutenant Delagrange. There was also the fact that C was undoubtedly displeased with me. I'd not submitted a report in over a week, and I'd ignored Finnegan's stringent suggestions that I return to London. This meant that finding some place north of the river to lie low for a few hours might be my best option. And only one place immediately sprang to mind.

The farther north I strode the more the crowd began to thin as people peeled off down the side streets. Once I'd deemed it safe enough, I climbed back on my bicycle and set off for Rutland Square. I leaned my bicycle against the wall outside Devlin's along with half a dozen others and entered the pub to find it already full. I'd not yet visited the establishment at such a late hour, usually being home preparing for one evening engagement or another by now, but apparently the pub did a bustling amount of business after the shops and first shift of workers at the various factories ended their workday.

Devlin nodded to me as I slid into an empty space at the bar. One from which I could conveniently survey most of the room. The publican poured me a dram of whisky from his hidden stash of Scots single-malt, for we'd fallen into a discussion of its merits one day when I'd expressed my appreciation for it over the Irish's lighter version. I might have feared this would appear a trifle suspicious, except for the fact that I'd claimed to be from County Antrim in the northwest corner of Ireland, neighboring Scotland, and there was much crossover between the cultures and people. In any case, it had enabled me to form a connection with the publican. One that afforded me some protection in his establishment and influenced him to believe me harmless. Even my presence at such an uncustomary hour didn't faze the Scotsman. He simply set my whisky before me with a wink before all but dismissing me from his thoughts as he returned to his conversation at the other end of the bar.

I took a sip, allowing the full smoky flavor to coat my tongue and savoring the burn as it slid down my throat, hoping it would help calm my nerves as I considered my options. There was really nothing for it but to stay put. Sidney was bound to grow concerned when I didn't return in another hour, but there was no way to contact him. Not without drawing unwanted attention to myself by asking to use the telephone, assuming they even had one. Many in Dublin didn't. No, he would prefer I use my head and return safely if not quickly.

So I breathed deep of the pipe and cigarette smoke, and the maltiness of my whisky, hoping to quell the quiver of uneasiness that had taken up residence along my spine. Another drink of whisky helped, as did the merry sound of lilting Irish voices filling the air as I listened to their conversations.

I'm not sure how long I sat at the bar, laughing at others' jests, and tapping my foot to the music of the fiddler and flute, but I knew some time had passed for I'd nursed one more dram of whisky than I normally allowed myself. Its warmth had spread through me clear to my fingertips, lulling me into a false sense of peace and belonging. That's when I heard a familiar voice raised across the room.

I slowly shifted so that I could see the men in the snug in the corner, confirming that the man who had cried out was, indeed, Tom. The chap I'd met in the Wicklow. The one who'd told me the rumor that the body of a spy could be found in a nearby bog.

And the man he'd hailed, the one who'd just entered the pub, was none other than the Big Fellow himself . . . Michael Collins.

My first instinct was to duck, but I knew that would do the exact opposite of what it was intended to by drawing attention to me. So instead, I calmly turned back toward the bar, attempting to steady my racing heart. Part of me couldn't believe it. After weeks of tailing him, I'd finally found Collins in a place where I might be able to question him. That is, if I could separate him from the group of men with which he'd gathered.

A wry smile curled my lips, acknowledging the irony of ultimately locating Collins in the place where the trail had begun. Was there anything more typical of a tale about Collins?

Knowing my sobriety was already slightly compromised

by my last sip of whisky, I ordered myself not to drink a drop more. However, I did intend to use the remaining dram as a cover. Lifting the glass to partially cover my face, I pretended to drink as I surveyed the pub once more. Discovering that no one at the table was paying me the least bit of notice, I lowered the glass.

I could see Collins now talking animatedly, a wide grin on his face and a ready laugh on his lips. Tom shifted to take the seat across from Collins, his eyes sparkling from whatever he'd been telling them. I realized that he must be, in fact, Tom Cullen, one of the members of Collins's intelligence staff, and a badly wanted man in his own right. And I had unwittingly helped him escape the raid at the Wicklow.

Which made me wonder, had he been telling me the truth all along? Perhaps Wick's intelligence was faulty. Perhaps Alec *was* dead in a bog somewhere. But then I forcibly shut down that line of thought. There was no way to know for sure. Not until I talked to Collins.

I risked another look in their direction, noting that Liam Tobin was seated in the booth, too, looking like a gaunt scarecrow compared to the others. *Were they all here?* I wondered in shock, surveying the faces of those I could see. If so, should a military patrol walk in right then, they could nab the whole lot of them, and probably end the rebellion. Or at least cripple it severely.

I was surprised by how torn I felt at this revelation. As a British citizen, a lover of law and order, and a British intelligence agent—albeit no longer officially—I should be pleased by the idea. I should be striding out into the night to search out just such a patrol.

But I wasn't pleased. In fact, if anything, I was horrified. I wanted to take Collins and them all to task and berate them for their foolishness.

As for the notion of approaching a patrol, I could only cringe at the very suggestion. Maybe it would be made up of the brave, courteous Tommies I knew from the war. Or maybe it would be a unit of the dreaded Black and Tans, more intent on harassing me, and mistrustful of anything I had to say. Even if I were to reveal my true identity, there was no guarantee of a respectful reception. They would question my presence and disguise, and the chances of them believing me outright were slim to none.

Devlin had been filling a tray with mostly lemonades and sherries, and I watched as Mrs. Devlin carried it over to their table. So much for the rumor that the Irish rebels were naught but a bunch of drunken sots. She laughed and flushed in pleasure as she bantered with them, making it clear this wasn't the first time they'd partaken of the pub's hospitality.

Knowing that they were welcomed here, and that I would *not* be if they knew who I really was, I felt an urgency to finish the business. After all, I was just here for information. Once I had it, I would leave them and this place behind and do my utmost to forget it.

Given our setting and the limited options available to me, it seemed I had no choice but to use the feminine wiles that male intelligence officers assumed were my only weapon, though I loathed and avoided using them at all costs. I might have risked following Collins from the room, that is *if* he ever ventured out alone, but I was unfamiliar with the layout of the pub, and what if he was merely intent on using the necessary. How awkward would that be? No, short of making a scene, wiles were all I had left. At least, to capture his attention and draw him away from Tom and the others.

Perching just so on the stool, I crossed my legs and positioned my split bicycle skirt so that a bit of ankle showed. Then I began to bob my foot up and down, hoping to catch his eye. I couldn't remove my hat because my bobbed auburn tresses would be a dead giveaway, but I could use the broad brim to my advantage if I cocked my head just so. Rather than stare, I cast subtle lingering glances his way. The trick was not alerting Devlin or his wife to this change in my demeanor, but fortunately he was engrossed in conversation once again at the opposite end of the bar and Mrs. Devlin had disappeared upstairs or into a back room.

Happily, this tactic didn't take long to bear fruit. By the third or fourth peek, I caught him watching me, and offered him a shy but artful smile of acknowledgment. He grinned in return before leaning over to say something to the man next to him, who also looked my way. I turned away, playing demure, and when I looked back something unexpected happened.

Collins was no longer just smiling, but a furrow had also creased his brow. One that suggested confusion or uncertainty. I realized he was trying to place me. I braced for Tom or even Liam Tobin to turn my way and identify me. But neither of them was the man with dark hair who twisted in his seat, his gaze colliding with mine.

I felt a wash of cold from my head to my toes as everything about me seemed to momentarily stand still, only to come back at me in a rush. For Alec Xavier was alive. He was alive and he was seated across the room with Collins and his intelligence officers, which meant one of two things.

Either he was deep into his assignment and had severed his connection—at least temporarily—with C and not approached me because whatever he was involved with was too precarious. In which case, my presence here had placed him in terrible danger.

Or Finnegan was right, and Alec had switched sides. He'd become a rebel in earnest, and should now, by all rights, be considered my enemy. In which case, my presence here had placed *me* in terrible danger.

My cheeks flushed as I turned away, berating myself for not anticipating this very scenario. I don't know what exactly I *had* expected, but it was not to find Alec drinking and laughing in the middle of a pub with the most wanted men in all of Ireland. And not knowing the answer to my conundrum, I decided my best option was to get out while I still could.

Pulling money from my pocket, I set it on the bar and slipped through the nearest doorway into a back room. After a brief pause, I located the rear door on the right and stumbled through it out into a narrow alley. It was then that I remembered I'd left my bicycle leaning against the wall at the front of the pub. Except I couldn't turn back now. Nor could I risk rounding the exterior of the building to fetch it. Instead. I hurried forward, gravel crunching beneath my feet in the falling twilight and deepening shadows of the tall buildings.

But I wasn't fast enough.

"Verity!" Alec called, exploding through the door after me.

I hastened on, wondering if I could outrun him. When he called my name again, I rounded on him, forcing him to skid to a stop just two feet from me.

I saw now that he'd donned as thorough a disguise as all the times before, transforming himself both externally and internally to fit the role. He'd grown an absurd little mustache and allowed his hair to become shaggy beneath the flat cap perched on his head. Gone were his stylish, well-cut suits and suave demeanor, and in its place sat a man rough and ready. Even his posture had shifted from easy confidence to a blunt assertion of the space around him. I had always possessed a healthy respect and admiration for his ability to shift personas, to become someone else, but I realized now that the transformation was so complete, he might have walked past me on the street a dozen times now without my recognizing him unless I looked directly into his whiskey-brown eyes.

I found myself crossing my arms over my chest, uncertain of this stranger. "I suppose that answers one question," I said finally. For he would never have risked chasing after me, he would never have called me Verity if Collins wasn't already aware of who he was.

He shifted his feet, turning his head to the side, and I realized he'd been watching me as closely as I'd been watching him. "Aye, well, I did warn ye to go home. Several times." He spoke in a light Dublin brogue, enough to give the suggestion of an Irish lilt. Enough that few natives would question it.

"Warnings you knew I wouldn't obey," I charged. "Not when I believed you were in trouble. Not when I suspected Finnegan wasn't to be trusted." I narrowed my eyes, considering our last interaction in a new light. "Which he isn't, is he? At least, not if one is loyal to the Crown."

Alec neither confirmed nor denied this suspicion, but I didn't really need him to.

"You should've gone," he said, growing angry. "Kent should've made ye." He took a step closer. "This is no place for you, Verity. Not now. When the entire country is a powder keg."

"I've been in dangerous situations before."

He shook his head. "Not like this."

I gazed up at him, a torrent of emotions flooding me. Relief that he was alive and whole. Anger that he hadn't simply found a way to tell me so. Apprehension of the man who now stood before me and wariness that the Alec I had known was gone, or perhaps had never been the real one at all. And fear that I already understood all too well the answer to my next question.

"Why?" I murmured in a broken voice, trusting he would know what I meant.

Why, after risking so much for his country during the war, had he turned his back on it and sided with the rebels? He wasn't even Irish.

Or was he?

I might at one time have been as close to Alec as he would let anyone get, but there was still a great deal I didn't know about him.

He lowered his chin, staring so intently into my eyes that

I felt my breathing hitch. "You, of all people, know why, Ver. Especially after havin' spent some time here." His brow furrowed. "More time than I wanted ye to."

Because he'd feared that I would come to the same conclusion he had.

I shivered with the awareness that that fear wasn't unjustified. Even now, I wanted to close my eyes and clasp my hands over my ears and run from it. To pretend I knew nothing of the situation in Ireland. But I knew no matter how far I ran, the knowledge would follow me.

CHAPTER 29

Alec glanced over his shoulder at the sound of the pub door opening before turning back to me. I couldn't quite decipher the look in his eyes—he donned his mask too well—but I comprehended enough to grasp that he wasn't completely at ease with the man approaching us. Or perhaps he wasn't completely at ease with that man meeting *me*.

"So this is Verity Kent," Michael Collins declared, his Cork accent more lilting than a Dubliner's. "I've heard quite a lot about ye the past few months." He nodded at Alec. "Not only from this one, though 'tis clear he's smitten."

Alec turned to scowl at him for this baiting remark, but Collins merely grinned.

"Nay, I'd say your name's been on the lips of about half my agents."

Though good-naturedly spoken, I could tell this remark was not as innocuous as it seemed. It also made clear that while I had been searching for Alec and marking several of Collins's men—and women—they had also been marking me.

"What can I say, I do get around," I replied flippantly.

Collins chuckled, rubbing his jaw as he paced around me. "That ye do."

I continued to meet Alec's gaze as Collins circled around my rear, hoping I could still trust Alec not to allow Collins to physically hurt me. Such attacks didn't seem to be the Big Fellow's style, but that didn't stop the hairs on the back of my neck from standing on end.

"Even inside the Castle. Where word is ye ruffled the Holy Terror's feathers quite thoroughly." Collins smiled broadly. "Now that's somethin' I would've liked to see."

"We call O the Holy Terror," Alec explained.

"I surmised," I said, though I wondered how Collins had known I'd ruffled O's feathers. Nancy couldn't have known I wasn't bluffing about that part. Unless she'd learned it from one of the men outside Smith's office. Some of them had probably overheard.

He came to a stop next to Alec, crossing his arms over his chest. "I haven't interfered with ye or your husband . . ."

I arched my eyebrows in challenge at this remark.

A corner of his mouth quirked upward in wry acknowledgment. "Well, not much. And only because MacAlister assures me you're here for him."

I knew the look I'd cast Alec's way conveyed my curiosity as to why Collins had still addressed him as MacAlister, but he didn't elucidate.

"Is that true?" Collins asked.

Once again Alec remained silent to my querying look, but I'd deduced enough about Collins by now to know he was testing me.

"Not strictly," I replied. "But you know that already."

"Aye. Miss Kavanagh, Collins said. "'Tis sad. But we had nothin' to do with it."

I knew that when he said "we" he meant the rebels, the IRA.

"No," I replied, my temper sparking. "It was Lieutenant Delagrange, the intelligence officer her parents wanted her to wed."

Collins and Alec shared a look that communicated they hadn't known this fact.

"You're certain?" Alec asked.

"Yes. Though I don't have proof. Not proof good enough for Dublin Castle anyway," I snapped indignantly. "But he and his mates assaulted Miss Kavanagh, sure enough. Likely murdered her cousin, too. And he may have killed her as well."

From the ensuing moments of silence, I realized I'd probably said too much, but I was still furious at the Castle, and both their treatment of Sidney and refusal to even open an inquiry of their own into the matter.

"So ye have no further reason to remain in Dublin," Alec said.

I glared at him, still furious at him as well. For his deception. For making me care. For being the reason I'd come here in the first place and been forced to confront all of these things.

Without Alec, I also never would have known about Miss Kavanagh. I never would have failed her. I turned my glare on Collins. Though perhaps there was one thing I could do in her honor.

"Your men may not have cut Miss Kavanagh's hair, but they have assaulted and forcibly cut the hair of other women. You need to order them to cease that tactic now. It reduces women to weapons of shame." I arched my chin. "And it is beneath you."

"Verity . . ." Alec warned, for Collins's expression had chilled.

"Mrs. Kent, I do believe ye think I have more power over the men than I actually do," he said. "I do not give orders to the brigades."

"Maybe not," I agreed, studying the determined line of his jaw, and seeking to sway it to my side. "But they all look to you for guidance. And if you wanted to, you could make it clear how intolerable such behavior is."

"Aye, but I think you're forgettin' the power of the sight of a man in uniform."

Implying that uniform-mad girls might forget to mind their tongue in the presence of soldiers.

"It's no more powerful than the sight of a pretty face," I responded tartly, for men were just as susceptible, if not more so.

He dipped his head, conceding this point.

"Well, lovely as this has been," I said, deciding it was time I make my exit before matters grew even more contentious. I began to back away. "But I think it's time for me to go."

"Hold on, Ver," Alec warned, halting me. "Ye don't think we're just going to let ye walk away, do ye?"

Alarm shot through me as I took in both of their implacable expressions. I had no idea what sort of combat training Collins might have had, but he was a fairly tall and robust fellow, and Alec could probably best me with one hand tied behind his back. So I held no illusions that I could escape. Not by speed or physical force.

However, Alec wasn't finished. "Not without your word of honor that ye won't reveal what ye know."

The demand rankled, and I thought about threatening them with the fact that Sidney would tear this city apart looking for me if they detained me. He knew enough to do serious damage to their organization, for I had shared nearly everything I knew with him for just this reason. But I didn't want to draw their attention to him. I didn't want to give Collins any reason to send his murder gang to Upper Fitzwilliam Street that night.

In any case, Collins didn't seem to be ready to let me go so easily. "Are you sure she can be trusted?"

Alec's jaw was firm, his gaze steady as he looked at me. "Aye. I'd sooner trust her than you or the .45 in my pocket."

His words left me feeling like I'd been punched. He trusted me that much, yet he'd not sought me out to tell me the truth and avoided this entire thorny dance. I wasn't sure if that said more about Alec or more about me, but I ignored my own complicated emotions and turned to Collins, expecting to find him displeased by Alec's statement. Instead, he appeared intrigued.

"If Verity gives you her word, she will honor it," Alec added, making the matter plain, and making it all but impossible for me not to give it now.

I scowled at him before relenting, telling Collins. "I'm not here to fight your war. I won't reveal what I know." My mouth twisted bitterly. "They wouldn't believe me anyway."

"More the fool them," Collins quipped.

I tilted my head, scrutinizing him. "At least you don't make the mistake of underestimating women."

Perhaps it was an observation I shouldn't have made, for it might be construed to allude to the fact that I knew he had female intelligence agents. It was the type of boneheaded remark Bennett might have made to show off. But after being discounted time and time again, I was suddenly finding it difficult to bite my tongue and not reveal how much I knew. To blurt out that I'd not just stumbled upon them here by chance, but that I knew perhaps half the locations on Collins's daily route. Only the certain knowledge that I would be signing Sidney's death warrant kept me silent.

"You are a dangerous woman, aren't ye, Mrs. Kent?" Collins said at last, his interest having sharpened.

I gave a humorous laugh, backing away with a shake of my head. "Not in the least. After all, what danger is there in knowing something when you can't do anything about it."

"Go home, Verity," Alec called after me as I turned to leave. "To London."

I lifted my hand in farewell, but didn't look back, still too stung by the truth of my last comment.

As I approached the end of the alley, I could see a man waiting there with a bicycle, smoking a cigarette. When I drew nearer, I could tell that it was Tom, and that the bicycle was mine. "Ye left somethin'," he said.

"Thank you, Mr. Cullen," I stated pointedly, but when I reached for the handlebars and began to pull it away, he held fast. I looked up to find him staring at me in puzzlement, as if I was an arithmetic problem he hadn't yet solved.

"We came there that day for ye, ye know? That day at the Wicklow," he clarified. "But then the Tans showed up and those intelligence officers. Collins had to distract 'em so we could slip out."

I was startled to discover Collins had been there that day. I wondered if it had been him who'd offered to buy the officers a drink. If so, reckless didn't begin to describe him.

"So I cooked up that excuse to ask ye to meet us in Capel Street at the library, but ye didn't show." He narrowed his eyes. "How'd ye know?"

He seemed earnest, but just because I'd given Collins my word that I wouldn't reveal what I'd uncovered about him didn't mean I was going to reveal the secrets of the British Secret Intelligence Service. My silence went both ways.

Instead, I smiled tightly, and pulled the bicycle more insistently from his grip. "Good night, Mr. Cullen."

With this, he stepped back, allowing me to ride off down Sackville Street.

It was later than I'd ever been out on my own in the city, with darkness having fallen and the streetlights casting haloed gleams over the pavement. By now Sidney must have learned of the firefight, which I'd overheard someone at the pub say had started when the IRA had disarmed two military police patrols, one outside Trinity College and the other in Westmoreland Street. When the army guards stationed at the Bank of Ireland had realized what was happening, they'd opened fire on the men, who had then returned shots. I imagined my prolonged absence was causing Sidney considerable worry, but I couldn't focus on that. Not when I needed to keep my wits about me to ensure I made it home without incident.

Fortunately, I was in an area filled with theaters and cinemas, as well as restaurants, hotels, and pubs. Two hours before curfew, there were still plenty of people about. Though I also couldn't help but note the increased police and military presence. Some people hailed them heartily, while others scurried past with their heads low. The majority did their best to ignore them while still keeping a wary eye in their direction. I was among the latter.

I was crossing the expanse of O'Connell Bridge when someone suddenly cried out my alias. "Dearbhla!"

It was a voice I would have known anywhere even if the attire was unfamiliar. I pulled to the edge of the pavement as Sidney retraced his steps, pulling me into his arms even as I awkwardly straddled the bicycle. "Thank God," he breathed into my hair.

Though I hadn't believed I was actually scared before, I found myself shaking as he held me close.

"What happened?" he asked as he pulled back, the flat cap on his head pulled low over his eyes. The rest of his clothing was that of an everyday Dublin laborer, and I realized at some point he must have acquired a disguise for just such an occasion. Though there was no hiding his memorable good looks.

But I could sense that we were drawing interest from others, including a pair of constables. Not wanting to face any awkward questions, I urged him, "Let's walk."

He helped me dismount and then took control of the bicycle, rolling it alongside him while his other hand held mine securely, our fingers interlaced.

I waited until we'd veered left onto D'Olier Street before attempting to speak. "I was cycling toward the bridge when the shots began, and everyone started running in the opposite direction. You heard about the firefight?" I confirmed.

"Yes."

I explained the logic behind my decision about what to do next and how I'd ended up in Devlin's pub.

"Yes, I see," Sidney agreed. "That was probably the wisest course of action. I knew you would have kept your head. But when one hears that the Crown Forces and rebels are volleying shots back and forth at each other in the middle of a public street, well, I suspect you can understand my unease."

I nodded, though the truth was that I was barely listening, all my thoughts being instead consumed by the momentous discovery I'd yet to share with him. "I found him," I finally murmured, an unconscious echo of my words a fortnight ago.

It took Sidney a moment to respond. Long enough for me to wonder if he'd heard me.

"Found him. You mean Collins?"

"You already knew that." I paused, bracing myself to get the words out. "I mean Alec."

He stumbled to a stop, turning me to face him in the gleam of the lights outside the Queen's Theatre on Great Brunswick Street. I could tell that I'd astonished him, but all of his concern seemed to be for me as he scoured my features. Whatever he saw there was enough for him to tuck me closer to his side as we continued to walk toward home. Or our temporary one anyway.

A sudden wave of longing for our flat in Berkeley Square struck me. There, at least, I was safe and secure, and I didn't have to confront any of this. I wanted nothing more than to curl up in our bed with Sidney's arms wrapped around me and pretend the rest of the world didn't exist.

Whenever the war had become too much, whenever I'd missed Sidney with that weary bone-deep ache that only love can cause, I would closet myself in our bedroom and imagine the war was over, and he was there with me. It would always be spring, and the windows would be open to let in the birdsong and the smell of flowers in the garden square below. We would be covered in nothing but the sheets tangled around our waists and the warm sunshine spilling through the window.

Sometimes imagining that was all that had gotten me through the day. Even during the months when I'd believed him dead.

But eventually the world always intruded. Eventually I had to return to reality. There was no permanent escape. Even if I were to flee physically, mentally I would still be here. Every illusion was but temporary, even the one found in a bottle.

Though that didn't stop Sidney from pouring me a glass of whiskey—Irish this time—once we reached our private sitting room still dressed in our disguises. Neither of us had bothered to change in my "writing room" upstairs, for Ginny was already long gone for the day and Mrs. Boyle was undoubtedly in bed. Only Nimble was about, and he already knew our secret. In fact, I suspected he'd been the one to acquire Sidney the necessary garments for his costume.

"And who are you supposed to be?" I asked as I took a sip of whiskey, never mind the fact I'd probably already had too much to drink that night.

Sidney had removed his coat and cap, and now stood before me in a linen shirt and rough trousers, gripping the suspenders. "Nimble thought something starting with an 'S' would be best. Something like Samuel. Samuel O'Shea."

I eyed him with amusement. "And is this the first time you've ventured out in that getup, Samuel O'Shea?"

"Sure, it is."

I shook my head at his accent. "Dreadful."

He took my criticism in good stride, but then he sobered. "I imagine Xavier's is flawless."

I stared down into the amber liquid in my glass. "It is," I admitted, setting the whiskey aside before I turned maudlin. At least, more maudlin than I already felt. "He's grown a mustache."

"Now that I'd like to see," Sidney jested, sitting beside me.

I cracked a weak smile. "It's ridiculous."

"He hasn't the face for it," he concurred. When I said nothing more, he prodded at the wound that was deepest. "He's switched sides, hasn't he."

"Yes," I squeaked out after a long exhale.

He nodded. "So Finnegan was right."

"But don't go thinking his disclosure was noble," I grumbled. "Alec all but confirmed Finnegan switched sides, too. Or maybe he's always been on the rebel side and C just didn't know it."

"Either way, I suppose Xavier is the one who instructed Finnegan to tell you. To convince you to leave, hopefully for good."

"No wonder the piker was so nervous when he told me," I replied, having already deduced all this. A tear slid down my cheek and I angrily dashed it away and the one that followed. Alec didn't deserve my tears. Not after everything.

Sidney reached out to me, but I pushed him away, rising to my feet. I didn't want to be comforted. My control was already too fragile. If I let him put his arms around me, if I gave myself over to his support, I feared I would fall apart completely.

He watched me pace for a moment, my arms crossed tightly over my chest, before asking. "What do you want to do, Ver?"

It was a repeat of the question he'd already asked me several times during our time here, and yet look what a hash my decisions had made of things. I didn't know what I wanted to do anymore. I didn't even know if I had the right to choose.

"I don't know," I admitted in a small voice as I stopped to stare into the cheval mirror. The powder I'd used to alter my complexion had streaked and my hair was matted and snarled from the hat I'd worn so far down on my head. There was even a splotch of something on the collar of my blouse.

I looked far from put together, far from capable of making good choices.

"What do *you* want to do?" I asked Sidney as I turned to look at him.

He crossed the room toward me slowly, I supposed wary of my pushing him away again. "What I want to do right now is to draw you a hot bath." Though he hadn't phrased it as a question, one glinted in his eyes, and I nodded, feeling a bit more of my resentment slip into resignation.

"And tomorrow"—he grimaced, tugging at his collar—"I want to burn this shirt."

One corner of my lips quirked at this absurdity.

"Seriously. How anyone can stand wearing this, I don't know."

"They have no choice, darling."

He mock shuddered, guiding me toward the bedroom. "And then Saturday, we'll go to Belgarde Castle for the Maudes' house party."

"I'd forgotten about that," I groaned.

"Yes, well, we've already confirmed we're coming. And it will be good to get out of Dublin for a few days."

"Gain some perspective, you mean."

"With the Maudes? Hardly." He turned me to look at him. "But it will give us time to think. To reassess before deciding our next step."

I liked his use of the word "us" and had to agree he was right. There was no need to pack up and rush off to catch the next ferry back to England. In fact, even in my muddled, aggrieved state, the very idea still smacked of cowardice.

So I lifted my hand to gently cradle his cheek in apology for my earlier rebuff and in acceptance of his proposal.

He pressed a kiss to my palm and then turned to draw the bath.

CHAPTER 30

Belgarde Castle was located west of Dublin in a lovely glade of trees surrounded by fields. It being the height of summer, the countryside was lush with greenery and growing crops and the garden was bursting with bright blooms and ripe fruit bushes. If any place could refresh my spirit and ease my soul, it was this.

Or it might have if it had been absent of people.

We arrived in the early afternoon, seemingly the last of about a dozen guests including Lord and Lady Powerscourt and a newly arrived civil servant from Dublin Castle, Mark Sturgis. Though I'd never met Mr. Sturgis, I was acquainted with his wife, Lady Rachel, the daughter of Lord Wharncliffe. Sturgis himself proved to be witty and charming with a genuine talent for moderating those who might have otherwise dominated the conversation. This latter quality soon proved invaluable, as our host, Anthony Maude, was a determined Tory. One who was prone to ranting about the rebels and the current state of Ireland in general. I'd developed a headache just from listening to him for the short time he'd held forth on the subject over tea.

And unfortunately, there was much to rage about given the fact that Frank Brooke, the railway director and privy councilor we'd dined with at the Viceregal Lodge the evening after the King's Inn raid, had been assassinated in his Westland Row office the day before. It had been shocking to hear considering the nature of his attack—in broad daylight in front of witnesses at his place of work—but also because we'd been acquainted with the man. I couldn't help but recall how O'Shaughnessy had warned Brooke that his determination to fire Irish railway workers and hire English ones because of the ongoing strike would paint a target on his back.

There was also the fact that I'd spoken with Collins the night before the attack. That I'd seen his intelligence team gathered in that snug at Devlin's. It troubled me to think that might have been where they'd planned the last-minute details of the attack. The notion made me feel a little queasy.

I understood the cost and method of war. I'd lived it for four years. But that didn't make any of it easier to stomach.

I didn't know whether Mrs. Maude had noticed my reaction to her husband's vociferous speech, or I simply appeared paler than I realized, but she suggested I might enjoy a walk in the garden before dressing for dinner. I readily accepted—anything to escape the house—and followed her directions out to the courtyard and past a thick iron gate. A set of wide terraced steps led me up a path through the trees and into the garden proper.

It was positively charming. Dahlias and marigolds nodded in the late afternoon sun while bees flitted between them and the trees heavy with ripening fruit. From this distance, I could see that the walls of the castle, and indeed every stone surface in sight, were covered in ivy and clematis. Only the windows and the top of the medieval tower could be seen peeking through.

I wandered for a time, breathing the scents of the earth and flowers and green things deep into my lungs. It was quiet and soothing, with nothing but the drone of the bees and the soft sigh of the wind through the leaves to disturb me. I rounded a corner to find a sundial, approaching it to see if it was accurate. Then spotting a bench nearby, I decided to sit.

I'd only been perched there for a few minutes with my face tipped up toward the warmth of the sun when something alerted me to the fact I was no longer alone. Whether it was a sound or a flickering shadow, or simply a disturbance in my equilibrium, I didn't know, but I opened my eyes to find Lord Ardmore watching me, a smile creasing his unctuous lips.

I should have been startled. I don't know why I wasn't. Except after seeing Captain Willoughby in Dublin, I supposed I'd been waiting for his employer to appear, and as always, where I least wanted him. It had been over six months since we'd met face to face, though he was always lurking on the periphery, casting his shadow over my peace of mind. Exactly where he wanted to be.

He crossed toward me, swinging his walking stick. He looked healthy and relaxed, and clearly unruffled by whatever his intentions were for those phosgene cylinders. I didn't know his exact age, but I'd pegged it at somewhere between forty-five and fifty, for his pale blond hair was streaked with gray and his figure, while still trim, was perhaps a stone heavier than it had likely been in his youth. As always, he appeared distinguished and respectable. Had I not known exactly what he was capable of, I never would have guessed what a Machiavellian mastermind I was facing.

"Careful, Mrs. Kent," he drawled before sitting beside me uninvited. "You'll give yourself freckles."

"Unlikely," I replied, apparently to his amusement, for he chuckled.

"That is one of the things I like most about you. You are undoubtedly beautiful, and you know how to dress and groom yourself to appear at your best, but you're not beholden to it and the more ridiculous practices and misconceptions about it."

I turned to pin him with a sardonic stare. Though a confirmed bachelor, Ardmore was known to have taken lovers, including a former friend of mine. But surely, he wasn't attempting to flatter *me*.

"Though I must say, you are looking rather wan today, my dear," he declared in mock concern, reverting to form.

"Has something happened to remove the bloom from your cheeks?" His gaze dipped to my abdomen. "Maybe it's merely a symptom of your present condition."

I turned back toward the sundial, not about to dignify that with a response. Though I supposed it answered the question of how far Bennett's report that I was expecting had traveled among the intelligence circles in London.

But Ardmore wasn't finished. "Or perhaps it's the fault of Dublin Castle." He shook his head. "I knew they were unimaginative, but not to this degree. Which is why I suggested to Lord French that he enlist your assistance in looking into the matter of Miss Kavanagh's assault."

My hands involuntarily clenched where they rested in my lap, such was my shock. "*You* asked Lord French to enlist us to investigate?"

"Of course, my dear." His mossy-green eyes glittered in satisfaction at my surprise. "I knew that you and your husband would be utterly fair and impartial."

I stared at him, feeling frustration and impotence and absolute wrath building up inside me. It was all I could do to turn away before I did or said something I would regret. I'd already given Ardmore exactly what he wanted—my shock and upset. I was not going to delight him further by raging at him.

Sidney and I had wondered what the real motivation had been behind Lord French asking us to investigate Miss Kavanagh's attack. Now we knew. It had been at Ardmore's behest. Ardmore!

As if summoned by my thoughts or my distress, my husband suddenly appeared around the corner, moving at a fast clip. But he checked his steps once he caught sight of us.

"Ah, Mr. Kent, there you are," Ardmore declared, rising to his feet. "And right on time. Don't worry, I've been looking after your wife for you." He paused as he was moving past him. "Though she does appear to be a trifle discomposed.

Might want to see to that, will you." With that he disappeared around the bend in the foliage.

Sidney turned to stare after the man, but then abandoned any idea of going after him, advancing toward me instead. "When Maude mentioned that Ardmore was to be a guest, that he'd already arrived, I knew immediately he would seek you out."

Perhaps our hosts had even arranged it.

He dropped down on the bench in the place Ardmore had vacated. "What did he say?"

"It was Ardmore," I ground out. "Ardmore who asked French to enlist our assistance. He's been toying with us!"

Sidney reared back as if he'd been struck, though I knew it was in response to the content of the words and not my delivery of them. "Bloody hell," he cursed, adding something even harsher than that.

"It's like Belgium all over again," I added bitterly.

For it was Ardmore's machinations that had forced us into a hunt for that report that had proved our government's complicity in prolonging the war. And it was now Ardmore who had drawn us into an investigation that had exposed some of the flaws in our government's response to the Irish situation. Not all of it, of course, could be laid at his feet. That had come from living among and interacting with those who lived here. From experiencing it firsthand. But our discoveries in the course of inquiring into Miss Kavanagh's assault and the Castle's response to our findings had certainly driven the wedge deeper.

"You see, *this* is what he does," I berated. "He doesn't just seek to outwit, but to demoralize, and manipulate, and . . . and corrupt. To do so in a way that we don't even know it's happening."

"That doesn't make the things we've uncovered any less true," Sidney pointed out.

I turned to grip his hand in mine, speaking in a low voice.

"No. But it's precisely because they're true that his maneuverings are so effective and dangerous."

Sidney knew that Ardmore had been attempting to burrow his way into my mind, to make me doubt myself and those around me, particularly C and British Intelligence. To make me disillusioned and distrustful, possibly even desperate. Since the moment we'd stumbled upon the truth of his treachery, he'd utilized every fact he'd learned about me, every instance we'd interfered with one of his agents to systematically pick away at me. And every step we thought we'd been taking away from him and toward thwarting his plans had really been drawing us deeper into his web.

Sidney's jaw firmed. "But Ardmore doesn't control everything, Ver. Even if he wants you to think he does. And whatever he's been planning"—he shook his head—"we know it can't be good. Don't lose sight of that."

I inhaled a shaky breath. "You're right." I reached for Sidney's other hand, drawing further strength from it and the confidence of his gaze, the faith he held in me, in us. "You're right," I repeated, stronger this time.

I couldn't let Ardmore distract me from that truth. Whatever his intentions were for that poisonous gas, whoever his intended target was, they were not to be borne. The very act of releasing such a deadly substance was horrifying enough without considering all of the ramifications and consequences, not only for those who succumbed to it, but for all of Ireland and Britain. And at the moment, all that he seemed to need in order to succeed was for us to take our eye off the ball.

No one else was suspicious of him, not with all of his government and intelligence contacts, and his own shadowy role with Naval Intelligence. No one but us and Alec, who was now a rebel, and C, whose suspicions were almost solely based on our reports. If Sidney and I failed to stop Ardmore, the world might be forever changed, and it was unlikely he would ever be held responsible.

I couldn't lose sight of that. Not for one instant.

Sidney squeezed my fingers in return. "Though we still have three days to endure in his company. Unless you want to leave. I'm sure we could make our excuses."

And let him win?

"No," I stated. "No, I can handle it. I can handle *him*."

"If you're sure?"

I turned to glare at him, and he smiled. I realized then he'd been testing me.

I leaned over to impulsively kiss him, hitting the corner of his mouth. When I drew back, he gripped the nape of my neck and pulled me toward him for a more substantial embrace.

We held hands as we made our way back toward the castle, and with each step, I regained more of my poise. I began to analyze Ardmore's confession from a different perspective.

"So Ardmore claims he convinced Lord French to ask us to look into Miss Kavanagh's assault. But how did *he* know about it?"

Sidney turned to look at me, perhaps struck as much by the quandary as I was.

"And how did he know that her assailants weren't members of the IRA as was suspected?" If they had been, the investigation and its findings would have been rather more straightforward and less fraught.

"I don't know," Sidney admitted. "But it would be worth finding out."

The remainder of the house party passed largely without incident. The weather was glorious, and we spent a great deal of time outdoors riding, picnicking, and playing lawn tennis. The men also went shooting, while the ladies toured some of the local churches and architectural sites.

Ardmore, for his part, mostly ignored me except when we were in mixed company at dinner or tea. I didn't know if this was because he thought the little seeds of doubt he'd planted in my head would grow more rapidly without him overshadowing them, or because he was more concerned I would ferret out something about him he didn't want me to. If the latter was his motivation, then he'd failed, and I had our host to thank for it.

During the midst of one of Maude's ranting soliloquys, he'd mentioned the fact that he'd heard that the Dublin Corporation—which encompassed the city government and all its administrative organizations—was facing bankruptcy and severely overdrawn on all its loans. Since Dublin Castle, as the seat of the British government in Ireland, had just withdrawn all aid to local authorities who had recognized and sworn allegiance to the Dáil—including the Dublin Corporation—the Corporation was forced to look for further funding elsewhere. For a time, like many councils, Dublin had attempted to have it both ways, taking the British government's money without giving them their loyalty. But the Castle had put a stop to that. And now none of the banks would advance the Corporation loans or buy corporation stock.

While Maude seemed to find this to be their just deserts, I had a different epiphany. One that stemmed from the dossier Alec had compiled on Ardmore while recuperating after being shot the previous summer. Alec had discovered that Ardmore was owner, or part-owner of a number of businesses throughout Ireland, albeit not in his own name. More pertinently, Alec had learned that Ardmore had his hands in a number of their banks. We'd speculated that he might be biding his time, seeking to take advantage, and wagering that an independent Ireland might mean greater profits for him in the long run. Assuming he possessed the capital, what better way was there to benefit from the country's upheaval—politically, professionally, and in the long term financially—than to bankroll it, both in Dublin and elsewhere.

If that was part of his plan, then this was a critical moment. The fact that the crisis also coincided with Ardmore's arrival in Ireland only heightened my suspicion. Though it still didn't tell us what his intentions were for the phosgene or where it was hidden.

Upon our return to Dublin, Sidney and I were met at the door by Nimble. The bruises on his face continued to heal and had now faded to a sickly yellow and green. Nevertheless, I could still smell the liniment Mrs. Boyle continued to apply to it daily. Though I couldn't deny that it appeared to be helping.

"Letter arrived for you, ma'am," he told me as I removed my gloves.

"From our mutual friend?" I asked.

"It appears so," he said, watching as I opened it.

It wasn't very lengthy. Mostly a reminder from Max that he would be away from London at his estate on the Isle of Wight for Cowes Week, a regatta held every year in August on the Solent. Presumably he'd not wanted me to worry like the last time he was away. Though there was also a notation at the bottom that might have proved useful had we received his letter before we'd departed for Belgarde Castle.

Ardmore is bound for Ireland. Uncertain of his plans.

To accost me, first and foremost, apparently.

Sidney looked at me in question as I refolded the letter, and I shook my head, letting him know there was nothing of import.

However, Nimble had yet to depart and I suddenly realized how anxious he appeared. I'd thought his impatience was about the letter, but perhaps I was wrong.

"Was there something else?" Sidney asked him.

"A Lieutenant Bennett called for you," he informed him.

A fact which, in and of itself, was not alarming, but for Nimble's demeanor.

"He said that Lieutenant Delagrange was murdered."

I stifled a gasp, gripping Sidney's arm.

"When?" he asked.

"Yesterday." Nimble's wide eyes flicked back and forth between us. "I told him ye were at Belgarde Castle. That he should look for ye there if it was urgent."

Since Bennett hadn't contacted Sidney, I could only presume he'd wished to ascertain our whereabouts. The fact that we'd been attending a house party with more than a dozen other guests afforded us rather solid alibis.

"Thank you, Nimble," Sidney stated calmly, though I could feel the tension in his frame. "I'll follow up with Bennett myself."

Nimble nodded and turned to go, though I could tell he was still conscious of the undercurrent flowing between me and Sidney.

Once he'd clumped out of sight, Sidney turned to look at me. "You don't think . . . ?"

"Who else?" I murmured faintly.

"Someone he'd wronged?" he suggested. "It's doubtful that Miss Kavanagh and her cousin were the only ones."

"Maybe," I allowed. But I also knew that I'd complained about Delagrange to Alec and Collins. I'd told them I was certain he was behind Miss Kavanagh's assault and Mr. Keogh's murder. That he might have even arranged Miss Kavanagh's death. And three days later, he was dead.

"It was certainly fortunate it occurred while we were away," Sidney dared to voice aloud.

"Yes."

Based on that remark alone, I knew we were both nursing the same unsettling suspicion, and it did not sit well with either of us. We'd wanted justice for Miss Kavanagh and the others, but not like this.

CHAPTER 31

Mater Misericordiae Hospital was located in north Dublin, not far from Mountjoy Prison. *Mater misericordiae* meant "Mother of Mercy" in Latin, so it made sense that the hospital treated all, no matter the patients' means. It had been founded by the Sisters of Mercy some seventy years ago and had grown considerably since. The hospital had treated the injured and dying from the 1916 Easter Rising as well as the hunger strikers released from Mountjoy Prison in April. It had also administered to injured soldiers transported from the front lines during the war and deployed its own doctors and nurses to work in the field hospitals and dressing stations.

Sister Mary Aloysius had the look of a woman who might have been dispatched in such a capacity. Stoic and severe, but with an underlying gentleness that I could imagine her employing to good effect in either a hospital near the Western Front or a young woman's sick room in south Dublin. Though she was younger than I'd expected—perhaps thirty-five—with a pair of brilliant blue eyes, made all the more arresting because of her coif and veil.

"Now, what is it ye hope I can tell ye?" she said after she'd finished pouring me a cup of tea. We were seated in a parlor with rose-covered wallpaper that I suspected was most often used to comfort the bereaved. When I'd briefly explained the reason for my visit, she'd not reacted with affront or rushed into denials, but calmly brought me to this room, which I viewed as an encouraging sign. It was also evident she knew something of my reputation. At least she'd not questioned my interest.

"You were engaged to care for Miss Kavanagh after her assault," I began carefully after taking a sip of tea. "But I've heard conflicting reports as to her state of being. Can you tell me what she was like? Obviously, she was distraught," I prompted, hoping she would take the cue.

"She was a modest girl. Kind. Obedient, from what I could gather. But she also knew her own mind. That much was clear." Sister Mary Aloysius paused, appearing to give the matter thoughtful consideration. "She had the normal symptoms of those who've experienced some shock or trauma. Agitation, fretfulness, the tendency to retreat within herself. Nightmares, too, of course."

Which would explain the need for a sleeping draught.

"Reliving the attack?" I guessed.

"Aye. But otherwise, I would have said she was recovering well. As best as she could anyway, under the circumstances."

"What do you mean?"

She frowned, turning slightly to the side as if she was uncertain whether she'd spoken out of turn. Perhaps it was a matter of patient privilege. In the end, I don't know what decided her in my favor.

"Mrs. Kavanagh struggled mightily with what happened to her daughter, and consequently, her behavior was somewhat erratic. She was the one who believed her daughter needed a nurse to see to her care, though her wounds were more mental than physical. But then she suggested Miss Kavanagh sequester herself in her room for her own good, not even allowing her to come downstairs for meals or to play the piano, as she often desired. She hired a hairdresser to come to the house to fix Miss Kavanagh's hair as best she could, but then ordered all of the mirrors removed from her daughter's room and certain parts of the house because she believed the sight of herself might distress her. Yet I know that Miss Kavanagh used a hand mirror she'd hidden from her daily for her ablutions."

I nodded, beginning to see what the sister meant. Mrs. Kavanagh took steps to see to her daughter's care and healing, but then sabotaged any good they might have done. "So it was Mrs. Kavanagh who confined Miss Kavanagh to her bedchamber?"

"At first." Her brow furrowed. "But once her mother relented, Miss Kavanagh began to refuse to leave it."

"Did this occur after she was forced to see Lieutenant Delagrange?" I asked on a hunch.

I could see in Sister Mary Aloysius's eyes that she'd made the same connection. "Aye. Her mother gave her no notice of his visit. Simply sent orders up one day that she was to come down to tea in her lavender gown. When Miss Kavanagh returned upstairs—" The nurse broke off, a troubled look crossing her features. "I had never seen her so distraught until that moment. I had to give her a sedative to calm her."

Because of Delagrange. Because he'd been her chief assailant and yet her parents expected her to receive him as if nothing had happened.

I couldn't imagine what she must have felt upon finding him in her drawing room, but the fact she'd required a sedative afterward said much.

"Did she confide in you?" I asked, wondering how much Miss Kavanagh might have told her. Whether she'd actually stated outright that Delagrange had been the one to assault and cut her hair.

"Not in words, no. But the fact that she asked me to bar entrance to everyone but her maid and her parents—who she couldn't refuse—said much."

"What about Miss Fairbanks?"

"Oh, aye. I'd forgotten about her." Her brow puckered briefly and I was about to ask why when she asked a question of her own. "Am I to understand that Lieutenant Delagrange is dead?"

"Yes," I answered quietly. Knifed in a street known to be frequented by prostitutes. That was what Sidney had learned when he'd spoken to Bennett the previous evening, though the official report had been worded a bit differently.

The sister nodded, crossing herself and murmuring something.

I'd considered abandoning this interview, wondering if there was really any need considering Delagrange had already been punished and was beyond our reach. But there were still questions I didn't have the answers to, and the nagging sensation that I was missing something. Perhaps it was only Ardmore's sudden appearance that made me think so, but I wouldn't be satisfied until I had explored every avenue.

I took another drink of tea before broaching the topic that was certain to be the most delicate. "Can you tell me about the day Miss Kavanagh died? What do you remember about it?"

Sister Mary Aloysius frowned, clasping her hands before her. "At the time, it seemed like any other day." She audibly inhaled and exhaled, perhaps restraining her own sorrow at losing a patient in such a way. "Though now I seem to remember the silence. But perhaps that's because of all the yellin' that occurred the evenin' before."

I sat forward in interest. "Who was yelling?"

"Mrs. Kavanagh. I didn't hear the exact words beyond a few aspersions she cast on her daughter's gratitude, but I gathered she was tryin' to convince Miss Kavanagh to leave her room."

"But Miss Kavanagh held firm?"

"Aye, to the best of my knowledge."

"Did she have any visitors?" I asked, leading her toward Miss Fairbanks's claim.

"In the afternoon. Her friend. Miss Fairbanks." She frowned. "She'd been there the day before as well. Heard part of the row between Miss Kavanagh and her mother."

"Did she have any other visitors?"

"Nay."

"Did Mr. and Mrs. Kavanagh?"

"Nay."

"You're certain?" I'd presumed that even if the nurse hadn't seen Delagrange enter Miss Kavanagh's room that she would have at least been cognizant that he was in the house.

"Aye." She stared back at me in confusion. "Why?"

I hesitated, considering whether I should share the source of my information, and then decided there was no way around it. In any case, Sister Mary Aloysius was unlikely to tell anyone else.

"Miss Fairbanks confessed to me that she'd helped Lieutenant Delagrange sneak into Miss Kavanagh's room to see her. That he persuaded her to do so with some sort of romantic drivel about her friend."

"I see," she replied, though the tone of her voice made it clear that whatever it was she saw, it wasn't to do with the romantic drivel.

"*Is* it possible Delagrange snuck into her room?"

"Nay. The Kavanaghs positioned a chair directly outside her door for me, so that if she had a guest or wished for privacy, I could still be close by in case she needed me. I never left that spot while Miss Fairbanks was there and after."

An unsettling feeling settled over me. "So Miss Fairbanks never drew you away from Miss Kavanagh's door? She never spoke to you?"

"Nay," she stated firmly, but then reconsidered. "Except when she left. She told me Miss Kavanagh had asked for privacy."

I scrutinized Sister Mary Aloysius's troubled countenance,

my uneasiness growing. For it was clear that one of them was lying. The question was, who?

"And I can tell ye one thing," she suddenly declared, sitting even straighter. "Had Lieutenant Delagrange been in the house, I would never have left her door. I knew how much his presence disturbed her. I'd not have chanced leavin' her alone. And neither would've her maid."

I realized then that it didn't make sense for the sister to lie. She had already been charged with carelessness and blamed for Miss Kavanagh's being able to commit suicide. Why wouldn't she leap at the chance to cast fault on Delagrange, who was already dead and therefore unable to either defend himself or face further punishment?

I leaned toward her, looking her squarely in the eye. "Did you leave out a bottle of sleeping medicine where Miss Kavanagh could get her hands on it?"

She leaned forward as well. "Nay."

"How can you be sure?"

"Because I kept it on me at all times. I wouldn't have trusted leavin' it anywhere else. And my bottle was still in my pocket."

"But they *did* find a bottle?"

"Aye, on the floor next to her wardrobe."

I puzzled over this, having assumed it had been found on or near her bed. "Then how did she take it?"

She nodded toward the table where the teapot and my cup still sat. "I believe 'twas poured in her tea. That's often how she took it."

"Did she take tea that afternoon?"

"Aye." Her brow furrowed again. "With Miss Fairbanks."

"Who brought it to them?"

"Mary."

"And did Miss Fairbanks drink any of it?"

"The second cup was used, so I assume so."

Then it was unlikely the entire pot had been poisoned. Not without it affecting Miss Fairbanks. Which meant the sleeping draught was added to Miss Kavanagh's cup. And the only person in the room with her at the time had been her friend.

I struggled with this realization, trying to imagine the sweet, mournful young lady I'd spoken with inside the Pepper Cannister church being capable of such a thing. But then I was perfectly aware of the darkness that could hide within the human heart, no matter the package it was wrapped in.

Sister Mary Aloysius sat quietly as I reconciled myself to this possibility. But there was still one alternative, and the simplest explanation was often the correct one. The nurse would know better than I.

"Do you think, in her extreme distress, seeing no way out, that Miss Kavanagh took her own life?"

She shook her head sorrowfully. "Nay, I don't."

"You're certain?" I asked doubtfully.

"Aye."

"How?"

"Because there *was* a way out." With this remark, she reached into her pocket and withdrew a folded piece of paper.

"What's this?" I asked, taking it from her.

"A letter. Miss Kavanagh gave it to me the evenin' before she died and asked me to post it."

I looked at her in startlement. "Yet, you didn't."

"Nay. Because I asked her to be certain. She'd just argued with her mother and I didn't want her to do anythin' hasty. I told her if she felt the same way in two days' time, I would send it."

This seemed to be wise counsel, allowing Miss Kavanagh time to reconsider and her mother time to reconcile with her. That is, unless it might have prevented her murder. It was clear this prospect troubled Sister Mary Aloysius.

"But why didn't you give this to the police?" I asked.

"Because they weren't called."

My shock must have been evident because she raised her eyebrows.

"They sent for Lieutenant Delagrange instead, and he said he would take care of the matter."

No wonder Miss Fairbanks had pointed me in his direction. Delagrange had his fingers all over the incident from beginning to end.

Except for Miss Kavanagh's death. He couldn't have done that.

I unfolded the paper, discovering it was addressed to Mrs. Keogh—Miss Kavanagh's aunt, I presumed. The mother of Daniel, her cousin who had died.

Mother won't see reason. She's insisting I marry him! I can't. I just can't! Please. You have to do something!

What Miss Kavanagh had expected her aunt to do, I didn't know, but Sister Mary Aloysius was right. Miss Kavanagh hadn't given up hope. Suicide didn't make sense.

I looked up into the sister's compassionate gaze, for she had realized the same thing I had. There was only one solution, and it was not easy to reconcile with, nor would it be easy to prove. In fact, it might be nigh impossible, unless she admitted to it herself.

The prospect seemed impossible, but I realized I had to try. For Miss Kavanagh. And also for Lieutenant Delagrange.

For I'd accused him of murdering her. I'd essentially declared it as truth. And it may have contributed to his being killed. Yes, he'd done some terrible things and had likely murdered Daniel Keogh. But he hadn't killed Miss Kavanagh. That sin could not be laid at his door.

CHAPTER 32

"Mrs. Kent, what are you doing here?" Miss Fairbanks demanded as she sank down on the settee beside me in her drawing room, glancing anxiously toward the door through which she'd entered and the one slightly ajar which led into the adjoining parlor.

A short time ago, I'd watched as her parents departed, waiting until they'd turned the corner before approaching the house. I'd encountered little trouble in convincing the butler to allow me to pay a call on the daughter of the house. After all, I was a respectable member of society dressed in the latest Paris fashions, and Miss Fairbanks was just a few years younger than me.

"I have a few more questions for you," I replied calmly.

"Yes, but why did you come here?" she implored softly. "Why didn't you arrange for us to meet as we did before? I *told* you my parents wouldn't approve."

"And you don't wish to have to explain the association, though I begin to wonder why."

She blinked at me before gesturing to my bobbed hair and the liberal amount of ankle revealed by my deep rose skirt. "Be-because you're rather too scandalous for my mother's taste." She arched her chin. "I'm sorry to be so blunt, but that's the truth." She pushed to her feet, her hands clasped primly before her. "If you go now, I can tell her you'd mistaken me for someone else."

What a brash little thing she was. I couldn't decide if she didn't realize how rude she was being, or if she simply didn't care. When I didn't budge, but continued to gaze up at her with a slight lift to my brows, I almost expected her to stamp her foot.

"I know what really happened, Miss Fairbanks."

A scowl rippled across her features. "I don't know what you're talking about."

"You heard about Lieutenant Delagrange, I'm sure."

"Yes, the poor man," she replied, sitting beside me once again. Her brow puckered in an approximation of distress. "To die in such a way."

"But you told me you helped him sneak into Miss Kavanagh's bedchamber shortly before she died. You implied he might have done something to aid her death along."

"I never meant to imply any such thing," she protested, now on the defensive. "You must have misunderstood me. Why, I just can't believe it of him. He *adored* Kitty."

"Then you lied? You *didn't* help him sneak into Miss Kavanagh's bedchamber?"

Her mouth clamped into an angry line as she appeared to struggle to formulate a response. "You're twisting all my words!"

"I'm not trying to twist anything, Miss Fairbanks. Merely to understand. Either you helped him sneak into Miss Kavanagh's bedchamber or you didn't."

She glared at me. "I think you should leave."

"Do you want to know what I think happened?" I continued evenly, ignoring her request.

Her glare only sharpened.

"I think Miss Kavanagh told you that she was refusing to marry the lieutenant. That she'd been fighting with her mother about it, but that she had a plan. And that afternoon when you called upon her, she told you she'd put it into action."

Thus far, nothing in her demeanor suggested I was wrong.

In fact, the twitch at the corner of her lip, as if she was desperate to speak but restraining herself, told me I was very, very right.

"She was anxious, hopeful, but wary of her next steps, and she wanted the reassurance of her dearest friend. Naturally, you tried to talk her out of it. After all, Delagrange was quite the catch. Handsome, distinguished, an officer on special assignment. She should have been grateful he'd taken an interest in her. So he'd behaved a bit . . . inappropriately," I settled on, nearly gagging on the word, but Miss Fairbanks's eyes only grew wider and her freckled cheeks more flushed. "But what was done was done. It couldn't be taken back. To refuse to marry him now was ludicrous. It would make her no better than—"

"A tart," Miss Fairbanks snapped, finishing the sentence for me. "She *met* him in her garden *in the dark* after everyone else had retired. I know she claimed she was going to tell him she no longer wished for him to court her, but it was perfectly obvious what she was doing. Forcing him into a compromising position so that he had to declare himself. My cousin tells me it's a trick as old as time."

For a moment I couldn't speak, such was my astonishment that she actually believed this.

"But even if it wasn't," she continued, appearing to give it a second thought, "it was too late. He *touched* her," she leaned forward to exclaim. "To not accept his proposal after that, to allow anyone else to woo her would have just been shameful. *Sinful.*" She spat the word as if its very utterance tainted her.

So horrified was I by her warped sense of propriety, of morality, that I struggled to press on. "So when the maid brought you tea . . ."

She straightened, smoothing out the wrinkles in her skirt. "I poured some of Mother's sleeping draught in her cup."

I thought I would have to prod her further, but she spoke matter-of-factly, without any further provocation.

She clasped her hands together primly in her lap. "I was saving her really. From her own sinful nature."

My lips snapped shut, for there really wasn't anything else to say. My silence clearly conveyed my shock and horror.

When Miss Fairbanks looked up, she narrowed her eyes spitefully. "You can't prove it, of course. It would be your word against mine, and I'll simply deny it." She arched her chin. "And we both know who they'll believe. Why, you couldn't even convince the Castle of Delagrange's guilt. They'll believe you've gone completely round the bend if you accuse a sweet, biddable girl like me of such a terrible thing." She sniffed, dabbing at the corners of her eyes in illustration. "Taking advantage of me in my grief."

Her words curdled in my gut, for she wasn't wrong. Had we only my word to rely on, she would have undoubtedly gotten away with it. But fortunately, we didn't.

Behind me, the parlor door slid open and Sidney, the Kavanaghs, and Mr. and Mrs. Fairbanks stepped through. Miss Fairbanks's face blanched, but then she straightened her back as if determined to brazen her way out of the situation despite the obvious distress stamped across both sets of parents' features.

I retreated to the parlor with Sidney, leaving the others to confront what Miss Fairbanks had done and decide how to proceed. It had been the deal we made in their allowing me to confront her in the first place while they listened in. When they'd made it, they'd clearly believed in her innocence and staunchly disapproved of me, and I'd admittedly exploited that and our closeness to Detective Inspector Burrows. However, I felt no remorse for it. Not given the truth we'd exposed.

"You did well," Sidney told me as we stood side by side, gazing out the parlor window at the Fairbankses' garden.

I felt too numb from Miss Fairbanks's revelations to discuss them. Particularly not her barb about Dublin Castle. The fact was, she had correctly read the situation. There was no denying it. Though she'd miscalculated in attempting to point the finger of blame for Miss Kavanagh's death at Delagrange. I could only assume that by doing so she'd hoped to divert any potential suspicion from herself. After all, she already knew we were looking at him for the other crimes. But clearly, she'd not counted on my speaking to the nurse or giving her words any credence. Otherwise, Miss Fairbanks wouldn't have overplayed her hand in trying to cover her tracks.

"Did you ask Mr. Kavanagh if he knows Lord Ardmore?" I asked Sidney after taking a long, shaky breath.

"He says not."

I turned to look at his profile. "Do you believe him?"

"Yes," he admitted reluctantly. He realized as well as I did that would be the simplest solution to how Ardmore had known about Miss Kavanagh's assault and its likely perpetrator. But if it hadn't been through Kavanagh, then that meant Ardmore had learned of it another way. Or perhaps he'd merely guessed the truth, though that wasn't his usual way of doing things.

Sometime later, the Kavanaghs and Mr. Fairbanks returned. Mrs. Fairbanks had presumably escorted Miss Fairbanks upstairs to prepare for whatever came next. I suspected a stay in a private institution. The men moved off to one corner to discuss it while Mrs. Kavanagh joined me at the window. It was evident she'd been weeping.

"You must think me a terrible mother," she whispered, clutching her handkerchief tightly in her fist just below her chin. "And you are probably right." Her face crumpled. "But I did love my daughter." She sobbed softly into her handkerchief for a moment before regaining her composure. "I only wanted what was best for her, wrongheaded as that might have turned out to be." She sniffed. "But I want you to know that in the end I intended to reconcile. I'd accepted her decision, and even come around to seeing that she was right.

Only I was *stubborn*, and I didn't want to admit it yet. So I . . . I never got to tell her."

I held her free hand, offering her what comfort I could while she wept, contemplating my own need for reconciliation with someone. I'd been angry with Alec when I walked away from him in that alley behind Devlin's pub. Furious, really. But since then, I'd had time to think. To realize that I was as angry at C and British Intelligence and Dublin Castle and the entire British government and the Irish rebels and *myself*, as I was at him.

It wasn't fair to blame Alec for the things that weren't his fault. And if Sidney and I ultimately decided to leave Dublin and return to London, I didn't want that parting behind Devlin's to be my and Alec's last goodbye. There was too much between us to end it that way.

"I see you got my message," I said without looking up from my contemplation of the late afternoon sunlight reflected off the River Liffey. I'd noticed Alec approaching out of the corner of my eye. Actually, I'd seen him crossing Grattan Bridge, for he was easier to spot now that I knew what guise I was searching for. Though, I noticed he was dressed in a respectable three-piece suit today, perhaps to better blend with my own attire.

Alec joined me at the cement embankment of Wellington Quay, peering west over the bridge toward the twin towers of the Ormond Quay Presbyterian Church and farther in the distance the distinctive dome of the Four Courts. "Finnegan said you didn't give him any choice."

This was true. I'd told the banker, in no uncertain terms, that he would deliver my message to Alec, or I would inform C of his deception. After all, I hadn't promised Collins that I wouldn't inform on his associates, just matters pertaining to *him*.

"You didn't give me any other way to contact you," I told him lightly.

"I wasn't sure you would."

I turned to look at him then, sensing his reticence, his hesitancy. It made me feel more on even ground. "Alec . . ." I began and then reconsidered. "Or should I be calling you MacAlister?"

His gaze met mine, warmer than the afternoon sun. "I'll always be Alec with you."

I inhaled through the tightness that had lodged in my chest. "Is either your real name?"

I knew before I asked it that he wouldn't answer, but it had to be said anyway.

"Alec," I tried again. "Are you certain about this?"

He knew what I meant.

"Yes, Ver," he answered solemnly, reverting to the more upper-crust British accent I had always known. At least, when he was speaking English. "I know at times it can seem I'm rash and reckless, but believe me, this wasn't a decision I made hastily. I've been here for nearly nine months now. I know the lay of the land, and I've seen enough to know my own mind." He began to grow irritated. "I expected you of all people to understand."

"No, you didn't," I countered. "Or else you would have approached me and told me yourself the moment you realized I was in Dublin."

He scowled. "I was trying to save you the necessity of lying for me. Credible deniability."

"Stop making excuses, Alec. You were windy."

His eyes narrowed dangerously at my calling him cowardly, but I wasn't finished.

"You didn't want me to know, so that you wouldn't have to face the possibility that I didn't approve. That I believed you were betraying your country and *me*." I tapped my chest. "Credible deniability, indeed."

He turned toward the river, his jaw hard and his breathing rapid, and I thought for a moment I'd pushed him too far. That he would simply walk away. But then he reached out to grip the cement bulwark. The knuckles of his right hand were busted, suggesting he'd recently been in a fight.

"Is that how you feel?"

Hearing the note of brittleness in his voice, I exhaled a long breath, pulling my gaze from his hand to stare out across the river. "I don't know how I feel," I told him honestly. "But . . . I do understand. Part of it. Though isn't there still *some* hope the government will offer better terms? At least for Dominion Home Rule."

Alec turned to glare at me. "They're republicans, Ver. They don't want Home Rule, Dominion or otherwise. They want their own republic. Like they had before the English took it from them." He adjusted his hat, glancing left and right, a disgusted grimace curdling his mouth. "As for hope, I would say our faith in the British government doing the right thing has just been effectively crushed by the coercion bill they rammed through Parliament."

The Restoration of Order in Ireland Act, or "coercion bill" as some were referring to it, had been conceived from the cabinet meetings Max had most recently reported to us. Though talk of peace and settlement had seemed to be on everyone's lips for weeks, including notoriously loyalist sources, the cabinet had instead sided with the war camp. The act confirmed Ireland's separateness in terms of policy and British law, empowering authorities to enforce curfews, limit movement of traffic, imprison suspects merely on suspicion, and replace coroners' inquests with military courts of inquiry which could try civilians by court-martial.

While most bills usually took a long time to become law—case in point the disputed Home Rule Bill passed in 1914, but suspended until the end of the war, and still mired in committees and controversy—the Restoration of Order in Ireland

Act had been guillotined through. Proving that the British government *could* act quickly. When it wanted to. The final step was Royal assent, which was expected to happen the following day.

"Don't try to tell me you're any more hopeful," Alec charged.

I had to admit, it was difficult to maintain any optimism in the face of it. I'd heard enough rumors concerning those within Dublin Castle to know that many of the civil servants possessed equally bleak outlooks. And there was no denying the government was perfectly aware of the effect this act would cause, because they'd ordered all their seconded civil service employees to move out of their current lodgings at the Royal Marine Hotel in Kingstown and inside the Castle walls for their own protection.

"No." I sighed. "Though I don't like to admit it." Then I scowled, growing angry with myself. "But I promised I wouldn't give in to despair, no matter what the circumstances. Or Ardmore's manipulation," I practically growled.

Alec looked to me in question and I explained what we'd recently learned about Ardmore convincing Lord French to solicit our services in investigating Miss Kavanagh's assault. When I finished, he was silent, seemingly absorbed in the flow of the river and the cigarette he'd lit.

"He's here, you know," I added, curious what his reaction would be.

"I know." His words and his resigned tone caught me off guard.

"You know?"

I could tell he was debating what to tell me, weighing the pros and cons of filling me in on whatever he knew. He took one last drag of his cigarette and pitched it in the river before turning to me in resignation.

"Mick has been in contact with him."

CHAPTER 33

I blinked at Alec in shock, unable at first to find my tongue. "Have you—"

He shook his head before I could finish the question. "Ardmore knows me, remember. I couldn't risk showing myself."

I'd momentarily forgotten Alec's history with Ardmore. How he'd questioned Alec's decision to flee Brussels when his position as a staff officer in the German Army had been compromised, rather than brazen it out. Never mind that Alec had been embedded with the Germans for over six years—since before the war—and never lost his nerve. Never mind that several of our intelligence sources had indicated he was about to be apprehended and almost certainly face torture and death. It was why I'd gone into Belgium after him to guide him back to relative safety in the neutral Netherlands.

Fortunately, the other officers in Alec's debriefing hadn't questioned his decision or his bravery. But then again, those officers also hadn't been mentioned in a confidential German Army report like Ardmore was. It had been the source of Alec's downfall when he'd bungled an attempt to get a better look at it. As such, he'd been understandably leery of Ardmore ever since, making his suspicions of His Lordship older than mine.

"Do you know why Collins is in contact with him?" I

asked, feeling the vague stirrings of my apprehension begin to solidify.

"Not entirely. But I know Mick seems to think Ardmore means to help. That he could be a valuable ally." Alec's voice was strained, telling me he wasn't pleased by this.

"Have you told him about your history with Ardmore? Have you told him what we know he's capable of?"

"Yes. And I warned him that Ardmore is almost certainly playing both sides and hoping to profit from it. Mick didn't seem surprised by anything I said. But then, he's no simpleton. He probably took Ardmore's measure long ago."

"I don't know. He seems to have a lot of people fooled." Including most of British Intelligence and the government.

"Aye, but those people aren't outwitting the might of the British Empire and its unlimited resources simply by willpower and strategic connivance. By refusing to play the game *their* way, no matter how often they change the rules, or how much they malign us for it," he muttered dryly.

He was right. We British did have a tendency to write the rule book and then expect everyone to play by it, whether it was to their benefit or not, and then cry foul when they didn't. It was a timeworn strategy, and the Restoration of Order in Ireland Act was merely the latest effort to enforce their playbook.

"Mick is no fool," he stated firmly. "If *we've* seen through Ardmore, he will, too."

"I'm glad you have so much faith in him considering all you've risked in joining his side," I replied, choosing my words with care. "But there's too much at stake for me to simply take you at your word, Alec. Does Collins know about the phosgene?"

Alec's brow furrowed, answering my question for me.

"Does he know where it is?"

"No. Though Ardmore has told him it's at his disposal."

"Alec," I gasped in alarm.

"Mick's not going to use it, Ver," he argued. "Not unless the Brits use it first. It's merely a precaution."

Then that letter Bennett had showed Sidney was correct. The rebels were looking to secure biological weapons at least as a means of retaliation.

"But Alec, even then."

"Eager to save our brave troops?" he sneered.

"From such a fate? Yes," I retorted angrily. "But I'm equally concerned about saving the innocent population of Ireland. You know as well as I do that poisonous gas is not so easily deployed. That it can billow where it wishes. Even as often as not, back at those who released it in the first place. And what of the reprisals that would follow?"

I shuddered at the thought of the Black and Tans and other Crown Forces running amuck after such an attack. Discipline was already lax—purposely or not. There would be no control if the republicans utilized such a weapon, regardless of the fact the British had used it first.

I could see that Alec was not unaffected by my words, and I pressed him further.

"You may trust Collins, but I know that you don't trust Ardmore any more than I do. And while that phosgene is in his hands, he could do anything with it. He may claim he's keeping it in reserve for the republicans' use if needed, but since when has he ever made his intentions so plain?"

"Never," he conceded.

"Mark me, he plans to use it for something unexpected, something heinous. Perhaps even blackmail or to frame Collins and the rebels. But certainly not the one he's stated."

Alec eyed me unhappily, but I could see I'd gotten my point across.

"So you're saving us now?" he quipped. "From infamy?"

"That's not what . . ." I began to retort until I caught sight of the tiny quirk at the corner of his lips. I might have retaliated for his twigging my tail, but I was simply too relieved to be on equal footing about something.

"I'll speak to Mick again," he assured me. "If nothing else, maybe he can convince Ardmore to at least hand the phosgene over into our care."

I shook my head. "He won't. You know he won't." He didn't counter this, and I took it as agreement, allowing my gaze to follow his across the water to the traffic passing along the opposite quay. "I'm worried, Alec," I confessed, allowing the nameless fear that had been lurking inside me to surface. "Why is Ardmore here? You know he doesn't do anything without a very specific reason. So why now? What is he planning?"

Yes, there was the financial crisis facing Dublin Corporation and many other local and county councils throughout Ireland, which Ardmore may or may not be intending to take advantage of. But he didn't need to be here to do that. He didn't need to come here himself to toy with me either. He could have tasked Willoughby to do it.

No, there must be a specific reason for him being here and now. But what?

Alec reached out to grip my hand where it rested against the cement bulwark, pulling me out of my fretful contemplation. "We'll figure it out, Ver. You and me." His gaze swept over my features, as tangible as a caress, and then retreated. "And Sidney." His hand moved away from mine. "Where is he, by the way?" He looked over his shoulder. "I'm surprised he let you come alone."

"I convinced him it would be less conspicuous." I turned to peer down the quay in the direction I'd come. "Though he could still be watching us from somewhere." Sidney trusted me. I knew that. But I also knew he didn't trust Alec. At least, not where I was concerned. And I couldn't blame him, considering my and Alec's past.

"I suppose this means we'll be remaining in Ireland a bit

longer," I replied, striving for a lightness I didn't feel. "That is, if Sidney agrees." My resolution from the week before remained firm. I wouldn't make any decisions without him.

But Alec was a different story. Though given how hard he'd been trying to convince me to leave, I was curious how he would react.

"You could always return home and let Sidney and me handle it," he suggested hopefully.

The glare I turned on him let him know how I felt about that.

He shrugged remorselessly. "It was worth a shot."

Church bells began to chime across the river and a second later from somewhere south of us, reminding us of the hour. The blue of the sky had deepened, sharpening the angles of the feathered clouds above. The smell of hot ink wafted from the printing works behind us, blown out toward the river by the same wind that played with the ends of my auburn hair curling out from beneath the brim of my ivory cloche hat.

"You should know," Alec said, trying to sound offhanded, but I noted the watchfulness in his gaze. "Mick seems determined to recruit you."

"That won't happen," I stated flatly.

He turned to lean his hip against the balustrade. "You sound confident, but he can be very persuasive."

I arched a single eyebrow, my voice turning wry. "Undoubtedly." He'd recruited Alec, hadn't he?

"He doesn't underestimate the value of women, or their minds," he assured me.

"I don't dispute it. Some of his best agents are female, no doubt." This was spoken lightly, but a spark of interest still lit Alec's eyes. "But I won't do it, Alec. I'll keep his secrets and yours. But I won't spy for Collins. Don't even try," I warned, wondering if Collins had tasked him with this very thing.

He dipped his head in acceptance, though I knew better than to think this discussion was over. "Neutral, then?"

"I suppose." I narrowed my eyes suspiciously. "Sidney and I are here to find those phosgene cylinders and stop Ardmore. Nothing more."

"Come on, love. Don't look at me like that," Alec cajoled, flashing me his blinding smile. "You may not trust Mick yet, but you know you can trust me."

I'd thought so, but I was just remembering something I'd meant to confront him about. "Interesting how Lieutenant Delagrange ended up dead just days after I was so injudicious as to grouse about his crimes in front of you both."

Alec held up his hands in a display of innocence. "That wasn't me. And it wasn't Mick either. Not after the way he called me on the mat after hearing about it. Mick has a strict policy about no unauthorized shootings and no revenge killings. It's detrimental to the cause, and considering the fact we're not all aware of who's working for who, might result in the murder of some of our own inside men. Or women."

"You truly didn't do it?" I pressed, easing down from the high dudgeon I was working myself into.

"No, Ver. I swear. And I don't know who did."

I'd thought for certain he or Collins was responsible. The timing had been right. But Alec's reaction was convincing, as were his arguments. I'd heard from other sources how selective Collins was about those he marked for assassination.

"Delagrange was knifed, not shot, right?"

I nodded.

"Not our method. It's too difficult to ensure the attack is fatal."

Inwardly, I shrank away from this comment, not wanting to imagine Alec in such a role.

"It was skillfully done," I told him, for Sidney had ferreted out a number of details about the attack from Bennett. Details that the general public wasn't aware of. "Whoever it was, they knew exactly what they were doing." Which certainly didn't suggest a random thief or a disgruntled prostitute.

Alec's expression turned pensive. "Could it be Ardmore?"

"Ardmore doesn't get his hands—" I began heatedly before breaking off. "Willoughby," I practically growled as I recalled his presence in Dublin.

"That captain who saved our bacon in Wiltshire?"

"At the behest of Ardmore," I reminded him. "And I assure you, he's done a lot less noble things at the behest of Ardmore as well. Including murder."

His brow furrowed in contemplation. "He was once a Naval Intelligence officer, right?"

"Yes. And the timing of his arrival here in Dublin is just about right." I frowned, not liking the picture that was forming. "Sidney and I have already been speculating about how Ardmore knew about Miss Kavanagh's assault and how her assailants were probably not members of the IRA. Maybe Ardmore's connection was directly to Delagrange."

"Making him a liability," Alec pronounced gravely.

One that perhaps had outlived his usefulness.

"Can you remember any connection to someone named Delagrange in that dossier you put together on Ardmore?" I asked.

Alec considered and then shook his head. "Not unless it was a detail so minor it slipped my notice."

I sighed in discouragement.

There was suddenly shouting from the direction of the bridge near the far shore, though we couldn't see who was making the ruckus. However, Alec seemed to have some idea.

"You should return home, Ver. Before it gets too late."

"Why?"

His brow furrowed. "The British Navy prevented Archbishop Daniel Mannix from landing in Ireland. Apparently, he drew massive crowds in New York, where he spoke out in opposition to English rule in Ireland, and the authorities weren't about to let that happen here. So instead they diverted him from his ship bound for Cork, to Penzance."

"They detained him in England?"

"At least, for the moment," Alec confirmed, surveying those around us guardedly. "But we expect trouble tonight. People are angry. About the coercion bill and everything else. This stunt is merely the latest provocation. I wouldn't be surprised if there are some clashes with Crown Forces before the night is through." He turned to look at me. "You should go home before the trouble starts. No one is safe in a mob," he pronounced solemnly.

I stepped away, knowing he was right.

"I'll be in touch," he promised, though the look in his eyes was conflicted.

"Be safe," I urged him before turning to go, a conscious echo of what I'd said to him the last time I'd seen him in London before he'd set out for Ireland. I'd wondered then if he had anyone else to tell him so. Now I felt fairly confident he didn't.

I didn't look back, allowing him at least the illusion that I didn't know he shadowed me for several blocks. Or perhaps he was merely bound for his next meeting. Near the corner of Nassau and Dawson Street I heard the distinctive rattle of Collins's bicycle chain and wondered.

Sidney was waiting for me in our private sitting room when I returned. I spared him the effort of poking and prodding, relaying everything Alec had told me up front, including his remark that Collins wished to recruit me. He listened intently, interrupting periodically for clarification, but otherwise remained quiet as I paced back and forth.

Once I'd finished, I plopped down on the settee next to him, staring down at the painted floor. "Once this bill receives Royal assent tomorrow, things are almost certain to get worse. Matters could seriously deteriorate. And quickly. Knowing that, knowing we have no idea where the phosgene actually is other than the vague notion that it's somewhere in or near Dublin . . ." I looked up, meeting his deep midnight-blue eyes. "Do we stay?"

The corners of his lips lifted unexpectedly. "Are you trying to talk me out of it?"

"No, but I am trying to be realistic." My eyes pleaded with him, wanting him to tell me what we should do.

Seeing this, his amusement faded, and he reached for my hand. "What do you want to do?"

"No! Don't ask me that," I exploded, pushing to my feet again.

"Why?" he asked calmly.

"Because I don't know. I'm . . . I'm terrified of what may happen to you, to me if we stay. And I'm terrified of what may happen if we don't. So don't ask me what the right thing to do is, because I don't know!"

Sidney stood, grasping hold of my shoulders as I paced past him again, forcing me to look at him. His eyes when I met them ached with uncertainty. "But here's the thing, Ver. I don't know either."

Contradictory as it may have been, this made me feel better. At least I wasn't the only one shaken by all this and frightened by what was to come. At least I wasn't alone.

I stepped into his embrace, clutching him as tightly as he held me. My breathing was shallow, and I forced myself to inhale deeply, drawing his scent into my lungs once, twice, and then a third time. Gradually, I began to feel the knots of dread loosen and the haze of my panic begin to recede.

One step at a time, I told myself. The same mantra that had seen me through countless difficult and perilous situations during the war and after. Just take it one step at a time.

"Bennett and Ames," I said, lifting my head from Sidney's shoulder. "Do you trust them to find this phosgene? Do you trust Ardmore not to somehow interfere or influence them if they do?"

In place of his answer, he posed a question of his own. "Collins and Xavier. Do you trust them to coax the phosgene out of Ardmore's hands? Do you trust them to do the right thing with it if they do?"

The simple answer was no. I wanted to trust Alec and that he would be able to convince Collins to do the right thing. But I also recognized that the Big Fellow exerted a strong influence over Alec. One that might be even stronger than his conscience.

However, there was no need to say this aloud, for Sidney could read my response as well as I could read his. There was no one here in Ireland we could trust to see this through to the end but ourselves.

"We can't leave, can we?" I murmured, daring to speak the truth.

"I'm afraid we'll never forgive ourselves if we do and the worst happens," he replied solemnly.

I sighed, resting my forehead against the center of his chest. "What an awfully noble pair we are," I quipped, sometimes wishing that wasn't the case.

Sidney chuckled humorlessly. "For better or for worse, it's who we are."

"I suppose at least we got that part of the vows right," I murmured.

He smiled sadly and I arched up onto my toes, wrapping my arms around his neck to hold him close. For a dreadful premonition had fluttered within me. And I could only pray this decision wasn't one we would eternally regret.

ACKNOWLEDGMENTS

What an intense two years it has been! And I have many people to thank for helping me through it.

First and foremost, I want to thank my husband and our daughters. None of this would be possible without you. You pick me up and cheer me on, you forgive me my distractions, and you help me remember what is most important when I'm over-anxious and in danger of losing perspective. I love you with all my heart.

Thank you to my mom and dad. You are always there for me and my family, in big ways and small. We're so fortunate to have you.

Thank you to my friends and family, who provide unending support and moments of much-needed laughter. Thank you in particular to my siblings and in-laws; my cousins Jackie and Kim; my friends Anita, Jessica, Karen, and Lauren, and all the ladies in my Mom's Group.

I'm also incredibly grateful to my author friends and the Lyonesses. You help keep me sane and offer advice and understanding in ways others cannot.

And of course, I can't forget to thank my stellar publishing team who shepherd my books into existence and make them shine. Thank you to my agent, Kevan Lyon; editor, Wendy McCurdy; and all of the amazing people at Kensington who work so hard to bring my books to life.

I would also like to express my appreciation for the many stellar researchers who made writing this book possible. Before I decided to send Verity into the heart of the Irish Revolution, I knew just a teaspoonful of the complex, surprising, often gut-wrenching history of that era. I'm grateful to those who continue to study and analyze and shed light on the past. However, any errors made within the pages of this book are, of course, my own.

One last note. I draw some of my research from the diaries of Mark Sturgis, a British civil servant within Dublin Castle during 1920-21. It is Sturgis who first calls O "a wicked little white snake," and I take the liberty of having Verity agree.